A War in Home waters

At Home and At sea,

1807

by

John G. Cragg

A War in Home Waters, 1807

.

Dedicated to

Reid Cragg

Who

Loves Horses

Table of Contents

Preface

This book is a work of fiction, both in terms of events and characters. It follows on from the first six volumes in this series, *A New War: at Home and at Sea, 1803, A Continuing War: at Home and at Sea, 1803-4, A War by Diplomacy: at Home and at Sea, 1804, A Stalemated War: at Home and at Sea, 1805, A Changing War: at Home and at sea, 1805-II,* and *A Widening: at Home and at sea, 1806.* They are available at Amazon.com and other Amazon sites by searching for my name or the title. The present tale takes place in 1807. A great many things have changed in the more than two centuries that have elapsed since that date, including items and phrases that may be unfamiliar to many readers. To help those who are curious, a glossary is provided at the end of the book. Items in the glossary are flagged on their first appearance in the text by an * as in, for example, tack*. A few notes on terms or institutions that may not be familiar to readers are found in the Author's Notes at the end of the text.

As always, I am indebted to my wife, Olga Browzin Cragg, for her encouragement and meticulous help in trying to make a readable manuscript. Many readers have also helped with their comments and criticisms.

Chapter I

"Lord Camshire! I thought it was you."

Sir Richard Giles, Earl of Camshire, looked up from the newspaper he was reading. "Sir Titus," he exclaimed. "Call me Giles. 'Lord Camshire' reminds me too much of my father. It has been a long time since we have seen each other. Do sit down."

The seemingly casual meeting in a gentlemen's club, in this case, Brooks Club in Pall Mall, was nothing of the sort. While the two men were acquaintances, indeed friends, this meeting had been pre-arranged. When Giles had returned from the House of Lords the previous evening, he found a terse note from Sir Titus Amery asking to meet the next day in the reading room of the Club but not announce the meeting to anyone else, including the Club's servants.

Giles had been intrigued. Sir Titus seemed always to be on leave from his judicial duties so that he could undertake tricky assignments for the government. Their paths had crossed several times, and Giles felt that he was in the other man's debt for the help he had given Giles's wife, Daphne, in solving problems that had fallen to her over the years while Giles had been at sea. Even if he did not feel that he owed Sir Titus anything, he would still have been intrigued. What could be so important that Sir Titus wanted to stage a seemingly casual meeting with Giles in his London club?

"I hear that congratulations are in order for Lady Camshire and yourself. A new son!" Sir Titus began in an unusually loud voice.

"Yes. We've called him 'Roger,'" responded Giles. "I was at the birth, in the birthing chamber, despite the tradition against husbands being present. You have no idea how terrifying the process is and how very wonderful it is when the child is born complaining loudly about his new status. Daphne was very brave, but that was no surprise; she always is."

"I imagine that she was. I've never been faced with having a child being born. If I did, I am sure that I would wait for news well away from the birthing room, unlike you. You and Lady Camshire do rather amaze me."

"Sir Titus," Giles changed the subject, "Daphne told me about your misadventures in Shropshire and how you were injured. Are you recovered?"

"Pretty much so. It took me a very long time to get over that bang on the head. I was surprised at how devastating the injury was. You always hear about people who are knocked senseless, quickly springing to their feet and resuming life as if nothing had happened. That wasn't my experience."

'I know. Though not as serious as your injury, I have found that confusion, tiredness, and lack of ability to concentrate last for some time after a blow to the head. It last happened to me quite a while ago, but it is only recently that I have felt that I have returned completely to normal."

"That is reassuring, I suppose," replied Sir Titus, "for not all my problems have gone away yet. I am still on leave from my judicial duties. I am just on my way back to my lodgings in St. James's, where I might have an afternoon nap after spending the morning with some colleagues at the Middle Temple. I decided to stop in at Brooks for a drink. Here, I think this chap is about to inquire whether we would like something.

"I'll have a Scotch Whisky." Sir Titus addressed the servant who was hovering near the two men. "And you, Giles?"

"Brandy."

When the servant departed, Sir Titus leaned forward and said quietly, "We can talk better over lunch upstairs."

Giles nodded. Although the statement made him even more curious about why Sir Titus wanted to see him, he followed the path that Sir Titus was signaling. "Tell me, Sir Titus. Daphne and I have heard no more about the mess that Edwards landed us in with that Shropshire property. Have you learned anything more since that confrontation by the river?"

"Some things. The ruffians who Lady Camshire had so large a hand in catching gave us quite a bit of information about what your former agent had been up to, though not enough to completely destroy the crime ring."

"Oh?" Giles prompted.

"Yes. Edwards, who embezzled so much money from you and other captains, appears to have had some other rackets going on. I haven't been involved in this matter since I got hit on the head, and I don't know how that man got involved in robbing from the Severn trade. I was looking into that series of thefts when I met up with Lady Camshire on your new estate, though I had no idea that you owned it."

"Quite frankly," Giles replied, "I wish I didn't, but since the title to it is still compromised by Edwards's theft, I can't easily get rid of it either."

The conversation continued in this vein for several minutes before Sir Titus pulled out his pocket watch and said, "I see that we should go up for luncheon if I am to have time for my nap later."

Only when they had found a table in the corner of the first-floor dining room and the waiters had supplied them with generous slices of beef and a bottle of claret did Sir Titus get down to the purpose of the meeting.

"What do you know about the Jacobites, Giles?" he asked.

"Very little. Something to do with Scottish revolts in the last century, weren't they?"

"Yes, somewhat. I'd better give you a bit of history — a very simplified bit of history.

"It all goes back to the seventeenth century, which for us could be called the century of the Stuarts, the Scottish kings who were on our throne. It was a period with a variety of struggles about how we would be governed and who would sit on the throne. The Stuarts were, in principle, in favor of the King being in charge of everything, with Parliament being a minor part of government at best. Others thought that Parliament should be more important and that the King should be somewhat subservient to it. The problems were supposed to be resolved in 1688 when King James II was deposed. Parliament selected his sister Mary and her Dutch husband, William of Orange, to be the reigning King and Queen — a very strange but successful arrangement.

"Not everyone was happy with this outcome, and over time there have been various attempts to restore the Stuart descendants of James II to the throne. You've probably heard of the 1745 rebellion, but the last somewhat-serious attempt to restore the Stuarts was cooked up by the French, who planned an invasion of England in 1759 in which Prince Charles, the 'Bonnie Prince Charlie' of 1745, would be restored to the throne. The Navy stopped that plan in the Battle of Quiberon Bay. Since then, the issue has been pretty quiet, but there are still people who long for the Stuart line of kings. That feeling is not helped by having a possibly mad king on our throne and a Prince of Wales, who would take over if his father's madness became serious once again, whom many consider a disgrace.

"Possibly not surprisingly, Napoleon seems to have realized that the Jacobite cause might be revived to raise problems for our government. I am amazed that he didn't try it as part of his plans to invade us — maybe he didn't know about the possibilities — but now we have information that he is trying to stir up trouble in Scotland."

"Oh, what could he do? Surely these issues are all dead as doornails."

"Not quite. And the embers of the revolts might be blown to life, even in England, but more likely in Scotland and Ireland.

"We have word that the French have found an heir — or rather a pretend heir — to the Prince Charles who led the revolt in 1745 and '46. He calls himself 'Prince David Stuart.' This man claims to be Prince Charles's son, born after the Prince's wife died to one of his aristocratic mistresses, but he claims that his father secretly married his mother before he was born, which would make him the King if you thought that Bonnie Prince Charlie should have been. It doesn't matter whether this story is true or not; there are people who are ready to believe it, especially in the Scottish highlands and western islands."

"This is all very interesting, Sir Titus, but how does it involve me?" Giles interrupted.

"I'm getting to that. I believe you know Lord MacCarthach?"

"Yes, I've met him. He is quite vocal in supporting the abolition of the slave trade, as I am, and we have talked about that issue a couple of times."

"That's him. He is the Earl of Pendrag, which is an island in the inner Hebrides. He is also the head of the Clan Carthach, the major clan in Glen Drayhag in Scotland on the mainland. His mainland clansmen are firm protestants, but some MacCarthachs who live on Pendrag are staunch Catholics who are not happy that their lord is a protestant. God, will we ever see the end of these religious hatreds?

"Now, if you will bear with me, there is a bit more to the story before I get to the current problem. Lord MacCarthach, whose first name is Robert, has a brother called Percy, and they are twins. Robert was born first. He was the fourth son of his father, while Percy was the fifth. As a result, it didn't matter much which one was born first. The midwife and others who observed the features of the babies at birth thought that there would be no trouble knowing which baby was which, so they took no special measures to prevent the babies from being mixed up, even though one newborn baby looks like another, and this seems to have been the case with these MacCarthach babies even though these two were not identical twins. It didn't seem to be really important at the time which one was which since there were already three males ahead of them in line for the title and the estate.

"Well, jump forward to today. The twins' father has died. Surprisingly, he survived his first three sons, so Robert and Percy are now his first and second living sons. Robert is the Lord and Chief of Clan MacCarthach. He inherited all his father's entailed properties, while Percy is still nobody and has received very little from his father's estate. It's all very clear, but Percy is not happy. He claims that he is Robert and that Robert is Percy, so the man who we know as Percy is truly the Lord and Chief of Clan MacCarthach because he is the male who was baptized 'Robert,' and Robert should really be called 'Percy' and treated as the junior son.

"Of course, there is not much evidence for Percy's claim. He has persuaded an old nanny, who is half-blind and has a wretched memory, to swear that they were mixed up soon after birth, though after they were christened, so that Robert is actually the second born, but his father, for some unknown reason, liked Robert better. To make matters worse, the twins' mother, who is also dead, was a MacCars, a staunchly Catholic clan, which backs Percy as the proper heir to his father since Percy claims to be a Catholic, even though the MacCarthach chiefs have always been firm Presbyterians."

"Where do I come into all this?" asked Giles.

"I'm getting to that. You see, the French have decided to intervene in this powder keg. They would dearly love to foment trouble in Scotland, using the old Jacobite cause. Of course, the Young Pretender is dead, and he left no legitimate male children, which you would think would end the possibility of restoring the throne to the Stuarts since the next in line is a man who is now a Catholic cardinal and has no legitimate children. He is the last legitimate male of the Royal Stuart line, but his religion bars him from the throne, and he isn't interested in any case. So, even if you think that the Stuart dynasty should be revived, you would end up with King George anyway.

Now along comes Percy MacCarthach with the man who calls himself 'Prince David Stuart.' It is quite possible that Bonnie Prince Charlie did have an illegitimate son after his wife died and that this man is that son, but that would be irrelevant. The claim that has emerged is that this son is legitimate since his father married his mother before he was born. She was a French aristocrat, but the evidence that she ever married his father is extremely questionable. This David Stuart would be excluded from the throne anyway because he is a baptized Catholic. However, there is still a lot of loyalty to the Stuart cause in parts of Scotland and some in England and Ireland, both from the old Catholic families and those who think that the Hanovers have been poor kings and that the Prince Regent is the worst of the lot.

"By himself, Percy MacCarthach could not raise the clans or appeal to others who are unhappy with King George and the Prince Regent to stage a revolt, and that would be his only real chance of replacing Robert as the Earl and Chief of the Clan MacCarthach. However, if the pretender to the throne were to be made king, thanks to Percy for putting him there, Percy MacCarthach would get what he wants. However, Percy also knows that he has no hope of leading a successful rebellion without strong backing from France.

"Someone in France found out about the two men, someone who must have Napoleon's ear. We don't know who that someone might be or how Percy approached him. Maybe it was the other way around, but it hardly matters. This person — it might even be a woman since David Stuart is quite the ladies' man — must have persuaded Napoleon or one of his cronies that causing a Scottish rebellion, even a forlorn one, would reduce our energies trying to interfere with his becoming Emperor of all of Europe, Egypt, Arabia, and even India. Napoleon may have felt that diverting our military force to cleaning up a mess at home and, more importantly, making us spend money to support a campaign in Scotland and possibly Ireland would mean less cash to try to get the Austrians, Prussians, and Russians to oppose that trumped-up emperor. This brings us to the next part of the story."

"I suspected that we would hear about Bonaparte soon," said Giles, mostly to confirm that he was still listening carefully to Sir Titus's tale.

"Our spies in Paris found out about Percy's approach to the French when the suggestion reached Napoleon that they should support the scheme to start a rebellion that would aim to give this Prince David the crown and, not incidentally, restore Percy to what he thinks is his by right. I doubt that the French believe that it could succeed or be the occasion to try seriously to invade us.

"What Napoleon approved is a plan to send a pair of brigs of war to Pendrag Island with a couple of companies of Skirmishers — that's what their light infantry is called. The idea seems to be that these troops, together with the local Catholic Scots, would seize control of Pendrag Island and proclaim Prince David the King of Scotland. They will then cross to the Scottish mainland to be joined by hoards of Catholic Scots and others who are fed up with the Hanoverian government and oppose Scotland being joined to England to the disadvantage of Scotland, as they see it.

"It sounds to me like an undertaking with very little chance of success, even of diverting many resources to killing it," Giles remarked

"Probably it is. We certainly expect so, but we see some advantage in letting it proceed so that we can catch the plotters in the act and remove any further threat from this pretender.

"That's why I am meeting with you, Giles, hopefully without anyone guessing what we are discussing. There are lots of French spies in London who would be very much aware of a distinguished frigate captain who has indicated that he is no longer interested in taking up routine commands, suddenly taking a new mission that might indicate that we have become aware of Percy's treachery. We can expect the French to be a bit wary of the consequences of their plan being exposed prematurely, and our taking steps that might be considered as getting ready to nip the plot in the bud would make them cancel, leaving us vulnerable to some other endeavor which we would know nothing about until it was being executed. We want to let the rebellion get started and then end it before it can do any serious damage or continue lurking as a possible danger to the country. So this is where we hope that you will come in, Giles."

"Oh? I was wondering when we would get to that. You know that I am not in command of a ship right now, don't you?"

"Well, yes and no."

"What?"

"You are not on active duty right now because your frigate, *Glaucus,* was so badly damaged on that voyage to try to assert the King's interest in Hanover, but no one else has been given her command. Because of the reputation she gained — you gained — the Navy Board decided to repair *Glaucus* and make her seaworthy again."

"Yes, I know. Luckily, the experts at the Board realized that the best yard for the job is Stewart's, who built her. Mr. Stewart tells me that the Navy Board have also acknowledged that they should have accepted his original design for the stern rather than the one some incompetent in the Navy Office insisted looked so much better than the one Mr. Stewart thought was structurally sounder for a vessel that might have to take a cannonball where the side meets the stern. So *Glaucus* should be better than new after he has finished the work."

"So I've heard. I've also heard that the Board and your first lieutenant want *Glaucus* to have a training cruise to make sure that everything is as it should be before she is put back in regular service. You'll have to make up your mind about continuing to command her when they have reached that stage."

"Yes, Daphne and I have been discussing my future. I am inclined to resign my commission and come ashore. I could be fully occupied as a member of the House of Lords and as a substantial landowner. I think I could be satisfied just doing that. However, Daphne believes that I would not be happy being permanently away from the sea. She claims she sometimes sees a wistful look in my eye, which means that I am thinking about and missing my ship. It's not that Daphne doesn't want me at home; it's that she wants me to be happy and satisfied with our life together. What she says about my missing the sea does have some truth to it, though I am fully reconciled to never commanding a warship again.

"I do know that I do not want a ship-of-the-line, and I don't want to be assigned to a distant fleet, like those in the Caribbean or the East Indies or even the Med. So I doubt that I will ever again command Glaucus or another naval ship. After Trafalgar, things should be pretty quiet in home waters."

"Yes, I can see your dilemma. I may have a temporary solution for you to see what you truly want: a final cruise to verify that you really desire to leave the Navy. I know that your last voyage left a bad taste in your mouth despite your capturing two frigates in the course of it."

"It did. On that trip, the basic mission was a flop, and I feel that I should have been able to prevent *Glaucus* from being hit in her very vulnerable stern. It seems silly, I know, but that is how I feel. What do you suggest?"

"A one-time endeavor to counter this pretender's efforts, using *Glaucus*, of course."

"Oh? I'd like to hear more, but I also want to have Daphne hear what it is all about. She has better judgment than me."

"Good, Giles, that makes a lot of sense to me, knowing Lady Camshire. But we want to keep this all as quiet as possible because of Napoleon's spies who may have been told to seek out anything that might indicate that we have learned about their plots. Do you like opera?"

"Yes, very much, but why do you ask?"

"Are you committed for this evening?"

"No, we will be going to a ball tomorrow, and Daphne has plans for us for the following night, I believe, but nothing tonight."

"Well, as you may know, they are performing an opera by Salieri at Covent Garden tonight. I reserved a box in your name. If you take it up, we can get together at the back of the box during the main break. There is often visiting between the boxes; no one is surprised when people vanish from sight into the curtained-off part of the boxes. I can arrange for several officials who are familiar with this situation and what we are thinking of doing about it, and they can explain to you our ideas and how you might be able to help."

"All right, I will try, but it also depends on whether Daphne has arranged anything for us to do this evening."

"Of course. And she can join us. I, for one, would value having her opinion on the plans."

"Just as well. I won't take another assignment without consulting her. Speaking of her, I have to run. I am meeting her at Camshire House, which we are renovating so that we don't have to impose any longer on Lord and Lady Struthers."

Giles said the last sentences in a louder voice that was sure to reach the servants at the side of the dining room. Later, when he and Sir Titus were retrieving their coats before leaving Brooks Club, he said, again loudly, "What luck that we ran into each other today, Sir Titus. Do have a good afternoon nap. It takes a long time to recover fully from a knock on the head."

If Sir Titus was right that French spies could be anywhere in London, Giles thought, it would be highly amusing to think that these remarks might help mislead them about the purpose of the meeting. He was now going to meet Daphne, who, he was sure, would appreciate the trick he was trying to play on the French.

Chapter II

Giles paused as he entered Mayfair's Camshire Square. Through the gardens in its center, he caught glimpses of Camshire house. The repainting of the outside woodwork, including the imposing double doors at the entrance, the repointing of the mortar, and the general cleaning up of the stonework, made for an imposing and harmonious mansion. He had never seen it looking better in all the times he had visited it when it was his father's London house.

The new architect and builder that Daphne had engaged when the criminal doings of the man she had first chosen had come to light proved to have done a magnificent job. Now Daphne was overseeing the placement of the new furniture and consulting with her senior servants about readying the house for their shift to London in a few weeks to stay there for the rest of the Season.

Giles found Daphne inside the house, consulting with the builder to ensure that all the details would be completed before the whole family arrived. Everything struck Giles as a great improvement on the mansion he had inherited. A smell of fresh paint lingered in the air, and the new furnishings that Daphne had ordered were mostly in place.

Missing still were paintings. Most of the good paintings that Giles's father had inherited had disappeared and been replaced by very routine ones. Many of those had been rehung until Giles and Daphne had time to explore the various galleries exhibiting items that they might be proud to hang on the walls. But three of the most prominent places were still empty. They were meant to be filled with pictures of their family. One of Daphne, one of Giles, and one, that would have pride of place, of the family as it had been until recently: Giles, Daphne, Bernard, and Christina. Should the latter one be repainted to include the new baby, Roger? Giles thought not because it would cause too radical a change to a grouping that they both thought was perfect. They could have another one painted with Roger included. There were plenty of places where it could be hung, and, anyway, they still had empty places in Dipton Hall, which these pictures were originally supposed to fill and for which others had to be commissioned. It was all very exciting but also overwhelming.

"Mr. Donahue," Giles broke off his examining the new furnishings to address the designer who had completed the work when his predecessor turned out to be a criminal. "You've done a good job here."

"Thank you, my Lord, but I was just finishing Mr. Beaver's work."

"Well, it strikes me as a very good job done under difficult circumstances. But speaking of Mr. Beaver, you know that he was supposed to be engaged in work for us in Shropshire when his other, nefarious activities were revealed. That work still needs to be done, basically from scratch. Mr. Beaver had hardly started when he was caught, but we still need the house there to be redone. Would you be interested in the job?"

"Not really, my Lord. I find that during construction, issues often arise which need my attention. Shropshire is a long way from London, so I would have trouble designing for you and overseeing the construction. I have a long list of projects that I am committed to finishing, so I cannot afford to be away from London for as much time as even a simple rebuilding would require. However, I know an excellent man in Birmingham who might be interested, a man called Meadows, Rupert Meadows. I am afraid that I know no one in Shrewsbury."

"I see. I would certainly appreciate your sending me a note about how to get in touch with Mr. Meadows. Now Daphne, if you have finished here, we need to stop at the artist's studio so that he can fill in any last-minute details of the paintings which need to be done before they can be hung up here before we move in."

"You're right. I am thinking that we also should order another set painted for the London house. Then we could hang the pictures he has already painted in Dipton Hall in the spaces for which they were intended."

"Good idea, though I hate the idea of posing again," Giles agreed. "And then we can include Roger in the group painting.

As they left Camshire House, Daphne introduced another subject which had been on her mind; "What was your meeting with Sir Titus all about? Has he recovered from his injuries?"

"He seems to have," Giles replied, "though he is still bothered by the effects of being hit in the head. But that is not what he wanted to talk to me about."

"Oh?"

Giles related what Sir Titus had told him about the French plan to revive the Jacobite cause.

"What does he expect you to do about it?" Daphne demanded rather aggressively.

"I'm not sure. He wasn't clear about that, only that it would somehow involve *Glaucus*. He wants to tell us tonight."

"Us?"

"Yes. I made it clear that I would have to consult you about the venture before I would commit to anything."

"Did you? I'm not sure I like that."

"Why? I thought you would be delighted to be part of the decision."

"I suppose I am. It's just that if you take on whatever the navy wants you to do and then you don't come back or are injured badly, I will feel responsible."

"That makes it simple. I won't go. The Admiralty can get someone else."

"No. Then I'd feel guilty about preventing you from doing something that you really should do. I know that I married a sailor and not just an ordinary one but a man who is especially good at undertaking difficult assignments. If someone else undertook it and it didn't work out, we would both feel guilty if you could have succeeded. But I would want it to be a sensible plan for an important business whose urgency is well defined, not like that stupid business with the Spanish galleon that didn't exist. Where are we supposed to meet with Sir Titus?"

Giles explained how a box had been arranged at Covent Garden for them, and the meeting would safely take place behind the curtain during the breaks. Daphne was delighted. She wanted to see the opera, but she had hesitated to suggest it when Giles, despite his love of operas, might feel obliged to attend sittings of the House of Lords. Now there was no conflict between what he had to do and what they wanted to do.

When Daphne and Giles reached the artist's, Mr. Findlay's house, they were shown immediately to the top floor studio. The painter seemed rather nervous as he greeted them. He had arranged the three paintings which they had commissioned on easels, and Giles realized that the painter was wondering what their reaction might be. Even though they had seen the images before at earlier stages of their development, this was the first time they had seen the three paintings together and in their almost-finished state. He had heard tales from Mr. Findlay and from other artists who had had pictures rejected at the last minute without the client paying anything for them. Was that why he was nervous?

The first painting, and already Giles's favorite though he had not seen it before, showed Daphne in summertime on the lawn in front of Dipton Hall. She was wearing a light-blue summer gown and a straw hat that did little to hide the color and fine texture of her hair. She had a rather wistful-looking smile, one that Giles knew well from times when she was making the best of his having to leave on a naval assignment. The next portrait was one of him at the stern windows of his cabin on *Glaucus*, holding his violin and leaning forward to turn the page of a musical score. Giles thought it a fine picture though he wasn't sure that the painter hadn't made some improvements to the face that Giles was used to seeing in the looking-glass. He thought the composition and treatment were far superior to the rigid poses he had seen so often of successful captains and admirals that decorated the walls of the Admiralty. The third painting was a family portrait with Daphne seated on a chair on the terrace of Dipton Hall, holding Christina while Bernard stood near the arm of her chair and Giles stood behind her looking fondly at his family. As always with such pictures, it looked a bit artificial, but then there probably was never a time when they would be together in a way that would produce a fine picture. It was a conventional pose but very well executed, and the artist had not included any dogs to divert the viewer's attention. Of course, Giles had only recently acquired a house dog, a rather scruffy-looking fox hound whose leg had been injured so he could no longer be part of the pack.

Both Giles and Daphne were very pleased with the portraits and their backgrounds and told the artist so. Surprisingly, Mr. Findlay was less so.

"I need to make a few little adjustments to the portraits if you can spare me a few minutes," the artist declared.

"Oh, they look very realistic to me, except you have left the little mole on Daphne's chin out of the picture," Giles remarked. "And her right eyebrow is not quite right.

"You're right about the eyebrow. Now that I see her face again, I realize what is wrong and will change it. The mole I left out deliberately. Most people think of them as flaws."

"Well, I don't," said Daphne.

"I am rather fond of that mole," declared Giles.

"Then I shall add it at the same time I get the eyebrows right," declared Mr. Findlay.

"I like the portrait of Giles more than his representation in the group picture, "said Daphne. "He is just too stiff. I don't suppose that you can get him to look more relaxed. That coiled-spring look, as if he is about to attack some poachers or some other intruders, is not how he is when standing, especially not when relaxing at home."

"I see what you mean. I confess that I wasn't concentrating on the realism of the face. Most of my clients would prefer the look I have given your husband, even if it is not quite how they look."

"I would prefer a more realistic representation. Even when Lord Camshire addressed the House of Lords in all that fancy clothing, he looked genuine rather than pompous. And while you are at it, I see that you have straightened his nose, but, as a result, he doesn't look quite like himself."

"You are right. Lord Camshire's actual nose gives him more character than the one I have drawn. I realize it is not just the straightness, but the shape isn't quite right. If you have the time, I will sketch it as it should be — and your eyebrow too, Lady Giles — so that it will be ready in plenty of time to be hung in Camshire House.

"I am surprised," continued the artist, "that you don't want me to remove what most people consider to be defects. Almost everyone who sits for me prefers pictures of how they would like to believe they should look rather than as they are."

"Well, that doesn't apply to me," declared Daphne. "I can understand if poor Lady Somerland wanted a portrait with the blemishes removed, but mine are just part of my face and always have been."

"Lady Somerland?" Giles asked.

"Yes, don't you remember what I told you," Daphne replied. "She caught smallpox after we met her last year. Luckily, she recovered and has suffered no debilitating consequences, but she is badly pock-marked, poor woman. She had a lovely, clear complexion, you know, and it is ruined. I recommended you to her, Mr. Findlay, to paint a portrait as she looked before becoming ill. I even mentioned that she or Lord Somerland might be interested in having one of your gentlemen's portraits painted since she tells me that the ugly scars are all over her body as well as her face. Did she call on you?"

To Daphne's surprise, Mr. Findlay blushed a bright red at Daphne's telling how she recommended him to paint a salacious picture. Didn't he realize that, in private, women discussed all sorts of things that they pretended they knew nothing about to their husbands and other men?

"Yes, she has. She visited a few days ago with Lord Somerland. Now let us get on with the touching up of the pictures." Mr. Findlay seemed to be very keen to leave the subject of gentlemen's pictures behind. Even though Daphne knew that he painted them, he seemed very nervous about discussing them with a couple who had not approached him about obtaining one from him.

After they left the artist's studio and were walking back to Struthers House, Daphne asked Giles, "Would you need a gentlemen's picture of me if I got smallpox?"

"I don't think so, my dear. It is not just your figure or your smooth face that excites me; it is just who you are, but, yes, your body most certainly does excite me. That is why I don't like to have the lights off when we go to bed and like to have the room well heated at this time of year. Goosebumps on either of us do not improve the passionate adventures we share."

"Oh, you! You are making me blush just imagining what you are referring to! Now, stop it! We have a lot to do today before we get to bed."

"There you go again, my love. My trousers have suddenly become quite uncomfortable."

Giles's uncle and aunt, Lord and Lady Struthers, were delighted when Giles suggested that they join Daphne and him at the Royal Opera House. Uncle Walter was a member of the government, while Aunt Gillian was the soul of discretion, quite capable of conversing all night if need be without ever revealing anything confidential. They were ideal companions to strengthen the ruse about the true purpose of the visit to Covent Garden.

Lady Struthers promptly ordered dinner to be moved forward and made less elaborate so that they could arrive in good time. She treated the sudden change of plans as nothing remarkable. Certainly, she wasn't going to miss the theatre just to keep to a domestic schedule. Of course, any bother involved fell on the servants, not on her, though the dinner might be somewhat less elaborate than usual.

When they entered the theatre, and before going to their box, Lady Struthers took well-disguised glee in telling all her friends how thoughtful her nephew had been to arrange this visit to the theatre when he realized that he would be staying with his aunt while attending to his duties in the House of Lords. No one would guess that it was a last-minute invitation arising from a purpose quite different from enjoying the theatre.

Daphne was careful to show enthusiasm for the performance even though, in reality, she thought both the singing and the staging were rather second-rate. Of course, that impression might be as much based on her impatience to find out what might be in store for Giles as on an impartial evaluation of the opera. Certainly, Daphne was relieved when the first act ended, and she and Giles could slip through the curtains at the back of the box to where several government officials waited who had entered the dining area of the box surreptitiously.

Quite a varied group was waiting for Daphne and Giles to appear. There was the First Sea Lord, Admiral Jerrycot, who, as Port Admiral in Portsmouth, had been very helpful to Giles in the past, and Mr. Newsome, the Second Secretary of the Admiralty. Besides Sir Titus Emery and a man from the Home office whose name Daphne did not get, the Permanent Secretary of the Foreign Office was present, who was introduced as Mr. MacPherson, and a rather unremarkable man named Mr. Jones also from the Forcign Office, who seemed to be very self-effacing. Finally, Lord MacCarthach was present..

The group got down to business right away. Mr. Jones started by spreading a chart of the east coast of France and Great Britain on the dining table. "It will be easiest to understand the plot we want to counter if I use this map," he announced.

"We start here at Rochefort, down behind these islands. The French have had the brig moved there. They will carry a small company of Chasseurs, hardly more than an honor guard, who are to provide the backbone and military skill that may be lacking in the Scottish rebels that your brother, Lord Pendrag, hopes to enlist in his rebellion. To permit carrying the soldiers and their equipment, the guns will be removed from the brig to reduce the weight she will be carrying.

"Right now, the brig is being provisioned, though loading will not be finished until she is almost ready to depart. Unfortunately, it takes quite some time for messages from our agent in Rochefort to reach us. However, he has engaged a fishing boat, which will sail for Portsmouth once the French ships have left. That news may come too late for any ship still anchored at Spithead or even at Plymouth to scuttle their plans. We'll need to set our trap ahead of time, but not so much that our intentions can get back to the French in time to postpone their venture.

"The French plan, our agent says, is to sail around the west side of Ireland to avoid being spotted or even captured, which might happen if they went the more direct route via the Irish Sea. Overall, their plan is to arrive at Pendrag Island on Wednesday, six weeks from today. For what is planned there, I turn to Mr. Lincoln from the Home Office — more precisely, the Secret Service."

"So that is who that man is," Daphne thought about the person whose name she had not caught.

"We are lucky to have had warnings from two public-minded citizens of Pendrag. They wrote to us about the plans they had discovered. They realized, independently of each other, that Percy MacCarthach was planning to make a Jacobite uprising using the Catholic resentments that still simmer on that island.

"We were tempted to ignore the warnings, thinking them implausible, but we decided to have our agent in Inverary look into the matter discreetly. I can't tell you who he is, but we trust him implicitly. He found out that the rumor was true and that the plans for the insurrection were well advanced, with various pockets of Catholic supporters warned to come to Pendrag or to the mainland near it on a particular day, about six weeks from now. Our man was tempted to raise the protestant clans to pinch this rebellion in the bud, but we persuaded him to wait so that we could catch the ring-leaders red-handed together with this David Stuart and thereby put an end to this nonsense once and for all.

"That pretty well sums up what we know about the plot and the plotters. For what we are thinking of doing about it, I will call on Admiral Jerrycot to tell us what we plan to do."

Admiral Jerrycot laid a new chart on the table. "This is the southwest corner of Pendrag Island. You will notice this area here," he said, indicating a slight indentation in the shoreline of the Island. "It has a sandy beach which is ideal for landing troops. That is where the French plan to come ashore with their troops. Behind the beach lie some fairly flat open fields, ideal for mustering the troops brought by boat and forces arriving by land, such as the Catholic residents of Pendrag Island.

Admiral Jeriycot then pointed to a small island shown on the chart a short distance to the southwest of the beach. "The beach is somewhat protected from the ocean waves and swells by this little island out here," the Admiral pointed to the chart, " known locally as 'Bird Island,' though it is not named on this chart. The chart does not show that it is an odd little bit of land, rising steeply to a height of several hundred feet. As you can see, there is a little bay opening to the southwest. The soundings show that bay is quite dept. You can hide a ship in there, and it is unlikely to be seen from Pendrag Island or from the ocean. The passage in front of the bay is little used by fish boats and other craft because there is a nasty tide-rip right about here and some reefs here, so traversing it can be hazardous." He had been pointing to bit of water shown on the chart as being between the end of Pendrag Island and the islet he was discussing.

"The one trouble with this bay," the Admiral continue, "is that the water is quite deep so, when anchoring, one has to use a stern line to keep the ship from swinging too widely when it is far enough into the bay to be largely hidden from passing ships while she would be virtually invisible to the surrounding area, including in particular Pandrag Island. Only a ship passing south of this little island might see it, and, as I said, that is unlikely to happen because the fishing boats from Pendrag always go around the north end of the island, and other ships steer clear of the hazards I mentioned.

"As a result, hiding a frigate there in advance to intervene just when the French brig is about to land their soldiers on the beach would certainly nip this rebellion in the bud. But it has to be done in secret and have a ship and captain of the highest quality. And for the ploy to work successfully, it has to come as a complete surprise to the attackers. If the French knew about the plan or discovered it prematurely, they might abandon the enterprise. More likely, they would adjust their plans to make our secret ship irrelevant to the early stages of the uprising when they might shift the landing place somewhere else and thereby make it more difficult to suppress the nefarious plotting that Napoleon no doubt hopes will divert our military efforts and expenditures.

"Luckily, we have just the ship and the captain for the job, but he will have to agree, and his participation in the ship's activities must not be evident to French spies in advance, lest they change their plans to frustrate ours. To that end, for I confess that I am very new to my job and not nearly as well acquainted with the resources of the navy as Mr. Newsome, I'll let him explain what we have in mind."

"Thank you, Admiral Jerrycot," the Second Secretary took the floor. "You have explained our requirements perfectly. The ideal situation would allow us to send *Glaucus* under Captain Giles to intercept the enemy. Because we want to capture them in the act, the frigate should hide at that little island until Giles can spring the trap. There two major problems with that. First, Captain Giles has to agree. In my opinion, our second choice to command our response to the French plot would have much less chance of success, and *Glaucus* is the best vessel for the job. Unfortunately, Captain Giles has every right to refuse the challenge, given his record. We hope that we can persuade you not to refuse, Captain Giles."

"Well, I would have to be convinced that this is not another wild-goose chase like my last two assignments. For that's what they were, even if they did turn out to be very rewarding. I would also have to talk it over with Lady Camshire since she has first call on my services, especially now that we have a third child. Iwon't take the job if she doesn't approve of my being away."

"Before considering that, let me tell you about the second problem. But it needs aa bit of a diversion, before I cana get into that. My Lord, I believe that you are short of a first lieutenant?"

"Yes, of course, as you know perfectly well, Mr. Newsome. Mr. Miller was promoted to commander as a result of the captures of those Dutch frigates, even though he was not the most satisfactory of first lieutenants or proved to be excellent when given command of that

Spanish frigate we captured. My second, Lieutenant Macreau, would be an ideal choice to take his place, even though he is rather junior. My acting third lieutenant, Mr. Stweart is very inexperienced, having just been promoted though he acted as acting third lieutenant in the last cruise. None of my present midshipmen is old enough for promotion, though I would certainly have complete faith in either Mr. Dunsmuir or Mr. Bush, who have passed their exams and only wait to become nineteen to get the rank of lieutenant. I would not hesitate to make them acting third lieutenants."

"That is good news because our suggested scheme would be improved by having those men as the officers of the frigate. It is particularly fortunate that Mr. Macreau is French. As you know, we have to guard against Napoleon's spies guessing that anything we do is in response to our becoming aware of their plot. They would find it ridiculous that your French lieutenant would be given an important role in such a sensitive endeavor as having *Glaucus* take the leading role in trying to put an end to this French-backed uprising.

"Let me explain. Our thought is that you, Captain Giles, should go to Baker's Hard to check over and approve the rebuilding of *Glaucus* before taking her on a short trip to check that everything is as it should be. Only after that would she be assigned another major endeavour. If Napoleon's spies discover that you are sailing on a "training" cruise, the French might suspect that we have discovered their plot to restore the new pretender and that *Glaucus* intends to interfere with it. That might be enough to make them cancel this effort and leave us with the possibility that they will renew it later without our learning about it. Since we would prefer to stop them now rather than wait and hope that we can discover the next time they plan to implement their attack, we want to make it unlikely that they will think that *Glaucus* is the heart of our plans to stop their uprising

"To that end comes the second aspect of our planning, which involves why it is important to have an unlikely set of lieutenants in charge of your frigate on a trial cruise. We were thinking that, after you have inspected *Glaucus* at the dockyard, word will come that you are needed in London or Dipton urgently. For that reason, Lieutenant Macreau will be ordered to take Glaucus into the Irish Sea. Rather than postpone the cruise, you will have Mr. Macreau take Glaucus to sea with orders — which will be loudly discussed in the tavern at Butler's Hard — to avoid conflict with French forces. That would make sense to the spies as being useful to remind our boat-owners operating out of that area that the Royal Navy is at sea to protect their shipping.

In reality, the purpose of the cruise is to meet you, Captain Giles, somewhere beyond the shores of Wales so that you can take over for the real purpose of *Glaucus*'s being in the area, namely to stop this nonsense at Pendrag Island. I was thinking that Liverpool might be a suitable place for *Glaucus* to pick you up. Then you would proceed north in your frigate to put an end to Lord MacCarthach's attempt at rebellion.

"I see," said Giles in a very noncommittal voice. "Well, I'll have to consider the proposal with Lady Camshire. It certainly sounds like a well-thought-out and feasible plan. The one thing that surprises me is going into Liverpool, where there could easily be French spies, and anyway, quite a fuss might be made over *Glaucus* just when we would prefer to have her whereabouts unknown. I would suggest the small town of Birkenhead for the rendezvous. It is nearer the ocean than Liverpool and is quite easy to reach from Chester."

Daphne, who was standing to one side, piped up. "If all that's holding you back, Giles, is me, then I would say this undertaking is ideal for you. It should be a short expedition at a rather slow time for us both at Dipton and in London. And it will get you to stop brooding about that last cruise."

"I wasn't brooding, Daphne! Nevertheless, since you think this enterprise might be worthwhile, my answer, Gentlemen, is 'yes.'" Giles said. "Just as well to get that settled now because the next act of the opera is about to start, and we wouldn't want to miss it or be trying to decide things while it is going on. I suggest, Mr. Newsome, that I call on you tomorrow morning, say at nine o'clock, which would be natural if I was about to request orders for *Glaucus*."

Everyone agreed with nods of their heads. Daphne and Giles slipped through their curtains as the orchestra started to tune up, though the musicians could hardly be heard over the ruckus that those attending the performance in the pit and the gallery were making. Daphne was hoping that she could better enjoy the rest of the performance now that she did not have to wonder what the mysterious meeting might be about. She was quite pleased to have been included in deliberations about

Giles's posting for the first time. Later it would feel less that his absence had been imposed on her and more that she was also responsible for it.

Chapter III

"Smallpox in Reading." Daniel Moorhouse read from the slate his brother was holding towards him. "Smallpox in Reading? What do you mean, George?"

An apoplectic fit had left George Moorhouse without the ability to walk or talk and with only the use of his right arm and hand, but reading and thinking had been left intact. He communicated by writing on his slate and by gestures, and now he pointed to the newspaper.

"In the paper, George? Let's see."

Daniel took up the broadsheet and scanned the articles. There it was, just a very short note saying that there had been a smallpox outbreak in the town affecting many people and businesses.

"Harold and Mary?" George wrote on his slate.

"Oh, Lord! Of course. How do we find out? Daphne would know, but she is away."

"Maybe the butler at Dipton Hall, Steves, has some way to contact them quickly."

As if writing his name on the slate had summoned him, the door to the room opened, and Tisdale, the butler, intoned, "Mr. Steves from Dipton Hall is here to see you, sir. Can I show him in?"

"Yes, of course, Tisdale."

Steves was right on Tisdale's heels. "Mr. Moorhouse, Mr. George. We have received a letter from Mr. Harold Moorhouse's bookshop in Reading marked very urgent. It is addressed to Lady Camshire, and I don't know if I should forward it to her and, if so, by post — which is how it arrived — or by messenger."

"Oh, goodness," said Mr. Daniel Moorhouse, "I don't know what to say. We just read that there is an outbreak of smallpox in Reading. I wonder if that is what the letter is about."

"Open it, Daniel! I'll take responsibility," wrote George.

"I suppose I should. Yes, Steves, give it here."

Daniel took the letter from Steves and broke the seal.

"Oh, no! Oh, no!" he cried, wringing his hands ineffectually. "George, this letter has terrible news from Reading. Both Harold and Nancy have smallpox."

"What about the children?" wrote George.

"The letter — from the bookshop attendant — doesn't say anything about them or much else. I suppose that I should go there at once." The way he spoke made it clear that Daniel would rather not go to the town to deal with whatever he might find there.

"Not much you can do there," George wrote. "You might make things more difficult. Anyway, it's too late to go today."

"I suppose that you are right," Daniel replied. "I wish Daphne were here — and Giles. They would know what to do."

"Mr. Moorhouse, sir," Steves broke in. "My thought exactly.

"Lord and Lady Camshire are at Butler's Hard now, which is hardly farther from Reading than we are here. I could order Walters, our groom, you know, who sometimes serves as a dispatch rider for Lord Camshire, a position he held in the army, to take the message to Lord and Lady Camshire. If Griffith leaves promptly, he could be in Butler's Hard by dawn, so Lord and Lady Camshire could get to Reading about as quickly as they would if they were here, or, for that matter, as you could if you went yourself."

"We'll do that," Daniel Moorhouse declared, not even hiding how relieved he was. "Send this letter with Griffith. Just have him mention that I will be happy to come to Reading if they think I would be useful."

"You should write that," George scrawled on his slate.

"I don't think we have time for that. The more daylight that this man Walters can have, the better, I would think," Daniel replied. "It's lucky that Daphne and Richard have had that cow-thing. It would keep them safe."

Daniel was referring to the new method of preventing smallpox, called vaccination. Mr. Jackson, the physician who liked to be called an apothecary to distinguish himself from the usual leaches who reveled in being called 'Doctor," had found out about it from his friend Jenner in Gloucestershire. Mr. Jackson had badgered everyone who would listen into having a preventive treatment he called 'vaccination.' Daphne had been very enthusiastic about the new method of preventing smallpox and had insisted that everyone at Dipton Hall and Dipton Manor have the treatment. Most of their tenants had followed suit, so Dipton was a town where a spread of smallpox was most unlikely.

"So have I," agreed Daniel. "That is not why I don't want to go. I do wish that I had tried harder to mend fences with Harold."

"Well, you did not," wrote George dismissively.

David Geoffreys had come to Dipton Hall after an accident invalided him out of the cavalry. He knew horses and had very good night vision. In the army, he had become used to riding at night with messages. When Giles discovered this ability and the man's complete honesty, he entrusted him with carrying messages that needed to be delivered as soon as possible.

Geoffreys was happy to ride through the night to Butler's Hard since it promised a clear night with a full moon, and there had been no rain for a week. He stopped only once on the way, at a posting inn, to change horses and to have a late-night supper. Then off he went again, more slowly since the hired horse was nothing like as good a mount as the one he had ridden from Dipton. He had paid extra to have the mare stabled at the inn until he could return. She was far too good a horse to be exchanged for the one he would take on the next stage of his journey.

Geoffreys arrived in Butler's Head well before dawn. The inn where he expected to find Giles reported that Lord and Lady Camshire were staying with Mr. Stewart, the owner and operator of the shipyard, in his house a few doors down the street. When Geoffreys knocked on the indicated door, it was opened by a servant, probably a footman, since it was not a large enough house to warrant a butler. In moments Giles emerged from the room where he had been eating breakfast.

"Geoffreys! What are you doing here?"

"Mr. Moorhouse and Mr. Steves told me to bring this letter to you, my lord, as quickly as possible. I left last evening."

'You've made good time, Geoffreys. You must be tired. Go to the inn and tell them to give you a good breakfast and a room to get some sleep. But first, let me see what this is all about," Giles said, holding the letter up to make his meaning clear.

As he was reading it, Daphne came from the breakfast room. "What is it, Giles?"

"Goeffreys has just brought this letter from Dipton. Harold and Nancy have smallpox. This letter arrived at Dipton from Reading yesterday afternoon. Steves and your father decided to forward it to us. Geoffrey rode all night to bring the news. Your father mentions that he thought we could get to Reading just as quickly as he could, and we would be better able to deal with whatever the situation turns out to be there."

"Well, that's probably true. We'd better leave as soon as possible," Daphne agreed. "Geoffreys," ordered Giles, "go to the inn and, before you arrange for your stay, see if you can contact Ted, our coachman. Tell him to come to Mr. Stewart's as soon as he can. You can tell him we are going to Reading as quickly as possible. Now, there are some things I have to arrange, though, Daphne, except for one item, they can wait until we have had our breakfast. And Betsey will have plenty of time to get everything ready to leave."

They returned to the breakfast room, where, even before he sat down again, Giles ordered, "Lieutenant Stewart, go out to *Glaucus* right away and ask Mr. Macreau to come here as soon as he can to get new orders."

Lieutenant Daniel Stewart rose to his feet, saying only, "Aye, aye, sir," before hustling out of the door.

"I am afraid that we have to leave as soon as Giles has instructed his officers," announced Daphne to the older Stewarts with whom they had been sitting at the breakfast table, dawdling over coffee as they chatted. Joshua Stewart, the owner of the shipyard at Butler's Hard, and his wife had become firm friends of Giles and Daphne, especially after Mrs. Stewart had gotten over her initial timidity in the presence of the wife of a Knight of the Bath when she discovered that they shared a passion for gardening. Luckily that had been before Giles inherited his Earldom. That might have produced too wide a gap between the two couples to be easily bridged. "My brother and his wife have contracted smallpox, and we have to go to Reading to see how we can help," she explained.

"Isn't it very dangerous for you to visit a house where there is smallpox, Lady Camshire, especially with your own young family needing you?" asked Mrs. Stewart.

"Not really, both Giles and I have been vaccinated against the disease, and it seems to work marvelously in stopping smallpox," Daphne replied.

"I should have thought of that," responded Mr. Stewart. "Daniel told us how Captain Giles had had every member of the crew vaccinated against smallpox. He mentioned that only knowing that you had had the treatment, Captain Giles persuaded every member of your crew to let your surgeon treat them as well."

"Yes, I am glad they agreed," Giles replied. You have no idea how an outbreak of a disease like smallpox can render a ship so short of crew members that she would have difficulty making port, where she would then have to be quarantined until there was no sickness left. You and Mrs. Stewart should get vaccinated, and you should get your doctor to vaccinate every one of your workers."

"Yes, you should do that, Mr. Stewart," chimed in Mrs. Stewart. "Daniel has shown no ill effects from the treatment. Lord Camshire is right: smallpox could wreak havoc on our town and the shipyard."

"I did try to get Dr. Butcher to vaccinate us and our people, but he said he didn't think anything of what he called "quack medicine," and so refused."

"Well," said Giles, "you can see, Mr. Stewart, from your son and the crew of *Glaucus* that the procedure is safe. If you want, I'll ask our physician, Mr. Jackson, if he would come here to vaccinate anyone who wants it. I am sure that if you lead the way, many of your workers will take the opportunity to get protected from the disease, but I warn you: many people are suspicious about the treatment and worry that it will do more harm than good. It is not dangerous like the old treatment, variolation, was. It gives you a mild case of cowpox. Cowpox is not fatal and leaves little scarring."

"I would be very honored if you could arrange for Mr. Jackson to visit, Captain Giles," concluded the shipbuilder.

Shortly after that, Lieutenant Stewart returned accompanied by Lieutenant Macreau. The two were closeted with Giles in Mr. Stewart's study. At the end of their meeting, Giles walked with them back to the landing stage.

"Good luck on the cruise.," Giles said in a loud, carrying voice, the sort used habitually by other captains, whatever the circumstances, so everyone in the vicinity knew what they were saying. "As you know, I have been called away to Reading to see about my wife's relatives. There is smallpox there, and I just got the news that they were infected. I don't know how long I will be, especially as my brother-in-law and his wife have children who may need special arrangements.

"I am sure that you can manage everything splendidly, Mr. Macreau. I'm sorry that I will not be with you to see how *Glaucus* is performing, but I know you are fully capable of handling this voyage up into the Irish Sea to check that Mr. Stewart's shipyard has once again done the repair job splendidly. Keep out of trouble. I am sure the Admiralty has something special for us to do after you get back, provided the frigate does not need more work done on her. I don't want you to cause any damage by being too adventurous, but be sure to look out for any weaknesses."

Giles winked at the two lieutenants before turning away to return to Mr. Stewart's residence. That little skit should mislead any spies that might be lurking in earshot. At the shipbuilder's house, he found that his traveling coach was just pulling up in front of the portico. The luggage had already been brought out ready for loading, and Betsey was standing, prepared to make sure that everything was stowed safely before getting in herself. Giles and Daphne said their goodbyes to the Stuarts. Then Giles handed Daphne into the carriage and climbed in himself. The footman closed the door and raised the steps before assuming his perch on the back of the coach. Off they went, keeping to a sedate pace until they reached the edge of the town where Ted, the coachman, cracked on the speed.

"How did it go with your lieutenants?" Daphne asked.

"Better than I expected. I think I put on a good act as a captain afraid that his subordinates wouldn't take good care of his ship, and they acted as if all the instructions were redundant because they knew their business, and anyway, it promised to be a routine, boring trip."

"If this keeps up, you will become an expert actor deceiving anyone who is paying attention about your intentions. Ted tells me that we only need to stop once to rest the horses. We should be in Reading well before dark if this weather holds."

They made good time, despite its being winter. There had been no rain for several days, and the road was in good condition. According to the clock on a church they passed as they entered the town, they reached Reading a little after two in the afternoon. After turning off the Turnpike, the road they followed led them to Broad Street, which seemed to be the town's high street. The coach turned off the street to enter the courtyard of an inn called the George, which Ted had heard was reliable. Of course, they had no reservations, but the crest on the carriage door guaranteed that fine rooms were available for the Earl and Countess of Camshire, no matter who else might already be staying at the inn.

The innkeeper and his wife were very helpful. They warned Giles and Daphne that there was an outbreak of smallpox, but they did not seem to be worried about it. That was not surprising: both bore the distinctive scars, called pockmarks, that indicated that they had survived the disease. Their host knew where Harold's bookshop was, just a few doors down on the opposite side of Broad Street.

"It's closed now, my lady," the innkeeper said. "Mr. and Mrs. Moorhouse both contracted smallpox and died."

"What happened to the children?" Daphne asked.

"Last I heard, they have not got the disease," his wife said. "The Moorhouses' servant left at the first sign of the illness — not that it did her much good. I hear she has the disease now. I think one of the safe maids is looking after the children."

"Safe maids?" Daphne asked.

"Yes. Someone who has had smallpox and recovered. Like my wife here, but, in this case, someone who can provide domestic service. The woman is called Marjorie, and terribly scared she is, too. But quite safe. One can't get smallpox twice, you know. I just hope that she is still there. Heaven knows how she will be paid. Kindness only goes so far, you know."

"Giles, we must get over there at once," Daphne pronounced.

"You can't go there, my lady. There is a quarantine. Unless you've had the smallpox, you can't enter."

"That's all right. We have both been vaccinated by our doctor, so we are safe."

"Is that like the var… var … something or other? You know, where you deliberately get smallpox so you can't get it again. You are supposed to get a mild dose, but it didn't work very well for poor Lady Susan at the corner house. She had a little party with three of her friends, and they were all given the var-something. They all got smallpox, all right. Lady Susan went blind, and one of her friends died. The other two are as badly scarred as anyone else who catches smallpox in the usual way."

"No, this is something quite different from variolation. There is no danger of getting smallpox, just cowpox. If you have had cowpox, then you are safe from smallpox. We have both had this vaccination, as it is called. It just produced one small pockmark where the material entered my hip."

"I don't know how many people would take to that. Most people don't like you treating them when they have nothing wrong with them just because they might catch a sickness," replied the innkeeper's wife.

"You are probably right. I'm not persuading anyone else to have the treatment, just that it seems to have worked for me and for others I know who have been vaccinated," Daphne replied. "Now, come on, Giles, let's get over to the shop at once!" Daphne declared, and she and Giles left the inn as quickly as they could.

There was no missing the bookshop. Over the main doorway of that building was a sign reading, 'Harold Moorhouse, Esq., Bookseller.' Giles and Daphne did not pause to examine the books in the shop window. At the side of the building was another door, probably one leading to a flight of stairs to the upper floors. There was a sign on the door warning of smallpox and instructing everyone not to enter. Giles, who was in the lead, ignored the sign and tried to open the door. It was not locked

"Is anyone here?" he bellowed even as he started to climb the stairs that began immediately after the door. Daphne was right on his heels. The stairway was poorly illuminated by a small window on the next floor. As Giles neared the top of the stairs, a woman appeared. Even in the poor light, he could see that she was covered in pockmarks.

"Here, what do you think you are doing?" the woman demanded. "You can't come up. It's a pest house."

Giles kept climbing. "You must be Marjorie," he declared. "I am Mr. Moorhouse's brother-in-law."

"He's dead. So is Mrs. Moorhouse. Dead and buried."

"And the children?"

"They haven't caught the disease — yet."

"Where are they?"

"In the room at the back of the house."

"Show me." But Giles didn't wait. He and Daphne barged past the woman to get to the door she had indicated. Surprisingly, he checked himself before throwing open the door. Instead, he opened it smoothly, saying in a surprisingly soft voice, "Hello, children. I am your Uncle Richard, and this is your Aunt Daphne."

Two small children were standing in the room, a boy and a smaller, younger girl.

"Thank you for coming," the little boy said solemnly. "I am Hugh, and this is my sister Mary. She's only five and doesn't understand anything. I am nine years old. Pater and Mater died, and some men came and took their bodies away. We couldn't see them after they became sick. Marjorie is looking after us because she has had the pox already," the child concluded in almost a monotone. Then his face crumpled. "What's going to happen? I've tried to be brave as Pater told me to, but I don't know what to do." He started to cry in a heart-breaking way that said he had been tested to the limit.

Giles squatted down on his heels and put his arms around the boy. "I am here with your Aunt Daphne, and we will take care of you and your sister. You have been very brave, and your father would have been very proud of you."

"But Pater said that boys don't cry," Hugh blubbered before weeping more voluminously.

"That's only when they have to do something brave that they can't do when crying. Just as you have been doing, Hugh. Otherwise, crying is all right. It's a way to recover from difficult things. So cry as much as you want since we are here now."

Daphne had squatted down to be on the same level as the little girl, who looked bewildered and on the verge of tears.

"Are Mater and Pater in heaven?" Mary asked.

"Yes, sweetheart, I'm sure they are."

"Then I won't see them again?"

"No, I am afraid that you won't."

Daphne gathered the child to her, even as the girl burst into a low howl. Daphne's eyes were far from dry, either.

"There ain't no food in the house," Marjorie interrupted. "And I ain't been paid."

Giles looked up. "Who engaged you, Marjorie, and what are you owed?

"That was Mr. Latimer, the accountant. After Mr. Moorhouse fell ill. He gave me two shillings to buy food and said we could settle up my pay later. Then he left for his brother's estate before Mr. and Mrs. Moorhouse became really ill and died."

"And this Mr. Latimer is involved how?"

"Mr. Moorhouse isn't very good at business, they say. Mr. Latimer handles all his bills and orders for books and pays Gordie Frederics, the shop assistant, and so on."

"I see. And Mr. Latimer has paid you how much?"

"He hasn't. Said it would depend on how long I was here and how serious was the illness, and whether the children lived. And now he has gone away, so I don't know where my money will come from, especially as I used some of mine to get food for the children. Two shillings don't go very far when there is smallpox."

"Do you know who the children's godparents are?"

"Yes, sir. They were Mr. and Mrs. Gatsby."

"For both children?"

"Yes, sir, even though it is unusual to have a husband and wife as godparents for all the children. Of course, Mr. and Mrs. Moorhouse didn't have many close friends here. Mrs. Gatsby died last November, and Mr. Gatsby got the smallpox even before Mr. Moorhouse. I heard that he died too. Mr. Latimer told me that no one else was designated to take care of Master Hugh and Miss Mary, but he would try to find out who should take charge of them. But then he left, and I have heard nothing more."

"What about Mrs. Moorhouse's parents. Do you know who they are or where they live?"

"No, sir, I don't. I never met Mr. or Mrs. Moorhouse. In fact, all I know is what Mr. Latimer told me. He said nothing about Mrs. Moorhouse's parents or about you, but everyone knows that Mr. Moorhouse was brother-in-law to Lord Camshire, and you look like your picture in the Illustrated News.

"All right," said Giles. "Then it is clearly up to us, as their aunt and uncle. We'll take care of the children from now on. At least, until Mr. Latimer can return or whoever takes over his practice, and we can find out whether their parents entrusted them to someone else. Here's some money, Marjorie, for you. We appreciate what you have done for the children."

Giles reached into his coin purse, extracted two gold guineas, and gave them to the woman. Almost by instinct, she bit each of them to check that they were actually gold before a smile broke out on her face. "Thank you, sir. Thank you. If there is anything else I can do, just call on me. The innkeeper can tell you how to get in touch with me."

"Did you really give her two guineas, Giles?" Daphne asked.

"Yes, I did."

"It was far too much."

"Possibly, but she took on the job and kept at it till help arrived. I think she earned it."

Daphne said no more. She didn't entirely agree with Giles, but it was not a point she wanted to dispute.

"Giles," Daphne changed the subject. "I think that we should take the children to stay with us at the inn tonight and then bring them to Dipton tomorrow. There is no one to care for them here."

"I agree. It is the right thing to do. Anyway, we are their closest kin, and it is up to us to make sure they are brought up properly. Unless their parents have made better arrangements for them, and it doesn't seem that they have, they should be our wards. When we get back, I will have Mr. Snodgravel look into it."

Daphne looked at Betsey, who had followed her mistress into the house. "Betsey, gather anything belonging to the children or that might be special to them and pack them up. There are likely clothes bags, boxes, cases, or something similar in the box room in the attic. Then get Freddie to help you carry them over to the inn." Freddie was the footman who had accompanied them on the trip. Betsey, Daphne had noticed, took great pleasure in telling him what to do.

"Now, Hugh," said Giles, "do you know where Mary's coat and mittens are and yours?"

"Yes, my lord," the boy stated.

"You shouldn't call me 'my lord,' Hugh. We're family. You and Mary can call me 'Uncle Richard,' and," Giles pointed to his wife, "she is called 'Aunt Daphne.'"

Daphne was astounded by how well Giles seemed to be dealing with this little boy he had never seen before. She'd had to teach her husband how to play with their son, Bernard, and knew that he had become much more relaxed in dealing with their daughter Christina than she had expected. No doubt he would have just as much success with their new baby, Roger.

Hugh proudly showed his aunt and uncle where the children's coats were, together with their boots and hats and mittens. He could put on his own coat by himself and button it up, but Giles had to help him with the boots. The only bit of laughter any of them had heard that day came when Giles tried to put Hugh's right boot on his left foot. Daphne found that Mary needed quite a bit more help and that she wasn't very good at getting the little girl into her outdoor clothes. Daphne was glad that Betsey was busy with other tasks: Daphne would rather her lady's maid did not observe how poorly she managed the job of dressing the little girl.

The innkeeper's wife was most accommodating. There was a connecting sitting room next to Giles and Daphne's bedroom, and it would be no trouble to move in a couple of cots for the children. Would the children eat alone or with Lord and Lady Camshire? Neither Daphne nor Giles had thought about how to care for the children, but they were in agreement. Hugh and Mary would join them for dinner as soon as possible, and they would see to getting the children to bed — with the aid of Betsey, of course.

At first, it appeared that dinner would proceed in silence since the adults didn't want to talk over the children's heads and couldn't think of anything to ask them that would not run the danger of opening the floodgates of grief. Suddenly, inspiration came to Daphne.

"Mary," she asked, "do you like dogs."

"I don't know. Small ones, I guess. Big ones scare me,'' the little girl replied.

"Did you ever want one as a pet? I have a small dog," Giles took up the theme.

"I did, but Mater and Pater said I couldn't. Mater said they make a lot of mess, and Mary is too young," Hugh answered.

"Did she say that? Well, she must have been right. I can understand why she said it, living in town as you do, but I don't think it applies if one has a house where a pet can go in and out when they want," Giles replied.

"Tell them about our dog, Giles," Daphne said, hoping to keep this conversation going.

"Yes, all right. He is called 'Scruffy.' Isn't that a silly name for a dog?" Giles asked Mary.

Mary giggled. "Yes. Why do you call him 'Scruffy?'"

"Because when your aunt and I first saw him, he had just come out of a muddy pond where he had tried to chase a duck. He was all wet and dirty, and his hair was all over the place. It was on a farm, and he went up to the farmer's wife and was about to shake all over her. She yelled at him, 'Get away from me, you scruffy dog.' So he went over to Aunt Daphne, and she stooped down to pet him, but instead, he shook himself, and dirty water sprayed all over her skirt. Oh, she was soaked!"

Mary giggled again and then looked worried when Hugh frowned at her.

"Yes, I was," Daphne agreed. "And I was furious. But Uncle Richard just laughed at me, Just like you did, Mary. It *was* funny. Then he said, 'Get away from her, you scruffy dog.' And that is when the dog got named 'Scruffy.'"

"Mrs. Kimberly, the farmer's wife, was very alarmed at what Scruffy had done," Giles took up the story. "'Bad Dog,' she yelled as she tried to shoo Scruffy away from Aunt Daphne. The poor dog didn't know what was wrong, of course. I don't think he had ever had a chance to spoil a dress before. He was an outside dog and didn't know any better, but Mrs. Kimberly didn't forgive him. 'I'm sorry, Lady Camshire' — that's what people call Aunt Daphne — 'we have to get rid of that dog,' Mrs. Kimberly said. 'We don't need him, and he just makes trouble. We're going to get rid of him.'"

To Daphne's surprise, Giles had adopted a high-pitch, silly voice that made the children laugh when he imitated the farmer's wife.

"Well," Giles continued, "Aunt Daphne didn't like that. She thought that Scruffy was just being a dog and didn't know any better. 'If you don't want him,' she said, 'we'll take him.' And we did, and he now lives with us. You'll see him when we all go to our home."

"Uncle Richard, is Scruffy a big dog?" Mary asked. "I'm afraid of big dogs."

"He's not very big. He's not as tall as you."

"Well, I'm not afraid of dogs," announced Hugh proudly. "I'll protect you, Mary."

After that discussion, the children were much less withdrawn, and they all talked about what else they would find at Dipton Hall. They were town children, knew very little about horses, and had trouble realizing that there would be no close neighbors. But interested as they were, the children were nodding off before the sugary last remove was even presented. They were promptly put to bed. It was fortunate that Betsey had come with Giles and Daphne since she was the only one with any idea of how to get small children ready for bed. At Dipton, that was the job of Nanny Weaver, aided by the nursery maid.

Soon, however, the children were in their nightgowns and tucked into their cots.

Giles and Daphne returned to their private dining room to eat the apple tart and finish their bottle of wine. It was the first chance they had since arriving in Reading to discuss the situation they had discovered. Things were not quite as bad as they had feared since the children had not caught the disease and hopefully would not, but that fact also presented major problems. The absence of Daphne's brother's solicitor, or man of business, or whatever the absent Mr. Latimer's role might be, did mean that all the matters affecting the property that her brother had owned or used could not be dealt with in the next day or two. And the absence of the children's godparents meant that they had no one to consult about how best to deal with the children.

It did not take Giles and Daphne long to resolve what they should do. The children had to be provided for, and the best solution to that problem was to take them to Dipton Hall the next day. To their surprise, they found that each had come separately to the conclusion that they should also adopt the children unless someone had a better claim, and each had feared that the other might not be all that keen on the idea. If Nancy had parents who wanted the children, they would deal with that problem when it arose. Nanny Weaver might not be happy to have two additional children added to the three she already had in her charge. Still, she had a big heart, and employing an extra nursery maid might reconcile her to the extra responsibility. The shop and other matters could be dealt with by their lawyer in Ameschester, especially as all the men who might be helpful in Reading seemed to have disappeared because of the epidemic. With the issue of what to do next resolved, the two were more than happy to go to bed themselves. They fell asleep almost at once.

However, that was not the end of how the smallpox outbreak in Reading affected their day. Sometime in the night, Daphne was woken up by the sound of a child crying. She got up to see what the problem was. Mary was weeping uncontrollably. Daphne gathered the little girl in her arms and murmured sympathetic words in her ear, careful not to promise that her mother or father would ever be back. The sobbing died down, and Daphne carried the child to the bed she was sharing with Giles. Somewhat later, it was Giles's turn to go next door to comfort a child, and soon he returned with Hugh, who snuggled up with Mary between the two adults and soon fell asleep. Giles did too. His long service at sea had taught him to sleep whenever possible and not worry about what the morrow might bring.

This was the first time that Giles and Daphne had children sleeping in their bed. What would Nanny Weaver think if she learned about this extraordinary occurrence, especially since their bed companions weren't even their own children?

Chapter IV

Lieutenants Etienne Macreau and Daniel Stewart were sitting in the stern of the boat rowing them back to *Glaucus.* Before boarding the frigate, they had both glanced at the waterfront in Butler's Hard, wondering if they would see urgent signals telling them to return to the land. It was almost impossible to believe that they would be sailing the frigate as captain and first lieutenant on a genuine ocean cruise. The only other time they had been in that position was when they were in charge of the badly damaged ship limping back to its builder to have major repairs.

There was no signal calling for their return. Instead, the lieutenants could see Captain Giles's coach pulling up in front of the Stewarts' residence. It looked like their voyage would proceed without any last-minute adjustments. Up they climbed to the entry port on Glaucus's main deck, where they were met by the master and bosun, but with no bosun's pipe* welcoming them aboard; Etienne was, after all, only a lieutenant.

Everything was ready for their departure. The tide had turned to ebb in the last half hour, and the wind was steady from the northwest. At nods from Etienne and the Master, Mr. Brooks, the crew raised the anchor, turned the frigate when she started to drift backward and set sails so that she could head down the river. Everything went smoothly; they turned to larboard when they reached the Solent; soon, *Glaucus* was at anchor. Their next tasks would be to take on supplies, including shot and gunpowder.

Large parts of the Channel Fleet were at anchor in Spithead, which did not bode well for *Glaucus* being served promptly by the port authorities. One independent frigate's needs were not likely to take precedence over the requirements of the fleet with the notoriously lackadaisical and unhelpful port suppliers who, though they were employed by government agencies, seemed to think that the Navy they supplied was a nuisance. Etienne had fired a salute to the Rear Admiral's flag flying over one of the ponderous ships of the line, which could blow *Glaucus* out of the water with one broadside. Even though the pennant *Glaucus* flew from her masthead indicated that she was under Admiralty orders and not those of the Admiral, that fact alone meant that he had little hope of getting the Admiral's support in meeting his needs.

Etienne had expected a great deal of trouble with the port authorities in obtaining what he needed from the various shore agencies in charge of victuals and all the other materials needed for even a short cruise. He had seen the frustrations that Giles had encountered with those in charge of supplying the Navy, who seemed to think that their job was to do everything in their power to curtail the transfer from their storehouses to the holds of the ships they allegedly served. In Etienne's early days with Giles, he had noticed how the naval success of a man with little influence led to particularly annoying and offhand responses to requests, couched in the most polite terms, and seemed to put his ship at the bottom of the list for acquiring whatever he needed. Now, here was

Etienne, aided by Mr. Stewart and Mr. Brooks, neither of whom had any smidgeon of influence, going up against the toadies of the anchored fleet. To make matters worse, *Glaucus* was short of hands due to casualties on their previous venture and the inevitable attrition as crew members had discovered convincing reasons for why they should end their naval careers. Giles had always been accommodating with such requests, and Etienne had continued his captain's practice when he was in charge of the injured frigate and her crew while the repairs had been made. Now he realized that the time had come when he would have to round out the crew, which Giles had done nothing about as *Glaucus* was being readied to re-enter active service. He lay awake that night worrying about what the morrow might bring.

Dawn found Etienne's worry about getting more crew members resolved. When he was summoned on deck by the midshipman of the watch, he discovered a collection of small craft surrounding *Glaucus*. They all had passengers on board who looked like they might be seamen. Indeed, he recognized some of the men as former shipmates who had left *Glaucus* for any number of reasons.

"What's going on?" Etienne asked the master, who was standing on the quarterdeck, looking a bit amused.

"Word must have gotten about that we are returning to active service. These boats are full of men who have come to enlist with us."

Etienne knew that, in the time he had served on *Glaucus,* Giles had never had to send out recruitment forays to try to lure men to sign up for naval service, let alone resort to press gangs, nor had he got additions to her crew from the receiving ships*. She had the reputation of being a lucky ship in the sense that she took many prizes and was not known for having many outbreaks of serious illness, while Giles himself and his officers had the reputation of being fair to all who were prepared to work hard.

"Then bring them aboard, one boat at a time, and we will sign up as many as we can. Mr. Stewart, Mr. Brooks, look after that. Now, I have to go ashore to try to get our supplies hurried up."

"Lots of luck with that, Mr. Macreau," said Mr. Brooks. "Portsmouth has a reputation for being extremely unhelpful in performing their duty."

"I know, but if I just sit here, we will never get to sea."

The crew of the captain's barge was turned out as if they were about to row royalty. That represented their pride in *Glaucus* even though the barge would be transporting only a lieutenant and with Carstairs, Giles's coxswain, absent. Etienne appreciated the gesture even though he suspected it would do nothing to advance his cause with the authorities. Their pride also told him they accepted his role and would continue to do their best for their ship and her absent captain.

When the barge arrived at the quay, Etienne found a man with both the insignia and the superior air of a flag lieutenant. Etienne saluted and was about to ask the stranger the way to the Port Admiral's office when the other man extended his hand. Etienne had been about to bow but instead reached out and shook the other lieutenant's hand.

"Lieutenant, are you from *Glaucus*?" asked the stranger.

"Yes, sir, I am."

"Good. I'm Lieutenant Bleay, flag lieutenant to Admiral Granger, the Port Admiral here. He would like to see you before you tackle the ordinance and victualling authorities. The Admiral's office is just down the way a little. I'm ordered to show you where it is."

Only the last sentence indicated the pique that the staff officer might feel about being sent to fetch a lieutenant who was undoubtedly junior to himself.

To Etienne's surprise, for he expected that any superior officer would tend to have him cool his heels for a while before deigning to see him, he was ushered into the presence of the port admiral at once.

"Admiral Granger, may I present Lieutenant Macreau of the frigate *Glaucus*?" intoned the flag lieutenant.

Etienne bowed to a somewhat elderly man sitting behind a table with a window behind him. The Admiral smiled as he nodded in reply to the bow and said in a tone unusually friendly for a senior officer. "Ah, of course, Giles's ship. Young man, you are lucky to be serving with him."

"Yes, sir, I realize that I am. Do you know Captain Giles?"

"Oh yes, he was attached to my North Sea Fleet for a while. Best frigate captain I ever had — made me a lot of prize money even as he was successful in harrying Bonaparte's forces. He was reassigned to *Glaucus* after losing his ship, *Patroclus*, and was no longer under my command. Of course, I had to go ashore soon after that because of this damned gout. I can still be of use, I hope, sitting behind this desk, but I would rather have a sea-going command.

"Well, enough of reminiscence. Captain Giles sent me a note asking me to do what I could to help you get *Glaucus* ready for sea. But that's not why I asked you to come here. Whatever he is up to now — and, no, I don't want to know even though I am curious — it must be very important. I received word from the First Lord that you were to be given every assistance and informed me that the same message had been given to the civilian authorities with orders countersigned by the Prime Minister. I've never known the like of it. Giles didn't have much influence when he served under me, though he had more than he seemed to realize. Even now that he is Earl of Camshire and a very rich man, he doesn't have the sort of influence that gets the Prime Minister to order the shore lazybones to act promptly. This must come from the center of government, whatever the reason for it may be.

"Now, I wanted to see you in advance so that you know that you have the unusual ability to get the suppliers to act quickly for once, especially as I don't imagine that you have the funds for the bribes that are sometimes needed to get these vultures to do their jobs. If there is any problem, you can let them know that you are aware of what they have been ordered to do and that you will not hesitate to complain to the highest quarters. You can also stress that I will be happy to back you up."

"Thank you, sir. That should be very helpful if needed," Etienne answered.

"I hope so. I will be delighted to call them out, especially as the landlubbers at Chatham caused my fleet more trouble than Bonaparte ever did. Tell me, how short of crew are you?"

"I think I have a full crew now, sir, even though we were very short-handed when we left the builder's yard at Butler's Hard. This morning a veritable swarm of experienced seamen showed up ready to serve with us."

The Admiral laughed. "So the tales about Giles not needing the fruits of press gangs are true. Would that there were more captains with his reputation! You can consider yourself lucky to serve under him, Mr. Macreau. Now, Mr. Bleay will take you to the Victualling Office first since they are usually the most difficult to get moving, and then, he will take you on to the Ordnance Office. Let me know if you run into any difficulties."

Etienne left in a daze and was fortunate to have Lieutenant Bleay accompany him. After Mr. Miller was promoted, he and Mr. Stewart had endless problems at Chatham to get work to proceed on the injured *Glaucus*, and Mr. Miller, *Glaucus*'s former first lieutenant, had had the same problems before he left. Now the way might be smoothed. Indeed, the special arrangements worked. Within the hour, Etienne was in the captain's barge, being rowed back to *Glaucus,* and the first of several lighters from the Victualling Office was approaching the frigate. Despite the unprecedented alacrity with which their needs were filled, it was late in the following day before all the gunpowder, shot, stores, food, and water were aboard, and the new crew members were assigned to watches and to tasks within their watches. Everyone was exhausted, so, despite the eagerness of the two lieutenants to start their independent adventure, they had to wait for the following morning before they could leave Spithead.

At Mr. Brooks's suggestion, Etienne waited until full morning light before having "all hands to leave harbor" piped. The lack of frantic activity on the decks of other ships made it evident that the fleet was not about to sail, but that did not mean that *Glaucus* could slip away unnoticed. Most officers and men not engaged in some activity paused to watch as the famous frigate raised her anchor, drifted backward with the ebbing tide and the westerly wind until the rudder bit, then turned, set sail, and proceeded to pick her way between the anchored vessels. Etienne knew well all the many things that could go wrong before they were clear of the fleet. It didn't help that Mr. Brooks tried to console him with the information that virtually all experienced ship handlers had got into trouble at some time leaving a crowded harbor; he didn't want it to be himself who needed to be comforted.

All went well. *Glaucus* had no trouble maintaining her reputation as a crack frigate despite the many new crew members on board who might have weakened her performance. Soon they were on a broad reach along the northeastern shore of the Isle of Wight, with Mr. Brooks murmuring directions to the helmsman to keep well clear of any underwater hazards. Soon they were abreast of the huts and storage sheds on Bembridge Island. The land started to drop away from them to starboard, and they could set a more westerly course. Soon *Glaucus* was full and bye, heading towards France even though their immediate destination was Land's End and the Irish Sea.

Both Etienne and Mr. Brooks knew that they were headed for the Cotinen Peninsula with its harbor of Cherbourg on their present course. For some unknown reason, the harbor was not a base of the French Navy but a haven for privateers and pirates. Cherbourg, however, was also a port frequented by French merchant ships, sometimes to ride out unfavorable weather, sometimes in the hope of evading English privateers when the conditions were too inviting for them to avoid the water near the mouth of the English Channel. The log would not account for the decision to take a long tack away from England. However, if questioned later, their action could be justified by their suspicion that the wind was about to back. When it did, *Glaucus* would make better progress towards their destination than if they had been tacking more frequently to take a more direct route to their destination. In truth, however, both Etienne and Mr. Brooks were hoping for the chance to pick up some prize money before turning back towards the English coast.

It was well past midday, with its change of watch and its ritual of taking the noon sights done before the welcome hail came from the top of the mainmast.

"Deck, there! Sail two points off the larboard bow."

"Mr. Dunsmuir," Etienne said to the midshipman of the watch, "Get aloft and see what she is."

The midshipman grabbed the telescope and headed for the ratlines. Etienne strolled over to the lee rail of the quarterdeck and then realized that he had no hope of seeing a sail that had just been sighted from the top of the mainmast. Sheepishly, he turned back to his position near the wheel. If anyone noticed his reflexive action, they were too wise to indicate what they thought.

Before long, Mr. Dunsmuir had settled himself at the top of the mainmast, put the telescope to his eye, and, after focussing it, found the upside-down image of the horizon where Carter, the lookout, had indicated the sail was. Quickly, the midshipman spotted not one sail but two, the first slightly higher than the second. After staring at the sails for several long seconds, he called down, “Deck there. There are two topsails. Too far away to determine their rigs.”

Etienne controlled his impatience at not knowing what was ahead only with effort. Then he thought of something to do that also would be advantageous in clearing off some of the cobwebs that had undoubtedly accumulated in a crew that had been idle so long. “Mr. Shearer,” he called to the bosun, “Clear for action!”

It was as if Etienne had kicked an anthill. In moments, the deck was covered with seamen emerging from below while the watch on deck moved to new positions. Etienne looked toward the helm, where the Master had taken up his station, while quirking his eyebrows in a decidedly skeptical way at Etienne as if to say, “Is this wise?”

“It’s good practice for the crew,” Etienne explained, then kicked himself mentally. Surely no ship’s captain would ever explain a straightforward order such as the one he had just given. Then he realized that that was not true. Captain Giles, in fact, made a point of explaining orders whenever he had time.

"Well, you or Mr. Stewart, as acting first lieutenant, should get your watch out to time how long it takes, don't you think?" the Master replied.

Etienne realized that Mr. Brooks was giving him an opportunity to save face. Instead of his nervous overreaction to the sighting of a strange sail, he could be thought to be showing a lack of concern about a distant threat that would not be a serious problem for at least an hour by practicing the crew in a much-needed routine. He pulled out his pocket watch, a gift from Giles, to check the time when the order had been given. As the minutes ticked away, he was glad to have ordered the practice while Giles was away. If he had not ordered the maneuver, he would likely be very embarrassed when Giles returned and routinely ordered the drill. The crew was definitely rusty in the coordination needed to clear for action speedily. The sooner he could get them up to form, the better.

Mr. Dunsmuir, who was still at the masthead, called down again, "Deck there! The sail is a brig. Her topsails are French cut. She is maintaining her course."

Mr. Brooks glanced aloft and murmured to Etienne, "With our royals furled, she probably has yet to see us. The royal yards are far harder to spot than the sails from that distance."

The implication was not lost on Etienne. Just because the distant ship was maintaining a converging course did not imply that she was friendly. As if to confirm this, the next cry was, “Deck there, there are two — no, three — other sails to leeward of the brig, possibly quite close to her. Still can’t determine what the others are, but they look like merchant ships.”

“Interesting,” remarked Mr. Brooks. “I wonder if they are prizes, or is she trying to protect them from privateers. In either case, we should investigate, don’t you agree, Mr. Macreau?”

“Quite right, Mr. Brooks. Helmsman, adjust course, steer a point and a half to larboard. Then steer by the course*. Mr. Carpenter, relay the instructions to the sail handlers to adjust appropriately.”

In his flurry of anxiety, Etienne was not at all sure that he had given the right command, but the response of his subordinates, the helmsman replying, “Aye, aye, sir,” and Daniel Stewart intoning, “Midshipmen, sail-handlers, sail by the course. Were the responses the correct ones? Etienne was not sure, but they were among the ones that Captain Giles used, even though he suspected that some of his captain’s practices were unconventional. However, Captain Giles, he knew, was not a stickler for clarity, putting more emphasis on having his orders understood by those to whom they were directed than according to standard and sometimes opaque jargon. He had learned a lot in his time in *Glaucus*. Would he have to unlearn it if he were appointed to another ship before getting his step?

“Mr. Macreau,” called Mr. Stewart. “Cleared for action.”

Etienne pulled out his watch. “Forty-seven minutes. Mr. Macauley, the marines can stand down from the fighting tops. We will not restore the other things until we know what these distant vessels are about."

"Deck there," Mr. Dunsmuir again called from the main-royal top. "The brig has worn around to go the opposite way, and the other ships are altering course similarly."

"Mr. Brooks," said Etienne, "set a course to intercept."

The orders were soon relayed, the master doing the calculations in his head that would have taken many minutes of head-scratching for Etienne to perform. It would undoubtedly be some time before any action would occur, Etienne mused, whether or not the clearing-for-action was complete.

Etienne heard another call, this time from the bow. "Sail ho, fine off the larboard bow." "That will be the ship we are pursuing," remarked Mr. Brooks.

"Mr. Dunsmuir," Etienne bellowed to the masthead. "Return to the deck."

"Forty-seven minutes! We'll have to do better than that, Daniel," remarked Etienne, "or Captain Giles will have our guts for garters. He is never happy if it takes over thirty minutes. Now get the cook to relight the stove and then pipe hands to dinner. It will be a good while before we are in action. Better to do it on a full stomach and get the marines out of the fighting tops. They can leave their rifles and muskets up there for now."

Etienne moved to the quarterdeck rail, looking down at the main deck. The crew was busy lashing down the guns and setting everything in order but not fully securing everything, leaving the possibility of springing into action quickly if needed. It had been a trying morning for the first lieutenant. He had commanded some prize ships before this, but he had never commanded *Glaucus* without Giles or Mr. Miller being at hand. Now he alone was in charge when action might be imminent. He was surprised how lacking in confidence he felt as they had sailed along, even how, at times, the commands, which he had heard over and over again when the Captain spoke them, sometimes came reluctantly or garbled to his tongue or even be forgotten without prompting from the Master. Had anyone noticed? Would this difficulty disappear with more experience, hopefully soon? Had Captain Giles ever had such problems. Somehow, it struck him as unlikely. He could not imagine Giles as a tongue-tied lieutenant or an inexperienced midshipman, even though he knew that his Captain had come up through the ranks with little influence to smooth his career, just like Etienne when he had received a minimal bit of help from an established relative to secure his first position, but with no further assistance from that source. Well, Etienne thought, he should get to dinner. It promised to be an even more trying afternoon when *Glaucus* came up with the unknown brig.

Chapter V

The afternoon watch dragged on as *Glaucus* pursued the brig and her attendant ships even though she was converging on them steadily. A shout from the masthead had announced that their target was flying a French flag, as were the others. That would account for her not cracking on all sail to escape when *Glaucus* came in sight. When they had turned to a more downwind course, Etienne had loosed the royals, and it was now clear that they were overhauling the enemy brig. The attendant vessels must account for the fact that the brig had not set more sails, though, if he were in the French ship's position, Etienne thought he might well abandon the ships accompanying him to their fate while he tried to escape from the large ship.

"We'll be in range in thirty minutes if she holds her course," Mr. Brooks told Etienne in an unexcited, matter-of-fact tone of voice. 'Was the Master trying to tell him something,' Etienne wondered. Of course he was!

"Mr. Stewart, prepare for action!" Etienne bellowed. The amount of scurrying around this time was less than when they had cleared for action. Nevertheless, the guns had to be unlashed, their gunpowder brought from the magazines, the bags of explosive put down the muzzles, then tamped down, and, finally, the balls inserted. The gun ports had to be readied for instant raising, and the lashings on the guns reduced so that they could be run out at a moment's warning. The marines who would be in the fighting tops awkwardly climbed the ratlines with their muskets while some of the topmen carried aloft the rifles that Lady Camshire had donated to Glaucus. The rifles would only be used when there was a good chance of their hitting someone because they took far more time to load than the inaccurate muskets, which were their standard guns.

Etienne could read the brig's name on her stern: '*Eclat.*' With no accents on capital letters, he could not tell if it was French or English, but he guessed she must be French, even though she had switched her flag from French to English as soon as she saw *Glaucus.* It was considered permissible to sail under false colors as long as the true flag was shown *before* battle started. The enemy might not have realized that her true colors had been spotted from *Glaucus* from the main royal topmast even while the royals were furled so that she could not see the British frigate.

Glaucus was on a course calculated to come up on the brig's larboard quarter. Both ships were on a starboard reach, with *Glaucus* slightly closer to the wind. Etienne could see through his telescope that an argument seemed to be raging on the brig's quarterdeck. 'What a way to run a navy!' he thought with the contempt that Frenchmen of the old regime felt about Napoleon's warriors. It didn't make sense, he thought. The time for the brig to come closer to the wind, giving *Glaucus* the dilemma of trying to capture the warship or go for her prizes, had passed. Even if the French ship sailed closer to the wind on the starboard tack, Etienne's frigate was now so close that she could catch the brig in minutes and still have time to catch up with the slower-moving merchant ships handily.

The dispute on the French ship ended. Orders were shouted that Etienne could not quite understand, but it was evident that the French crew was preparing to change course. 'Well,' he thought, 'They have left it too long.'

"Larboard your helm, steer two points to starboard!" the first lieutenant bellowed. 'This will teach them!' he thought. To his complete surprise, *Eclat* turned downwind rather than upwind. What was she doing? It became obvious even as Etienne's helm order was being obeyed. The brig was trying to ram *Glaucus*! On Etienne's new course, with the brig now pointing straight at where the frigate would be in moments, she would ram the larger ship almost at once. It was too late for Etienne to do anything: trying to cancel his previous order would do more harm than good.

Eclat's bow thrusters fired. They were only nine-pounders and did no serious damage. Even before the smoke had cleared, a call came from Mr. Jenks, the youngest of *Glaucus*'s midshipmen, who had been given the job of watching *Eclat*'s flag, which would signal surrender. "She's struck."

"Hold your fire!" Etienne roared even as the French brig's bowsprit came into contact with *Glaucus*'s

"Let go sheets and tacks. Topmen, furl the sails," Mr. Brooks commanded.

The two bowsprits ground against each other as the ships' ways forced each spar across the other with *Glaucus*'s on top. On each ship, some forestays failed.

Then as a wave raised *Eclat*'s bow faster than *Glaucus*'s, it put irresistible pressure on the bowsprits of both ships, and so loud, ominous cracks sounded from both. In *Eclat*'s case, the remaining stays of the foremast snapped, smothering the focsle in sailcloth from the headsails. The foremast swayed most alarmingly but held, except that the fore topgallant mast went by the board. Only prompt action by the sail handlers prevented more extensive destruction of her masts and rigging.

Glaucus fared even worse. The pressure on her bowsprit caused the bobstays* to fail, with the result that the spar bent upward until it cracked, the gammoning* was pulled upward, and all the forestays went limp. From bottom to top, her now poorly supported foremast swayed alarmingly but somehow remained vertical, thanks to very quick work with the sheets and tacks by the sail-handling crew. Even so, the royal foreyard was left hanging cockeyed as its sail flapped loudly.

"Whooo! That was close to being a disaster," said Mr. Brooks when the worst of the destructive motions had ended. "Now, all we have to do is take command of the prize and start putting things to order."

Etienne realized that the Master was again guiding him to the most important thing he had to do now.

"Mr. Stewart, Mr. Macauley, borders away; take her surrender. Mr. Evans, examine the damage to the bowsprit and recommend the best way to repair it."

Suddenly, Etienne found himself at a loss. Everything that needed to be done was being undertaken. The petty officers, topmen, and experienced able seamen had everything under control. His giving more orders would just slow things down. Now that he thought of it, Captain Giles's habit in similar circumstances was to step aside once the jobs had been assigned and wait until he was needed again to make a decision. Was it as difficult for the Captain not to interfere as he was finding it?

Etienne realized that, possibly, no one was keeping track of the French brig's prizes. Of course, with all that had happened, they were probably now well away, and *Glaucus* was in no state to chase them. He looked leeward, and there they were, but they were not hurrying downwind to get away. Instead, they appeared to have rafted together and backed the mainsail on the nearest ship to hold them in place. That seemed strange, but, right now, Etienne didn't think he had a boat's crew to spare to visit the other ships to satisfy his curiosity. The next time he glanced, he saw a boat being launched from the leading merchant ship, and his following glance showed that it was being rowed toward him. As it seemed to be always the case, he would have to wait to satisfy his curiosity; there was no way to speed the answer. In the meantime, reports were starting to come in from the various subordinates assigned to the wide variety of tasks arising from the French brig colliding with *Glaucus.*

Etienne was discussing the problems from the cracking of the bowsprit with the carpenter, Mr. Evans, when Midshipman Jenks called, "Boat approaching larboard side." In moments, a burly, bearded man came through the entry port. In response to Etienne's greeting, the man replied, "Michael Forth, sir. Captain of *The Pride of Rye,* one of the ships that the goddamned Frenchman captured."

"Lieutenant Etienne Macreau, Captain Forth. Welcome aboard H.M. Frigate *Glaucus*."

"Another bloody Frenchman pretending to be English!" Captain Forth exclaimed. "Where is your captain?"

"I command this ship, sir, in the absence of her captain," replied Etienne amicably. "What can I do for you?"

"I hate to say it, but we need your help."

"I am afraid that we cannot discuss this in my cabin since we are still cleared for action, Captain Forth. Please tell me what you need."

"Those three ships were all taken by that French pirate. They were taking us into Cherbourg when you appeared. They left minimal crews onboard us — they must have been short of men. Captain Walter, who commanded one of the other captives, said that the frogs had sent most of their excess crew back on other captures they had made. Anyway, the frogs kept us three ships close together, with their brig somewhat to windward. I suppose they thought they could recapture us without trouble if we tried to overwhelm their prize crew.

I don't know what happened exactly, but suddenly there was a great deal of confusion. After the frogs captured us, most of my crew and I had been shut up in the focsle. Its door doesn't lock, so they tried to lash down the door, but they didn't do much of a job of it. They left cracks that we could see through.

We saw these two ships collide and realized that we could retake our ship and might be able to get away since the brig could not come down on us for a while, if ever. We got out of the focsle and overwhelmed the few Frenchmen who were trying to sail our ship. The other ships were similarly successful. We thought of just trying to sail away, but then we would be vulnerable to being captured again by the frogs who had been our jailers. So, after seeing that you had clearly beaten our captors and after some discussion between ourselves, I have come over here to see if you could take our prisoners with you. Otherwise, we would each be at hazard for being retaken."

Etienne thought for a minute. "Yes, we can do that, Captain Forth. I'll send our launch over with our lieutenant of marines as soon as he has finished securing the brig. How did you come to be captured, Captain?"

"We were sailing from Cardiff with a cargo for London. We left quite late in the day because of various delays and waiting for the turn of the tide. It was almost dark before we were out of the Bristol Channel. We were standing out to sea when we saw a brig coming towards us. She was flying British colors, so we held our course. She would pass quite close to windward. That close to England, it never occurred to me that she might not be a Royal Navy ship. There were a couple of merchant ships behind her. They might have been accompanying her, but I thought nothing of it. Only when she was directly to windward of us did I realize that something was wrong. She hauled down her colors, raised the French tricolor, opened her gunports, and fired a ball across our bow. There was nothing I could do, and no help was in sight. We backed our mainsail, and she sent a boat to take us. And that was that.

'I learned later," Captain Forth continued, "that it was the same story with the other two ships, though they are bound for London from Bristol. It was a good ruse the frogs used, I must admit. Unless there was a ship of the Royal Navy at hand, they would get away scot-free. Indeed, it is just our good fortune that you came along, or we would have ended up rotting in some French prison. I shall make sure that my owners know about what you did."

At that point, Lieutenant Macauley crossed from the brig with a uniformed officer in tow. "Lieutenant Macreau, may I present Captain Alarie of the Brig *Eclat*. Captain Alarie and his officers have given their parole. Captain Alarie speaks fluent English."

"Welcome, Captain," said Etienne. He had largely lost his French accent while serving in Giles's frigates and thought it best if the French officers were unaware that he was completely fluent in French.

"Jamieson," he continued to the wardroom steward who was standing nearby expecting a command, "See Captain Alarie and his officers to the wardroom. Captain, I trust you will join the wardroom for dinner."

Etienne turned back to Lieutenant Macauley. "What is the state of the brig?"

"We've secured the crew members in a couple of locked storerooms. Had to smash the locks, but eyebolts will keep the crew locked away. I will leave a dozen marines to guard them. Mr. Stewart should be completing his inspection soon, but he thinks the damage is minimal except for the bowsprit. He already has men aloft taking down the fore topgallant yard and mast since he is doubtful they can be supported. He has two carpenter's mates with him, examining the bowsprit. They think that it will be a simple job to make one of the spars she carries serve as the bowsprit, at least temporarily. The gammoning* and so on have not been affected since their bowsprit broke so completely before the hull could be damaged. He'll be reporting to you as soon as he can."

"Very good, Mr. Macauley. This is Captain Forth of one of *Eclat*'s prizes, which their original crews have liberated. Take the launch and some of your men. Bring back the French seamen and officers who were on board. I understand they are under control but that the merchantmen don't have the facilities to imprison them safely."

The marine lieutenant quickly assembled his troops and set off in the barge accompanied by Captain Forth. Etienne turned to Daniel, who was standing to one side after returning from *Eclat*. "Mr. Stewart, how are things on the brig?"

"Temporary foremast stays have been rigged, Mr. Macreau, and the carpenter's mates and other hands are in the process of taking out the broken bowsprit and rigging a replacement. None of their spars are long enough, unfortunately, or as sturdy as the ruined one, so we will have to go easy on the foremast when we have her stayed up as well as possible. Otherwise, all is well. I have brought over her log and other papers. They apparently did not get time to sink them, even though they were already in a weighted bag."

"Very good. We are very short of officers, as you know. We will head for Plymouth when we are finished here. Only a short voyage overnight, I hope. I don't think Mr. Dunsmuir is ready for command yet, so you will have to captain her. I suggest that you take Whitley, the master's mate, as your second to stand watches with you. As you know, Mr. Brooks thinks very highly of him, thinks he is ready to become a master of his own ship, or else take the lieutenant's exam if he prefers that route. You should have Mr. Richardson while I will take Mr. Dunsmuir as my second. That leaves Jenks among the midshipmen, doesn't it? I'll keep him on *Glaucus* for signals.

"Now, before you return to *Eclat*, Mr. Stewart, can you have a look at our bowsprit here. You know far more about how *Glaucus* is put together than I ever will, especially after all that work you did in the boatyard while we were waiting for *Glaucus* to be repaired."

The two lieutenants went to the bow where the carpenter, Mr.Evans, was feeling with his hands all around the bowsprit where it was attached to the hull, even under the figurehead. After a few minutes, he looked up."As I thought, sir," he told Etienne," The knighthead* is cracked. How much and how seriously, I can't tell from here, but the crack does not go down to the waterline —at least not yet. There is no sign of leaking, luckily.

"It would be a very major job, requiring a drydock, to replace it. That will have to be done eventually, but for the time being, when I reinforce it with stout planks bolted on each side, it should work as it always did. The weakness may be that, when she pitches, the crack will likely increase until the bow needs to be rebuilt. For now, I will use two of our spare spars fished together as a bowsprit, and we will have headsails that allow us to proceed. We don't have a stout enough spar to fully replace the old bowsprit, but we should have no problem reaching Plymouth if we take down the royal foremast."

"What are your thoughts, Mr. Stewart?" asked Etienne.

"I agree with Mr. Evans. I am sure the repairs he proposes will take us to Plymouth, and they should have a strong enough spar to properly replace the bowsprit. The problem with the bow will have to be dealt with better in the future, but what is needed can only be determined by a much closer examination of the knighthead* all the way down than we can make at sea. Indeed that examination may need to be made below the waterline as well. I am surprised that the knighthead split. I remember that piece of wood from when my father was building *Glaucus*. It seemed perfect then, so I am very surprised at its failing now."

"I see," said Etienne, just to fill up the silence as they all three reflected on the bad news. "Well, all we are able to do now is make the repairs we can and sail to Plymouth when we are ready. It will be only an overnight voyage, I expect. I will be happier if we stay close together. I will have a lantern on the stern, and *Eclat* should show a light on the bow.

It was almost dusk before Mr. Evans declared that he had done everything he could while at sea. He was now confident that the bow would stay whole for a good, long time, so there was no immediate need for *Glaucus* to go into drydock. The three British merchantmen that

Glaucus had rescued had disappeared over the eastern horizon several hours before that. Mr. Brooks calculated his best guess as to the course to sail to arrive at Plymouth in the morning, provided that the westerly wind held through the night. Off *Glaucus* sailed with *Eclat* following her. It took some time for Daniel on the brig to find the right combination of sails to keep pace with *Glaucus,* after which both enjoyed an uneventful night on their way to the unscheduled stop at Plymouth.

Etienne did not have a restful night, even though he had stood the first watch, so he could sleep from midnight to four a.m. Through his mind, again and again, went worries about what Giles might say about his ruining *Glaucus*'s bow. Giles had not explicitly forbidden it, but his conversation with Etienne before he left had indicated that he did not expect *Glaucus* to be involved in any action while her very junior lieutenant was in command. Such independent action without Captain Giles should properly have had to await the appointment of a more senior officer as First Lieutenant. It was no good Etienne trying to reassure himself that Giles would have done the same thing in his shoes and that the destruction of the bowsprit was not Etienne's fault. He was in charge, and his decisions had produced the result. Obviously, he would just have to face the music when the time came, and he would also have to carry on being in charge when they reached Plymouth as if nothing had happened. Nevertheless, those consoling thoughts did not prevent him from tossing and turning while wide awake until the morning watch was called.

Chapter VI

Daphne found that her arm had gone to sleep when their coach turned into the drive at Dipton Hall. It was the turn that had awakened her, and her arm was tingling because Mary was using it as a pillow while Daphne was jammed against the side of the coach. Beside Mary, Hugh was sleeping while slumped against Giles, who was staring out the window.

A footman opened the carriage door as soon as it stopped. Daphne accepted his help to be the first one to emerge. She turned immediately to lift out Mary and then stood to one side holding the child while the footman helped Hugh descend. Giles emerged immediately after, needing no help, and he bent down immediately to get to Hugh's level.

"This is Dipton Hall, Hugh, where Aunt Daphne and I live. As you can see, it's very big, so we have lots of room for you and Mary. The child looked around wide-eyed and then clutched at Giles.

"It's huge," he declared. "Mary and I will get lost in such a big place."

"No, you won't. Nanny Weaver will start you in the nursery, and then she'll bring you to us in the drawing room, and, before long, you will know your way all over the house, and you can explore outside too."

"Is Scruffy here?"

"I don't see him. When people arrive, the footmen often keep him in the house because he is too friendly to some visitors. He might knock you over, even though he wouldn't mean to, because of being so excited to meet you and Mary. You'll see him soon. Now let's go to meet all those people who are waiting for us."

As usual, when Daphne or Giles had been away for any length of time, Steves, their butler, Mrs. Wilson, the housekeeper, and various footmen and maids would line up on the parterre in front of the main door to welcome home their master and mistress. Daphne had thought it an excessive ritual, except possibly when they returned from a very lengthy absence. Steves thought differently and tended to arrange it on any but the most trivial of returns. She and Steves had reached a compromise. They would only have the full performance when she or Giles had been away for at least a week. Otherwise, one footman, if he were near the door, could open it for her or Giles.

It was clear that Steves did not think this arrival was a routine return, and Daphne could understand why all the servants who could were lined up. They were all vaccinated at Giles's and Daphne's insistence and wore their single scars with pride, though some may have been skeptical of the effectiveness of the treatment. If their Master and Mistress did return home with the disease, would they become infected anyway? Even those who knew that it took a long time before people who had caught the disease showed any sign of ill health still had to appear at the ceremony and appear cheerful that their mistress and master were back. Luckily most did not have to pretend very much, especially as they realized that if there was smallpox in the house, they would get it if that was their fate.

Giles took Hugh's hand to start going up the stairs, but he waited for Daphne to go first. Mary had taken one look at the huge house and the people all lined up waiting and was overwhelmed. She firmly stuck the knuckle of her index finger in her mouth, something that Daphne had noticed the little girl tended to do when something bothered her. She grabbed Daphne's dress with her other hand and hid her face in its folds.

"It's all right, Mary," Daphne said, picking the girl up. "Let's go and meet all these people who are waiting to greet you and show how happy they are that you are here."

At the top of the steps, the imposing figure of Steves wearing, as always, the full regalia of a butler, waited, first in line among the servants.

"Mary," Daphne told the little girl who had glanced around to see what was going on, "this is Mr. Steves, our butler. Steves, this is Mary, my niece. She and my nephew, Hugh, will be staying with us."

"Welcome to Dipton Hall, Miss Mary," intoned the imposing man in a deep, booming voice. That was too much for the child, who buried her face in Daphne's shoulder again and only peeked out after several moments as Daphne moved on to Mrs. Wilson, the housekeeper.

Giles held Hugh's hand as they followed Daphne up the steps. When it was the boy's turn to be greeted by the butler, He stuck out his hand to shake the dignified figure's hand. "It is a pleasure to meet you, Mr. Steves," he intoned as his father had taught him how to greet gentlemen. Steves was flustered by the action. In all his years as a servant, he had never had a gentleman shake his hand, and certainly not one as young as this boy. Only when Hugh persisted in the gesture did the butler reach down and shake the lad's hand. As Giles moved on to be greeted by Mrs. Wilson, Steves shook his head, not knowing how to live down the incident where the other servants might presume that he had been presumptuous.

Giles noticed Steves's discomfort. He bent down and whispered to Hugh. "That was very friendly of you, Hugh," he told the boy, "but we don't usually shake hands with servants." Hugh picked up the meaning and did not offer his hand to Mrs. Wilson when she was introduced to him.

Nanny Weaver did not attend the parade of servants when Daphne and Giles returned from a trip, being in a different category of employee from the other servants. One of the nursery maids, Agnes, realized that with two small children accompanying the master and mistress, her superior was needed immediately. She slipped away from the lineup and rushed to the nursery.

Nanny Weaver was none too happy about being summoned to the lineup by her subordinate, but her bad-tempered frown evaporated when she saw Daphne carrying a child that seemed to be quite young and a bit overwhelmed by Steves's ritual. She surmised what must be the situation at once, though it saddened her greatly since she had also been Harold's nanny. Nanny Weaver had been Daphne's nanny, and she could not recall ever having seen Daphne's mother carrying her daughter at that age, while Mr. Moorhouse had certainly not taken his son's hand the way that Giles was guiding a quite large boy.

"Can I take the child, my lady?" the nanny asked.

"Ah, there you are, Nanny Weaver," Daphne replied. "This is Mary, and the boy holding Giles's hand is Hugh. I am afraid that Harold and Nancy have perished from smallpox, so we are now looking after their children. The nursery may be a bit crowded initially until we can expand the area, but I want you to look after them."

"Very well, my lady. Let me take this little tyke. We'll settle the children down right away. I'm sure that Mr. Steves can arrange for the extra furniture I will need to be brought to the nursery right away."

"Did you hear that, Steves?" Daphne demanded.

"I did, my lady," replied the butler. "Thomas, see to everything that Nanny Weaver requires."

"Now, Nanny," said Daphne. "The children have just lost their parents and were quarantined for a few days with only a strange servant to care for them. They need a lot of sympathetic and understanding treatment before having much stress on how to behave in a large house. Mary, particularly is very much at sea. Hugh is trying to be brave, but I am not sure how long he can keep that up. They both will need a lot of understanding and affection. Take them to the nursery now, and Lord Camshire and I will be up to see them shortly."

"Hugh," Giles broke in as he and the child finished Hugh's introduction to Mrs. Wilson. "This is Nanny Weaver, who was Aunt Daphne's nanny and looks after your three cousins that you will meet soon. Go with her now, and she will show you where the children's space is."

The nanny somehow had no trouble taking Hugh's hand even though Daphne had already transferred Mary to her arms. "Come along with me, Master Hugh. I imagine that you are hungry and thirsty after your long trip, and you too, little one," turning her words to Mary as well. "We'll just see what we have in the nursery to tide you over until Mrs. Darling, our cook, can make you a specially good meal."

The nanny had such a warm voice and confident manner that neither child objected to being separated from the adults who had been caring for them. After the children disappeared through the doors into Dipton Hall, Daphne and Giles made quick work of greeting the remaining servants and then heading into the mansion themselves. Both wanted a good wash and some fresh clothes after the coach trip.

"Giles," Daphne said, "I think that we will have to adopt the children. Nancy's father was hardly more than a greengrocer. Harold married her partly from necessity and also to rub my father's nose in how he disagreed with his plans for Harold to be a gentleman. Letting Nancy's parents take care of the children — even if they are alive and they may not be — is no way to honor my grandfather's wish that the Moorhouses rise in the world, and Harold was his only grandson to carry the name forward. But Hugh can fill that role now that his father has perished, and the children are my only close kin in the next generation. We can provide for the children as gentlefolk should be brought up and give them the appropriate aid to reach their proper status in life, like our own children, except, of course, for Bernard, who will inherit the earldom and all your still entailed property. I don't know if I could ever love them as much as our own children because I bore them, but I will try."

"We definitely should adopt them," Giles replied. "as you say, Hugh and Mary are kin, and we can look after them better than any alternative that Nancy's side of the family, I am sure. As for providing for them when they are grown or helping them achieve a satisfactory level of society, I suspect that your father and Uncle George may want to be involved in meeting the children's needs. They are both well off, and your father would have made sure that his grandchildren were well-off except for that row they had over Harold's role in life."

"Well, that's settled. We can arrange the legal aspects when we see Mr. Snodgravel," declared Daphne, quite forgetting that such money matters really should be taken care of by her husband.

With that issue resolved and after a short visit with Giles to the nursery to see their own children, Daphne went to Dipton Manor to tell her father the result of the visit to Reading. Giles went to Daphne's workroom. It was a time of year when the stewards' reports about the states of their many properties were coming in. Giles had started to go over them with Daphne, partly to ease her burden but mainly because he was learning how the seeming dull reports could tell him a lot about the condition of the fields and animals in their various farms. While Daphne could learn much more than Giles from the dry records about the monetary well-being of their holdings and spot glaring inefficiencies, Giles was the one who was becoming better at recognizing other possibilities revealed by how the detailed figures fitted together to reveal weak farming techniques. Before long, however, Daphne returned just as the dinner gong rang, and they proceeded to dinner. Only Lady Clara, Giles's mother, was in residence, so there was no special fuss about going to dinner.

The discussion at dinner centered on the children and the situation they had found in Reading. Lady Clara was surprisingly critical about Daphne and Giles adopting Hugh and Mary, or at least treating them on an equal footing as their own children. She wanted her grandchildren to be treated better than the newly orphaned children, at least financially. She thought that any extra money not needed to provide for Giles's children should be allocated to her other son's children if there were any. Lord David, Giles's younger brother, was a clergyman who had recently married the only daughter of a nobleman who was influential in church matters. Already he had been named Dean of Ameschester Cathedral, and Giles was certain that his brother was well on the way to becoming a bishop. No one would call a bishop poor, and Giles and Daphne had already helped his brother with funds to be able to live in the lavish style that his wife and her parents wanted. Giles was not at all happy with his brother, who retained his seat as one of the two members of parliament for Dipton even though most of his time seemed to be spent on pursuing matters that would aid his ecclesiastical ambitions and those of his father-in-law rather than subjects on which Giles had strong notions. Lord David was also vicar of Dipton's church, though he performed none of the duties attached to that position but kept most of its income.

His brother had become a problem that Giles knew he had to face soon. On matters about which Giles felt strongly, especially the slave trade, Lord David had done everything possible to avoid expressing opinions, including missing votes in the House of Commons, in agreement with Giles's very clear beliefs. Indeed, Lord David never consulted with his brother and benefactor about matters before the House of Commons. Instead, he aligned himself as a Member of Parliament with his ecclesiastical faction. Giles was also annoyed that his brother had not conducted a service in the church at Dipton for several years, though he always seemed ready to preach wherever his father-in-law wished. Fortunately, the curate whom Lord David had appointed to take on his duties was a first-class clergyman, even though the stipend the vicar paid his substitute was ridiculously low. Giles and Daphne did not want the parish to lose this treasure, but almost anywhere else might offer him a more lucrative position and the certainty that would come from having his own parish.

Giles was not looking forward to having a showdown with his brother, but it was necessary. David could either do the jobs his brother had found for him or resign from them to pursue his own interest. The present situation was intolerable.

These problems with his brother passed through Giles's head while Lady Clara kept making her pitch for her other son. "As I said, Richard, David has no fortune, and clergymen do not make much money. His children need to be supported in keeping with his father's status. I can't do it since most of my money will go to you when I die. He needs it more than these children of Daphne's brother."

"Mother, enough of this. My father showed no interest in the position of his own grandchildren. Just look how he treated my half-sister Marianne. I had to find dowries for both of her daughters because he would not lift a finger. I had to provide them, or else they would have had no dowries. I was glad to do it, of course. They are my nieces — in fact, only half-nieces. Hugh and Mary are Daphne's nieces, and it is up to us to make sure that they are well provided for."

"But Marianne's position was different. Lord Camshire's property was all entailed, and he couldn't raise any money. You should treat David's children in at least the same way, and you are richer now."

"Blast it, Mother," Giles burst out, further irritated by his mother using his father's title now that it was his own. "David has been acting more like my father than like you. He has already conned me out of a living for which he does nothing, a seat in parliament, and a small fortune in advances to impress his new father-in-law. David can look after himself now as far as I am concerned."

That outburst put a damper on conversation for the rest of dinner. The group finished eating quickly, not doing justice to the special dishes that Mrs. Darling had prepared. Giles was still fuming when he was alone with Daphne.

"What I do with my money is none of her business."

"Of course it isn't, my love," Daphne agreed. "It's none of mine either."

"I didn't mean that," Giles protested.

"It's true, nevertheless, in law. I think your mother was just worried about David showing some of his father's habits and getting cut out of his father-in-law's will. However, Lady Clara is indeed getting well beyond herself. Lord David doesn't even have any children yet."

"You're right. But I sometimes wish that we weren't so rich. Then no one would worry about what I will do with my money. Maybe I should just give it away to some good cause."

"Well, most of it is entailed, so that isn't possible. But, of course, what you do with the rest is up to you. I don't get much say, though I would get my widow's portion if you die."

"I know that is unfair. Anyway, a lot of our fortune is still tied up until the consequences of Mr. Edwards's thievery are decided. But It's all your money as much as mine, you know. I've asked Mr. Snodgrass to look into ways to have you keep the unentailed property when I die. He says it's complicated, especially with our properties spread over so many counties. Still, I will remind him that I need the information soon, even if it is incomplete, so I can start making the proper provisions for you and the children.."

"Speaking of Mr. Edwards," Daphne said, "I certainly wish that we had not trusted your former prize agent so completely. Do you remember that we still have to deal with Sallycroft in Shropshire? In case you have forgotten, that's the name of the estate that we believe that Mr. Edwards bought for us and where I had that adventure with those crooks that Sir Titus was involved with. We really should go back to see about establishing our claim on the property more thoroughly."

"Good point. You know, Sallycroft is on the way to Cheshire. Maybe we should visit it on my way to meeting with *Glaucus*."

"We could stop in Birmingham also for a day or two. George is anxious about his company there, even though he tries to hide it."

"Yes. Sometimes it seems to be never-ending, doesn't it, this running around looking after our duties and our properties?"

"Yes, it was simpler when we first got married. Let's get to bed."

"Yes, let's."

Later, when they were starting to fall asleep, Daphny murmured. "Do you know, Giles, I am surprised that we found your mother here and not at Dipton Manor discussing the situation at Reading with my father. They seem to get on so well together, and it would be a fine excuse for her to visit Dipton Manor."

"That's probably why she was here, so no one thinks they get on too well together."

"Really? No! Surely that's ridiculous? You don't suppose that they feel — well, you know —?"

"Carnal desire?"

"Yes," Daphne said, glad that the dim candlelight hid her blushing. "Surely not at their age."

"Why not. My mother is less than twenty years older than me. I hope I will still be feeling 'carnal desire' for you at that age. I seem to still be doing all right in that area, as are you."

"Really, Giles! Of course, I will also feel that way. I *am* younger than you!"

"There you are. We all know that it is not supposed to happen — carnal desire, I mean — but we think it will be, given a chance, so we have all these rules to make it unlikely for anyone to believe that it has — or at least that it might have led to anything."

"Well, maybe you are right. Though you *are* the only man for me. I have never felt 'carnal desire' for anyone else, and I don't imagine that I ever will."

"So I hope. We just have to keep making sure that there is no room for anyone else in our affections."

It took them some time to fall asleep after that. Both were wondering if the other was ever going to feel 'carnal desire' for someone else. Surely it wouldn't happen if they continued to demonstrate their affection for each other in the way they had after their conversation about 'carnal desire.'

Chapter VII

Giles left the breakfast room as dawn was breaking. He was surprised to see Hugh standing in the gloom in the passageway. He had expected that his nephew would still be sleeping after the trip from Reading the previous day. The boy still wore his nightclothes, so he couldn't have been up very long.

"What are you doing here, Hugh?" Giles asked.

"'Sploring, Uncle Giles," was the reply.

"Exploring? Exploring what?"

"This house. But it's so large that I got lost."

Examining Hugh properly for the first time, Giles saw that the boy was on the edge of tears.

"Getting lost is easy in this big house, especially when it's dark. You should wait for daylight before leaving the nursery. I don't suppose that Nanny Weaver knows that you have decided to explore on your own."

"No, she was busy with Mary and had sent Agnes to get something, so I'm 'sploring on my own."

"Then I think we had better go and tell Nanny where you found me. She will be worried. Hugh, you should never leave the nursery without telling Nanny

Weaver. She gets terribly anxious if she doesn't know where the children are."

Giles and Hugh climbed the main staircase, which the rising sun was starting to illuminate properly, and then along the first-floor corridor, which was only lighted by a few candles.

"Your candles smell much better than the candles we have at home," Hugh mentioned.

"Do they? I think it must be because Aunt Daphne likes ones that smell nicer and give more light, but they are very, very expensive, so most people use ordinary candles."

Giles wondered how many other things in everyday life Hugh and Mary might find were of better quality at Dipton Hall than their parents had been able to afford and whether that would do something to spoil their memories of their early years. Would it add to their stress in being so completely uprooted?

They turned right at the end of the corridor and were faced by the door that shut the nursery off from the rest of the house. Giles opened the door to find Nanny Weaver on the other side, talking to Agnes. One look at Hugh told Nanny Weaver the whole story. To Giles's surprise, her first words were addressed to the nursery maid, not to Hugh or himself. "Agnes, you told me that Master Hugh was still sleeping."

"I thought he was, Nanny Weaver. When I checked on him earlier, I was sure that I saw a big lump under the covers that I guessed was him, so I decided that he should be allowed to sleep after his busy day yesterday."

"That was probably that big stuffed horse he brought with him yesterday, which I allowed him to take to bed with him last night. In the future, Agnes, when you check on the children, make sure that you actually see them. Don't just presume that a child is in bed because something large is under the covers. When they are older, they may try to fool you in that way."

Turning to Giles, Nanny weaver continued. "I'm sorry, my lord, it is my fault that he is not in the nursery. Where did you find him?"

"At the foot of the main staircase, Nanny. He just wanted to explore his new surroundings. I told him that he has to tell you before he leaves the nursery."

"Quite right, my lord. Master Hugh, you haven't had your breakfast yet, and you are in yesterday's clothes. Now come along."

"Can I go 'sploring after breakfast?"

"Of course not. We don't leave the nursery in the morning until everyone has finished their tasks. And even though you are a big boy now, you have to tell me whenever you leave and where you are going."

Hugh's face fell. Giles knew that, for his own safety, the child would have to obey the rules, but he was getting to an age where surely more leeway would be warranted in where he could go 'sploring.

"Nanny," Giles said. "Of course, Master Hugh has to obey the rules, but I am not surprised that he is curious about where he is now. I have to go to the stables in about an hour. Maybe, he can come with me."

"Would you like to accompany Lord Camshire to the stables, Master Hugh?" Nanny Weaver asked.

"Yes."

" 'Yes, please, Nanny Weaver.'" Even in the presence of her master, the nanny wanted to instill her rules.

"Yes, please, Nanny Weaver," Hugh intoned, catching on quickly to what was required of him.

"Very good. I'll be up to get him in an hour, Nanny." Giles announced, turning to leave, entrusting Hugh to Nanny Weaver's hands. He hoped that he had succeeded in maintaining the nanny's authority without dampening the child's curiosity.

Giles had not originally planned to visit the stables that morning. Instead, he and Daphne had intended to visit the nursery to play with their three children. But Giles was now committed to Hugh, and he certainly wanted to check on the stables. Daphne was left to play with the children and find a way to incorporate Mary into the time she spent with them.

Nanny Weaver had Hugh dressed in his warmest coat and sturdiest boots. It was evident to her that the children needed new clothes for both indoors and outdoors. She also had to start thinking about having more vigorous activities for the newly acquired children. Luckily, she had had much experience with other children and looked forward to the added challenge. While she dearly loved infant children, she had long found older children more interesting. Indeed, Bernard was just reaching that age. Unfortunately, the age gap between Hugh and Bernard was too large to bridge, but maybe Mary could be induced to accept the role of older sister to Bernard, just as before long, he could start acting as Christina's older brother. Nanny Weaver clearly was not anticipating that the two additional children might move on to some other relative's house.

Giles was always delighted to find an excuse to visit the stables. The stud farm he and Daphne had established to breed hunting horses was his favorite place on the estate, and he had become firm friends with Henry Griffiths, the stable master. They had spent hours talking about horses, horse breeding, horse racing, and how to steal a march on competitors. Giles was punctilious in always calling the horse expert 'Mr. Griffiths' because he knew that his friend would never be comfortable calling him 'Richard' or even 'Giles.' How Giles had come by the 'common touch' was a mystery to Daphne. He had grown up in the midshipmen's berth on navy ships. That was a place where familiarity between officers and crew was firmly discouraged. Having herself a father who was always very aware of his high status, as Giles's father also had been, Daphne was surprised at times about how little importance his position was to her husband. It didn't occur to her that she had the same ability to get on easily with all ranks despite being the daughter of a man whose very existence had been based on not being 'common.'

Someone must have told Mr. Griffiths that Giles was approaching, for he emerged from the stables office before Giles and Hugh reached it. Giles had become used to people who worked on the estate keeping track of where he and Daphne were. Nevertheless, he remained surprised when their practice exhibited itself, even though, on his ships, he had learned early on that everyone always knew where the captain was and what was his mood.

"Welcome home, my lord," the stable master greeted his employer. "I was sorry to hear about the death of Mr. and Mrs. Moorhouse."

"Thank you, Mr. Griffiths. This young man is Master Hugh, their son, who will be staying with us. Hugh, this is Mr. Griffiths, our stable master. He runs the Dipton Hunters Stable and is in charge of all our horses. Another stablemaster looks after our riding and carriage horses at the stables beside the house. You'll meet him sometime soon."

Mr. Griffiths knelt down and offered his hand to the youngster. Hugh glanced at Giles before taking it. Giles nodded, realizing that he should suggest to Nanny Weaver that a bit of instruction should be given in the difficult subject of how children were supposed to greet the various levels of servants and employees of the estate.

"Do you like horses, Master Hugh," Mr. Griffiths asked.

"I don't know," Hugh replied. "I've only seen them on the street where my mother warned me to keep well away from them."

"She was right. It is a good idea to stay away from working horses, especially from their rear hooves. They have been known to kick. But most horses are quite safe and great fun to ride. Have you ever been on a horse?"

"Oh, no. Isn't that scary?"

"Not on a well-trained horse. It's just very exciting."

"Hugh," Giles broke in, "would you like to go for a short ride sitting in front of me on the horse just to see what it is like?"

"Oh, yes, please, Uncle Giles, please, please!" the little boy begged.

"Might I suggest that you take the horse over there, my lord? The one that Phil, the stable boy, is about to exercise? She is very placid. Do you see her, Master Hugh? She is called 'Daisy.'" Mr. Griffiths pointed to a fully equipped riding horse being led across the paddock at the back of the stables.

"She looks very big. How can I get on?" Hugh's enthusiasm seemed a bit dampened by the magnitude of the task in front of him.

"That's easy," Giles replied. "I'll get on, and Mr. Griffiths will lift you up to me. There will be plenty of room for both of us on her. Let's try riding her, Hugh."

Mr. Griffiths signaled to the stable boy, who had started staring at them just before mounting the mare. Instead of getting on the horse, the servant led the horse to the waiting trio and adjusted the stirrups to Giles's height. After checking that all the riding equipment was properly fitted, Giles swung himself into the saddle, steadied the mare, and reached down for the little boy. Hugh seemed a bit nervous as Giles settled the boy in front of him, anchored by the pommel horn and Giles's arm.

Giles made the mare begin walking very slowly, rocking the lad hardly at all. When he felt Hugh relax, Giles increased the pace a little. Then a little more. Before long, Giles had Daisy going at a slow trot with his small charge starting to bounce up and down. After a few moments, Giles turned Daisy around to return to the barn.

"Giddy-gup, giddy-up," yelled the excited Hugh.

Giles let the horse speed up some more so that they were trotting along quite quickly before he reined in at the stable office. Mr. Griffiths reached up, lifted Hugh from the saddle, and set him on the ground.

"Do you like horseback riding, Master Hugh?" the stable master asked.

"Oh, yes! It's fun! Uncle Giles, can we go riding again?"

"Not right now, but maybe tomorrow, Hugh."

"Oh, I hope so."

"You'll be riding on your own before long, Master Hugh," Mr. Griffiths added, much to Giles's annoyance because he was far from sure that Hugh was old enough — or large enough — to start riding by himself. When the boy was old enough, Giles wanted to introduce him to the activity himself.

"We'll have to see about that," Giles said noncommittally as he dismounted. "Mr. Griffiths, I'll be by later to discuss the horses. Come along, Hugh, we should get back to the Hall."

When they reached the mansion, Giles took Hugh up to the nursery and made sure that he was entrusted to Nanny Weaver's care.

"Well, Master Hugh, did you have a good walk with your uncle?" the nanny asked.

"Oh, yes! We went riding together. The horse was ever so big and fast, but I wasn't scared a bit, was I, Uncle Giles?"

"No, you were very brave."

"And he's going to take me again tomorrow, aren't you, Uncle Giles?"

Giles had no idea how 'maybe' had disappeared from his commitment. He resolved to try to be clearer if he made more promises to the children. It was not the last he would hear about children and horses that day.

For dinner that night, Daphne had invited her father and uncle and Giles's mother and half-sister, Lady Marianne, to come to the dinner to hear first-hand about the situation that they had found in Reading and to introduce the two new members of their household. When they assembled before dinner, Nanny Weaver and the nursery maids brought Hugh and Mary, as well as Giles and Daphne's two older children, to meet the guests. After shyly shaking hands with their relatives, Berns and Christina played quietly on the carpet. Mary looked no one in the eye and then snuggled on Daphne's lap, hiding her eyes on her aunt's shoulder. By contrast, Hugh decided to be precocious, talking freely to the adults to hide his shyness. Asked by his grandfather how he liked Dipton Hall, he launched into a recitation about how Giles had taken him for an exciting ride on a big horse, which went very fast but had not scared him a bit. Both Daniel Moorhouse and Major Stoner were interested in horses and pursued the subject of horses and riding them with the boy.

The episode caught the attention of several of the guests, for, at dinner, the subject came up again right after the report on what Giles and Daphne had encountered in Reading and its implications. Daniel Moorhouse raised the subject of the horse ride that Giles had given Hugh.

"Giles, was it really safe to have such a small boy on a horse?"

"Of course it was! Hugh was sitting on the saddle right in front of me, and we only went at a very modest trot."

"Yes, but won't that make him want to ride himself."

“Possibly, but I imagine that he will be riding soon if he wants to. I was riding at his age, wasn’t I, Mother?”

“I don’t remember when you started to ride, but I am sure that you were larger than Hugh is, and I do remember that I was furious with your father for letting you start riding. He was not much of a father, you know?”

“That’s true. His idea was to put me up on the saddle of one of our riding horses without any instruction or even shortening the stirrups and then whacking the horse’s rump to get the animal moving. I did stay on the horse’s back somehow, I remember, for quite a while. In fact, what happened is that the horse stopped, and I slid off. I’m not going to do anything like that with Hugh!”

“I was certainly smaller than Hugh is now when I started to ride,” said Daphne. “And possibly younger. It was before my ninth birthday, I remember, because I wanted you to get a horse for me as a ninth-birthday present, but you didn’t.“

“I remember you wanting a horse then, but it must have been a couple of years later before your governess told me that all ladies should learn to ride properly.”

“Oh, yes. I can hear her now. She insisted loudly that I ride side-saddle. ‘Ladies only ride zide zaddle,’” Daphne quoted with a bogus French accent.

“That was the only way that ladies should ride, Mademoiselle Lafont maintained,” Daphne continued. “Of course, I had been riding long before that; you just didn’t know about it, Father. Before I was eight, one of the stable boys challenged me to get on a horse since, at that time, I was climbing all over things, especially, of course, trees. I took him up on it and somehow climbed onto that old mare we had, using a stool and pulling myself up by her tail. I got far enough forward to hold onto her mane, and then she started to move. She was in that paddock behind the stable, and no one could see that area from the house. We walked around a bit, and then she stopped, having lost interest, and I couldn't get her going again. So I slid off her, with the stable boy's help — I don't remember his name. But after that, I made him harness her so I could control her and forced him to boost me up on her back. I rode her quite a lot when I could get away from that governess who liked to drink a little sherry in the middle of the day and go to sleep."

"Well, I don't remember any of that," said her father.

"Of course, you don't. I always made sure that you were safely in your library before I went riding, and Mademoiselle Lafont didn't care what I did as long as I learned my lessons. She had long ago stopped trying to make me 'a proper lady.' If you saw me returning from the stable area, I always told you that I had been for a walk. Anyway, if Hugh wants to ride, I say that we let him when he is large enough to get on a horse."

Conversation then turned to other matters, and the topic was not revived until Giles and Daphne were alone at the end of the evening.

"Giles," Daphne said, "I've been thinking about Hugh and horses and also about the other children. I probably sounded enthusiastic about how I started riding, but that was partly to annoy my father and the others. It was a dangerous and stupid thing to do, even though I succeeded and I've been more comfortable on horseback ever since. I don't want Hugh to take after me, and he is enough of an adventurous scamp to do so."

"What do you suggest?"

"We should get a gentle, small horse for him and have the stableboys teach him how to ride properly. They are better on horseback than any of us, you know."

"I'd never thought about it, but you are right. Working with the horses every day, putting them through their paces, and training them for all aspects of the hunt may make them experts at following the hounds, but do we have any horses that are small enough and gentle enough? I think all our hunters are too big, even the ones we are raising with women in mind," Giles reflected.

"There is Moonbeam."

"Your old mare?"

"Yes, she is very gentle and biddable even though she is a bit old. I don't ride her often anymore because I prefer the more lively, younger horses even if I am not riding my hunter, Serene Masham."

"I think trying Moonbeam for Hugh is a good idea. I'll mention it to Griffiths when I see him tomorrow."

Giles was as good as his word. After giving Hugh another ride on his pommel, he mentioned having him learn to ride to Mr. Griffiths. The stable master thought it was a good idea. "Of course," he added, "we need to get him a saddle. We don't have any that are nearly small enough."

"Won't it take quite a while to have one made? I want Hugh to start as soon as possible to take his mind off having lost his parents."

"Let me think — Last time I was at Marcher's, the saddler in Ameschester, they had a small saddle that someone had failed to pay for and so was for sale. It might be about the right size for Master Hugh. After all, saddles are not like boots that have to fit well or are useless. I have to order some materials from Marcher's, and I can have Roger, who is becoming a very good stable hand, go to Ameschester with my order and see if the saddle is still available."

"Sounds good. Tell Roger to get it if it is suitable."

Later in the day, Giles returned to the stables to find out if the saddle had been available. It was, and Giles also found a very excited Mr. Griffiths.

"I have been thinking, Captain Giles, that there is no one near here breeding first-class riding horses or ponies for smaller riders like some ladies and children. We only sell as riding horses those hunters who have not made the grade as hunting steeds we can be proud of. Most are very good riding horses, but they come to the market with too much expensive, specialized training for hunting to be profitable when sold as just riding horses. I was thinking that we could expand our stables into raising more riding horses, especially small ones for ladies and children, possibly even ponies."

"It's an idea I'd like to think about. But talking of new ventures, don't forget that we have talked of going into thoroughbred racing, which is very expensive. Maybe widening the profitable side of things would compensate for also undertaking a losing operation."

Giles walked back to the Hall, deep in thought. Somehow, no matter how much he and Daphne resolved just to enjoy their holdings, both were attracted by the idea of expanding and facing the new challenges that would bring. Wouldn't his naval service, like the present duty to go to Scotland, interfere with their following more interesting avenues? He wondered how his lieutenants were getting on with *Glaucus* in his absence. He was getting a yearning to go back to the sea.

Chapter VIII

"I believe, Mr. Macreau," said the Master, Mr. Brooks, "that we can easily clear Land's End if we come about now."

"Stand by to come about," Etienne bellowed. The watch on deck finished what they were doing or secured it and rushed to their sail-handling positions. In a couple of minutes, all was quiet again as they reached their positions.

"Ready — About!" Etienne called. The business of tacking *Glaucus* and the intricate process of bringing the ship onto the other course began. On a full-rigged ship, the success of the maneuver depended on every crew member performing their tasks at the right moment in the elaborate dance that would get the frigate turned. It was initiated by the helmsman calling "Helm's a lee." That started the frenzied loosening and hauling on lines all over the frigate until the moment when the bow turned through the wind and completion of the remaining tasks became less urgent as *Glaucus* settled onto the opposite tack.

Even after Etienne indicated the end of the maneuver by ordering, "Full and Bye*," to the helmsman, there was still work to be done furling lines and getting everything shipshape.

"We should be able to hold this tack for a long time, Mr. Macreau," the Master remarked when *Glaucus* had settled onto her new course. "This northerly wind may hold all night, and, if so, we don't have to worry about anything until we come close to the Irish coast tomorrow morning. If my guess is right, this wind will drop overnight and veer a bit, so going west a bit more makes sense. We can check how it's going later. I believe that Mr. Stewart has this watch, so we can have supper together before reevaluating the situation.

By midnight, the wind had dropped somewhat and had veered a little. Dead reckoning put them a third of the way between Land's End and Wexford. Etienne emerged on the quarterdeck just as eight bells sounded the beginning of the middle watch. Mr. Brooks was already there and explained exactly where he thought they were after Mr. Stewart had formally handed over the control of the ship to Mr. Macreau.

"Mr. Macreau, sir," said the Master, knowing that technically giving advice to the man in command of the warship on destinations and targets was improper, "may I make some suggestions on where we should go?"

Etienne was surprised. Only recently, he had been a midshipman, and Mr. Brooks had been his instructor on large parts of what he had had to learn before becoming a lieutenant. "Mr. Brooks," Etienne said, "always feel free to tell me your thoughts."

"Well, sir," the Master responded, "we have some time before we have to be in Birkenhead, and I think that Captain Giles, even though there is some mysterious mission for *Glaucus* after he joins us, would want us to harry the enemy in any way we can, though he would wish us not to be noticed by possible French spies. That means, I think, trying to catch privateers and pirates and even smugglers, all of whom are known to operate in these waters. There could even be naval ships on the lookout for prizes, like *Eclat*. Most of the traffic is likely to be on the eastern side of the Irish Sea, coming from the Bristol Channel or the Mersey. I believe that there isn't much material shipping from the western part of Wales. Merchandise being shipped from Ireland is, I believe, more likely to be carried down the western side of the Irish Sea, though there is, I believe, much less of it than on the eastern side.

"I expect that the small ships that the Navy uses to try to catch privateers are concentrated on the eastern side of the sea, though, as we learned from *Eclat*, they are not entirely successful. Now, where should we look for privateers? Despite there being more ships for them to prey on, I would not be surprised to find them along the coast of Ireland. If we don't find them there, we can go to the other side of the Irish Sea."

"That makes sense to me. We shall keep the present course until we see Ireland."

"One other thing, Mr. Macreau."

"Yes?"

"I would suggest that we take down the skysails and yards but leave their masts up. That way, we can spot other ships from the crow's nest before they can see us, and that may give us a better chance to catch them."

"Good suggestion. We won't need the speed unless we are in very light winds, and then we can refit the yards quickly. I'll tell the bosun to see to it after our routine clearing for action. Anything else?"

"No, sir."

"Well, feel free to tell me anything or make suggestions. I know I am very green to be commanding this vessel and need all the help I can get."

Word spread rapidly through the ship that they were on the lookout for prize money — easy-to-earn prize money. Everyone was eager to gain some; jobs were done with even more of a swing than usual, and crew members who were sent aloft were encouraged by their comrades and the officers to keep their eyes open and their wits about them.

Glaucus made landfall just south of Wexford. After consulting Mr. Stewart and Mr. Brooks, Etienne decided to hug the coast on the way north, the reason being to make it more difficult for their prey to find refuge in landlocked bays where it would be difficult for the frigate to follow the suspicious craft.

There was no reason for *Glaucus* to go into Wexford. Out of curiosity, Etienne climbed to the masthead to see into the port. It appeared to him that the entry to the bay leading to the town featured sandbanks that were probably shifting, so safe entry might well have required a pilot. He could spot a few ship's masts farther in where the town appeared to be, but none looked large enough to attract pirates. He wondered idly what cargos were shipped from Wexford. Would they attract French privateers or pirates?

Glaucus came about and stood out to sea. The masthead lookout reported some small fishing boats but nothing of interest. The wind was still light from the north-northeast. *Glaucus*'s search for other ships was going very slowly, both because her own progress was minimal and also because any other ships at sea would be moving very sluggishly. When the lookout at the masthead reported that the Irish coast had disappeared in a light mist, *Glaucus* came about, and the search continued. Still, nothing of interest appeared, and so things continued as the frigate slowly beat to windward, changing tack with each turn of the glass.*

Only when they were well into the afternoon watch with sunset only an hour and a half away did the cry come from the masthead that a sail was in sight to the northwest headed their way. Hopes rose but were soon dashed by Mr. Brooks observing, "She is unlikely to be a French privateer or a pirate."

When Etienne asked for his reasoning, the Master explained: 'She has been holding the same course since we first spotted her. Now that we can make out her topsails from the deck, she must be aware of our presence, while no other ship looks like a frigate. Holding her course suggests that she has nothing to fear from us, for we are flying the British flag."

"Of course," Etienne responded, "it could be a ruse de guerre. If she doesn't react, she may be hoping that we will think her one of ours even if she is not."

"Quite right," agreed Mr. Brooks, "and it will do no harm to speak with her. She may be English, but she could be carrying goods that cannot be shipped to Napoleon's allies or some other sort of contraband, and she may presume that a frigate would never be engaged in enforcing those laws."

The two vessels were on converging courses and got closer and closer to each other quite quickly.

"Deck there," called Midshipman Jenks from the masthead. "She has four guns per side. Eighteen pounders, I guess."

"Clear for action," Etienne yelled. "We can't be too cautious," he remarked to the Master, "can we?"

"Practice never hurts with a rusty crew, Mr. Macreau," replied Mr. Brooks, clearly indicating that he thought Mr. Macreau was overreacting. However, his point was made when the action was performed more smoothly than on the earlier occasion when Etienne had ordered it. When the operation was complete, it was already time for Etienne to give orders for the next step.

"Mr. Jenks, signal the merchantman to heave to. Mr. Stewart, prepare to put a ball across her bows if she does not respond to the signal. Not too close, of course. If she does not comply, we are faster than she is, so we can catch her up again if she slips past us. Better not run out the other guns just yet."

A pair of 'Aye, aye, sir's responded to his orders, giving Etienne the proud feeling that he really was in command of *Glaucus*.

The merchant ship responded promptly, luffing up* and backing* her mainsail. At Etienne's order, *Glaucus* stopped quite close to the other ship.

"What ship is that?" Etienne shouted.

“The *Pride of Merseyside,*” came the reply. “Out of Liverpool, bound for the Slave Coast* with a cargo of trade goods.”

“‘Trade goods’ — what are they?” Etienne called back.

“Bright cloth and things like that.”

“Any iron goods?” broke in Mr. Brooks unexpectedly.

“Oh, yes. Some hoes and shovels and so on.”

“What is that all about, Mr. Brooks?” Etienne asked Mr. Brooks in a tone of voice that would not carry to the other ship.

“They are slavers, Mr. Macreau. Captain Giles hates slavers, as you know, and would want us to harass them as much as we legally can. Most iron goods are banned from export to countries or colonies aligned with Bonaparte,”

“I see. Well, Mr. Brooks, continue to find a way to interfere with their voyage.”

“Aye, aye, sir.

“*Pride of Merseyside*, stand by to receive some of our officers and crew members who will inspect your registration certificate, bills of lading, and cargo,” bellowed the Master.

“Mr. Stuart, raise the gunports and run out the guns,” ordered Etienne.

“Mr. Brooks and Mr. Macauley, take the captain’s barge and a file of marines over to that ship and see if you can find a reason to detain her.”

The marines boarded the barge quickly, quite undercutting the usual seaman's claim that they were a useless bunch of clodhoppers on a ship. Mr. Macauley and Mr. Brooks followed immediately. The barge wasted no time rowing to the boarding slats on the *Pride of Merseyside,* where they did not meet a friendly welcome. A rotund, gray-harried man leaned over the rail above them.

"You can't board a British ship in British waters," he stated firmly.

"Yes, we can, and you should know it. Now let us on board, or I'll signal to *Glaucus* to fire on you. Her guns are loaded with grapeshot, so I doubt that many of you will survive," Mr. Macauley called back. He was dressed in his standard, scarlet uniform intended to convince an observer of the martial prowess of the wearer. While the standard weapon of the marines was a musket with bayonet fixed, Mr. Macauley's men carried cutlasses, and these were the weapons they would use if force was needed on the ship they were boarding. Ignoring the standard rule that officers should leave a boat first, they swarmed up the side, hopped over the rail, and were lined up with their cutlasses at the ready before anyone on the merchant ship had time to relax. Mr. Macauley and Mr. Brooks followed more sedately.

"I am Lieutenant Hamish Macauley of HMF *Glaucus*," announced Mr. Macauley, "and this is her Master, Mr. Brooks. We need to examine your certificates, bills of lading, and manifests. Captain, please take me to your cabin or wherever the ship's documents are kept. Mr. Brooks will inspect the cargo while we are doing so. Then we will compare what he finds with what the documents say about the cargo."

"Lieutenant, you have no right. You have no reason to stop us and are exceeding your authority. The *Pride of Merseyside* is a British Ship registered in the British port of Liverpool and sailing in British waters."

"I have every right, and the guns of *Glaucus* confirm it. Take me to the cabin and have your first mate arrange to show the cargo to Mr. Brooks. If you don't comply, I will have you and your officers arrested by these marines and have you taken to *Glaucus*. Now, let's get going."

Reluctantly, the captain of the merchant ship led the marine officer and two other marines to his cabin. It was not very neat, not at all like the captain's cabin on *Glaucus.* There was, however, a chest of drawers where the ship's documents were kept in the top drawer. The registration certificate said that the *Pride of Merseyside* was registered as being the property of four owners in Liverpool. Among the owners' names, Hamish noted, was 'Baron Otterly,' a man whom Hamish had read of in the newspapers as being very much in favor of the slave trade, though the reporting had not mentioned his being engaged in it. Hamish had noticed the article because the same issue of the paper had reported on Giles's opposition to the trade. On other documents, the cargo was listed as cotton textiles, agricultural tools, and miscellaneous iron goods. They were all being transported from Liverpool to the Slave Coast and were owned by the same consortium which owned the ship.

"Jenkins," Hamish addressed one of the marines. "Take this bill of lading to Mr. Brooks so that he can compare it with the actual cargo." When the marine left with the document, Hamish turned again to the captain.

"The statement of your destination is very vague, is it not Captain — ?"

"Bogie, sir. Richard Bogie."

"Ah, one of the owners, I note. But where are you bound?"

"The Slave Coast, sir. We can't be more precise because where we trade depends on which of the various factories have recent acquisitions of slaves to sell and where there are not many competitors."

"Ah, I see. Part of the Slave Coast is controlled by the French, I believe, with whom trading is prohibited. Show me the logs of your previous journeys so that I can see where you have been trading."

"I cannot do that. I turn all those documents over to the owners after each voyage."

"Do you? What is in that next drawer?"

"It is locked, and I don't have a key."

"Sergeant, open that drawer," Hamish addressed the marine petty officer who had accompanied him.

The burly marine lost no time in bringing the hilt of his cutlass into contact with the drawer's lock. That was too much for the drawer's front as one of its dovetailed corners cracked open. A fast application of the weapon's blade tore the front off the drawer. Inside was a pile of documents.

"Well done, sergeant," Hamish said, even though his training as a marine officer had discouraged praise for actions taken by his subordinates. He had learned and adopted the more generous practice from observing how Giles and his officers got enthusiastic cooperation from their crew. "Now pass me those documents."

The sergeant took the top layer of documents from the drawer and handed them to Hamish. The first one on the pile proclaimed in large letters, 'The High Court of Admiralty,' and in even larger letters, 'Letter of Marque.' Skimming through the document, Hamish found the words, 'Pride of Merseyside.'

"So, Captain Bogie, this ship is a privateer. According to your certificate and bill of lading, you are a merchant ship engaged in the slave trade. Which are you?"

"Both. Presently my vessel is a merchant ship."

"So you are just a pirate of opportunity?"

"Oh, no, sir! A privateer, not a pirate."

"I see. Well, let me examine some more of these documents."

The next two seemed to be contracts of some sort that Hamish thought he should examine only if he found some reason to read their poorly written words. Then came a page that changed the situation completely. It was in French, which Hamish did not understand. He would have to ask Mr. Macreau what it said when he returned to *Glaucus*. Many other pages in the stack appeared to be of the same sort of document. Then came another one that aroused Hamish's interest far more.

The new page was headed ‘Lettre de Marque’ in elaborate printing. It was then filled with much handwriting, which Hamish had trouble deciphering, let alone understanding. Two things stuck out for him. One space following the printed word ‘vaisseau,’ which looked like ‘vessel,’ was filled with the words ‘Pride du Loire.’ Another line contained the name ‘Richard Bougie.’ That looked suspiciously like Richard Bogie, while the name was the pride of a river, like that of the vessel they were on. Could the *Pride of Merseyside* also be known as the *Pride du Loire*? Looking at Captain Bogie, Hamish realized that the captain had turned quite pale at what had been discovered.

“Captain Bogie,” Hamish addressed the merchantman’s captain, “it looks like you are a French privateer as well as an English one. This is well beyond my ability to assess or my commanding officer’s. I imagine that he will have to take you and your ship into port to have the officials there decide what will be done with your ship and you. I shall make sure that my marines do not allow you to destroy any material before my commanding officer can decide our next steps. Pirates, I believe, usually hang, so we have to be scrupulous to preserve any evidence that would prove that that is what you are.

“Sergeant, assign two reliable men to guard this cabin and prevent anyone from entering until we can inform Mr. Macreau.”

“Yes, sir.” The marine shouted out, stamping his boots at the same time.

Hamish restacked the papers he had been examining. “I’ll need a portfolio or portmanteau to carry these documents to *Glaucus*. Captain Bogie, what do you have that would do?”

“Nothing, sir.”

“Pity. I’ll just have to use this fine case then.” Hamish pointed to an elaborately worked leather carrying case set next to the table.

“I think the canvas bag behind that one might be better,” Captain Bogie muttered hurriedly.

“Very well. Sergeant, place the documents we have found in the drawers of this chest in the canvas bag and bring it on deck when we go there. Captain Bogie, I see that this cabin has a lock. Please give me the key.”

“You have no right.” Captain Bogie sputtered.

“Sergeant,” said Hamish in response, ignoring the protest, “check the Captain’s clothes for the key, and if it is not there, proceed to ransack this cabin until it is found.”

“Oh, all right!” said the ship’s captain. “Here it is.”

“Thank you, Captain. That is so much easier than destroying the cabin searching for it. Now let us go on deck. Sergeant, lock the door with the key Captain Bogie is holding out and give it to me when we are on deck. Now Captain, lead the way to your quarterdeck.”

Back in the open, Hamish conferred with Mr. Brooks to compare what was in the hold with the bill of lading.

"That paper doesn't really represent the cargo," said the Master. "For instance, there is not as much of the cloth as the bill of lading states. The agricultural goods include a large number of sharp, bladed instruments that could equally be taken as weapons: more like cutlasses or sabers than sythes. The miscellaneous iron goods are, in fact, shackles, chains, and locks, far more of them than even a full cargo of slaves would require. Similarly, there are twenty stands of muskets and a goodly amount of ammunition and fine gunpowder: more than enough to allow everyman aboard to have three or four muskets and to fire a great many shots from each. They were not mentioned on the bill of lading you sent to me, and shackles in that number are hardly 'miscellaneous iron goods,' are they? The very fact that they are not listed specifically could be taken to suggest that they are meant for the enemy. I believe, Mr. Macauley, that we should have these oddities brought to the attention of the authorities before we allow this vessel to continue."

"I agree, especially as she seems to engage in piracy when the opportunity presents itself."

"Does she? That will account for the large number of cutlasses we found in the hold."

"It might, Mr. Brooks, it might."

"Captain Bogie," Hamish addressed the *Pride of Merseyside*'s captain. "There are too many irregularities here for me to allow you to proceed. My commanding officer will likely require you to have your documents validated by the authorities. Mr. Brooks and I will return to *Glaucus* to report to our captain. I will leave my marines here to make sure that you do not try to destroy evidence or sail away.

"Sergeant, you and your men are to remain here and make sure that Captain Bogie does not do anything or try to sail away.

"Come along, Mr. Brooks. I am sure that Captain Macreau will want to hear about what makes Merseyside Proud."

Onboard *Glaucus*, the officers conferred about the situation. Though none doubted that what happened next was up to Etienne, he welcomed any suggestions, especially from the Master, who had far more experience than the other three put together. He summed up their considerations well before it was Etienne's time to decide.

"That ship is obviously suspicious. At the very least, her cargo documents are inadequate. At worst, her captain and crew are pirates. We are in no position to decide what her crimes are, and we have time before we have to meet Captain Giles to take that ship into port and let the authorities deal with her. The nearest major naval base is Plymouth. Going there might make us late for our meeting with Captain Giles. Belfast is also far away and closer to the island to which we are heading secretly. Captain Giles would probably prefer that our presence close to that island not be known. Liverpool and Bristol would be better, but the first suffers the problem of being too near where spies may congregate, and reaching the latter may take us too far out of our way. That leaves Dublin or maybe Wexford or even Waterford. I've never been into any of them, but none of them has an easy entrance. Dublin is the nearest, and it is the largest city, so it is most likely to have useful officials. I recommend that we take that ship into Dublin, though we may have to wait for high tide to safely cross the sandbar at the entrance."

"Then we shall go to Dublin," said Etienne. "Incidentally, Captain Giles gave me a list of prize agents associated with his new one in London. That fellow we dealt with in Plymouth was excellent, and the Dublin one is marked on the list as being particularly energetic and knowledgeable. It will be helpful to have someone in Dublin who knows the ropes to figure out whether the *Pride of Merseyside* or her cargo are prizes.."

"If they are, we'll all have some more money to add to what we will get from *Eclat*," said Hamish greedily.

"Captain Giles still is captain of *Glaucus*," said Mr. Stuart. "I imagine that he will get three-eights of anything we capture as if he were here."

"Don't be so sure," replied Mr. Brooks. "Captain Giles has always seen to it that we got at least everything that was owing us and sometimes more. Remember that in the last two occasions when we took prizes, somehow his agent arranged for the division to occur before the various fees were paid, and the captain then paid the various levies himself. I would wager that he takes his one-eighth as if he were an admiral and distributes the rest of his share among us."

The others nodded, and no one took up the Master's wager.

"Right. Now we will treat that ship as hostile, even more so than a normal prize since her captain may hang," Etienne announced in decisive tones that indicated that the discussion was over, and now he was giving orders. "Mr. Stuart will be in command of the *Pride of Merseyside.* Take Mr. Dunsmuir as your backup watchstander. Mr. Macauley, we should treat the crew and officers as hostile. Take some more marines across to that ship and stay there until we reach Dublin. Also, send the captain — Captain Bogie, did you say his name is? — and his first mate over to *Glaucus*. In fact, now that I think of it, it might be a good idea to lock the crew in the hold. Mr. Stuart, select enough of our sailors to manage that ship for a couple of days. Luckily, we do have a full crew, even if we are short of officers, so we can spare as many men as you need."

Once the designated crew members of *Glaucus* had been transferred to the *Pride of Merseyside,* and Captain Bogie, or Bougie, or whatever his name was, had been brought to the frigate, the two ships headed for Dublin. The wind was favorable though light. Morning found that the coast around Dublin was in sight, and, before long, they were met by a pilot boat offering to bring them safely into the harbor. Etienne did not look forward to having to deal with whatever authorities might turn out to have jurisdiction over their capture, but he at least had a plan. He would go ashore and find his way to the agent Giles had told him about. Then the whole matter would be out of his hands if the agent was competent. He realized that he would be quite happy if *Glaucus* found nothing more of interest until she arrived in Birkenhead to rendezvous with his captain. As he had found out in

Plymouth, being a successful captain brought its own headaches.

Chapter IX

"I am glad to be out of Dublin," Etienne Macreau remarked as he watched the pilot boat head back to the port across the sandbar over which *Glaucus* had just been guided.

"I don't know about that, Captain," replied Mr. Stuart. "I found it fascinating. All those splendid buildings, though most look like they need some upkeep soon."

"Yes. Dublin reminded me of Paris a bit," replied Etienne. "Not the buildings, of course; they are quite different. Nor the taverns. They were nothing like Parisian cafés, at least not as my parents used to describe them to me after we came to England, but The Irish pubs were certainly all right. Quite different from English ones too."

"Yes, that stout! We have nothing like that in Hampshire," Mr. Stewart agreed.

"No, I think it was the look of decay that Dublin has that made me think of Paris," Etienne continued his earlier thought. “Rather like, what I am told happened to Paris when the king moved to Versailles. As I recall, Paris’s decay was worse, but Dublin has been going downhill only recently, while it had been happening in Paris for much longer. The reason for that shabbiness in Dublin, I am told, is that the town lost its parliament and, with it, the gathering of the nobility that happened when parliament was in session. I am told they had a Season in Dublin rather like the one in London. Now, there is no such social event leading to everything being spruced up the way it is in London.”

“Well, there is a bright side to its being a less important place than it used to be,” Mr. Stewart remarked.

“What is that?”

“The doctor tells me that Dublin is a far healthier place for the crew than London or Portsmouth, at least in terms of the pox and the clap.”

“Is it?” said Etienne. “I didn’t know that, but what I was really thinking about when I expressed my pleasure in leaving the town was not having to deal anymore with all the muddle that was caused by us bringing in that pirate ship. The prize agent on Captain Giles’s list, Mr. O’Donnell, tried to be helpful, but the authorities we had to deal with were anything but that. They really wanted nothing to do with the matter. They seemed to think that the sooner the *Pride of Merseyside* was on her way and out of their hair, the better.”

“Well, Mr. O’Donnell put paid to that, didn’t he?”

“He certainly did. He insisted that the ship was our prize unless the Court of Admiralty in London ruled differently and should be kept in Dublin until a ruling could be obtained. But the locals still insisted on having their way until that Indian general, Sir Arthur Wellesley, got involved, and it became a completely different story. He made sure that Captain Bogie would be held over for the Assizes and that the rest of the crew be locked up as being possible pirates so that they could be tried and hung if Captain Bogie was convicted. It seemed that he would have impressed some sailors from the *Pride* if we had had any need for crew. I wouldn't be surprised if he ships them all off to Portsmouth to serve in the navy no matter what the ruling of the court is."

"Anyway, we are clear of Dublin now, aren't we?" Mr. Stewart concluded the reminiscences. "We still have some time before we have to cross to Birkenhead to pick up the Captain. I wonder what challenges will come our way in the next few days."

"I'll be quite happy if there are none," replied Etienne. "I've learned a great deal while commanding *Glaucus,* but I have had no chance to absorb it properly. Now I'll be learning more. But I'll be quite happy to have no more excitement until we meet up with him. Do you suppose that Captain Giles ever lies awake at night pondering what to do next?"

"I doubt it. He always seems to know what he is doing or, if he doesn't, promptly asks for advice from us or Mr. Brooks or anyone else who might have ideas."

The next few days saw calm seas with light winds interspersed with showers. Mr. Brooks devised several drills to keep the crew on their toes, and they practiced clearing for action and running out the guns each day. If the weather had been warmer and sunnier, it would have been an ideal way to enjoy the ocean, though there was no slackening in scanning the horizon for ships.

As the crew cleared for action repeatedly, they became more coordinated and the time taken diminished. On the first occasion when they matched the time that had become standard before *Glaucus* had gone into drydock, Etienne decided they could have some fun. Casks were set adrift and became targets for the guns firing separately. Each gun crew strove to surpass the others, and everyone wanted to hit the target when it was their turn. Near misses were recorded carefully, for the results were subject to friendly betting. When number three gun hit its cask and blew it to smithereens, the cheering and enthusiasm seemed boundless, far more than Etienne had ever seen when they were firing the guns in battle. Of course, there was no time to celebrate before getting ready for the next shot when an enemy was firing back.

They spoke with several small merchant ships, but nothing suspicious was uncovered. Only one of the craft was a full-rigged ship. She was bound for Baltimore with a load of textiles from Liverpool. Like *The Pride of Merseyside*, this ship was armed with four cannon on each side and, like many East Indiamen, had gunports all along her sides even though there were no guns behind them. Her captain, a small, weatherbeaten man with a Yorkshire accent, who introduced himself as "Hardy," complained bitterly about the need to carry the guns and the extra crew to be able to fire them while still meeting the everyday needs of a sailing ship.

This captain was happy, indeed eager, to have himself rowed over to *Glaucus*. Like many others, he had heard of the frigate and was clearly disappointed that Giles was not aboard, though he tried to hide his feeling out of respect for those in command of the ship. Captain Hardy was also more than happy to sample Giles's wine in his absence, as the captain had told Etienne he should use it for entertaining officers from other ships.

"You know, Captain Macreau, we all know of *Glaucus* and wish there were far more such ships devoted to putting down piracy and other commerce raiders, whether privateers or French navy ships. It's not as glamorous as what you have been doing by fighting the enemy directly, but it is just as important. Indeed, if piracy and privateers were not such a threat, we would not have to carry the guns and the powder and shot for trying to protect ourselves from those thieves. As you know, guns and ammunition are very heavy. Carrying them is your job. For us, what they are is cargo we can't carry and insurance rates that make shipping much more expensive than it needs to be. If I had my way, the navy would have far more ships like yours. They would pay for themselves in the losses they would prevent and the extra cargo we could carry."

Captain Hardy left the officers on *Glaucus* feeling much better about their role. Maybe stopping privateers and pirates was about something more important than getting prize money; what they were doing was worthwhile even if they did not enrich themselves. However, sailing the Irish Sea with no more excitement was a bit tedious, and they were glad when the time came to set sail to meet Giles at Birkenhead. Etienne discussed when they should make the move with Mr. Brooks, and he decided that at the end of their present tack, which was taking them to the Irish Coast again, they could set a course for the mouth of the Mersey and the Wirral Peninsula near whose northwest end Birkenhead was situated.

The wind was lively from the north-northeast as *Glaucus* settled onto the next tack. It would take them across to the mouth of the Mersey in good time if it did not veer much or die. Indeed, even if it turned foul, they had plenty of time to arrive at their rendezvous with their captain. *Glaucus* had just come about and settled onto her new course after approaching close to the Irish coast north of Dublin when a call came from the masthead, "Ship to larboard, emerging from behind the headland, three leagues away. Funny looking ship, sir; don't know what to make of her."

"Mr. Jenks, take the telescope aloft and see what she is," ordered Mr. Stewart, the officer of the watch.

"You, Charlie," he addressed a nipper who was on the quarterdeck for no apparent reason, "inform Mr. Macreau that there is a strange ship to the north of us."

Etienne arrived on deck promptly and strode over to the rail. The strange ship was only now emerging from the headland. The lookout must have spotted it while it was still behind the sloping end of the point. She was flying a flag where a ship's nationality would usually be proclaimed, but Etienne did not recognize what little of the gaudy yellow and green banner he could make out as it streamed toward him.

A weird-looking ship she certainly was. At first glance, she looked like a standard three-masted merchant ship, but the mainsail and the driver were lateen-rigged instead of being square-rigged. They made the stranger look a bit like the ships he had seen sailed by Arabs on a previous trip, but the square foresail and topsails looked like the standard sails of a full-rigged ship. By contrast, her bowsprit was considerably shorter than he would have expected, and the jibs, as a result, looked less effective than the ones on ships with which he was familiar.

What was this strange rig doing in a bay along the Irish Sea? Would she be faster than *Glaucus*? Etienne guessed that the lateen sails would be much less effective than square sails going downwind, but it might be a different story if they were close to the wind, though, on that tack, the abbreviated jibs should prove a very great weakness.

As Etienne watched, the strange ship came closer to the wind, onto a narrow reach, probably her best point of sailing. That would be her best course to get away from *Glaucus* if she were faster. It was certainly highly suspicious that she seemed to be maneuvering to avoid the British frigate. Etienne would try to catch up with her.

"Helmsman, steer towards the stranger, but keep three points to starboard of her."

"That should do the trick," Etienne thought. *Glaucus* would try to avoid the strange ship escaping him by turning upwind. As long as she wasn't faster than his frigate or couldn't sail closer to the wind, they should succeed, and she should be easy to capture. The very fact of her changing course when his frigate came in sight made Etienne suspicious of what she was up to. It didn't take long for him to see that *Glaucus* was faster, but the strange ship could point just a bit higher, but that advantage was offset by the more pronounced leeway she suffered from. Etienne could see what looked like covered, square openings along the middle of the side of the strange ship. Possibly they were gunports, though they didn't look quite right for that purpose and didn't match what looked like gunports on the side of the ship towards the bow and the stern.

"Mr. Jenks," he called aloft. "Does she have any guns?"

"Yes, sir. Three each at the bow and the stern. Look like they might be eighteen-pounders, maybe smaller. There are oars stowed along the center of the ship, it looks like, and rowers' benches. There are no guns behind those covered ports amidships."

More and more suspicious, thought Etienne. This ship had to be looked into, and he had better take proper precautions because she might be dangerous. But what in the world could a ship that looked like some form of Barbary pirate be doing in the Irish Sea?

"Clear for action," Etienne ordered, none too soon. If the wind held and the strange ship maintained her course, they would come up with her within the hour since *Glaucus* seemed to be going considerably faster.

"What do you make of that ship?" Etienne asked Mr. Brooks as they drew closer to the strange ship.

"It looks like they have captured a frigate — maybe a Dutch or Neapolitan one — and converted it to their uses," the Master replied. "The Mohammedans like the lateen rig and have changed the ship to have those two sails, one instead of the mainsail and the other instead of the driver. Similarly, those people are usually happier with galleys than with the usual sailing ships that can be becalmed, so maybe they have converted that ship to allow some rowing. It looks like they have also radically shortened the bowsprit, maybe so that they can find it easier to come up with their prey and go across to her from the bow. I think they may have raised the sides a bit too, but I don't really know or understand the reasons for the things that they have done and how they affect her sailing properties. It is certainly a mystery to me what the advantages of this strange rig may be, not to mention what she is doing off the coast of Ireland."

"I guess that we will find out the answers soon enough, Mr. Brooks," replied Etienne. "We seem to be closing with her rapidly."

"We are. That ship must have a foul bottom for us to be catching up so quickly."

It did not take long for Mr. Brooks's point to be illustrated. "Larboard bow chaser, fire a shot across her bow," ordered Etienne.

"Aye, aye, sir," called back Mr. Dunsmuir.

The cannon crashed out. Moments later, the ball could be seen splashing some distance beyond their opponent's bow.

"Prepare to fire," called Etienne to Mr. Dunsmuir, who commanded the larboard guns. At the order, all the larboard cannon were run out simultaneously. It was a more impressive demonstration than if they had been fully ready when the warning shot was fired. It emphasized what a fatal threat *Glaucus* posed to the fleeing ship if she tried to thwart the British frigate.

The ploy was effective; the strange craft spilled the wind from her lateen sails and backed her mainmast topsail. *Glaucus* backed hers. It was time to solve the mystery of what they had found.

"Mr. Stewart, Mr. Macauley," ordered Etienne. "Take the longboat with some marines, go over to her, and find out what she is all about."

When they reached the strange ship, Mr. Stewart led the way up the boarding slats. He emerged on the quarterdeck to be met by a huddle of men dressed in Arabic clothes.

"I am Lieutenant Daniel Stewart of His Majesty's Frigate *Glaucus*."

The men waiting for the arrival of the British officers clearly listened to this pronouncement, but it was also obvious that they did not understand the words. They started murmuring to each other in puzzlement.

"Does anyone here speak English?" Daniel asked in a loud voice.

There was no reply from the men in front of him. After a pause, a voice came from the starboard well forward of the quarterdeck. "I do, sir,"

Daniel moved over to examine where the voice came from. A gangway ran between the quarterdeck and the focsle. In the wells on each side were benches to which men were chained — galley slaves, Daniel presumed. He'd heard the term — who hadn't? — but he had never before seen the reality. The shackled men were all dressed in rough clothing that looked hardly adequate for people exposed to the elements in the Irish Sea. One of them, a couple of rows forward, was waving his hand.

Daniel turned back to address the huddle of Arabs. "Release that man and bring him here," he ordered, accompanying the instruction with signals indicating unlocking the man's chains. Some of the men in front of him looked confused, but others nodded their heads. No one moved. Mr. Macauley nodded to his sergeant, who brandished his pistol and put a bullet into the deck only inches from where the best-dressed of the nodders stood.

That produced action! The man whose toes had been in danger suddenly came to life and roared to one of the less well-dressed among the crowd. That man, in turn, quickly started down the ladder leading to the well where the slaves were tethered to their benches. He rushed to the bench where the man who spoke English was sitting and unlocked the slave's shackles with a key attached to his belt.

The released man jumped up, kicked his liberator in the crotch, and rushed to climb to the quarterdeck. He knuckled his forehead to Mr. Stewart and said in a firm voice, "Dixon, sir, from Newcastle-on-Tyne."

"Dixon, why are you here?"

"The brig I was on was captured near Tangiers, sir. We got caught in a sudden storm and were on a lee shore when a galley came and captured us. They didn't try to save our ship, and it must have washed ashore. The galley took our crew into Tangiers, where they sold us as slaves. I have been in the galleys ever since, though I was only recently sold onto this one."

"How long ago were you captured?"

“Four years, three months, and two days, sir.”

”What an ordeal! You’re free now or will be as soon as we reach port, Dixon. Now, do you know what this ship is doing here?”

“Yes, sir. She has been making raids on small villages along this coast to capture people for slaves.”

“What? They are enslaving people? Where are these captives?”

“Locked in the hold, I imagine.”

“Good Lord! Can you tell whichever of the men in that group is in charge to give Mr. Macauley here — our Marine officer —the key to the hold and show him where the access to it is.”

“I’ll be glad to, sir, but Mr. Macauley will also need the key to the shackles. I imagine that they already have the newly acquired slaves all fastened down securely.”

Dixon shouted out a long speech at the assembled sailors. He seemed to enjoy giving the orders for a change rather than taking them. The face of one of the better dressed of the ship’s crew got noticeably more furious at his former captive’s words, but a gesture from Mr. Macauley, which resulted in one of the marines taking aim at the man, induced rather unwilling compliance with what was needed. The marine lieutenant, accompanied by a couple of his men and the crew member pointed out by Dixon, went off to find the entrance to the hold.

“Dixon,” asked Mr. Stewart, “exactly where are these galley slaves from?”

"All over, sir, but they are mainly Spanish and Italians. That is where these thugs usually go hunting for slaves, but their victims do come from many other places."

"Do they speak English? If we release them, will there be a problem?"

"Well, we would all like to kill most of these Barbers, sir, but I am sure there should be no trouble, not with your ship ready to blow us out of the water. We all have old scores to settle with our captors, especially those bastards who wielded the whips to make us row faster, but there should be no difficulty as long as you can tell us that we will be free to go after you have got us to a port provided that none of us attack the slave mongers."

"All right. Wilcox," Mr. Stewart addressed a bosun's mate who was part of his boarding party, "go with Dixon here and that creature who has the keys, and unlock all the men chained to the benches. Dixon, tell the galley slaves that they are now free men. We will disembark them when we reach a suitable port. Oh, and Dixon, make clear to them that we will not tolerate any violence towards the men who have kept them in slavery. Those villains will be dealt with properly, I can assure you, but I cannot tolerate murder, even though I expect that all these thugs will hang eventually."

"Yes, sir," said Dixon in surly tones.

Hardly had Daniel finished dealing with the galley slaves than a crowd of bewildered-looking people, men, women, and even some children started to mount the companionway that led to the hold. Several were rubbing their wrists where welts, probably from shackles, were evident. They were chattering in some language that Daniel did not know, indeed one that he had never heard before.

"Do any of you speak English?" he called out.

This was met by blank stares and some murmuring among the arrivals on deck. Daniel had heard vaguely that some people in Ireland — or was it Scotland — spoke some strange language quite different from English. This must be it. What was it called? Gaelic or something like that.

Daniel raised his voice and cried to the men and marines from *Glaucus*, "Do any of you understand what these people are saying."

There was silence for a moment, and then one of the marines spoke up, "I know a bit of it, sir." He spoke with such a thick Irish accent that he was almost incomprehensible to the Hampshire-raised lieutenant.

"Very good, Hagarty. See if you can discover what happened to them."

The marine stepped forward and addressed the crowd.

The response was incomprehensible gabble, with most of the crowd trying to talk at once.

"Silence!" roared Daniel, surprising even himself with his volume. "Haggarty, tell them to speak one at a time."

Presumably, the marine did so since the subsequent discussion was much more orderly. After a while, Haggarty turned to Daniel and reported. "Sir, they all live in small coves by the sea with only poor tracks to more populated places or their lords' holdings. These raiders arrived after dusk and somehow captured the inhabitants — or at least some of them. I'm not clear just how that happened. Then the raiders would take their captives to the ship, chain them up and lock them in the hold. These people have no idea about what happened next or what is going to happen to them, for they have been unable to communicate with their captors except by sign language. Sir, they seem to be very simple people, but they all tell very similar stories, at least the people who said anything much to me."

"I see," said Daniel, though, in fact, there was a lot he did not understand, and he was having trouble wrapping his mind around the idea that capturing slaves could happen anywhere in the British Islands in the nineteenth century. Slavery was something that happened far away and did not involve his sort of people at all, at least not as slaves.

"Haggarty," Daniel again addressed the marine, "tell them that we will make sure that they return to their homes, but we can't do it right away because of our other duties. Also, promise them that their captors will be punished." Even as the words were out of his mouth, he realized that he might have gone too far. He really couldn't promise that *Glaucus,* or the navy, would see that the captives were returned to their homes. Well, he could hardly reverse himself. He would just have to hope for the best.

With his immediate problems dealt with, Daniel returned to *Glaucus* though he thought it wise to leave Mr. Macauley and his marines on the captured ship. Etienne was as stumped as Daniel about what to do with the captives they had acquired. The time spent dealing with the slaver had eaten up much of the spare time they had had before it became urgent that they meet with Giles on the other side of the Irish Sea. Could they just send the captured ship into Dublin? That would undoubtedly tie up a significant number of *Glaucus*'s crew with no obvious possibility of rejoining their ship in time to be of use in whatever secret venture Giles had planned. Also, could they even control this weird ship? It was certainly different from anything that either of the lieutenants had sailed in before. But they would have to try. With the captives and the slaves, there were far too many people on this strange ship to transfer them all to *Glaucus,* which had a full crew already.

Mr. Brooks came to their rescue. "That ship can't be all that difficult to sail, though I don't think we can safely use any of their crew to do so, even though they should know how to handle her. I think it is quite likely that they know that they will all hang, so they will try to do everything they can to stop us. Not that I don't think they should be executed. I think they should! Indeed, hanging is too good for them!

"I believe that I can make a decent job of sailing that unusual ship, even if the rigging is a bit strange. Wind is wind, and water is water! I have examined a lot of strange rigs in my years at sea. My master's mate and I should be able to handle her for the short trip to the Mersey, and then we can let Captain Giles decide what to do about her. Of course, I'll also need some of our crew members to sail her."

"I appreciate your offer, Mr. Brooks, and I am happy to take you up on it," Etienne responded. "I am sure that Daniel and I can get *Glaucus* to Birkenhead by ourselves; after all, we were both trained by you. Pick out the people you need; you know their capabilities as well as I do. I would suggest that you take Mr. Jenks with you for signaling. It would be good experience for him."

"Mr. Macreau," broke in Daniel, "can I suggest that Mr. Macauley and his marines stay on that ship? All those Arabs we took as prisoners will be desperate to try to retake the ship to avoid hanging, and those galley slaves would like nothing better than to kill the lot of them. It would be asking a great deal of Mr. Brooks to sail a strange ship while putting down a battle among the people on board."

Having made up his mind, Etienne wasted no time carrying out the plans. It took Mr. Brooks about twenty minutes to feel confident that he could handle the slave ship. Then off they sailed. The prize made so much leeway when close-hauled that *Glaucus* had to sail a bit off the wind. She was also considerably slower than *Glaucus*. Mr. Brooks led the way in the former slave ship realizing the course after allowing for the leeway* which he had calculated would get them to the northwest corner of the Wirral peninsula where Birkenhead was located. Both ships then settled in for the long night passage across the Irish Sea.

Etienne and Daniel shared a bottle of Giles's best claret after doing everything to ensure a quiet passage. "This has been quite a baptism of fire for you in the responsibilities of being a captain, Etienne," Daniel remarked. “Do you feel ready to have your own command now?”

“It’s a scary thought. But, somehow, we have come through some unusual incidents successfully. I will be quite happy to remain a lieutenant for the time being, but yes, I would like to have my own ship before too long.”

Chapter X

Daphne was late, by her standards, in getting to work at her table in the morning room of Dipton Hall, though, in fact, it was becoming her new norm after her return from Reading to start late. Bringing her brother's children into the nursery had somewhat upset the established routines that Nanny Weaver had dictated for taking care of three infants, and Daphne had been drawn into the care of children much more than before. Mary had found the transition to Dipton Hall rather frightening, though she tried to hide her anxiety and had taken to seeking comfort with Scruffy, the rejected foxhound. She would sit for hours telling him how they had to be brave and how wonderful it was that Uncle Giles and Aunt Daphne had taken them to live in such a wonderful castle, a description that Mary felt fitted her new home better than 'house' or 'manor' or even 'hall.' The dog, who was normally rather impatient with people who were not going to do something interesting with him, seemed quite happy to let her hug him for as long as she wanted. He would often show his sympathy by licking her face, much to Nanny Weaver's annoyance.

Mary regularly woke up in the night crying softly, and if she was not heard by the nursery maid, she would sneak out of the nursery to go looking for Scruffy, who was firmly banished from the nursery when the children were put to bed. Scruffy could always be found in Giles's and Daphne's bedroom, and Mary would climb into bed with her aunt and uncle. If anyone had suggested to Nanny Weaver or Daphne before Mary arrived that this was acceptable behavior for a five-year-old, they would have been laughed out of court. But Daphne felt that it was the least she could do for the child. She remembered all too clearly how her own mother's death had distressed her when she was about Mary's age. As a result, Daphne rose later than usual to make sure that the child had enough sleep.

Hugh had also had problems adapting to his new surroundings and the loss of his parents. He tried to put a good face on the situation during the daytime, but at night he had reverted to wetting his bed. Nanny Weaver told Daphne that she had no idea how to deal with this problem. He was clearly not at fault, but she knew that somehow he had to be encouraged to stop it, especially as he found it terribly embarrassing. While Mary's source of comfort and distraction was Scruffy, Hugh's was Mr. Griffiths. Given the chance, Hugh would sneak off to visit the stables, and the stable master always found time to include Hugh in his chores and to give him a ride on Moonbeam. Hugh was still too small to handle the big horse by himself, or so Mr. Griffiths thought, but he was a quick learner on how to get the horse to turn and stop, though old Moonbeam could rarely be induced to go faster than a sedate walk unless Mr. Griffiths dictated the speed. Nanny Weaver was surprisingly tolerant of the boy's sneaking off to the stables once she realized that both Giles and Daphne thought it was good for the child. However, the nanny did point out several times to Daphne that she should make arrangements for the lad's education.

Daphne had a tickle at the back of her throat and a stuffy nose that she had to blow before settling into her work. She had just reached for the first of the accounts she intended to go over that morning when Steves announced that Reverend the Honorable David Giles would like to see her. Despite the resounding title, which rolled off Steves's tongue as if he were introducing the Crown Prince, the visitor was only Giles's younger brother, known to the family as Lord David. He was the Vicar of Dipton, but recently he had been absent from the parish most of the time, his duties being assumed by his curate, Mr. Foster. Lord David had helped Daphne with some tricky problems arising from Giles's older brother's death, while Daphne had had a major hand in ensuring that Lord David was elected Member of Parliament for Dipton. Lord David was not content to be just a vicar, even one who doubled as an MP. He had his eye on becoming a bishop as soon as possible. Daphne had helped that endeavor by giving him a substantial annuity to allow him to put on the elegant front, which he claimed was essential to show support for Giles's brother's plans.

"Lord David," Daphne greeted her visitor. "It's good of you to visit. I haven't seen you since your election last year when Giles and I had to be away. What brings you to Dipton — pastoral duties, I suppose."

"Oh, no. my curate, Mr. Foster, handles all that. No, I came to Dipton to see you — and, of course, my brother."

Giles entered the room as if this was the cue for him to appear.

"David," Giles said. "Welcome back to Dipton. It has been a long time since you have been here. The parish has also not seen you from long before your last election."

"Yes, well, I have been busy. Parliament, you know, and church matters."

"Oh? Your attendance at the House has not been stellar. I have been disappointed by that. I understand that you didn't get the rural dean position despite Daphne's best efforts, did you?"

"Well, no. How was I to know that the Bishop detested Lord Tamerstead?"

"That sort of knowledge would have come to your attention if you had been attending to Parliamentary matters as closely as you should have. After all, the Bishop expressed his loathing of Lord Temerstead when Tamerstead so aggressively defended the practice of seriously underpaying curates, claiming that it was necessary to maintain the dignity of the placeholders who made, according to him, such a great — and unspecified — contribution to the life of the country. Lord Tamerstead also said that there was no need for curates to live well since their real job was to look after the routine church matters for the common people. Poppy cock, if you ask me. If those who have a particular living don't want to perform the duties that come with it, they should pay their substitutes as befits a gentleman, not like some laborer. Your devotion to Lord Tamerstead has cost you other positions as well, you know, or is about to."

"What do you mean?"

"It is simple. Mr. Moorhouse — Daniel Moorhouse — and I detest slavery, especially the trade in slaves from Africa. Thank heavens the right side prevailed on that issue, and the trade is about to end, but that happened with no thanks to you, who vociferously took the side of Lord Tamerstead and the slave owners of the Caribbean Islands."

"I had no choice in that matter! Stopping the slave trade would be ruinous to Lord Tamerstead if it passed. If that happened, Lord Tamerstead declared that he would not be able to provide his daughter, Cecelia, with her dowry unless I did my best to see that the measure failed."

"I am not surprised at Tamerstead's taking that line. He has the reputation of being one of the worst slave owners on Antigua. He has found it cheaper to treat his Africans very badly and to feed them even worse so that many die, and he has to replenish them regularly from the new arrivals on the Island. His agent must be a truly terrible man with his constant need for slaves even though Tamerstead's estate is not getting any more profitable. His plantation's lack of success reflects very badly on its owner.

"Lord Tamerstead has made a lot of money by being a silent partner in the slave-auction on Antigua. That activity is finished now, thank heavens, though I wouldn't put it past him to try to smuggle African slaves into the country using illegal ships and clandestine auctions. His estate on Antigua never made much money, and now, I expect, it will make none."

"Surely that is not true! How can you even think it? Lady Cecelia has always spent lavishly." Lord David stated, even though his voice sounded as if he had doubts about his patron's financial security and was just whistling in the dark.

"I was a lieutenant on a couple of ships in the West Indies and spent quite a bit of time in a frigate based at English Harbour on Antigua. I made some good friends there with officers from other ships when we were serving together and had quite a lot of shore time. One of the lieutenants on another ship wooed and won one of the planters' daughters. My friend settled there and, I suspect, has become fabulously wealthy. We correspond occasionally, and I asked him about your patron in one of my letters. His reply was long and specific. It was clear that he thought that Lord Tamerstead is a disgrace to the peerage, as well as being a very deficient plantation owner.

"Are you sure you want to go ahead with marrying Lady Cecelia, given what her father has threatened and how he treats people?"

"Yes. What choice do I have? Even if what you say is true, Lord Tamerstead still has great influence in the Church that will advance my clerical career."

"Will it?" Daphne broke in. "His influence was supposed to get Bishop Chesterton to appoint you as rural dean. That certainly didn't happen, did it?"

"That is hardly my fault. How was I to know that Lady Chesterton despised Lady Temerstead and the Bishop had little respect for what Lord Tamerstead was doing for the Church? Your bright idea scuttled my chances there, Daphne."

"I am quite sure that that is not the case, and Daphne was only doing what you wanted." interrupted Giles. "You brought it upon yourself by not finding out enough about the men you want to deal with."

"What do you mean? I had no way of knowing that the two women detested each other, and the Bishop's wife scuttled my chances because of not liking my patron's wife. Why else would the Bishop block my appointment? It is one that I could fulfill quite profitably without its taking much of my time, if any."

"Bishop Chesterton and I have become quite good friends over several issues before the House of Lords in the short time that I have been a member. What he did not like was your vociferous attempt to influence the vote on the pay of curates. Even though it did not come before the House of Commons, you were active in getting men to take up Lord Tamerstead's position, which would also benefit you personally. I agree with the Bishop on that. Curates should be paid a decent wage."

"Surely, you don't take those problems seriously, Richard? They are entirely an internal matter for the Church." Lord David replied. "They don't concern you."

"Well, I *do* think they are a matter of general interest," intervened Daphne. "I was expecting that you would pay your curate properly when you became our MP and that you have not done. Mr. Foster is an excellent minister, and he is grossly underpaid. He has trouble dressing appropriately in reasonably new clothes. He couldn't possibly get married on that stipend. And his principles won't allow him to take a subsidy from us. He claims that that practice leads to the provider having a special relationship with the minister, which isn't right, even if he is not treating his benefactor differently from others. Too many other clergymen are doing just that — pandering to the local nobility or richest gentry. We provide you with a very generous allowance, and you don't even pay Mr. Foster appropriately."

"Well, Mr. Foster hasn't complained to me."

"Not surprisingly, since you are never here, and he undoubtedly also knows your views on "overpaying" curates who should not rise above their station — at least, that is what the press reported you to have said about the matter."

"Yes, that is my position. Dipton, you know, is not a very rich living."

"Why do you say that?" asked Giles. "We are certainly prosperous enough, surely."

"It is prosperous, indeed, but it is not a very large parish, and it is a vicarage, not a rectory."

"Why does that matter?" asked Giles

"Rectors get all the tithes, the great ones and the small ones. Vicars, like me, only get the small ones. Dipton would be a much more attractive living if it were a rectory."

"I thought that every parish priest got just the lesser tithes though I am unsure what they are."

"No. That is not the case. Rectors get the greater tithes as well."

"Still, the lesser tithes are quite substantial here at Dipton, and I know that, as our estates have become more productive, so have our tithes. As you know, we pay them in cash as a percentage of what we take in, and they have been going up since we took over Dipton Hall."

"So have prices," interjected Lord David.

"True. But it still leaves the payment to the church just from us, which is enough to keep you very comfortably, even without the tithes from other estates here, and their tithes also must be considerable. The annuity was just to help you put on the appearance of a very, very well-to-do, independent MP. Maybe that was a mistake; it certainly hasn't weakened your subservience to Lord Tamerstead. You have acted as the lackey of Tamerstead, which is no way to get his respect, let alone that of Bishop Chesterton."

"Daphne is quite right, David," Giles rejoined the conversation. "Your behavior has been disgraceful, especially as an MP where there is very strong reason for people to think that your support is for sale, particularly when it is quite clearly opposed to the opinion of the most influential person in the riding you represent. You know my views on slavery, which are shared by most of the prominent men in this riding, and I know of none that think that Mr. Foster should not be properly paid. As you know, Mr. Moorhouse and I completely control your election. I have to tell you now — I would have told you earlier, but you are never here, and you have been avoiding invitations to visit Lord Struthers's residence when I was staying there — I have to tell you that we have decided not to support you in the next election. You have not consulted with your main constituents about where you should stand on major items. You are rarely in your constituency and have not bothered to communicate your thoughts or ask for advice by post. Even the other member for Dipton, who is a holdover from the previous owner of Dipton Hall and lives in London, communicates regularly with Mr. Moorhouse and me about his thinking and asks our opinions. I wouldn't necessarily expect you to follow them, but I would expect you to find out what they are and tell us why you disagree if you do. The other member has not always followed our advice, but he has had more cogent reasons for his choices than blatant self-interest."

"You can't stop me from being the MP for Dipton! I won't have any influence if I lose my seat. Lord Tamerstead will not give me a dowry for marrying Cecelia."

"And you won't marry her without a substantial dowry?" Daphne asked.

"Of course not."

"I have mentioned your situation to Bishop Chesterton," Giles continued, ignoring the interruption. "To my surprise, David, he might be willing to consider you for the Dean of his cathedral, provided that you are prepared to give up your living here. Without a seat in Parliament and the presumption that you must be in league with me and so can speak for me — even when you don't — he thinks that your more disgraceful tendencies would be stopped and, if you performed well, he might be able to advance you further. I am sure that the Dean's House at Ameschester is superior to the vicarage here at Dipton. And it is a much more important position to use as a stepping stone to even more prestigious positions in the Church. Of course, you would have to give up your living here. It would be a condition of your taking the position at the cathedral. After what he knows of you, I am surprised that the Bishop might consider giving you a second chance in the Church, but he says he believes that you are better than you have demonstrated."

"What about my annuity?" asked David, somewhat to Giles's annoyance.

"That ends as soon as Parliament dissolves, or you are lucky enough to get the deanship that Bishop Chesterton may offer you. He still could change his mind after all.

"Now, I promised Hugh to take him to the stables," Giles continued. "Make up your mind about whether I should approach Bishop Chesterton again. Remember that you will not be in our seat in Parliament after the next election, which may come soon, and that your annuity will disappear if you do not reward Mr. Foster properly."

Giles turned and left the room. His voice had become very soft and cold when he said his concluding words. It left Daphne worried. She had never seen Giles so angry. His brother had pushed him to the edge by not admitting his wrongdoing. Another minute and her husband would have taken a stand he would later regret, but she knew that Giles was too proud to admit his error in this case. Daphne agreed completely with Giles but was more prepared to remain diplomatic to try to save the situation. She didn't want her children to grow up unfamiliar with their only uncle.

"You know, David," Daphne remarked, "you would do better to admit you had stepped out of line rather than try to defend the indefensible. What is the state of your wooing Cecelia now?"

"I don't see any point in going on with it. If I'm not to be of use to her father, he'll keep the dowry for someone who would be useful to him."

"Would you marry her without a dowry and if you were only vicar of Dipton?"

"No. I wouldn't. Cecelia isn't very bright, you know. Her conversation is all about things in society and how to spend money on fashions and so on. I don't think that she has ever read a book. I can't see her as the wife of the vicar of Dipton or even of the dean of the cathedral in a small county town."

"If that is how you feel, I don't see why you wanted to marry her in the first place."

"I thought her father would advance my career. Many prominent men in the capital spend a minimum amount of time with their wives, mainly on social occasions such as dinners, where they can have little to do with each other. So it doesn't matter if their wives are as shallow as a goldfish pond. That's what I expected in marrying Lady Westerly, but I can't imagine having that sort of life when my only source of income is the vicarage of this village. We could not ignore each other without it being noticed, which would mean the end of ambitions in the Church. Things would be hardly better as the cathedral dean of a small town. We would have far too many public occasions to be amiable with each other, and I doubt that I could do that.

"No, marrying Cecelia if she brings no dowry and no influence is out of the question. That would be stupid. It's out! If I anger Bishop Chesterton anymore, I don't believe I can ever expect preferment in the Church. I don't believe he would look favorably on his dean having only a token marriage. Cecelia's only virtue besides the dowry was the influence of Lord Tamerstead that would come with the marriage, and both have disappeared. No, I think I had best see if Richard is still willing to get Bishop Chesterton to offer me the position of Dean of Ameschester Cathedral and hope that more preferment may spring from that. Of course, if I want to be a bishop, having a wife does help the cause, so I shall have to look for a suitable mate."

With that, Lord David left, looking as if he was hoping that his last words would horrify the romantic, which he believed that Daphne was, despite much evidence to the contrary. Admittedly, Daphne wasn't happy with what this little speech revealed about Lord David's character. Nevertheless, she realized that Giles really shouldn't drop his brother entirely. She felt that she should make sure that Lord David's annuity should continue as long as he gave up the living at Dipton. Financially, the annuity was larger than Lord David's income as the Vicar of Dipton. What Daphne had been most concerned about was that they not lose Mr. Foster's services. Mr. Foster was highly respected and likable.

Lord David was, in Daphne's eyes, a most unsatisfactory substitute.

Most importantly, Mr. Foster was the only preacher Dipton had had that had not resulted in a deluge of ill-tempered commentary on the unsoundness of his sermon from her father at lunch on Sundays. Mr. Daniel Moorhouse, despite being an atheist, had paid close attention to the Christian subjects, which were so large a part of the curriculum at Oxford when he studied there. Her father was all too happy to enlighten Sunday luncheon with the unbiblical nature of most of the claims that came from the pulpit about what God wanted. Mr. Thompson somehow avoided such pitfalls, partly because he never claimed he knew what God or his Son wanted but instead gave sensible homilies on what could be learned from the Bible, as he interpreted it, about improving his congregants' daily lives and understanding of life around them.

After Lord David left, Daphne returned to her work, but she had only gotten through one report when Steves announced another visitor. This time it was Mr. Foster. Daphne had asked him to visit before she knew that he would be the subject of a lively discussion that morning. She had wanted to ask him about a tutor for Hugh, even though she knew that Mr. Foster would not have time without giving up his position as curate. Mr. Foster becoming Hugh's tutor would solve her immediate problem, and he could become Bernard's and Roger's tutor when her own boys were older. It went without question that they would each go to public school when they reached age thirteen.

"Mr. Foster, thank you for coming today. I wanted to consult with you about my nephew Hugh, who is, it seems, also our ward since his father and mother have died, and no other relatives are available to take him while we feel that looking after him is our duty as well as our desire. Have you met him?"

"I haven't had that pleasure, though, of course, I have heard a lot about Hugh from Mr. Jackson and Mr. Griffiths as well as from your father, Lady Camshire."

"I'm not surprised," commented Daphne. "I suppose our bringing my brother's children to Dipton is bound to be news in our village. Anyway, Hugh is nine. So far, his formal instruction has only been conducted by his parents, and he needs to continue his studies now. His sister will need a governess, but not, we think, before next year.

"I wanted to consult with you about getting a tutor for Hugh. He needs one until he is ready to go to one of the good schools, maybe Eton or Rugby. His father and grandfather went to Rugby. Lord Camshire never did go to one of the public schools; his school was the Navy."

"Well, I must say, Lord Camshhire seems none the worse for that!"

"In any case, we need to continue Hugh's education. His father was an Oxford graduate and a bookstore owner, and he was in charge of Hugh's education up to now, though I suspect that his wife may have contributed greatly. I never knew her. Anyway, Hugh's tutor is the problem right now; We won't need a governess for Mary for a while."

"So, are you thinking of getting a tutor for Hugh as soon as possible?"

"Yes, we are. It should be quite a good position. When Hugh is ready to go to school, Berns will need a tutor, and then Roger will be the student. Would you be interested, by any chance?"

"I'm afraid not, Lady Camshire. I am committed to my duties as a clergyman. Admittedly, the financial rewards are not great here in Dipton, but I still hope to find a more lucrative position that would allow me to marry."

"I am sure that we would pay quite enough to you as a tutor that you could easily afford marriage and a comfortable status."

"I appreciate the offer, my lady, but I have to refuse."

"Why?"

"No matter how you look at it, a tutor or, for that matter, a governess is still a servant. A very high-ranking servant, admittedly, but still a servant. My grandfather and my own father struggled mightily to be of the gentry. They succeeded and have made sure that my older brother could maintain that position without difficulty. They provided me with a good education, but I have been on my own since then. I don't want to slip back to a position they worked so far to evade."

"I see; I think I can understand. As you must know, my father was the first of our family who jumped the barriers to becoming a gentleman. I've never faced the problem of being accepted by society since I intended to remain single with resources more than adequate to maintain the status provided by my father. Of course, those plans did not include falling madly in love with a man who would ask me to marry him. It was just my good luck that Giles had been very successful in his own right before any inherited status or wealth was in sight.

"Well, I am disappointed by your answer, Mr. Foster. We certainly don't want to lose you from our community; you have been a great addition to Dipton! My husband has been disappointed by how little his brother is paying you. I believe he is planning something that will better your lot.

"Since you are not interested in being our tutor, do you have anyone to suggest?"

"I've already thought about it, anticipating that you might ask. I am afraid that I don't though I can make inquiries. None of the people I admired at Cambridge are at a loose end, but I don't know what has happened to all of them."

On that note, Mr. Foster's visit was about to end when Giles reappeared.

"Mr. Foster. Good to see you. It has been too long," said Giles striding forward to shake Mr. Foster's hand.

"My lord, it has. I hear that you have been busy."

"Somewhat. Has Lady Camshire told you of our dilemma?"

"About Master Hugh? Yes, she has."

"I am afraid that Mr. Foster is not interested in being a tutor, not even for us, and he doesn't know of anyone who might be available," Daphne reported.

"I'm sorry to hear it, Mr. Foster," said Giles. "And I've only recently become aware of what a miserable salary my brother is paying you. Quite outrageous, especially as he has funds beyond those he gets from the living. "Now, about Hugh, I was just speaking with Mr. Griffiths, and he had an interesting suggestion about what to do about Hugh's education."

"What was that, Giles?" asked Daphne.

"He suggested that the educated men in the village could each lend a hand in his education. Well, not only the educated men. He included himself among them since he believes, as do I, that the care and uses of horses should be part of every gentleman's education. Mr. Griffiths has seen many men of the upper classes who have no idea how to look after, judge, or even handle horses. Horses usually play a large role in gentlemen's lives, though they didn't for Hugh's father after he left Dipton. Then Mr. Griffiths speculated that Mr. Jackson might allow Hugh to accompany him on some of his trips when he is being a vet rather than a physician. You cannot find a better-educated man here than Mr. Jackson."

"I learned an awful amount by following him around," said Daphne.

" I know. And so does Mr. Griffiths. That is where the idea came from, basically. You did very well without a governess by relying on Mr. Jackson."

"And my father."

"Quite right, and I know that your father would like to have a part in Hugh's education, as would your uncle."

"What about me?" asked Mr. Foster.

"That would be excellent if you have the time. We thought that Hugh would benefit from the Sunday school you run on Sunday afternoons."

"I am not sure that that is a good idea, my lord," replied the pastor. "The Sunday school is to teach the older children in the parish how to read and write and figure. Sunday afternoon is the only free time many of them have, strange as that may seem to us. I give very little religious instruction in the classes, in fact hardly any, though some of the reading material is from the Bible or the Hymnal. I imagine that Hugh is far too advanced for those lessons to be useful since we concentrate on the very basics of reading, writing, and arithmetic. He will already have learned what I am teaching at the Sunday school. I feel that I have succeeded in those classes if my pupils can easily add and subtract, read simple instructions or reports, and write a simple message. Hugh should know all these things from his parents' lessons. I am afraid that he would start to feel superior to the others, and they would resent his lording it over them. Maybe that is the way that society really is, but I don't think it is good to teach that lesson in Sunday school."

"I understand. I just presumed that you give religious instruction, which I am not sure that either Daphne or I are qualified to provide."

"That makes a difference if what you want is instruction in religion. I could easily find time for a couple of hours a week. I don't think more would be beneficial for a nine-year-old. I have to warn you that I am not very doctrinal in my interpretation of Christianity. Like many men from Cambridge, I am quite a bit more liberal in my interpretation than my colleagues from Oxford. However, I am much less of a free-thinker than Mr. Moorhouse, with whom I have had many good verbal tussles about Christianity. We do agree that the Church provides firm support for the community."

"That rather lines up with my own views of the Church's role in society. If Hugh knows what other people believe, he can decide what he himself believes when he grows up."

"Well, if you could spare a few hours for Hugh a week, that would be wonderful," Daphne announced. "I don't think that either Lord Camshire or I are equipped to instruct Hugh in religious matters."

"Then let's make it Tuesday mornings if that is convenient," said Mr. Foster. "Of course, as I explained to Lady Camshire, my Lord, I cannot accept any remuneration for my efforts. It would not agree with my status as a clergyman."

"As you like, Mr. Foster," replied Giles. "However, I wanted to speak with you on a different subject since you turned down our offer to become Hugh's tutor. Lady Camshire and I agree that you have been doing an excellent job as my brother's curate. Indeed, you look after the parish far better than he did when he was acting as our vicar. As you no doubt know, his appointment as vicar of Dipton is his for his life, if he wishes, and the associated income is his alone. How he performs his duties is for the Bishop to decide, not his parishioners. I recently learned that my brother is underpaying you, and I am surprised that you have not yet sought out another parish. As I said, we do not want to lose you, and I cannot force my brother to pay you more. However, nothing stops me from donating an annuity to the church to supplement the curate's salary. I believe that £250 per annum should go a long way to correct my brother's impropriety. I am informed that that should be enough to let you enjoy the life of a gentleman, including being able to afford to marry if you choose."

"That is very good of you, my Lord. Thank you. I will not lose any time before searching for a soulmate. I hope you and Lady Camshire will be the guests of honor at my wedding."

"No need to thank me, Mr. Foster. What is it you people say? 'The labourer is worthy of his hire,' isn't it? And I would definitely consider preaching and all the other duties of a clergyman as labour, just as is captaining a ship."

At that point, Hugh burst into the room yelling, 'Uncle Richard, come quickly. Mr. Griffiths says someone has stolen Moonbeam He wants you to help get her back. Come quickly."

Message delivered, Hugh turned and ran out of the room, not waiting to see what might be Giles's reaction.

"Excuse me, Mr. Foster," said Giles. "I had better see what this is all about."

He left immediately but Daphne and Mr. Foster were hot on his heels. They were as eager to learn what was afoot as Giles.

Chapter XI

Giles strode quickly to the main entrance of Dipton Hall. An agitated Mr. Griffiths was standing just outside the door, telling Steves why he wanted to see Giles urgently.

"My Lord," the stable master greeted Giles, bypassing the butler. "Several of our horses have been taken from the paddock at the Red House fields. As you know, we have been using those fields for training the hunters and for grazing them. Today, one of the stable boys, Charlie, took a handful of them over to the paddock soon after dawn, and he included Moonbeam among them. He was supposed to bring them back around eleven, but instead, Joe, the groom at the Red House, came to tell us that they had found Charlie in the paddock, just recovering from a knock on the head. There was no sign of the horses except for some fresh dung."

"How's Charlie?" Giles asked.

"Bit doozy. Based on the lump that he has developed on the side of his head, someone hit him with something big. He was still out when Joe found him. He sent one of the outside servants at the Red House to get Mr. Jackson, but right now, Charlie can't tell us anything."

"Right. Then we had better get after the horse thieves as quickly as possible. I see that you have brought our hunters, Dark Paul and Serene Masham, with you."

"Yes, my lord. I thought you and possibly Lady Camshire would like to join the chase. And I have one more horse as an extra."

"Of course, I will come," replied Giles. "Daphne, I suppose that you are not dressed for riding."

"I'm wearing my split skirt," Daphne retorted. "All I need is my coat and gloves, just as you do. Where is Hugh, Mr. Griffiths?"

"With Nanny Weaver, my lady. I brought him here and had one of the maids take him to the nursery."

"Good, then all we need are our coats and those rifles that Uncle George had made for us," Giles stated. "Would you like to accompany us, Mr. Foster?"

"I would, my lord, but I don't have a horse."

"Mr. Griffiths has brought an extra one, as you can see. I know you ride well. Take that one."

Betsy, Lady Giles's lady's maid, and Phillip, the first footman from Struthers House in London who was learning to be Giles's valet, had anticipated the needs of Daphne and Giles to have suitable clothing for riding on a winter's day. Soon they were ready, and off the party went from the stables, joined by those from the Hall, riding at a gallop. No one noticed that Scruffy was running along behind the group.

It took only a few minutes to reach the paddock at the Red House. Charlie was sitting on the ground with Mr. Jackson examining him as several other men watched. The doctor, who liked to be called an apothecary, looked up when Giles and Daphne arrived.

"This man has suffered a very nasty concussion to the left side of his head. It hasn't fractured the skull, but whether it has caused lasting damage to the brain remains to be seen. It's too early to know if it has produced permanent injury, but you can warn his family that it may have. He should be taken home as gently as possible and watched for the next couple of days. Let me know if his condition gets worse. In any case, I will call by in a couple of days to see how he is getting on," Mr. Jackson addressed the men who were already in the paddock as well as those who had just arrived.

"See to it, Mr. Griffiths," ordered Giles. "He should rest and not come to the stables until Mr. Jackson says he can."

"Very good, my lord. That is a very generous way to treat one of our workers."

"It's the least we can do. Now, what do we know about the theft?"

"The paddock gate to the road was left open. If it weren't for poor Charlie, we might have presumed that someone left the gate not properly closed when they left, so the horses escaped. Suppose George hadn't been sent to help Charlie with the horses or he hadn't arrived only a little behind Charlie. In that case, we might not have known about the theft for a very long time," said Mr. Griffiths, who had spent the time while Mr. Jackson was examining Charlie, studying the ground around the gate. "You can see from the hoof marks at the gate that there were only three horses with riders who moved the herd along. They took the road to Dipton. Probably no one would remark on horses being driven through the town at a walk as they were doing. I can't tell how long ago that was, though Charlie was not supposed to get here very early."

"I see," said Giles. "Then we had better follow them at a less leisurely pace. Mr. Griffiths, let's go."

Giles and Daphne led the way along the road to Dipton. Daphne thought it was unlikely that the horse thieves had been able to drive their herd right through the village without anyone noticing, but they might not have been wary of being seen. Parties of men with groups of horses were common as horses were returned from one destination to another. In Dipton, the group might well get news of the passage of the thieves. They were heading towards the village where they might be able to get news.

Scruffy had trailed the group going to the paddock from Dipton Hall and now attached himself to them as they started after the thieves. He excitedly ran ahead of the riders and then came racing back again to make sure that they were still following him and that there were no stragglers for him to round up. He played this game to the mild amusement of Giles while Daphne was engaged in a conversation with Mr. Foster about how he had become a proficient rider. They passed a gate in the hedge, but no one took any interest in it since the hoof prints they were following suggested that the thieves had not gone that way. Indeed, there were no hoofprints at all leading up to the gate.

The troop pursuing the horse thieves continued on along the road to Dipton. Scruffy, surprisingly, stopped leading them and started sniffing around the gate in the hedge. Then the dog started barking agitatedly. When that had no effect on the riders, he raced back to Giles and tried to get his attention by jumping up in front of him. Luckily Giles's horse, Dark Paul, was familiar with Scruffy and did not panic, though his rider had to deal with the unstable gait produced by Dark Paul's trying to kick Scruffy when the dog got close to his hoofs. This behavior was not at all like Scruffy. What could the dog be trying to communicate?

Giles turned Dark Paul and headed back to the gate. At first, he could not see what had Scruffy so excited. Then he realized that no hoof prints led up to the gate. Instead, it looked as if the ground had been roughly swept with a branch or something similar. He moved Dark Paul to the gate to look over it. On the other side, the track continued, but now the hoofmarks showed that many horses had passed that way recently.

"Ahoy," Giles bellowed in a voice that could reach the masthead of his frigate during a full gale. "Come back here."

The cavalcade stopped and turned their horses. Mr. Griffiths was the first to respond, turning his horse and returning at a gallop.

"What is it, my Lord?" he asked.

"Look over the gate. You will see where our horses have gone."

"So they have. Geraldson, open the gate!" commanded the stable master.

As soon as the gate opened, Mr. Griffiths rode through, dismounted, and examined the ground. He kicked over a couple of the turds on the road. "This is where those horse thieves went. They have about an hour and a half lead on us," he stated. "There are only three thieves; the other prints are of our horses."

"Daphne," called Giles, too excited to remember to address her formally, "do you know where this track leads?"

"Yes, Giles, I do. It is a route for farm carts and so on to Rolfstead. That is what the path was designed for, and it goes in a large loop to the ford over the creek. Though it is not much used, this cart track is a public right of way. It leads to a main road. Soon after it joins that road, there are several main turnoffs. If we can't get ahead of the thieves before they reach those junctions, we may have a real problem guessing which road they have taken.

There is a quicker way for us to take since we are on horseback and do not have a cart with us, and we can jump over some hedges in the way. If we use the shortcut, we may get ahead of the thieves."

"Oh?" Giles sounded doubtful.

"Yes. This cart track goes out of the way to take a wide loop so that it can use the ford across Rolf creek. My way meets the creek much higher up, where it is smaller, and we can easily ride across it. If we go cross country, we can cut out several miles and hopefully get ahead of the robbers. Riding more directly to the junction, we might get ahead of them, or if not, we will have much more chance of finding out where they have gone. We have enough people with us so that we can split up, and each party will still be a match for the thieves."

"That might be a good idea," Mr. Griffiths chimed in. "I can take some of the men along this track, so if the thieves turn off somewhere or go to earth for the night in one of the copses along the route, we can catch them, but if they are making such good speed that we can't catch them, but you have got ahead of them, you can double back, and we will have them caught after all. I am afraid that with their head start, we may not catch up with them before it is too late. "

"Good. The cross-country group should take the men on the best hunters since there are quite a few obstacles to jump along Lady Camshire's route. Mr. Foster, that is a splendid hunter you are riding. Would you like to accompany us?" Giles asked.

"Thank you, my lord, I would be delighted to, though it is some time since I did any hunting," replied the clergyman.

The trio set off with Daphne leading the way confidently, leaving the cart track to mount a hillside where sheep were grazing. At the top, they came to the first hedge, which Daphne made Serene Masham sail over, apparently effortlessly. Giles held back to make sure that Mr. Foster would have no trouble getting his horse to follow Daphne's lead. He had worried that the curate, who had not ridden a hunting horse for some time, might have trouble getting his mount to jump hedges or fences easily. After the borrowed horse cleared the hedge without trouble, Giles had no reason to worry about the curate's ability to handle his horse. Of course, the hedge posed little challenge to Dark Paul.

The trio proceeded rapidly. Daphne, in the lead, jumped barriers wherever needed without worrying about what lay on the other side since she had been over this route several times. Mr. Foster and Giles were happy to follow her without checking ahead of each barrier whether jumping it was actually a good idea. At first, their route led uphill, crossing several fields that had not yet been plowed for the spring plantings, then through some woodland where there was a well-defined deer track, with no major branches slowing their progress. They came to the creek as they traversed a wooded hillside that sloped to the left. It posed no problem for them, though it was flowing rapidly, and the footing in the creek looked treacherous. They did not have to have the horses splash through it. Instead, all three jumped it with ease. Soon after that, they emerged from the woods onto fields where sheep were grazing, again with hedges easily jumped. Eventually, Daphne led them to a gate. When they jumped it with no difficulty, they found that it was the last barrier to reaching a track that looked much the same as the one from which they had started.

"Here we are," Daphne declared. "This is where that cart track that the thieves took comes out. The main road is just around the corner over there. It doesn't look as if anyone has been over this lane today. We must have the horse thieves caught in a vice between Mr. Griffiths' group and us."

"That is good news," said Giles. "We must have them trapped. I suggest we ready our weapons in case we meet the thieves unexpectedly. Daphne, is your rifle loaded?"

"Of course it is, and so is my fowling piece. After the events at Sallycroft, you pointed out to me that if you are going to carry a weapon, it should be loaded with the trigger locked. All our pieces have trigger locks that are easy to unlock if needed. I hope you have followed your own advice about riding with a loaded rifle."

Daphne turned to Mr. Foster. "I am afraid that you do not have a weapon. May I lend you my fowling-piece, or would you rather not accompany us into possible danger?"

"I'll come with you, my lady. I have not had so much excitement since I went up to Cambridge."

"Then you had better take my fowling piece. It's primed and loaded, and the trigger lock is under the trigger guard."

The winter afternoon was now well advanced, and the shadows were getting long. The trio trotted back along the track, sure they would meet up with the horse thieves and the party led by Mr. Griffiths before dark. Still, they had to ride for another half hour before they heard raised voices ahead. Advancing cautiously, Giles's group rounded a corner and saw a stretch of wasteland before the track disappeared back into the woods. A short distance from the track's mouth clustered the stable hands with Mr. Griffiths. A good way farther into the clearing, horses were feeding, their legs hobbled to prevent them from running away. Several carts were scattered about haphazardly, some distance behind the grazing horses, while several low tents were near the carts.

"I'd heard that there were gypsies in the neighborhood," remarked Mr. Foster, "but I had no idea where they were or how many. They have a bad reputation for thieving. I think we must have caught up with the thieves, but there are far more people than just the three who we know took the horses."

Daphne had heard all her life about gypsies, but this was the first time she had seen one of their encampments. It seemed a strange place to camp, quite a distance from Dipton or the other villages where these gypsies could ply their special trades, such as sharpening knives and tools.

Between the horses and the men from Dipton were a dozen or so rough-looking men. Several of them held muskets, and one even had a rifle that looked well cared for. The others had cudgels. Mr. Griffiths's men were outnumbered, and they were also unarmed, with the exception of the stable master himself, who had a pistol. It did not seem to Daphne that the imbalance in firepower bothered him, even though his opponents appeared confident that their weapons gave them an upper hand. Was Mr. Griffiths bluffing?

The stable master glanced at the new arrivals and turned back to the threatening thieves.

"My reinforcements have arrived," he bellowed. "Now, lay down your arms, and untether our horses. We need not involve the militia and the courts to deal with your thievery if you do that. You must know that you could all hang for stealing our horses."

"Begone, you old fool," came the reply. "They are now our horses; you can't prove differently since they are not branded. Leave us alone, or there will be trouble."

"Don't be stupid. Of course, they are our horses; we can prove it because we know them all well, and they know us. It is easy to show that you have stolen and driven them here. If you don't comply immediately, we'll have to haul you before the magistrates, and you know that they love to hang gypsies."

"Get out of here before I lose my temper," came the reply.

"Kashi," the leader of the thieves said to the man with a rifle. "Put a bullet over this man's head to show that we mean business."

"Stop it at once," Giles bellowed. "You're cut off, and more of our reinforcements are on the way. Lay down your arms now!"

The response was for all the gypsies to turn to look at the newcomers, and a shot rang out from the rifleman among the thieves. Whether the shot was deliberate or a nervous accident was not clear. What was clear was that the bullet passed through Daphne's skirts, possibly grazing her horse, who shied away, but did not bolt.

Giles's response to the shot aimed at his wife was immediate. He drew his rifle from its scabbard, flicked the trigger lock aside, and returned the shot, all in one smooth motion. To everyone's surprise, the bullet hit the rifleman called Kashi in the chest. It knocked him over, and his jacket rapidly turned blood-red as he collapsed on the ground. Only Giles was not surprised. In his meticulous way, when it came to weapons, he had been practicing with Daphne's gift until he became proficient.

A frozen moment ensued as everyone tried to take in what had happened. Daphne was the first to recover. She slid quickly from her horse, not thinking at all about the display she would be making if her skirts caught on some piece of equipment. Pausing only to check that Sereen Masham had not been hit by the bullet, she ran towards the man Giles had shot. He was lying on his back, with a red stain spreading on his chest. Even as Daphne knelt down to see if she could help. The man raised his head, coughed up a glob of blood, and then lay still.

This was not the first seriously injured man that Daphne had seen. As a young girl, she had accompanied Mr. Jackson on his visits to the ill and injured, and he had shown her how to detect if a victim was still living. She reached forward and touched the man's neck, where she could feel for a heartbeat. There was none.

"I think he is dead," Daphne declared. "There is nothing we can do."

A moment of shocked silence followed her pronouncement. Then bedlam broke out. Giles, who had dismounted in a more relaxed way than Daphne, rushed forward to help her. Not sure what happened, Mr. Griffiths spurred his horse towards the fallen man, followed by his group of stable hands. Their opponents, however, produced the most dramatic response. To a man, they turned away from the confrontation with the men from Dipton and rushed towards their wagons. Ignoring the horses they had stolen and, aided by the women of their encampment, they threw their tents and other possessions into their carts, harnessed their horses to the vehicles, and headed towards the track that Daphne, Giles, and Mr. Foster had used to reach the clearing. No one tried to stop them. Mr. Griffiths and the other stable hands were fully engaged in trying to calm the many horses, especially the stolen ones, that had been distressed by the sudden violence to which they were unaccustomed. The creatures were starting to panic because the hobbles prevented them from racing away from the threatening situation they did not understand.

Daphne was in a bit of a state of shock because she was unused to witnessing and responding to sudden, violent death. Giles was more accustomed to killing opponents in battle without a second thought, but he was saddened by how good his aim had been and worried by Daphne's reaction once there was no need for immediate action. Daphne was shaking and holding Giles desperately as he tried to calm her after she realized how close she had come to being shot and how serious the consequences of Giles's immediate reaction were. The headache and sore throat, which had been bothering her all day, had intensified, and she was almost shaking.

Being wrapped in Giles's arms seemed to calm Daphne. The horses had to be unhobbled and rounded up, and Mr. Griffiths had to direct the tying of the dead gypsy to one of the horses before they were ready to proceed. Nightfall had fallen while the group was preparing to depart, but an almost full moon rose as darkness became complete. Since the night was clear, there was enough light that the group could proceed at a rapid clip. But the clear night meant that it was also cold. Before long, most of the men were getting uncomfortably cold. Daphne felt the cold particularly strongly; before long, her teeth were chattering, and she was trembling. When they reached Dipton Hall, Giles had Daphne slide into his arms and immediately carried her upstairs to their bed, pausing only to order Steves to summon Mr. Jackson immediately. Betsey was summoned, stripped off Daphne's clothes, and dressed her mistress in a warm flannel nightgown. Giles took the unusual step of building up the fire in the room without waiting for the scullery maid, whose job it would normally be. Then he climbed onto the bed, slid under the covers, and held his wife as her shivers lessened.

Mr. Jackson arrived remarkably quickly, with the disheveled look of a man who had been woken from a good sleep and then dressed as quickly as possible to get away from home without wasting any time. He rushed to Daphne's bedroom. Ignoring the presence of Giles in the bed, Mr. Jackson felt Daphne's forehead and neck and listened to her chest. He didn't have to ask her to cough: she did it while his ear was on her chest.

"You have caught a nasty cold. Daphne," Mr. Jackson stated. "Luckily, it is not the flu. It didn't help that you traipsed around the countryside for a whole day and most of the night. Stay in bed now and drink lots. Boiled water, mind you, or tea, rather than small beer. I'll send over an elixir of birch bark that may help your sore throat and a syrup that may help your cough. There is nothing to worry about, but you will recover faster if you stay in bed today with a good fire in the room. I'll be by in the morning to see how you are."

With that, Mr. Jackson left. Giles debated sleeping in his dressing room so as not to disturb Daphne, something he had never done since he married her. He changed his mind when he thought about what he would prefer if the roles were reversed. His place was with his wife. If he caught her cold, that was just too bad.

Chapter XII

Giles was up early the next morning, getting up quietly to let Daphne sleep. "Keep the fire going, Betsey," he ordered, "and try to persuade her ladyship to remain in bed. Remind her that it's by Mr. Jackson's and my orders."

After he had come downstairs, he addressed his butler even before entering the breakfast room: "Steves, can you send for Lord David to come on an urgent matter."

"My lord, Lord David left yesterday afternoon for London."

"Drat the man. He happens to be a justice of the peace because he is our MP. We need a magistrate to deal with the matter of the dead gypsy as soon as possible. I have to go north imminently. Indeed, as you know, Lady Giles and I were supposed to be traveling up to Birmingham and Shropshire today. That, of course, is canceled, but I have to leave soon anyway. I don't want any issues arising from my shooting the criminal who tried to murder Lady Camshire hanging over our heads when I leave to go to Birmingham. Lord David, as a magistrate, could have dealt with the matter expeditiously. Now, I will have to waste time finding someone else."

"Mr. Halliday is in residence at Laidly under Harmon, my Lord, and I am sure he would be eager to be of use."

Reginald Halliday was a fairly recent addition to the neighborhood. He was a younger son of a Northumberland baronet who had had a career in one of the private banks in London. He had prospered there, indeed, become rich. After his physician suggested that the air in London was very bad for his health, Mr. Halliday decided to become a country squire not too far from London. The manor at Laidly under Harmon, about nine miles from Dipton, had become available when he was looking for a property to serve his purposes.

Mr. Halliday had wanted some status in the area of his new home. He was open to becoming a justice of the peace, especially as the duties would relieve some of the boredom that he discovered arose from his not being in the city anymore. He and his wife had been entertained at Dipton Manor a couple of times, even though Daphne had developed a poor view of Mrs. Halliday as an unctuous social climber. Nevertheless, Giles realized that Mr. Halliday was a man of sound judgment. As a result, Giles had suggested that the newcomer be appointed a justice of the peace, much to the recipient's joy. The other magistrates for the area lived much farther away from Dipton.

"Excellent suggestion, Steves. I'll just write a note indicating why Mr. Halliday must come here at once. Have one of the stable hands deliver it to him."

Giles wrote the note explaining why the magistrate should visit Dipton as soon as convenient. After giving it to Steves to have it delivered, he went into the breakfast room, selected some ham, eggs, and toast to take to the table, and settled down to enjoy his food and tea while reading the newspaper that had been delivered soon after dawn. He had only read a third of a report on a debate in the House of Lords when he was interrupted by Daphne appearing in the breakfast room fully dressed, though with somewhat reddened eyes indicating that she was still not well.

"What are you doing here, my love?" he asked. "Mr. Jackson said you should remain in bed."

"I'm too busy to lie in bed. We are supposed to leave for Birmingham today, or have you forgotten?"

Daphne punctuated her statement with a concluding sneeze. She was blowing her nose on her handkerchief as Giles replied. "We can't go possibly go today or even tomorrow. You are far too sick. Mr. Jackson said explicitly that you should stay in bed. Anyway, we must stay here to clear up any issues arising from my killing that gypsy last night."

To Giles's surprise, Daphne, after suffering a nasty round of coughing, agreed with him. She allowed him to take her back to bed and then accepted a cup of tea, which the servants rushed up to their bedroom, docilely took the medicines that Mr. Jackson had prescribed, and settled back into bed. She then fell asleep even before Giles had a chance to tell Betsey to make sure the fire was burning brightly.

Giles returned to his breakfast and paper, but on the way, he told Steves to summon Mr. Jackson. In fact, Giles still did not get to complete his breakfast because the physician showed up before he could re-enter the breakfast room.

“How is Daphne?” Mr. Jackson asked the moment he saw Giles. His concern was indicated by his calling her by the name he had known her all her life rather than the ‘Lady Camshire’ he had adopted after Giles became an Earl.

“Still pretty sick, I guess. She tried to get up this morning, but I persuaded her to go back to bed. She did not give me much resistance.”

“I’m glad that she didn’t remain as stubborn as usual,” Mr. Jackson remarked. “If Daphne takes care of herself now, she’ll be feeling better much sooner. Still, even though your report is very helpful, my lord, I’ll just go upstairs to see her to make sure that we are doing everything we can to speed her recovery and make her comfortable in the interim.

“No, my lord, I am more likely to find out how she really feels if you are not there. With you present, she will try to play down her symptoms so as not to worry you, even though that is not really what you want. I have put a little laudanum in the medicine to help her sleep. Rest is the best tonic for this illness. I’ll stop by later in the day to check on her progress. Keep the fire going in her room.”

Mr. Jackson left, so Giles hastened upstairs to see Daphne. But she had fallen asleep. The room was toasty warm, and Daphne had thrown off most of her covers. Giles stayed a couple of minutes admiring the sight of his wife sleeping, apparently peacefully. Then he tiptoed out of the room and closed the door quietly.

Outside the room, Giles found Mary and Scruffy. Mary looked very perturbed. She must have sneaked out of the nursery when Nanny Weavers' back was turned.

"Uncle Giles," Mary asked in a hushed voice. "Is Aunt Daphne going to die and go to heaven?"

"No, Mary, she is not. Mr. Jackson was here, and he told me that Aunt Daphne will recover completely. But she does have to stay indoors, in bed, and not get chilled. And, for a while, you should not get too close to her so that you don't catch her cold."

"Does that mean I can't sleep in your bed?"

"I'm sorry, but it does. Nanny Weaver will make sure that you are comfortable."

"Can Scruffy sleep with me?"

"Let's go ask Nanny Weaver."

To Giles's surprise, Nanny Weaver let Scruffy stay in the nursery until Daphne was better.

"But, my lord, this cannot continue after Lady Camshire has recovered. I am agreeing to it only because, this way, Scruffy won't be bothering my lady while she is ill."

Giles was surprised, though not very. Nanny Weaver didn't want either Mary or Scruffy in Daphne's bed, and she was fiercely protective of Daphne. If Scruffy wasn't with Mary, he would probably somehow find a way into Daphne and Giles's bedroom during the night or early morning. That was something Nanny Weaver did not approve of at all! She thought it was better to have the dog in the nursery.

As Giles reached the landing on the main stairs, Hugh came dashing up to meet him.

"Uncle Giles. You rescued Moonbeam! I've been down at the stables, and Hank told me that you and Aunt Daphne and Mr. Griffiths and all the stablemen had rescued her last night. I couldn't find Mr. Griffiths, and Hank said he was busy. Can we go and see her?"

"Of course, we can. Get your coat and tell Nanny Weaver where we are going. You always should tell her when you leave the house."

"But then she will tell me I can't."

"Even so, you should tell her."

When Giles and Hugh reached the stables, Mr. Griffiths came out of his office. "My lord, I am glad you have come. I was about to go up to the Hall, but we can discuss what's on my mind here just as well."

"Good. Hugh is worried about Moon Beam. Can he see her?

"Of course. And ride her if he wants. She is none the worse for her adventure. In fact, none of the horses was harmed by the thieves.

"Hank," Mr. Griffiths called to the nearby stableman. "Take Master Hugh to see Moonbeam and help him ride her if he wants.

"That lad," continued Mr. Griffiths in his normal voice, "is learning very quickly how to ride and take care of horses. It will still be two or three years before he is ready to handle our hunters. You really do need to get him a pony or a small horse.

"Now, I wanted to talk to you about those thieving gypsies. And especially about what to do with the dead one. I don't think there is much point in trying to get the law to find them and bring them to justice. Once they got away, there would be no chance of proving that they were the criminals, even if we could find them. The word about gypsies is that they usually do not leave their dead behind when one dies, or so I am told. I was half expecting them to try to raid us last night to get the body back, but there was no sign of them. They are probably well out of the county by now. So, we are stuck with the corpse, and the question is, 'what do we do about the man you shot?'"

"Yes. I've sent a rider to ask Mr. Halliday, the magistrate, to come here as soon as possible."

"Good idea. That should deal with the matter, I guess. Actually, here comes Walters now. He must have missed you up at the Hall."

Walters was the rider entrusted with taking the message to Mr. Halliday, the magistrate. He reined in his horse, dismounted, and addressed Giles.

"My lord, Mr. Halliday is away from the county. Furthermore, his butler informed me that all the magistrates, except Lord David Giles, have gone to the races at Silverstead and won't be back for several days."

"Thank you, Walters," Giles replied. "Mr. Griffiths, have you any idea what I should do now. I have to leave Dipton soon, and the matter of the dead gypsy should be dealt with first."

"I can see why you may not want to leave before that matter is settled, my lord," replied the stablemaster, "though I don't imagine anyone would challenge you if you just left the matter until it is convenient for you to deal with it. Do you suppose this might be a matter for the Coroner? I think he is supposed to examine any bodies that show up unexpectedly and decide what to do about them. I am afraid that I have no idea who the Coroner might be or how to contact him."

"You're right; that's the official we need!" exclaimed Giles. "My Ameschester lawyer, Mr. Snodgrass, will know who he is and can arrange for him to visit. Walters, Mr. Snodgrass knows you, I think?"

"Yes, my lord."

"Then ride to Ameschester and tell him that I need him here as soon as possible and what the reason is."

"Yes, my lord."

Walters left on his new mission. Giles remarked to Mr. Griffiths, "I am surprised that all the magistrates have gone away to some race meeting."

"It's not that surprising. Except for Lord David, the present group of magistrates is all keen on horse racing. After their most recent hearing, when they retreated to the pub, they got to talking about horses and horse racing and which horse was faster than another one, and so on. I'm told the discussion grew quite heated. I've heard that some wagers were made on the spot about which horses would win at Silverstead. They must have decided to go and see the racing for themselves and not just wait for the results to filter down here."

"I confess that I have never heard of this Silverstead meeting. Of course, I don't follow the results of various races when I can't attend them. Do you know anything about it?"

"It's a fairly new meet, but I hear it is well run and well attended by the more reputable bookmakers, and it attracts some major racing stables."

"Well, we'll have to think again about extending our stables to racing horses or ponies. Ponies to serve a need. Thoroughbreds just scratch an itch."

Mr. Griffiths laughed at Giles's jest but suspected that, before long, they might have a racing stable and be providing the neighborhood with ponies as well. Both Giles and Daphne seemed to have boundless energy, and if Mr. Griffiths needed more hands or subordinates to help run a more complex establishment, he knew they would not hesitate to provide what was needed. Nevertheless, his reply was non-committal: "Very good, my lord. — My goodness, isn't that Walters coming back with two other horsemen?"

"Yes, it is. And one of the two is my lawyer, Mr. Snodgrass. Who do you suppose the third man is?"

It did not take long to find out. The three riders drew up to Giles and Mr. Griffiths. Even before dismounting, Mr. Snodgrass addressed Giles, "My lord. I heard about the horse theft and how you got your horses back. This is Mr. Breecher, the Coroner for the county. I have asked him to come with me to see if the rumored matter of the thief's death can be resolved quickly."

"Thank you, Mr. Snodgrass. Mr. Breecher, welcome to Dipton Hall. I am afraid that I didn't know the right procedure to follow in such a case and was trying to find a magistrate, but they are all from home. I quite forgot that there must be a coroner for Ameschester."

"Very understandable, my lord, though my purview is the whole county. I hear that you killed a man. Do you know where the body is?"

"Yes. We brought it here. We couldn't just leave it out in the open, could we? And the rest of the gypsies had disappeared."

Giles related to the Coroner what had occurred, supported by remarks from Mr. Griffiths.

"Now, let me be sure that I understand what happened," said the Coroner. "The gypsy, who was among the horse thieves you caught up with, fired first, did he?"

"Yes. He shot at my wife, Lady Camshire."

"Did he hit her?"

"Luckily, no, though the bullet did go through her skirt. She, herself, was uninjured."

"And then you shot the man?"

"Yes. Just one shot."

"I see. I suppose that the only people who saw the event were Mr. Griffiths and your stablehands and, of course, the other horse thieves who have undoubtedly left the county. I am surprised that they didn't take the corpse with them as gypsies usually do when there is trouble," said the Coroner.

"Mr. Foster, the curate in our parish, was also among our party."

“Ah. Very good. An independent witness. I suppose that I will have to interview him. I’ll do it after I see the corpse. Where is it?”

They all trudged to the shed where the gypsy’s body had been placed. Mr. Breecher knelt down to examine it. There was no problem seeing where Giles’s bullet had struck the man and where it had exited. It must have killed him instantly since there was very little blood around the holes in his coat. The Coroner examined the corpse and turned it over but did not suggest undressing the man or doing anything else.

“No question about what killed him, I believe,” Mr. Breecher remarked. “A remarkably accurate shot, my lord.”

“Thank you. It is a remarkably good rifle, so it is easy to be accurate.”

“Well, everything seems clear to me. I am sure I need not bother Lady Camshire, but I suppose I should interview the curate. The gypsies are not rushing forward to give their side of the story, thank heavens.”

“Thank you for coming, Mr. Breecher and Mr. Snodgrass. Let me offer you a stirrup cup before you leave. We can easily walk up to the Hall. Mr. Griffiths will have your horses brought up to the house when they are needed.”

“With pleasure, my lord,” replied the Coroner.

When they reached Dipton Hall, Giles discovered that Mr. Foster was at the portico, having come to ask how Daphne was after her ordeal with the horse thieves.

"Mr. Breecher," said Giles, "I'd like you to meet Mr. Foster, the curate I was telling you about who accompanied us on our pursuit of the horse thieves."

"Mr. Foster," said the Coroner. "I am glad to meet you. Otherwise, I would have had to seek you out. A word with you in private about what happened last night, and then I should be able to conclude this matter."

The two stepped aside and conversed in low voices while Giles addressed his butler, "Steves, how is Lady Camshire?"

"She is sleeping right now, my lord," was the reply. "Betsey reports that her fever is steady. Betsey also says that she doesn't understand how the bullet missed my lady's leg judging by the holes in her garments. She was very lucky, I believe."

"Good to hear how well she is doing, Steves. It was a close-run thing, but she came out unharmed. I'll look in on her later rather than disturb her while she is asleep."

Giles and Mr. Snodgrass waited while the Coroner and the curate conferred. "Are you thinking of visiting that property you acquired in Shropshire in the near future, my lord?" the lawyer asked.

"Yes. Lady Camshire and I were intending to visit Birmingham this week and take a side trip to Sallycroft—that's what the estate is called. Unfortunately, I suspect Lady Camshire's illness will put paid to those plans, so we will have to wait for a more favorable time to go.

"That may be as well, my lord. My colleague in Shrewsbury tells me there are more complications to that title. No, it is not about whether it is yours or is part of the loot of that crooked agent you had. He seems to have embroiled you in another dispute, having to do with relations with another landowner there about a claim that the other man owes your property some fields that were loaned to him rather than sold, or so your agent claimed, who filed a suit to get it back. Luckily, he still claimed in that suit that you were the owner. If you are in Shrewsbury, you might consult with my colleague, or I can find out more about the situation so that you can give him instructions through me on how to proceed."

"I'll do that when I have a chance," Giles replied ambiguously. Privately he was thinking that maybe these men were called 'solicitors' because they were continuously soliciting business to bring in large fees. He was quite happy to leave all the legal aspects of the Sallycroft acquisition to his London agent and solicitor. With the delays produced by the horse theft and Daphne's illness, he wouldn't be going to Sallycroft soon, nor even Birmingham. Indeed, he might be hard-pressed to get to Birkenhead in time to deal with this ridiculous Jacobite plot. Why was he so unable to say 'no' to tasks alleged to be in the national interest? After all, the Royal Navy was full of officers as capable as he was; they just hadn't been as lucky. Of course, it was too late now to turn down that assignment, even though he had lost all his enthusiasm for it. What he would do was to wait in Dipton as long as he could in order to see how Daphne was getting on. If he was very pressed for time to get to Cheshire, that was just too bad.

The Coroner had finished his conversation with Mr. Foster. "My Lord," he said, "my discussion with Mr.

Foster was very helpful. I am now quite certain of what the cause of death of that gypsy was. I shall declare it a justifiable homicide in defense of your wife and the other members of your party. The evidence is so clear that I do not need to convene a coroner's jury to validate my judgment. I commend you on your prompt response to the crimes. I am surprised that gypsies were at the heart of all your troubles. That sort of organized crime, taking a large number of horses so blatantly, is not like them at all, just as I have never heard of gypsies leaving a body behind when they could take it with them for proper burial. I am sure they are now far away from our county, but I will circulate the news of what happened here and warnings to be on the lookout for the group of criminals."

"I welcome your decision, Mr. Breecher, and again, thank you for coming here so expeditiously," Giles replied formally. "Now, all this talking is, I believe, dry work. Steeves, show the gentlemen into the billiards room where we can enjoy a glass before they leave."

Giles turned away to stifle a sneeze before he followed his guests. There seemed to be a tickle at the back of his throat, and he felt a distinct need to clear his throat. That was all he needed: to catch Daphne's cold when he needed to ride hard to join *Glaucus*.

Chapter XIII

Hector Fitzroy Blenkinsop was a middle-aged Royal Navy Post Captain of only a few years seniority. He had been at sea since 1792, but his career had advanced very slowly. Most of it had been spent in the Caribbean. For more years than was usual, Blenkinsop had been a midshipman on a ship of the line, where he had succeeded in twice failing the exam to become lieutenant, largely because he had paid little attention to the lessons he was supposed to learn on seamanship under a captain who made a modest income from their fathers for keeping midshipmen on his ship but taking no interest in their training.

Blenkinsop's chance came when yellow fever hit *Circe*, one of the brigs of war on the station, wiping out all but one of her lieutenants. Blenkinsop was appointed acting lieutenant in the vessel, and when the supply of qualified lieutenants was not soon increased, his promotion was made permanent. He stayed with *Circe*, doing very well from her capturing merchant ships engaged in trade with the many enemy islands in the Leeward Islands.

The Treaty of Amiens ended the profitable use of *Circe* to further the war efforts and enrich the admiral under whose command she sailed. Her captain gave up his command to marry a Jamaica planter's daughter, and the brig was decommissioned as excessive to the navy's peacetime needs. Lieutenant Blenkinsop was able to find a birth as second lieutenant on a 32-gun frigate called *Cicero*, which was ordered to return to England just before she lost two of her lieutenants to yellow fever. *Figaro*'s captain, an experienced sailer called Harold Brasewait. was only too happy to accept the long-serving lieutenant for the journey home. Captain Brasewait believed in constantly exercising his crew, preparing for all sorts of situations. Blenkinsop, of course, could only feign enthusiasm for what he thought was excessive practice and work for all men aboard, but especially, in his view, the officers.

Cicero left Jamaica before news of the renewal of hostilities between Britain and France had reached the island. She crossed the Atlantic in complete ignorance of the changed state of affairs. Off Brest, she met a 36-gun frigate flying British colors. As the two vessels converged, the other frigate displayed what looked like it was the private signal used to prevent French ships from masquerading as English until they were in range. However, what was flown was not the appropriate signal that *Cicero* had expected and the number of the ship was not one found in *Cicero*'s list of active vessels. Captain Brasewait replied with the correct reply from the list he had been using in Jamaica and explained that *Cicero* was returning from Jamaica with an out-of-date signal book. The other frigate replied that they should meet so that *Cicero* could get the latest information.

None of the officers on the deck of *Cicero* suspected a trap. There were no enemy ships at sea after the peace treaty had been signed. Only when a lookout in the foremast crow's nest reported that the strange vessel had her guns ready to run out and fire the minute her gunports were opened did the captain of *Cicero* guess the trap he was sailing into. He reacted instantly. "Fog Drill," he bellowed.

This was a drill that Captain Brasewait had practiced several times on the trip from Jamaica. The imaginary situation was that an enemy vessel had just appeared from a fog bank when *Cicero* was unprepared for action. Though in the present situation, the hostile vessel had been in sight for some time, the presumption that she was British had lulled the crew to a state similar to what they would have been in if there had been a sudden encounter in fog.

The plan called for *Cicero* to sail towards the hostile ship so that they would meet bow to bow so closely that they could be tied together as they came alongside each other. Captain Brasewait would lead the boarding charge as soon as the ships had come together. The first lieutenant would lead all the seamen who were on deck and had grabbed their weapons to board the hostile ship. Similarly, the marine lieutenant mustered his men to board from slightly forward of the first lieutenant's group. Blenkinsop's assignment was to remain on the quarterdeck with the Master and supervise the backing and furling of the sails at the right moments. The third lieutenant was tasked with getting the watch below to come on deck and participate in the attack as quickly as possible.

Everything worked like clockwork. In minutes after the bows came together, the French crew, for the strange frigate was indeed French, had surrendered. The butcher's bill was huge, especially considering the short period of the fighting. The major casualties were Captain Brasenose, who was killed by a musket ball fired from the French marines from the foremast fighting top, and the first lieutenant, who lost a duel with one of the French officers before the latter was laid low by a cutlass slash.

The marine lieutenant returned to *Cicero* to report that he had received the surrender of the thirty-six-gun French frigate *Mephistopheles* and that Lieutenant Blenkinsop was now in command of both ships. Thanks to the high level of training that Captain Brasenose had maintained, there was no trouble manning both ships, and two days later, he sailed into the Solent in command of *Cicero* and the captured French frigate.

The capture of a more powerful frigate at the start of the renewed war, with a very large number killed and injured, made *Cicero* and her acting captain, Lieutenant Blenkinsop, famous. The admiralty had no choice but to promote him to Post Captain, skipping the intermediate rank of Commander. They also rewarded this new hero with the command of *Cicero* and attached her to the fleet blockading Brest.

Though sometimes detached by the admiral to go looking for merchant prizes, Captain Blenkinsop and *Cicero* disappointed both the admiral and himself. His stock of consols, in which he had invested his prize money earned in Jamaica, steadily shrank. This happened because members of the fleet, including *Cicero,* were regularly sent into port for fresh food and other supplies. On shore, Blenkinsop pursued his two expensive pastimes of gambling and consorting with concubines. Both were expensive as he usually lost far more at cards than he could afford if he were to be generous to the women whose time he purchased. Unfortunately, his chances of taking prizes were now few and far apart, and he did not want to economize.

Blenkinsop realized that he needed a more lucrative vehicle to invest his funds, even though his salary was large as a Post Captain. He chose a shipping firm based in Liverpool engaged in trading voyages to Africa and the Caribbean colonies. The investments consisted in buying shares in individual voyages the company sponsored. Needless to say, the main source of profit from these voyages was slaves. On a wink-wink, nudge-nudge basis, Captain Blenkinsop learned that their ships might masquerade as French vessels transporting slaves to the French Island or even as privateers capturing other merchant ships. Because of the risks, the returns were very high with successful voyages, though unsuccessful ones could lead to no return or less than the investment.

Blenkinsop had made handsome, if not spectacular, profits from his association with the "merchant" company, but recently they had tailed off. Sickness among the cargo in unusual amounts and piracy had been blamed for two major losses, and other vessels returned hardly anything on Blenkinsop's investment. He was tempted to go to Liverpool to investigate why such sure-fire ventures were not making him rich.

Captain Blensinsop had reached this conclusion while the fleet was still anchored in Torbay, the admiral having gone there in the face of one gale and had not chosen to move back to his station from another winter storm being imminent. Rumour arrived from Plymouth of the arrival there of *Glaucus* with a captured French ship and several merchant ships that were prizes of the French ship. When the frigate captains of the fleet met for dinner and wine aboard one of their vessels that evening, *Glaucus* and Captain Giles were the main subjects of conversation. It was grossly unfair that she habitually sailed under Admiralty orders, giving her the freedom of action to pursue prizes that was denied them. The fact that much of Giles's success had come from defeating enemy naval vessels rather than from capturing merchant ships was conveniently forgotten. To add insult to injury, it was reported that Captain Giles had not even been aboard *Glaucus* when she had captured the French ship, but instead, she was being commanded by her first lieutenant.

When Blenkinsop went on board the flagship to discuss the reports about *Glaucus,* of more importance to Captain Blenkinsop and his admiral than the scandalous treatment of *Glaucus* was that the French ship's prizes, which the privileged frigate had liberated, had been captured in the Irish Sea. One could argue, and Blenkinsop did, that that body of water was within the area assigned to the admiral blockading Brest, so it would be sensible to send one of the admiral's frigates to make sure that no other French raiders were operating there. The admiral was skeptical that there would be any positive reward for sending *Cicero* around Land's End looking for French marauders. Still, he was sure that his own commander and the Admiralty would be pleased to be able to announce that steps had been taken to make the Irish Sea safe again.

While Captain Blenkinsop was also skeptical that he would find any French vessels in the Irish Sea that he could capture, patrolling the Irish Sea looking for targets would undoubtedly require a visit to Liverpool, the other main English harbor on that body of water, to learn if there was any news or rumors of French ships, whether naval ones or privateers, in the area. That would permit a visit to the firm in which he had invested his money and see if he could get to the bottom of the lack of success that they had been exhibiting.

Cicero did no serious searching for French ships once she got her orders. Captain Blenkinsop wanted to lose no time getting to Liverpool. There the news was not good. Blenkinsop had invested heavily in two voyages. One was six weeks overdue reaching Barbados and was presumed to be lost. The other ship was called the *Pride of Merseyside.* It had recently sailed for the Slave Coast, intending to get ahead of the ban on the slave trade. However, the firm had just received word that she had been intercepted by the frigate *Glaucus* and taken into Dublin for reasons that were not entirely clear as yet.

"How does that affect my investment?" Blenkinsop asked.

"We don't really know," the partner he was dealing with announced. "One of the principals of our firm will be taking the next packet to Dublin, but it is almost certain that the delay arising from *Glaucus*'s interference will seriously reduce the profits of the voyage. It may even have to be called off in view of the coming ban on the slave trade. In that case, Captain Blenkinsop, your losses will be substantial."

"How can that be?"

"Well, if we are held up too long, the authorities may confiscate our restraint equipment. They may find evidence of our privateering work that is not always above board, which will cause further delays that may make it more difficult to continue with a slaving voyage. It doesn't help that our ship was carrying a significant number of gold coins, mainly five-guinea coins but also some one-guinea pieces. There was an unusual number of them aboard because of the current shortage of the usual trade goods, so we would not have enough goods to trade for slaves and would have to use money. Guineas have a way of disappearing when there is interference from the Navy. There may also be some documents on board our ship reflecting that she sometimes acts as a privateer in ways that some might regard as piracy. You, of course, were fully aware of these features of our ventures, Captain Blenkinsop."

"I didn't realize that the hazards were so great."

"No? Why did you think that the rewards were so great? Of course, many other legitimate merchant ships involved in the trade are also in dire straights because of the embargo. Some are trying to get in one last slaving voyage before it becomes law, even though they cannot obtain the usual trade goods. You may have noticed the two ships in the harbor which are getting ready to sail this morning. My clerk was in the bank earlier today. There he saw their captains collecting as much gold as the bank had on hand so they could sail today even though they do not have the usual trade goods in their holds. He tells me they intend to sail north around Ireland to avoid interference from our navy like our ship encountered.

Blenkinsop returned to *Cicero* fuming. That god-damned Captain the Honorable Richard Giles KB, Earl of Camshire, was out to do honest ship's captains in. First, he seemed to be assigned to voyages that always led to prize money — unfairly since Blenkinsop was never given good chances to profit from his activities. Second, he had been a strong supporter of the ban on the slave trade, which would greatly reduce the honest earnings that Blenkinsop achieved by supporting British trade. Third, the bloody nobleman had maliciously interfered with the commendable voyage to assist the British Colonies that would restore Blenkinsop's fortunes. As a result, he, Blenkinsop, faced ruin.

Blenkinsop ordered *Cicero* to leave harbor and head down the Mersey to continue her voyage. Then, he went to his cabin to ruminate some more over how unfairly circumstances and the Navy had been treating him. He was well into his fourth glass of Madeira when there was a hail from a lookout: "Frigate anchored off a town on the larboard bank of the channel — the frigate looks like *Glaucus* — seems to have a prize with her."

Through his open cabin windows, Blenkinsop could hear the officer of the watch acknowledge the hail, order the midshipman of the watch to signal *Cicero*'s identification number, and direct someone else to tell the captain. He didn't wait to be officially informed. Pausing only to replenish his wine glass and grab his telescope, he went on deck.

"That frigate is indeed *Glaucus*: her signal agreed with who we thought she was," said the first lieutenant who had the watch. "I don't know what to make of the prize. She looks like a frigate at first glance, but the rig is wrong, and those gunports in the center are strange. Too big and too low. Also, you will note that the flag flying below the union jack. I have never seen anything like it before."

Blenkinsop stared at the two ships through his telescope. The situation certainly looked strange. The only officer to be seen on *Glaucus* was wearing a lieutenant's uniform, as was the officer on the strange ship. Could it be that *Glaucus* had been captured by some French ship that had then come to the Mersey to try to capture other vessels? Blenkinsop dearly wished that that bloody Captain Giles had come a cropper and had his ship captured by some enemy frigate. Indeed maybe the French used that weird sort of frigate in the Mediterranian, where Blenkinsop had never served. It didn't take long for Blenkinsop, as he examined the ships carefully, to convince himself that *Glaucus* had been captured by that weird frigate and needed to be rescued by *Cicero*.

"Mr. Lester," Blenkinsop ordered his first lieutenant. "Alter course to converge on *Glaucus* and clear for action."

On *Glaucus*, Lieutenant Etienne Macreau was leaning on the rail, idly looking at *Cicero*. All he knew about her came from the exchange of signals and the slight entry in the signal book next to her number. She was a thirty-two-gun frigate commanded by Captain Hector Fitzroy Blenkinsop.

"What do you know about that frigate, Mr. Brooks," Etienne asked Mr. Brooks, the master who had had himself rowed over from their prize.

"Not much, sir. She was in the Caribbean until the pause, and then she has been serving in the blockading fleet off Brest."

"Well, it seems that we shall soon know more about her. She has altered course towards us. I wonder," Etienne continued, "where Captain Giles is. It is not like him to be late."

"But he only stated that he would be here by yesterday or today and would wait for us for several days if we were late, as we should wait for him if he were delayed."

"That frigate seems to have set course for us."

Mr. Brooks turned back to the rail to take a closer look at the other frigate. "She is. … By God, she seems to be clearing for action."

Mr. Brooks raised his telescope and focused on *Cicero*. "She is! That's strange behavior. Do you suppose that a Frenchie has captured her and is trying to trick us? Have a look."

Etienne turned from the rail and bellowed, "Clear for action, Mr. Stewart, and rig a spring to the anchor line." More quietly, he told Mr. Brooks. "A ship, none of whose officers we know, approaching us under a union jack but clearing for action. We need to be prepared if she turns out to be hostile."

On board *Cicero*, all the officers were watching *Glaucus* carefully.

"*Glaucus* is clearing for action, sir," announced the first lieutenant.

"I have noticed that," Captain Blenkinsop replied acidly. "Just what I expected. It confirms that *Glaucus* must now be a French frigate masquerading as one of ours. No English frigate would worry about our approaching them."

Mr. Lester shook his head. That was exactly the sort of reasoning that had got *Cicero* clearing for action in the first place. But there was no point in telling the captain what he thought: Captain Blenkinsop did not welcome comments from his subordinates that disagreed with his ideas or observations.

"She has cleared for action, sir," *Cicero*'s master remarked.

"She can't be," retorted Captain Blenkinsop. "We started first and are not yet done."

"Yes, sir, just as we might expect from a crack frigate like *Glaucus*," muttered one of the few petty officers left on *Cicero,* who had been aboard when she was fooled by the French frigate. He was clearly much less impressed with his current captain than with his previous one.

"Of course. Any French ship which bested *Glaucus* would have to be an exceptional one, wouldn't she?" replied Blensinsop, quite missing the point that *Cicero* was showing herself to be anything but a crack frigate.

Cicero completed her clearing for action. She was getting close to the other frigate. Soon she would be close enough that her broadside would reach *Glaucus* effectively.

"Run out the larboard cannon," Blenkinsop ordered.

"Raise the larboard gunports and run out the cannon," Etienne commanded. "Adjust the spring so that the broadside is square on her."

Etienne's order could be heard on *Cicero*. "Sir," said her first lieutenant, "did you notice that their order was given in English? Maybe they are not hostile."

"I don't think so, Mr. Lester. Didn't you notice that the order was given in a decidedly French accent, not a good English or even a Scottish one? That accent convinces me that *Glaucus* has been taken by the French. Her officers could have told their crews in French the content of that order.

Tension on both ships was rising to fever pitch. Would they all be blown to pieces and, more importantly, into the next world? Was the other ship really an enemy, or were they about to die for nothing? On each ship, dozens of eyes watched the opposing gunners closely to spot the moment one of them pulled a firing lanyard.

Luckily, on board *Glaucus*, the lookouts were still performing their duty of looking elsewhere. The one on the ship's starboard side called out, "Boat approaching from abeam."

From his station at the wheel, Etienne glanced to starboard. There was a boat, and the man in the sternsheets looked like Captain Giles. At the top of his lungs, he bellowed, ”Mr. Stewart, prepare to welcome the captain aboard. He just hoped that might do something to convince the captain of *Cicero* that they were English. If it didn’t, it would indicate that the threatening ship had been captured by the French.

On board *Cicero,* everyone could hear Etienne’s order. *Glaucus*’s captain was being welcomed aboard. That didn’t square with the notion that she had been captured by the French. Blenkinsop ordered, “Hold your fire, but stay alert.”

‘Could this really be Captain Giles about to return to his ship?’ Blenkinsop wondered. The man in question could soon be seen coming onto *Glaucus* through the entry port, and the sound of bosun’s pipes welcoming him aboard could be heard on *Cicero*. ‘Is this actually Captain Giles arriving? If so, *Cicero* was embarked on a dangerous fool’s errand.’ The man in question was dressed in civilian clothes, but that was the norm for British captains when ashore on private business.

“Mr. Lester,” Blenkinsop addressed his first lieutenant. “Does that man in civilian clothes boarding *Glaucus* look like Captain Giles to you?”

“It’s very hard to tell, sir. I’ve never seen Captain Giles, just sketches and caricatures of him. But he certainly does resemble them.”

On board *Glaucus*, Giles wasted no time. “What is that ship, Mr. Macreau, and why are you about to fight each other?” he asked?

“I don’t really know, sir. She is His Majesty’s Frigate *Cicero*, 32, Captain Hector Blenkinsop, but no one aboard *Glaucus* has ever seen him. She was coming down the Mersey, sir, when she challenged us, and soon after we answered, she changed course towards us. When she got close, she cleared for action without sending any message about why she was doing it. I wondered whether she might have been captured by the French and was just masquerading as British, so we cleared too and had a spring line rigged to the anchor rode so that we could aim at her. If she fires first at us, we shall respond in kind, sir."

"Quite right, Mr. Macreau. I'll hail her to see what she thinks she's doing."

Giles strode to the larboard rail. "Ahoy, *Cicero*. I am Lord Richard Giles, captain of this ship. What do you think you are doing? Run in your cannon and unload them at once. Otherwise, I shall blow you out of the water."

On *Cicero*, there could be no more doubt. This time the hail was clearly called in an English accent, moreover, in that pretentious accent that only the highest level of the nobility seemed able to use faultlessly. There was no chance that this was some Frenchman masquerading as an English officer. Blenkinsop realized he might be in very severe trouble.

"Do as he says, Mr. Lester, at once," he said loudly enough for his words to reach *Glaucus*. He then approached the larboard rail and called, "My lord, I believed that *Glaucus* had been captured by the French and posed a serious threat to shipping coming from the Mersey. I apologize for my mistake."

"I see," called back Giles. "Report to me at once."

While waiting for the rival captain, Giles went to his cabin and quickly changed into his full-dress uniform.

That costume made it clear that he was a very senior officer with decorations to show that he had already had an illustrious career. He wanted to impress on this Captain Blenkinsop that he had taken on the wrong opponent and should do what Giles ordered. Though Blenkinsop sailed under an admiral who clearly outranked Giles, Giles was the senior captain of the two and was sailing under Admiralty orders, a man whose suggestions were bound to be followed unless they were explicitly contrary to Blenkinsop's orders.

Giles was back on deck by the time that *Cicero*'s captain's barge pulled alongside *Glaucus*. His respect for the customs of the Navy and discipline made him reluctantly order that Blenkinsop be piped aboard with all the usual honors, but he sent Etienne to welcome the rival captain aboard. He was entitled to order the subordinate captain to come to wherever was convenient, but it went against custom. He was sure that this Blenkinsop fellow would recognize the snub.

Blenkinsop had suspected that he was not being invited to come to *Glaucus* for a comfortable chat. He had concluded that it would be wise not to be accompanied by any of his officers and to order his boat's crew and cox'un to remain in the barge. His conclusion was shown to be correct. He was greeted at the entry by the cocky French lieutenant who, Blenkinsop had already concluded, was at the heart of his problem.

Etienne was polite but not servile in his greeting of *Cicero*'s captain. He made no mention of the reason for this visit and confined himself to telling Captain

Blenkinsop that Captain Giles was waiting for him on the quarterdeck.

Giles was indeed ready to give Captain Blenkinsop a piece of his mind. He was standing near the "What the devil did you think you were playing at, Captain Blenkinsop? Clearing for action against one of our frigates and threatening my ship?"

Giles paused to allow the other captain to answer.

"My first lieutenant, my lord, thought that you were a hostile ship masquerading as a British one, sir," replied Blenkinsop, hoping that his putting the blame on Mr. Lester would get him out of trouble.

"So you didn't think to check for yourself. If your first lieutenant suggested that you jump overboard, you would do so? Incidentally, I don't use my civilian title while I am on naval duty."

"No, my lord — sir — I take full responsibility. We found it very strange that your frigate was moored on that side of the estuary with that weird prize with you. We thought you must be a French frigate masquerading as an English one."

"Didn't you send the private signal?"

"Of course we did."

"And the reply?"

"It announced that this frigate was *Glaucus*. But there was no reason for her to be there, so we concluded that she must have been captured by the French along with her signal book, sir."

"So you were about to try to blow us out of the water, were you?"

"Well, sir, everything pointed to your ship having been captured by the French. Your lieutenant even issued commands with a thick French accent."

"Well, Captain Blenkinsop, I have no idea how you became post when you are clearly unfit to command. I shall report this to your admiral and let him deal with your stupidities before they cause real damage. Now return to your ship and get out of here."

Giles turned away in disgust. Blenkinsop bowed at his back and then was led by Lieutenant Macreau to the entryway.

All the way back to *Cicero*. Blenkinsop's brain was working furiously. There was no doubt that Giles's report to his admiral would not be favorable. Blenkinsop badly needed some sort of success to quell his superior's anger. He needed a prize, or if not a prize, at least some sign that he was of use to the admiral and not just an embarrassment. But how to get one? The chances of happening of a French privateer or brig were remote if he just sailed back to the blockading fleet. Suddenly the answer came to him. The two ships that had just left Liverpool had turned north, presumably to try to avoid the sort of encounter that had such a terrible effect on Blenkinsop's prospects. He could cause the same sorts of trouble to these ships, and if he wasn't able to recoup his losses by stopping them with their gold on board, he would also send them into Dublin for trying to evade the law. It wouldn't guarantee a favorable response from his admiral, but he knew that his superior was not indifferent to having his fortune increased. If Glaucus could get away with such behavior, why shouldn't Blenkinsop? That should mitigate the losses he stood to suffer because of that self-righteous Captain Giles.

Chapter XIV

Daphne waved as Giles's carriage left Dipton Hall. It was the last she would see of him until he returned in a few weeks from the mission to contain a Jacobite rebellion. Because of Daphne's cold, Giles was now somewhat short of time to make the rendezvous with *Glaucus* near Chester. Originally Daphne and Giles had planned to go together to Birmingham and their estate in Shropshire before he left her to meet his ship. Instead, Daphne's indisposition and the need not to leave her brothers' children until they were settled in their new home had kept Giles in Dipton much longer than they had intended. Now he would have to travel without stopping to reach Birkenhead on time.

Daphne turned to re-enter the house. A large, damp sneeze interrupted her, and she had to blow her nose before going to her workroom. There she suffered a coughing spell before sitting down to start on the paperwork that had accumulated over the past few days. Mr. Jackson said that the worst of the cold was over. She would just have a stuffy nose and the cough and sore throat that were related to it. Now she had no fever and no danger, only discomfort.

Mr. Jackson had been distinctly unhelpful in relieving her illness. "Daphne, do whatever will make you feel better, and drink a lot, but it won't make your cold go away any sooner. A cold lasts two weeks if you treat it and fourteen days if you don't," was one of the apothecary's unhelpful sayings. The worst part of his repeating it was that Daphne knew he was likely to be right, as usual. She didn't want to be ill. She didn't want to feel that she couldn't do anything she wished. In particular, she wished that she could attack the papers with enthusiasm rather than as an annoying chore.

Luckily, Daphne soon found a distraction from the tedious task when Steves entered the room to announce, "Major Stoner is here to see you, my lady."

"Show him in, Steves.

"Good morning, Major. What can I do for you?" Daphne did not sound exactly welcoming. Her cold was making her very irritable. Did the Major really need to see her? Couldn't she just tell him she was busy and to go away, even though he was family and a close ally in the canal business? But, really, seeing the Major was better than going over some more accounts, which Daphne would feel bound to do if she sent the Major away.

"A couple of things, my lady," replied the Major calmly, "if you have the time."

"Of course, I do. And do call me 'Daphne.'"

"As you wish, but I do love having the chance to call someone 'my lady,'" the Major replied teasingly.

"Well then, I won't stop your pleasures. I suppose it is about the Hunt?"

"Among other things. Mr. Summers does not believe that he should continue as President of the Hunt.

The man doesn't want the job anymore. Just doesn't want it!"

"Understandably. He has been ill, quite seriously ill, I believe."

"Yes, he has, Daphne. Truly, he hasn't been performing the duties of the President for some time. I want to ask you to take on the job."

"That is ridiculous, Major. I couldn't possibly be President. It has to be a man. Otherwise, we'd lose half our members, especially those from the other side of Ameschester. The members have enough trouble accepting that a woman can ride to hounds at all, even more so when some of us ride astride rather than side-saddle. They believe that it is most inappropriate that sometimes we are in at the kill, especially when they are not. Anyway, Major, the President should be the most prominent figure at the Ameschester Hunt Dinners, and women are not even allowed to attend them."

"That is something I would like to change. Really change."

"Small steps at a time, Major, small steps. Let them accept that we can ride to hounds just as well as most men. Then you can tackle the next barrier."

"You are probably right, quite right.

"Daphne, do you suppose that Giles would take on the position of President?"

"I doubt it. Giles is scrupulous about fulfilling any role he assumes, and he is away at sea or seeing to his duties in the House of Lords too often to be able to do justice to the position of President. I think that the most he could do officially is to be the patron of the Hunt. You could ask him when he gets back if you like. We certainly actively support the Hunt, as you well know."

"I do, Daphne. We all do and are most grateful, most grateful. You have given us much more prominence than we would have otherwise. You certainly have!"

"Thank you, Major. The person who should be President is you, I believe. Everyone knows that you have been doing most of the work for some time, and I think you should get the credit for it by being named President. We would certainly support you strongly if you want the position. When will the next President be named?"

"The decision will be made at the next Hunt dinner. Some others may want the prestige they believe goes with the position, but I don't believe that they are willing to devote the time needed to do the job properly—not properly at all. I am not prepared to shore up another President in the way that I have Mr. Summers. I believe the Hunt is much more successful and respected than it used to be before Mr. Summers took on the job, but that is mainly due to your interest and contributions, Daphne. Definitely the case! You and Giles have contributed greatly. Really greatly!"

"Fiddlesticks! Giles and I wouldn't be so involved in the Hunt if you hadn't asked me to participate. That's where the credit lies – with you and Mr. Summers, primarily you. Anyway, I'll be sure to put out the word that I think that you should be the next President. That should ensure that the members make the right choice. The only right choice!"

Major Stoner's habit of emphatically repeating everything seemed to be catching.

"Thank you, Daphne. I'd hate to see all that hard work wiped out by someone who doesn't know what is involved in keeping a hunt going successfully— really successfully."

"As I said, I'll do what I can to make sure that doesn't happen. After all, with our commercial stables, Giles and I want the Ameschester Hunt to be the best showcase of our horses we can manage.

"Was there anything else, Major?"

The words were hardly out of Daphne's mouth when she realized how rude they must sound and how pointing that out to the Major would just make things worse, even though he always seemed oblivious to the rudeness.

"There is one other thing, Daphne. It's about the horse thefts in the area."

"What? Have there been other thefts besides ours? I think Mr. Griffiths is investigating a horse we bred that went missing from an estate on the other side of Ameschester but are there other thefts of horses we bred?"

"Yes, I heard about the one he is investigating. However, another one was stolen, I am told. It is also a horse that came from your stables originally. I only got word of it second-hand from a friend who heard it from someone else. I didn't think to follow up at the time."

"This is very disturbing. Especially after the attempt to take a large number of our hunters. Why would people want to steal horses we raised rather than other ones? Surely the thieves cannot hope to cash in on our reputation, can they?" Daphne wondered.

"I don't see how. Are the horses branded?"

"Branded? No, I don't think so. Do some people brand horses?"

"I believe so, though it can't be a common practice, for I have never seen a branded horse," replied the Major, "not even in India."

The Major took his leave, and Daphne returned to her accounts. But now, the figures seemed to carry no messages to her about how the enterprises were going. After a few minutes, she realized she was wasting her time. The numbers were not singing to her as they usually did. In particular, her Uncle George's numbers were not letting her imagine the gun factory and its workings as she had seen them not so long ago. She couldn't fit the numbers into a tale about what was happening in the gun factory. Specifically, the accounts just lay there as a tedious set of numbers that did not suggest today where difficulties might occur and what new directions might be followed.

Daphne gave up trying to get enlightenment from the dull figures suggesting nothing of interest. It was too early for luncheon, so she wandered down the corridor to the library. It was one of her favorite rooms, with south-facing windows, comfortable chairs, and a wide range of books that she added to steadily. Despite the low-lying winter sun that cheered up the room, a fire was blazing in the hearth. It must have been burning all morning since the cheerful room was warm. Daphne did not feel like picking up one of the serious books about mathematics she was studying but instead took one of the new novels that had been delivered earlier in the week and started to read it.

Daphne was soon lost in the tale, devouring it swiftly, pausing only to blow her nose occasionally. She was so engrossed in the fictional characters that she didn't notice her five-year-old niece, Mary, entering the room. Only when the girl picked up a new book and started climbing onto her aunt's lap did Daphne realize that she had a visitor.

"Read to me, Aunt Daphne. Please!" said the child.

Daphne could hardly resist the request, even though she knew she should take a stand about Mary wandering away from the nursery whenever she wanted to. The nursery staff had enough trouble with the three younger children and didn't pay as much attention to where Mary was as they should. They knew that Daphne didn't get truly angry if Mary strayed from the nursery. Steves was also hopeless in keeping Mary in the nursery. He was always happy to see Mary and talk with her as he went about his very light duties in the middle of the morning and the afternoon. The butler said it reminded him of the days when Giles was a small boy, much more full of interest in the world around him than in the rules of the nursery. Even Mr. Jackson was no help keeping Mary in her place; he had already told Daphne that he didn't believe that the children could catch a cold from her any longer, and he thought that being confined to a couple of rooms was not good for their health and development. Daphne knew that the common belief among the gentry was that she should insist that the children be supervised by servants at all times, but she also didn't really feel that way.

"Let's see what we have here," Daphne suggested. "It is the new book that Hatchard's bookstore in London sent me. I think it is a very good story that you can help me read."

Mary looked at the book carefully for the first time and squealed with delight. Its cover had a sketch as well as some writing, a little nursery rhyme.

"Look here, Mary," Daphne said. "Do you see the dog in the picture?"

Mary studied the three figures in the drawing. “Is it this one?” she asked, pointing to a black blob that looked slightly like a dog standing on its back legs. “This is a boy,” she added, pointing to one figure, “and this is a girl, but the black one doesn’t look like a dog.”

“I think it does, but only in a very silly way,” replied Daphne. “Look, he’s standing on his back legs, and the little boy is holding his front paw. Do you see the dog’s tail now?”

“Oh, there it is,’ said Mary, taking her thumb and index finger from her mouth to touch the figure on the cover. Do you think that Scruffy could walk like that?”

“Not if you didn’t help him, and I don’t think he would like it very much.”

“It’s silly, isn’t it, Aunt Daphne?”

“Maybe a bit. Do you want to hear what the writing below the picture says?”

“Oh, yes.”

“Yes?”

“Yes, please, Aunt Daphne. Please! Please!”

“All right. Follow my finger as I speak the words.

Says Will to his sister
My dog here proposes,
To take a nice walk
And follow our noses.

“Oh, my. Mary, can you see their noses?”

“There,” replied Mary, pointing at the girl’s nose. “She has a very large nose — longer than yours, Aunt

Daphne," Mary giggled. "The boy has hardly any nose, but the dog has a big one."

"Do you think that we can find out what any of the words on the page say, Mary? Let's try. I think that we should look for 'dog.' Let's look for the 'dee' letter. You liked that one last time we played this game, and there is only one 'dee' on the page."

Mary looked carefully at the book. Daphne didn't know whether the little girl would remember the letter from her last lesson or whether the hint would work, but she thought that, in either case, it would be good practice. Her hopes were soon rewarded.

"There it is," squealed Mary, placing her damp index finger on the 'd' in 'dog.'"

"That's very good, Mary. And look, the 'd' is followed by 'oh' and 'gee.' 'Oh and gee' when they are next to each other represents the sound 'og.' 'Og" sounds very silly, but not when you put the 'dee' sound in front of it, which is 'duh.' Now here we have 'duh' joined to 'og.'" What do you think that tells us what the word is?"

Mary immediately cried excitedly, "dog."

"That's right! See how we can use the letter sounds to build word sounds so that we can read. That's enough for now, Mary. Rachel, the nursery maid, is here to take you to luncheon, isn't that so, Rachel?"

"Yes, my lady. I'm sorry that I allowed Mary to slip away. I hope she wasn't bothering you. Nanny Weaver already isn't happy with me."

"I don't mind at all, Rachel, Daphne replied. Don't be upset. With Mr. Steves guarding the front door and Cook the back one, Mary should be perfectly safe exploring the Hall."

"Thank you, my lady. Are you teaching Mary how to read?"

"Yes, I'm starting to. At her age, we can make a game of it."

"I wish someonc had taught me to read when I was young," Rachel said woefully.

"Can't you read? It's not too late to learn."

"Oh, where would I find a teacher, my lady?"

"Let me see. I think Mr. Foster has a Sunday School on Sunday afternoons, where he teaches reading and writing. I can ask if he would allow you to attend."

"That would be very good of you, my lady, but I wouldn't be free on Sundays until it is time for evensong."

"Well, I'll talk to Nanny Wilson about that, and I'll ask Mr. Foster if you can attend even though you are a little older than most of his students. I'll tell you what he says as soon as I can. I think everyone should have a chance to learn to read and write."

"Oh, thank you, my lady."

"You're welcome."

As Mary and the nursemaid departed, Daphne exploded in an enormous sneeze. She must have been holding it back when she was reading with Mary, or maybe she had just been blowing her nose often enough that nothing built up. Now Daphne realized that her cold had not mysteriously gone away. Maybe she should have a nap, much as she hated sleeping in the middle of the day. Before lying down, however, Daphne realized that she should have something to eat. She had had little breakfast. The morning had somehow gone, and it was time she had her usual luncheon. Mrs. Darling would have prepared something special, so Daphne might as well see what it was. She didn't want to disappoint the cook, who went out of her way to try to persuade Daphne to eat when she wasn't feeling well. Somehow, Daphne had not picked up the common belief among the gentry that servants' feelings were no concern of theirs.

Daphne's plans for an afternoon nap seemed less necessary after the food had done quite a bit to revive her spirits; the special raisin and dried cherry flan had induced her to eat more than she intended. She was just debating with herself what to do in the afternoon when that problem was solved for her. Steves announced that Mr. Griffiths wanted to see her on a matter of some importance.

Daphne's first reaction to the news was to direct Steves to tell the stable master to come back another day when she felt better, but then she thought better of that idea. Partly it was because she thought it was childish to petulantly refuse to see a busy man.

Mr. Griffiths must have been almost on Steves's heels, for the minute Daphne told Steves that she would see the horse expert, he strode into the room. The stable master was still dressed in riding clothes, and their dusty nature suggested that he had not paused to clean up before coming to the Hall.

"My lady," he burst out even before engaging in the usual pleasantries of greeting, "I have some terrible news."

"Calm down, Mr. Griffiths, do calm down and have a chair before you tell me what is on your mind. You look like you have just returned to Dipton after a substantial journey. A few minutes to put things in context will pay off in making sure that I understand what is agitating you.

"Steves, Mr. Griffiths could use some refreshment. Get him some cider and ask Mrs. Darling to prepare some food. What she made for me will do nicely if there is any left.

"Now, Mr. Griffiths, do sit down. And tell me what is on your mind. You have been on a journey, it seems."

"Yes, my lady. I have just returned from Wallingford. I went there yesterday morning to see about ponies. As I mentioned to you earlier, they were holding a pony fair, and I thought it was a good place to investigate ponies for Mary and Hugh and find out more about what was involved in breeding them."

"Did you find anything interesting?"

"Yes, I did, though that is not what I wanted to talk to you about."

"Well, tell me about it first, anyway. Then we can get on with the new business."

"Very well. I spent the night in Wallingford, though the fair did not open until noon. It was a place for exchanging information about ponies as much as about selling them. I learned a lot, I must tell you. About the many different types of ponies and the different uses to which they can be put.

"Anyway, after talking to quite a few people, both those who breed ponies, but more those who had them for sale, I was surprised to learn how many different types of ponies are and how they are used.

"Well, to make a very long story short, I purchased two ponies, one a very small one of the type called 'Shetland ponies' and a larger one, intermediate between the smallest one and a horse called a 'New Forest pony.' You may have seen New Forest ponies running wild near Butler's Hard."

"I believe we must have, but at such a distance that I could tell little about them."

"I thought that the little one, the Shetland pony, might be suitable for Miss Mary when she starts to ride. The other pony would be suitable for Master Hugh. It may be a bit big for him now, but not too much so. Very soon, he will shoot up but still be too small to handle a proper hunting horse. The New Forest ponies might also be suitable for small, less adventuresome ladies who would like to ride with the Hunt or might want to have a smaller horse just for getting about. If we like these ponies, I thought that we might consider getting some others to start breeding them."

"Did you bring the ponies you bought with you, Mr. Griffiths?"

"No, my lady. Both sellers were happy to come here on their way to their next engagement. I confess that the reputation of Dipton Hall Stables is now such that they said they were keen to see our establishment. They should be here in a day or two."

"Well, that is very exciting. I will look forward to seeing these ponies. Now, there was something else you wanted to talk to me about."

"Yes, my lady. When I was at Wallingford, a gentleman approached me asking if I was the stable master of Dipton Hall Stables. When I said I was, he told me that he had recently acquired one of our horses and that he was very pleased with it. I hadn't noticed his horse before, but when I looked at it, I realized that it was Thistledown Dipton, one of the earliest stallions we bred here at Dipton, a very well-trained hunter that I was very proud to have produced. I knew I had not sold the horse to the man who now owned him, a gentleman named Hitchens from Ridley Grange near Wallingford.

"Since I knew he had not acquired the horse from us directly, I asked him how he obtained the stallion. He told me that a Mister Geoffry Snider had sold the horse to him. The reason for this Mr. Snider selling the horse, he said, was because the seller said he was about to voyage to India and couldn't take the horse with him. He mentioned that Snider showed him the bill of sale for the horse from our stables, signed by Lord Camshire and me.

"Well, my lady, I knew I had not sold that horse, nor any other horse, to a Mr. Snider, so I suggested that he must have the name wrong. No, he said, he was sure of it. Indeed he had retained that original bill of sale for the horse, which transferred the ownership from us to this Mr. Snider. He invited me to come with him to see the bill of sale in question when I expressed my surprise at his story.

"I took him up on his offer. With an apparently valid bill of sale for the horse, backed by a previous one, I assured him that I believed his ownership was secure. — I hope I did right, my lady."

"Yes … Yes, of course, you did. We can't have people believing that there is something suspicious about our bills of sale. Do you recall who you sold that horse, Thistledown Dipton, to?"

"Yes, I do. I'm not likely to forget those early sales. We sold it to Mr. H.W. Grossling of St. Joseph in the Dell. His estate is on the other side of Ameschester, quite a distance away from here. He doesn't attend meetings of our Hunt, so I haven't seen the animal since we sold him."

"I am afraid that I don't recall him at all or even the sale," Daphne stated. "It is possible that we have never met. But this is very disturbing. Major Stoner was here this morning talking about rumors that some of our horses were being stolen more frequently than one would expect by chance. We don't want to get a reputation that we are somehow connected to horse thieves, do we? I wonder what we should do."

"I think that, as a first step, we should see Mr. Grossling, my lady."

"Quite right, Mr. Griffiths, "and I'll ask Major Stoner if he has more information about the other horse. The more we learn about what is going on, the more likely we are to find a way to stop it."

Chapter XV

"We were lucky that Captain Giles showed up to sort out the situation at the last possible moment," Mr. Lester suggested to Captain Blenkinsop once *Cicero* had settled on a course to take her farther down the Mersey estuary.

"Yes, it was fortunate," replied the captain. "Otherwise, we would have had no choice but to blow that incompetent French lieutenant out of the water. Imagine the problems that action might have caused us – and his Lord High Highness Captain Giles! Can you believe he left a frog in charge of that ship — particularly one who dared to clear for action against us? Just as well it ended safely. We would have been tied up in red tape forever otherwise. We'd never get any prize money or recognition from that initiative either. Lord High Camshire had no business leaving his ship in the hands of that Frenchie! Especially not with that crazy prize of his in tow."

Mr. Lester thought it would be impolitic to point out that if they had come to exchanging broadsides, *Cicero* would undoubtedly have come out second-best.

"I heard something interesting about that damn Earl's ship while I was in Liverpool," Captain Blenkinsop continued. "She stopped a merchant ship engaged in the slave trade on some pretense or other, even though the anti-slavery act has not yet come into effect. *Glaucus* took her into Dublin on some shady charges.

"I also learned something interesting about those two merchant ships which passed us while we were dealing with that damn Earl and the mess he created. They were getting ready to sail at very short notice to escape being stopped as potential slavers, which they most certainly are. Apparently, they are also even shadier than the ship that that damned *Glaucus* took into Dublin. I believe, Mr. Lester, that it is our duty to examine those two merchantmen. More sail now, Mr. Lester. Make more sail so that we can overhaul her as quickly as possible now that we are out of sight of the blasted *Glaucus*."

Mr. Lester felt it would be unwise to question the Captain's instructions. He gave the orders that had *Cicero* loose her topgallants and shake a reef out of the topsails.

Cicero bent more to the wind when the extra area of her sails was filled by the wind. Still, it was not clear that she gained much speed, a view that Mr. Lester had confirmed by the ship's master, Mr. Harrison, raising his eyebrows in silent condemnation of the Captain's order, a form of communication with the first lieutenant he had used often when dismayed by Captain Blenkinsop's orders.

It took the best part of two hours for *Cicero* to catch up with her prey, during which time Captain Blenkinsop ordered that the guns on the leeward side be loaded and run out. When finally they came abreast of their target, whose name turned out to be *Jennifer*, Captain Blenkinsop ordered a shot across her bow to get her to back her sails. When he saw the merchant ship comply, he ordered *Cicero*'s topsail also backed and called across to *Jennifer* to await a party of inspection from the frigate.

After *Jennifer* had complied, Captain Blenkinsop addressed Mr. Lester, "Have my barge readied and tell Lieutenant Harrison of the marines that I will go across to this merchant ship with him and several of his men. You will be in command of *Cicero* until I return."

Though the order was unexpected — usually, the First Lieutenant would visit ships that *Cicero* stopped — Mr. Lester obeyed without comment. In minutes the captain's launch was manned, and Captain Blenkinsop followed the marine lieutenant onto the barge. Soon they arrived at the merchant ship, and Captain Blenkinsop led the way on board her, followed by his marines. There he was greeted by the merchant ship's captain with his mates arrayed behind him.

"Welcome aboard my vessel, Captain. George Wesley at your service, sir," a burly man dressed in a neat, serviceable jacket and trousers greeted Blenbskinsop. "I am the master of this ship. What can I do for you?"

"As you must know, Captain Wesley, the prohibition of the slave trade is about to take effect. It is no longer possible for any vessel to reach the Slave Coast from Britain before the prohibition takes effect. I have been ordered to make sure that no vessel leaves our waters intending to break the law. Now let me see your bills of lading and your logs.

"Lieutenant Harrison," Blenkinsop continued, addressing *Cicero*'s marine officer, "check the hold to see what cargo this ship is carrying. I will take a couple of your men with me to make sure that there is no funny business while I examine the ship's papers. "

Blenkinsop concluded this little speech by signaling to Captain Wesley that he should take him to his cabin.

"Captain Wesley," Blenkinsop started the conversation with the merchant ship's captain, "I know, and you know, that this is a slaving ship trying to avoid the newly passed ban on trading in slaves. I know that your hold contains nothing except the shackles to hold down the slaves you intend to acquire in Africa, a fact that my marine lieutenant is verifying. Of course, the acquisition of slaves will be illegal by the time you reach the Slave Coast, but you may be able to sell the shackles to foreign ships coming to trade there, which may now be attracted to the business since British ships are banned from it. I imagine that you have letters of marque so that you may go on a trip for legalized piracy since you cannot trade in slaves anymore."

Captain Wesley started to protest all these allegations by Blenkinsop, but he waved them away.

"None of that is my business, Captain Wesley," Blenkinsop assured the master of *Jennifer,* "though I do hope you don't also have French letters permitting piracy against British vessels. My only concern is guaranteeing that you don't participate in the slave trade."

"How can you do that, Captain Blenkinsop?" the puzzled Captain Wesley asked.

"Simple. I understand that you have many guineas with which you wish to purchase slaves, a remarkably large number since you have not had time to acquire the usual trade goods to exchange on the Slave Coast, and so, you will need hard coins to purchase your cargo. My officer is in the process of confirming that that is the case.

I shall impound those gold guineas that you were going to use to buy slaves. That will guarantee that you cannot have a profitable slaving voyage. Of course, you can still go to the Slave Coast to sell the shackles to some enterprising Portuguese trader or someone else who can still trade in slaves, but you will not then be able to participate in the abominable trade."

"You can't do that!" protested Captain Wesley. "It is thievery! How can I complete my voyage without the coins to buy a cargo?"

"That's your problem, Captain. Of course, the Admiralty will return your coins after the enforcement of the act takes effect. This is just a transition measure. Now, where is that gold?"

"You can't do this!"

"Yes, I can. Either you hand it over, or I will have my men wreck your cabin, and anywhere else, you may have stashed these coins. It's your choice."

"Oh, all right, Captain Blenkinsop, though it is theft, and you know it," replied Captain Wesley. "I will expect a receipt, of course."

"Of course not. It would be too easy for every Tom, Dick, and Harry to fake a receipt in my name and claim they are owed money. No. I will enter the sum in my ship's log, which is turned into the Admiralty when my cruise is finished, and you can claim your gold in London based on that entry after the act goes into force."

"Damn you, Captain Blenkinsop, you are going to ruin me."

"Not me, personally. I am simply obeying my orders. Now, where are those golden guineas?"

"All right! All right! Here they are!" Captain Wesley opened a drawer and took out a small cloth bag which he handed to Captain Blenkinsop. The naval captain hefted it in his hand. The bag was heavy, but not very heavy. Blenkinsop emptied the bag onto Captain Wesley's dining table. The result was a small pile of gold coins, all one-guinea pieces. Blenkinsop quickly counted them.

"Fifty guineas," announced Captain Blenkinsop. "You don't expect me to believe that you will be able to buy a cargo of slaves and the provisions for a lengthy trip with them with fifty-two pounds and ten pence, surely. What is this? Your own private cache to trade on your own account when you get to the slave coast?

"Marines, start searching the cabin to find the money that Captain Wesley has hidden here. We don't want to waste time, so you don't have to be overly careful not to damage things."

With this encouragement, the two marines got to work, roughly treating the possible hiding places.

"Captain Blenkinsop," one of them called after pulling the front off a locked drawer, "Are these papers of interest?"

The documents were a jumble of papers concerning the ship and its past cargos. Two, however, struck Captain Blenkinsop as being of special interest.

One was a letter of marque, in French. The other was a receipt for a cargo of slaves sold in Martinique. It was, of course, also in French. Martinique was also a French Island.

"Well, well, well, Captain Wesley," Blenkinsop remarked. "You seem to have been acting as a French pirate and trading with the enemy. Either offense is enough to get you hanged, don't you think? Certainly, both together will guarantee that you swing — if these documents come to the attention of our authorities. Unfortunately, I have pressing matters to attend to. They will make it very inconvenient for me to take you to the nearest port and make sure that justice is done. But you must tell me where your gold is hidden, or I will have no choice but to make sure that you are punished to the full extent of the law. Now, let's not waste any more time. Where is the money?"

"All right, all right, you win!" conceded Captain Wesley. "The coins are in my sea chest under the bed."

"Look there," Blenkinsop ordered his marines. They hauled the chest out to the center of the cabin so that they could open it with the key that Captain Wesley produced in response to a threatening gesture for the naval captain. The top layers of materials in the chest were clothes. In moments they were scattered about as the marines dug deeper into the trunk. Success was signaled by finding a large canvas sack, whose neck was closed with wire and an elaborate wax seal with the imprint of a bank in Liverpool.

"That looks more like it," declared Blenkinsop. "Put the sack on the table and open the seal."

The marine complied, using a knife that was lying on the table to deal with the seal. When the bag was opened, everyone in the cabin immediately spotted the glint of gold coins.

"How much do you have in there, Captain Wesley?" demanded Blenkinsop.

"Four hundred guineas."

"Well, that would pay for quite a good cargo of slaves, I would think."

"It and my own guineas would fill my hold and all the provisions needed for the voyage unless the price of prime slaves has already risen on the Slave Coast because of the last-minute demand. Of course, some people expect the price to rise with the need to acquire as many slaves as possible before the impending embargo comes into force, but other people believed it would fall even before the law comes into effect. If that happens, I will have some spare cash to bring back to my principals."

"Well, you won't be taking this gold to the Slave Coast, I can assure you.

"Right. I'll just put these sacks of gold in that sea bag with the incriminating documents, though not these owners' papers that state you are a French ship out of St. Etienne, wherever that is. You can recoup your losses by capturing one of the smaller slave ships scurrying to the English Caribbean islands before the embargo goes into effect and then sealing your profit by selling the slaves in Martinique. Of course, if I hear anything about these guineas again, I will have to use the documents I have seized."

"Now, you two marines," Blenkinsop continued. "Put these gold coins into the sea bag with the documents, but first, let me take ten guineas from the hoard. If you keep your mouths firmly shut about what was found, there will be five of them for each of you. — Here are two of them for each of you now. The rest will come when we reach port. Of course, if you tell your shipmates about this money, I will accuse you of stealing them and have you flogged almost to death."

Back on deck, Captain Blenkinsop met with his marine lieutenant, who verified that there was nothing in the hold except the shackles ready to restrain the human cargo that *Jennifer* had been fitted out to carry.

"I cannot believe how crowded that hold must be when all the shackles are in use," Lieutenant Harrison remarked to his captain. "It is totally inhuman and disgusting."

"I know. That's why it is so good that the trade is being halted," Blenkinsop agreed sanctimoniously. Listening to him, one would never guess how he had been trying to counter his gambling losses by participating in slaving voyages or how opposed he had been to ending the trade in Africans.

"Captain Wesley, I am sure we understand each other now. Tell me, are you related to the famous preacher?"

"That man! I most certainly am not. The old ways of religion are good enough for me. Church on Sunday: that is all there is to religion as far am I am concerned."

Blenkinsop returned to *Cicero* well pleased with his visit to *Jennifer*. He also had thought of a story that would mean that he could keep his hoard of guineas secret.

"Mr. Lester, we were right to take action against that ship. She was indeed trying to get away to fit in one more somewhat legal slaving voyage before the embargo becomes law. She was not carrying coins to pay for the slaves, as I had presumed. Instead, she had a bill written on a bank in Lisbon that would provide her with the needed cash. I tore it into pieces. He won't get his money back easily, certainly not in time to legally engage in the slave trade. I have many damaging documents about that ship in this bag too. I don't expect to hear anything more of that ship or her Captain Wesley.

"Now, what of the other merchant ship?"

"Only her topsails were in sight when we came up with *Jennifer*, sir. Then she turned northeast and now is below the horizon.

"We won't catch up with her before dark, unfortunately. Mr. Jollicot, plot me a course to the northeast corner of Ireland. As I recall, there is an island there, is there not?"

"Yes, sir," *Cicero*'s master replied. "It is called 'Rathlin Island.' We could use it to hide our presence from other ships taking that route to and from the Atlantic, making it easy to catch them."

"That's what I have in mind. Set a course that will get us there before dawn, Mr. Jolliccot. It will be interesting to see what ships try to escape the ban on slavery by taking that route."

It was a beautiful night for sailing, a waning moon giving plenty of light for navigation and a steady, moderate wind from the west-southwest driving *Cicero* along easily. By dawn, they were in position.

Rathlin Island is shaped like a capital L with the corner in the northeast. *Cicero* was inside the L, coasting back and forth, north to south. She would be invisible to ships coming from the east. Blenkinsop expected that would be the route any escaping slave ships would take. Positioning Cicero where he did would make it a simple matter for Cicero to apprehend the ships since vessels coming from the east would be unable to see *Cicero* much in advance.

As the first hint of light came the next morning, Captain Blenkinsop came on deck. The fresh wind was still from the west. *Cicero* was proceeding south slowly, a half mile from the coast of Rathlin Island. She was under only mainsail and one jib, just maintaining steerage way. Mr. Lester had the deck and gave this information to Captain Blenkinsop.

“Shall we clear for action, Captain?” the first lieutenant asked. Most naval ships cleared for action routinely at dawn, but Captain Blenkinsop had decided to abandon that custom since it invariably disturbed his sleep in a most inconvenient way. Mr. Lester was hoping for a chance to practice the crucial drill at first light, but his captain still did not agree, even though he was already out of bed.

“There’s no need, Mr. Lester,” the captain explained. We are in home waters. Clearing will delay scrubbing the deck. We don’t know what the new day holds, but we don't want to be found with filthy decks, do we? Carry on as you were."

Mr. Lester had long ago learned that there was no point in arguing against his Captain's orders. He turned to stare over the taff rail as he tried to hide his anger.

The light was increasing. It promised to be a fine day. To make things better, there came a hail from the masthead: "Deck there, ship off the starboard beam. Only topsails showing. She is coming towards us."

Time passed as dawn broke, and the newly sighted ship drew closer to *Cicero*.

"Ship is a frigate," was the next hail. Presumably, the lookout was judging solely on the basis of the stranger's sails and rigging, for her hull would still be below the horizon, even from the masthead.

"You there," Captain Blenkinsop addressed one of the midshipmen whose name he couldn't remember. "Get aloft with the telescope and tell me what you see."

The next report came in the midshipman's voice, but Mr. Lester suspected that the experienced lookout provided the information: "The frigate is British built; can't see her flags in this wind," the hail continued.

"Not surprising in this wind. She won't be able to see ours either," declared Captain Blenkinsop. "They are streaming out directly at her. Still, make our number, Mr. Lester."

The appropriate flags soared to their position and streamed away from the approaching vessel.

More time passed without more information being obtained about the converging vessel, though it was confirmed that she was British-built and flying the Union Jack.

"Shouldn't we clear for action, Captain Blenkinsop?" suggested Mr. Lester.

"Of course not. She is British-built, and that main flag looks like the Union Jack. She is British without question, Mr. Lester. Definitely British."

"But what is she doing here, Captain?" asked Mr. Lester. "Isn't that suspicious?"

"I don't see why it should be."

"But, Captain Blenkinsop, isn't it surprising to find one of our frigates approaching along the north coast of Ireland?"

"I don't believe so. She may have been looking for dubious merchant ships just as we are. Or she could have been blown off course, coming from America or Canada, and found this the convenient way to reach her destination. Maybe she's from Newfoundland. Or Halifax. Nothing suspicious. No reason for an enemy frigate to be here. She is certainly flying British colors."

"But, Captain, that could be a ruse. If an enemy were looking to make mischief here, wouldn't she be flying the Union Jack? Shouldn't we take precautions?"

"What? Like clearing for action? Mr. Lester, really! That sort of reasoning is how you led us into problems with *Glaucus*. Didn't you learn anything from it? Indeed, with us seeming to be hiding behind that island, it's probably we that look suspicious. If we start clearing for action, she will have to respond, and things may get out of control. Just remember what happened with *Glaucus,* where we had much better reason to be suspicious. I can think of no reason why a French frigate would be in these waters. There is nothing to worry about, and that's that!" Captain Blenkinsop concluded decisively.

Mr. Lester looked at Mr. Jellicot, who shrugged his shoulders in a 'what can we do?' gesture.

The other frigate approached steadily. It was now clear that she intended to meet with *Cicero* for her course if it was extended, would have her pass only a few yards in front of *Cicero* but not by a great margin. All eyes on *Cicero* were trained on the approaching frigate, including those of the midshipman whose task was to watch for signal flags, but who forgot to check if he might be able finally to see the recognition flags that she should be flying.

"Back the sail," Captain Blenkinsop ordered, for the approaching frigate might run into *Cicero* if they both held their own course. At what seemed to be the last moment, the strange frigate turned hard to larboard and backed her main topsail so that she would slip up to windward of *Cicero* and stop, close enough for a comfortable discussion. At the same time, she lowered her Union Jack and hoisted the French tricolor instead. This was accompanied by her larboard gun ports rising and her broadside guns being run out.

Captain Blenkinsop stared speechless at this development for several seconds. It dawned on him that his order had led them into a complete disaster. But if Blenkinsop was waiting for his first lieutenant to surrender, he was mistaken. Mr. Lester knew that Captain

Blenkinsop would try to pin the blame for this fiasco on his subordinate officer if one of his lieutenants gave the life-saving order. Lester's career was likely over due to this development, but he wanted his captain to accept the blame for the situation. Getting into this fiasco was entirely Captain Blenkinsop's doing. Shame made Mr. Lester resolve to perish rather than to accept any responsibility for the disaster.

After a short pause, but before the French captain gave the order to fire, Captain Blenkinsop snapped out of his stunned inaction. "Lower our flag, Mr. Lester," he said in a resigned voice. "We have to surrender because none of you realized that she was French. I must go and get my sword to hand over to them."

Following that speech, the First Lieutenant was tempted to ignore the order and let the French frigate blow them all to kingdom come. Shame filled him, but the flag had to be lowered. He did it himself. And then he went to the entry port to welcome whoever the French sent to take possession of *Cicero*. It was his duty, even though he knew it marked the end of his career in the Royal Navy. But it was his pride to do what he knew to be his duty. *Cicero* had surrendered without a shot being fired because of Captain Blenkinsop's unreasonable orders. But he could not just abandon the last tasks he was likely to take on as an officer of the Navy.

Chapter XVI

Giles, Etienne, Daniel, and Mr. Brooks stood at *Glaucus*'s rail as *Cicero* sailed off to the northwest.

"What a disgrace to the Navy that captain is! I wonder how he got his step, let alone his ship," Giles commented. "Making him a post captain must reflect the worst abuses of the Influence System."

"Not in this case, I believe," said Mr. Brooks. "His promotion was a mistake, obviously, but it was not made because of influence. Somehow I clearly recall the name of the captain and of the ship. It was just after the war resumed, ending the Peace of Amiens. *Cicero* was returning from Jamaica under a very good captain though I don't remember his name. The captain, and everyone else on board, had no idea that the war had resumed.

"A frigate appeared on the reciprocal course to *Cicero*'s as *Cicero* approached the mouth of the Channel. The stranger was British-built and flying British colors; if both ships held their courses, they would pass close to one another. Since the men on *Cicero* believed that it was peacetime and the ship appeared to be British, *Cicero*'s captain and her other officers had no reason to suspect that the approaching ship might be an enemy. However, the ship approaching was no longer a British frigate, for she had been one of the few frigates that the French had captured in the earlier war. That fate was unknown, of course, to every one of *Cicero*.

"The ruse that the approaching ship was making almost paid off. The two ships were very close to each other before someone on *Cicero* realized that the approaching ship was hostile. What they spotted was that she was cleared for action and needed only to raise her gunports and run out her cannon to fire what would be a devastating broadside.

"*Cicero*'s captain reacted immediately to the danger when he perceived it. He altered his ship's course so that she met the other one bow-to-bow rendering the enemy broadside inoperative, boarded her, and took her. The butcher's bill was terrible, even though it was all hand-to-hand fighting, for the two crews were about the same size. *Cicero* prevailed despite having had no time to prepare for the fight. Unfortunately, her captain and first lieutenant were killed in the battle, so Blenkinsop, who was not involved in the melee, but was assigned to sailing the British ship, was the senior officer on the British frigate when the French surrendered.

"The reports of the battle caught the attention of the public, which was eager for good news to help to justify the resumption of hostilities, and Blenkinsop was a hero despite having had no real role in the encounter. In recognition of his new status, he was made post-captain, without ever having been a commander, and given *Cicero*. I've heard nothing about her since then. Her performance here clearly suggests that Blenkinsop's reward was a mistake."

"Yes, that may explain why *Cicero*'s captain is such an incompetent," remarked Giles. "Let's hope we don't have anything to do with him in the future. Now tell me, Mr. Macreau, what you have been doing since you brought that French brig into Plymouth as your prize. I received news of that success while I was still at Dipton. Since then, I can see that you have acquired a very strange-looking prize. What is the story behind her being with us?"

Etienne told the tale, aided by comments from Daniel and Mr. Brooks, of how they discovered and captured the slave-gathering ship.

"Incredible!" exclaimed Giles. "Barbery raiders are still taking slaves here? Unbelievable. But obviously, you have the full evidence. I'll have to inspect your prize before I can decide what we shall do with her. Before we go over to her, are there any other adventures you have had that I should know about?"

"Yes, sir, we did have one other significant adventure." Etienne went on to tell the tale of how they had taken the *Pride of Merseyside* into Dublin to deal with the suspected pirates aboard.

"You did very well, all of you. You took the right attitude towards a suspicious vessel, and your actions were proved to be justified later," Giles said. "Now tell me about that ship anchored there flying that strange flag below the jack. Is she another prize, and how did you take her?"

The three officers took turns relating how they had captured the slave-catching, square-rigged galley.

"Let me check that I understand what happened, Mr. Macreau. You decided to investigate a strange-looking ship flying an unknown flag when you spotted her emerging from behind a headland on the Irish Coast?"

"Yes, sir."

"And when she saw you, she altered course as if to avoid you?

"Yes, sir."

"And further examination suggested that she might have been a frigate that had been modified so that she could be rowed as well as sailed, but she still carried at least six cannon on each side?"

"Yes, sir."

"Well, you certainly had sound justification for investigating her. Then you stopped her?"

"Yes, sir. We fired a shot across her bow, and she hove to."

"Mr. Stewart, you accepted the surrender, did you not?"

"Yes, sir. That's when we started to learn about how she had been taking slaves along the Irish Coast."

"How did you communicate with these Berbers or whatever they are?"

"One of the galley slaves spoke English, sir. Indeed, he is English, enslaved by the Mohammedans. He had learned their language and could translate for us. So we learned what the ship had been doing. They had been capturing new slaves along the Irish Coast. We couldn't talk to these unfortunate captives, sir, since they don't speak English. However, one of the marines, Haggarty, told us he spoke some of their language, so we found out their story."

"What about the ship's papers?"

"I think we found them, sir, but they are written in some strange script, so we couldn't read them."

"I'm sorry to quiz you like this, Mr. Stewert and Mr. Macreau, but I had to know the details of the capture. I needed to make sure that whatever government this ship sails under would have no basis for objecting to our capturing her and seizing the ship for conducting piracy against us, as well as for illegally imprisoning British subjects. Our government takes a very lenient view of the Berber states' pirate and slave businesses, offensive as they are to us. The claim is that we need access to supplies and port facilities on the south side of the Med., so we turn a blind eye to their activities. I don't see how our officials will have any reason to object to our seizing her, though I will be surprised if any of these pirates hang, as they all should. I'm sure that our government will take no action against the Berbers until we have disposed of Napoleon.

"Now tell me, Mr. Brooks, how does your pirate ship sail?"

"She is a bit slow, sir, partly because of her rig and partly because her bottom is foul. On the other hand, she can point quite high, though not as high as *Glaucus*, sir."

"I don't suppose you were able to test her as a galley."

"No, sir. I didn't think I had the authority to have our people pull on the oars."

"Well, we may have to see to that. I recall seeing something like that vessel in the Med when I was a midshipman. They were less beamy than this ship, but they had the same feature: they could be sailed as well as, or instead of, being rowed. What were they called? — xebecs, that's what it was, I believe. Maybe we should refer to your capture as a xebec since she isn't a frigate, a galley, or a plain merchant ship.

"Mr. Macreau, did you indicate to the Irishmen that we would return them to their homes?"

"Yes, sir. I'm afraid that I did so without thinking carefully about the implications."

"Next time, not that there is likely to be a next time of this sort, think more carefully before you make a promise. However, I think you are right about what we should do. If we leave the Irish captives here in England, and even if we take them to Belfast, they would not likely find their way home easily, and I doubt the authorities would do much for them except to try to move them along to avoid charges to the parish. We may have trouble taking them to the coast where they were kidnapped. We don't have time before we have to be in Scotland, I am afraid, something I didn't tell you about. I think that we should take that boat with us and then see them safely home when our task in Scotland is finished."

"Now, I'd better go over to her — what shall we call her?"

"We never thought of that, sir," said Mr. Macreau.

"Well, you caught her. You can name her."

"Good heavens, let me think. She was a slave ship, and now the slaves are free. Let's name her 'Freedom.'"

"'Freedom,' she is," said Giles. "Now, come with me, Mr. Stewart, over to *Freedom.* I want to see her for myself. When we are ready, I'll signal to you, Mr. Macreau, to get *Glaucus* underway to come with us. Our course will pass the Isle of Man to larboard on our way to the Inner Hebrides, but I'll probably be back on board *Glaucus* before we get to the North Channel."

Giles and Mr. Stewart took the captain's barge to *Freedom*. It felt strange to Giles to have his barge steered by someone other than his long-term cox'n Carstairs, though he believed that Harrison, his new cox'n, would do an adequate job. He'd miss Carstairs, who had sailed with him from the time Giles had been a midshipman, somehow succeeding in changing ships when Giles was appointed to a different vessel even before the time when Giles became a post-captain and could take his cox'n with him.

Midshipman Jenks and Master's mate Whitley had been left on the newly-named *Freedom* while the officers who had brought her across the Irish Sea had returned to *Glaucus*. They seemed very glad to see Giles, even if they could not welcome him properly without bosun's mates and their whistles.

Giles wasted no time dealing with the problems caused by having three distinct groups of people on board *Freedom* when she was captured. He dealt first with the Irish who had been captured by the slavers. He had them gather on the rear deck of the vessel, which he thought of as the quarterdeck. He used Haggarty, the Irish marine, to translate for him.

"I know that you were kidnapped illegally," Giles announced to the group, "and I imagine that you want to go home. Your Irish Government let you down, but luckily the slave catchers did not get away and take you to a distant country. I could arrange for you to be taken to Dublin sometime soon. The trouble with that is that I cannot guarantee that officials there will take to your homes quickly, or at all. I cannot take you to your homes immediately because I have to take my ship to Scotland on a critical and urgent mission. That task should take no longer than two weeks; after that, we can return you to your homes along the coast of your country. However, being on my ships will not be without danger, but trying to get home in any other way may be equally hazardous. Now take a few minutes to discuss what you want to do while we, including marine Haggarty, check into the other aspects of this ship."

Giles's next problem was what to do with the rescued galley slaves. He didn't feel that he owed much to them since they were from various parts of Europe, with one exception. That one was Dixon, the seaman from Newcastle-on-Tyne, who had helped Mr. Stewart when he took charge of the xebec. He called the former galley slaves together on the rowing deck, where they could sit, and his voice would carry. Speaking through Dixon, Giles addressed them.

"I am sure that you are glad to be rescued from slavery. Now the question is, 'what is your next step.' Mr. Dixon here tells me that most of you are from

Mediterranean countries. It will not be easy to get home while the war is still raging, especially as many of the areas you come from have been seized by the French with whom we are at war. Unfortunately, I can't provide you with any money or arrange transportation. In fact, I cannot do anything to help you get home.

"Now, if you wish, we will set you ashore here. There is a major port not far from here; indeed, it's only a short ferry ride away, but I can warn you that trying to live without money, even for a short time, will be hazardous. The people are very suspicious of strangers.

"I can offer you an alternative. If you come with us and help to sail this ship, I'll arrange for you to be paid for the time you spend with us, and I will not require you to stay in the Navy after this voyage is finished. No, you won't have to row, though you may find some satisfaction in helping those who will be learning how to row perform better. Did I mention that we will use the former crew of this ship to do the rowing? Yes, and we will shackle them to the rowing benches, treating them as they treated you. That seems fair to me."

Those remarks produced cheers from the former slaves. They would be very happy to see the tables turned on the slave drivers.

"I will leave you for a moment to discuss things among yourselves," Giles concluded.

He went back to the displaced Irish. "Any progress yet, Haggarty?"

"Yes, sir. They have decided to stay with us until we can take them home."

"Excellent. Tell them that I am very pleased."

"One thing, sir. The men offered to help in any way they can. They know nothing about ships, but they are strong and believe they might be useful."

"Thank them for me, Haggarty, and tell them we will take them up on their offer as much as possible."

Giles turned to Mr. Stewart. "Send back to *Glaucus* for the purser to arrange for — Haggarty, how many of these Irish people are there?"

"Thirty-seven men, twenty-two women, and twelve children, sir."

"That many! I didn't realize how large a contingent they are," Giles remarked. "The women can camp in whatever the Berbers were using as a wardroom, and the men can have hammocks in the focsle. Mr. Stewart, arrange for *Glaucus* to send us hammocks for the Irish men and for our crew members who will be here for the time being. The purser will not be happy about this, but tell him I will see that his accounts are made good. We'll also need a third of our people from *Glaucus* to be able to sail this ship properly, though I believe that you had fewer for your trip here."

"Yes, sir, we did," Daniel confirmed.

"Then, you'll also need purser's supplies for them."

Daniel arranged for the request to be sent to *Glaucus* while Giles returned to the galley slaves.

"Any results, Dixon?" he asked.

"Yes, sir, we have all decided to try our luck with you for the immediate future."

"Even you?"

"Yes, sir. I'm done with the merchant service. I am not sure that I want to join the Navy, but you said we could wait and see, and I will need some money, even if I am just returning to Newcastle."

"I am very pleased. Tell your companions that I said so. Now, let's get on with the next step, which is to get ourselves some new rowers. I expect that you will all enjoy what's going to happen to your former tormentors."

It was a slow process assembling the new rowers on the benches. The former galley slaves selected likely candidates to row the xebec, selecting ones by whom they had been treated worst. That still left a number of Barbers shackled in the hold.

The former slaves unlocked their former masters one at a time and locked them to the rowers' benches. The process was not quiet; the new slave drivers enjoyed jeering at their former masters. When the benches were full, Dixon turned to Giles.

"Captain, I suggest that we make them practice unshipping and shipping the oars before we set them rowing. We have placed the former slave masters on the sternmost benches so that they can show the others how to do it. I hope you won't object to us encouraging the new rowers with the whips they used on us."

Giles had to think about that request for a moment. He abhorred everything about slavery, but he could understand the abused victims of slavery wanting to get their own back. It wasn't as if he had never seen the lash employed to encourage performance by slaves. He had seen a lot of that while serving in the Caribbean; that was one of the reasons he was so against slavery in general. But he could certainly understand and even approve of the desire for retribution held by the former victims of his new rowers. He was also very aware of the widespread use of the cat in the Navy, though very rarely on *Glaucus* and then only as the main punishment for stealing from other crew members.

"All right, but in moderation. No settling of old scores, tempting as that may be. I don't want the rowers rendered incapable of doing their tasks because of the harshness of the whip. Let's see if they can get the oars in the water and back again before we try anything more adventuresome."

Practice with getting the oars back and forth into the water took several tries, but finally, Giles and his slave drivers got it down to ten minutes to get them in and four to get them back out.

"That is enough for today," announced Giles. "We can try some more oar handling and rowing when we are underway.

"Mr. Brooks, are we ready to set sail?"

"Yes, sir. The topmen and others are now quite proficient at handling the sails and lines on this ship, even though some of the rigging strikes us as peculiar. All we need is to designate some strong men to raise the anchor. I brought some nippers over from *Glaucus,* but no one is detailed to man the capstan. I suppose we could use some of those newly enslaved Berbers. I noticed that there are places to chain them to the windless on this vessel."

"It's an idea, but given our recent experience with the oars, I am not sure that we could raise the anchor. Possibly all we would do is get the workers all tangled up in their chains just at a crucial moment. It might be feasible without the shackles, but that might be asking for trouble with desperate men who are probably expecting to face the noose. I suppose we could bring some more marines from *Glaucus* to keep them from rebelling, but it would not be the easiest way to start out."

Haggarty, the Irish marine, was nearby and perked up his ears when he heard the word marines. "Captain, sir," he interrupted Giles's discussion. "The Irishmen we rescued are very strong. They could certainly man the capstan with little instruction and are eager to help. They are not used to having nothing to do."

"That's a good suggestion, Haggarty," Giles praised the marine. "Let's try it.

"Mr. Stewart, prepare to get underway. Mr. Jenks, signal to *Glaucus* that we are about to raise anchor. Tell her to take station off our weather quarter, ready to come to our aid if we get into trouble."

It took longer than usual for Mr. Stewart to report that all was ready, for Haggarty required some time to explain to the eager but inexperienced new deckhands what was involved in raising an anchor. Now the first clank of the windlass heralded the beginning of the next and critical stage of *Glaucus*'s mission. This task went surprisingly smoothly. In came the anchor line, clank by clank. Some of the weaker-looking Irishmen had been put to the task of helping the nippers who had been brought from *Glaucus*. Every stage of getting underway worked, if not always, very smoothly, but eventually, *Freedom* was settled on her course. Giles was pleased. While *Glaucus* had taken half the time before being ready to sheet home the sails, he had seen many ships of the Navy leaving Portsmouth with more dither and confusion. All he needed was for the ships to reach their appointment in Scotland in time, and that task was certainly on schedule.

The wind was light from the south. *Glaucus* and *Freedom* proceeded to the north-northwest with *Glaucus* on *Freedom*'s larboard quarter, all ready to quell any signs of revolt or other problems on the captured ship. The winter sun was sinking towards the southwest horizon when Giles decided to try *Freedom*'s rowing properties again. He alerted his slave drivers to get ready and ordered that the oars be unshipped. That exercise went reasonably smoothly, and then Dixon ordered that rowing begin. The performance was rather ragged to begin with, but before long, the slaves settled down enough to propel the xebec through the water effectively. The rowing trial ended abruptly when the starboard bow rowers caught a crab and went sprawling onto the bottom of the rowing deck with the oar entangled with the ones forward of them. Only the facts that the rowers were shackled to the deck and that their captors had fastened wrist shackles to rings on their oars prevented any rowers or oars from going by the board.

Giles called a halt to further rowing for the day, pleased with the result. The strange vessel his lieutenants had captured might find use in this expedition. He returned to *Glaucus* before it was fully dark, satisfied with his day. The two ships continued northwards throughout the night, a gibbous moon providing more than adequate illumination until they were well past the Isle of Manx and entering the North Channel. Though there must have been shipping around with Glasgow and the Firth of Clyde to the east of them, they saw no ships during the night, and dawn revealed only a few distant sails. Giles was well pleased. He could now hope that no news of a British frigate heading up to the Hebrides would precede him and warn the would-be traitors of his coming.

The wind stayed light but steady as the two ships proceeded northwards. It would take at least another day to reach their destination, but that would still allow them to arrive ahead of the scheduled gathering of the Jacobites. Giles again went over to *Freedom* to oversee the development of rowing skills. It would be a long process if he wanted to make an effective warship of the xebec, but his intention was only to see what could be learned about rowing a ship. He had no experience in galleys, but he had seen them in use when he visited Russia and had wondered then whether the sacrifice of broadside guns could be compensated by the ability to maneuver effectively into the eye of the wind.

Giles concluded that it would not be worth introducing galleys or xebecs to the Royal Navy, but he would continue his rowing efforts on *Freedom.* They provided amusement and some satisfaction to the people on the overcrowded xebec to see the tables turned on their former captors. He certainly enjoyed having the slave gatherers and drivers receiving some of their own medicine, even if he also felt slightly guilty about that satisfaction. Certainly, he thought those men deserved that treatment and the humiliation that came with it. Giles even wondered how he could make the rest of the slavers, who were still chained in the hold, receive their share of the payback. Maybe, once the Jacobite rebellion was dealt with and he was still using the xebec to return the Irishmen to their homes, he could rotate the rowers and anchor raisers, so all the Berbers received the same share of the punishment before the ship anchored in the Solent, and he turned them over to the authorities who, for diplomatic reasons, would likely not hang them.

The next day was just as uneventful. A steady southern wind, quite atypical for the time of year, carried them steadily northwards as they stayed several leagues off the coast of Scotland. Mr. Brooks kept checking his charts and comparing them to what he could see, sometimes using his telescope to verify items on the distant shore that his charts pointed out. When about two hours of daylight remained, he put down his telescope and turned to Giles.

"I think that that is our island ahead."

Giles took the telescope. He pointed it towards what looked, with the naked eye, like another of the many headlands that they had been passing. The telescope emphasized that behind this headland, the shoreline seemed to be usually far away, suggesting that he might be looking at an island rather than another point stretching out into the sea from the land. The island or headland was notable in that it rose sharply to a conical summit covered by pine trees. The telescope also revealed that there was quite a deep bay at the foot of the steep hill, with flatter arms extending towards *Glaucus*. This fitted the description that he had been given when this voyage was being planned. Ahead must be the little island where he could hide *Glaucus,* and behind it would be Pendrag

Island, where the Jacobite insurrection was supposed to start shortly.

Glaucus reached the little, unnamed island as the day faded and the wind dropped. Good anchorage was found near the shore, and Giles was sure their presence would be hidden from Pendrag Island. They would have to hope that no one had seen them arrive. He was ready to spring the trap on the rebels and their French allies. At first light the next day, he would climb to the top of the island to see if there were any signs of the action that was supposed to take place in two days if everything was still on schedule. Tonight he would enjoy a light supper with some of the fine wine that his wife always made sure was among his cabin stores, write the next installment of his letter to Daphne, and get to bed early.

Chapter XVII

Daphne's cold had become much less annoying in the two days she had had to wait before investigating the horse thieves. The first day had been marked by a blizzardy snowfall and the second by cold rain and mist. Now everything had changed. The sun was rising to show a sparkling day with a brilliant blue sky and no wind. There were still large patches of glistening white snow on the fields beyond Dipton Hall, but it looked as if the roads would be passable. Steves announced that Mr. Griffiths had arrived with the horses, and Daphne and Major Stoner came out the front door and stopped to admire the view. It was a perfect day for a horseback ride, with little danger of getting bogged down in any slush left from the storm in shaded valleys along their route.

It was certainly a brisk day for a ride, but Daphne reveled in it, even if her nose ran a little more than it usually would. Once away from Dipton, there was less slush on the road, and no snow drifts obstructed their passage. Their route took them through the center of Ameschester, and after they passed through the market square, Mr. Griffiths took the lead, guiding their way to the road that led to their destination. When they reached the edge of town, Mr. Griffiths indicated that they should pull up at an inn.

“Why are we stopping?” Daphne asked.

“I think we need a break, and this is the best place to pause between here and our destination. In my opinion, it is the best inn in the Ameschester area.”

“Are we stopping to rest the horses?” Daphne asked.

“Partly, but it is more to rest ourselves. I have often noted that people who have been riding for a while do not seem to be as alert as usual when they reach the end of their journey. It may be an uncomfortable interview that we will have with Mr. Gossling since I think it is highly likely that his horse has been stolen, and he may want to blame us when he finds out we know something about it. We may need to have all our wits about us to get him to help us, so we don’t want to arrive shivering and wanting a warm fire more than polite conversation. Also, I know that this pub has excellent cakes and so on, so I think we should refresh ourselves before pushing on. I would certainly enjoy having something to eat and drink.”

Large windows brightly lit the large taproom of the inn, and a cheerfully blazing fire made it pleasantly warm. All three travelers had tankards of the ale for which, Mr. Griffiths claimed, the inn was famous. Daphne’s companions were not surprised that she also ordered ale, but the serving girl seemed puzzled when such a well-dressed woman wanted the common beverage.

The servant told the landlady of the pub, who approached Daphne. “Madam, wouldn’t you prefer a private parlor to the common taproom?”

"Why should I?" asked Daphne. "This room is bright and cheerful and spacious. Private parlors are always stuffy and small."

"But madam, I can't allow this. What will people say if it seems that fine ladies have to share the common space? I can't allow it, for no one of quality will stop here once the word gets out."

"*Madam*," Major Stoner spoke up, using the title sarcastically, "When the Countess of Camshire wishes to sit in your taproom, you should welcome her with open arms."

"The Countess of Camshire … The famous Countess of Camshire… is in my taproom?"

"Yes, indeed," confirmed Mr.Griffiths. "You should be glad to have her here, especially as a recommendation from her is worth a hundred from other travelers."

"Oh, I'm very sorry, your grace," the landlady said. "Of course, if you wish, you may sit in the taproom, though I am afraid it cannot be up to your usual standards."

"It's all right, Mrs…."

"Jamieson, your grace."

"Mrs. Jamieson. 'My lady' is the right way to address me, and 'madam' suffices. You have a very pleasant room here, and I suspect you will find that the less stuffy ladies will also appreciate it as long as it does not get too rowdy. If I were you, I wouldn't push them away."

"Well, I will consider it, my lady. But won't other ladies think we are very common if we have gentle women in our taproom? In the evening, we sometimes get women in here, but they are of a very unrefined type; many of them are no better than they should be if you get my meaning."

"Well, you may be right. But in the daytime, when business is light and orderly, I think you will gain from encouraging ladies who are traveling to stop here for refreshment and enjoy this friendly space."

"Yes, my lady. Since you have been so understanding, I hope we can provide you with some sweetmeats to try. We are very proud of them."

"That would be excellent. Thank you, Mrs. Jamieson," Daphne replied.

The landlady bustled off to make sure that their order was fulfilled promptly.

Daphne opened the conversation while they waited. "Mr. Griffiths, how should we go about talking with Mr. Gossling?"

"I think, my lady, that we should first confirm that the horse we sold him is not still at St. Joseph in the Dell. I am sure that I saw the horse, Dipton Thistle, at the Wallingford pony fair, but it is always possible that it was some other horse. On the bill of sale for that horse, he was called Dipton Rover. It may be another horse, though a very similar horse, masquerading as one of ours because all our horses have 'Dipton' in their names. We have never sold a horse with that name, though it is on the list of names we might use in the future. The description of the animal is exactly what we might have written."

“Well, that all makes sense, implausible as it seems. If Mr. Gossling still has Dipton Thistle, we can say we were passing by and wondered how he is performing. Maybe we could suggest that we would like to see him at the Ameschester Hunt. What do you think, Major?”

“Splendid idea! Splendid! Terrible thing having your horse stolen! Terrible! Especially as it is bound to imply a whisp of carelessness, wouldn’t it? Don’t want to give that impression! No, we don’t! I had not thought about the awkwardness of asking a man if his horse had been stolen.”

It took the trio another three-quarters of an hour to reach St. Joseph in the Dell and to be directed to Summit Manor, the estate of Mr. Gossling. The house was at the end of a short driveway, quite pleasantly situated with no other houses visible, though it seemed that the property might not be extensive.

A well-dressed man, whom Mr. Griffiths recognized as Mr. Gossling, was standing before the front door, pulling on warm gloves. He waited at the top of the steps as they arrived, but when they stopped, he came down to welcome them.

“Mr. Griffiths from Dipton Stables, aren’t you?” he welcomed the stable master, “and who are these guests? Do dismount, please, unless you are pressed for time.”

“Yes, that’s me,” Mr. Griffiths could finally get a word in as he swung down from his horse, “and this is Lady Camshire and Major Stoner.”

"The real Lady Camshire? Of course, you are; how rude of me. Welcome to Summit Manor, my lady. What brings you here? How rude of me, again, as if you won't tell me as soon as I stop nattering on. You must come in. Mrs. Gossling would never forgive me if the Countess of Camshire came here and I didn't invite her in."

Daphne was amused. She was used to people recognizing her with excitement, though not usually as enthusiastically as Mr. Gossling. It may not have been what she expected when she married Giles. Still, now it seemed to be the result of the publicity about his successes as well as of her own adventures, all of which had been reported at far too much length in the newspapers, she thought, but all she could do about her fame was cheerfully to make the best of it.

"That would be delightful, Mr. Gossling. You have a lovely estate here and a charming house. We hesitated to intrude, but we had some things to discuss with you, and it is a nice day for a ride."

"Come in, come in, please, all of you.

"Trent," Mr. Gossling directed his butler, who had opened the front door the minute he realized that Mr. Gossling had visitors, "get someone to take their horses to the stables."

Mr. Gossling led the way into the house and turned down a hallway. He threw open the door to a well-lit, cozy sitting room with a fire blazing in the grate. "Mrs. Gossling, may I present the Countess of Camshire, Major Stoner, and Mr. Griffiths," he said in a loud voice.

A middle-aged woman, who had been working on some needlework, put it aside, rose to her feet, and curtseyed deeply to Daphne.

"My lady, it is an honor to have you visit our house."

"It is very good of you to welcome us uninvited, Mrs. Gossling. We had business with Mr. Grossing but did not intend to intrude on you."

"Oh, you are most welcome, my lady. You and the gentlemen must stay for some tea.."

"That sounds delightful, but we don't want to be a bother."

"No bother at all. Trent, we'll have tea with our guests."

Daphne could have kicked herself. She didn't want to have tea and chit-chat before she could get down to business, but it would be the height of rudeness to visit Mrs. Gossling's estate and not spend some social time with the woman of the house. She should have thought of it when they rode up and, at that time, claimed to Mr. Gossling that they only had a few moments for a visit, implausible as that might seem when arriving at a somewhat out-of-the-way manor. Now that they were here, politeness demanded that they remain a while. Luckily, Mrs. Gossling turned out to be a no-nonsense woman who appreciated that it was unlikely that the Countess of Camshire would drop in uninvited to spend the afternoon, especially since Dipton Hall was not close to Summit Manor.

When everyone had been served tea and offered sandwiches and pastries, Mrs. Gossling got down to business: “My lady, pleased as I am to see you, I would guess this is not just a social call. You and these gentlemen no doubt came to see my husband. He keeps me in his confidence on all things concerning the manor. You can speak freely with me since I always get my husband to tell me everything.”

Daphne hoped that she hid her surprise at the offer. She was aware that her involvement with the management of Giles’s estates was a subject of gossip throughout the area, with most men thinking it was scandalous. She also knew that some women thought it was marvelous, and even more of them were well aware of their husbands’ business matters and often helped in dealing with them, but usually did so behind the scenes while maintaining the fiction that their husbands managed everything unassisted. Of course, there was nothing in what she wanted to discuss with Mr. Gossling that Mrs. Gossling shouldn’t hear; nevertheless, the acknowledgment of her interest was the surprise. It certainly made this visit more pleasant not having to conceal its purpose until they had Mr. Gossling by himself again.

“That is good news, Mrs. Gossling. It is so much easier when couples can share important information, isn’t it? We wanted to ask you about the hunter Mr. Gossling bought from Dipton Stables, a horse called Dipton Thistle.”

“Oh, yes. He was a wonderful horse. My husband was very pleased with him!”

"I'm glad you were satisfied with him, Mr. Gossling. Do you mind me asking what has happened to him?"

"He was stolen, my lady."

"Oh, no! we were afraid that that must have happened. Tell us how the horse was stolen, please, Mr. Gossling."

"It was really my own fault. We had just returned from a meeting of the hunt — our hunt, of course, not your Ameschester Hunt. We had invited some friends from Rocky Dell to visit and enjoy the Hunt. He is a very keen rider, but their local hunt has had some difficulties recently, and he jumped at the chance of riding with us. He brought his hunter, a big brute of a horse, not all that well trained. Anyway, the fox led the hunt through a rough ravine. Sensible people went around the hollow, keeping track of the hounds from the sound and counting on catching up with them before the kill. Unfortunately, Mr. Kinghorn, my guest, went straight ahead, relying on his horse to see him safe. Something went wrong, though no one saw exactly what happened, and he was thrown. That knocked Mr.Kinghorn unconscious, and he also broke his arm. I was nearby, so that was also the end of my hunting for the day.

"We brought Mr.Kinghorn back here. I told the stable boy to take the tack off the horses and put them in the paddock. I am afraid that I forgot all about the horses while dealing with Kinghorn's accident and getting a doctor to look after him and sending word to Mrs. Kinghorn, and so on.

"The paddock is next to some thick woods, and, without orders, the stable boy left the horses there. It was late in the afternoon before he returned to bring them in, and he discovered that, while Mr. Kinghorn's horse was still there, Dipton Thistle was gone. When I got the news, we went looking for the horse. Even if something had scared him into jumping the fence, I knew that he would not then wander off without returning. You trained him too well for him just to disappear, Mr. Griffiths.

"Hoof tracks in the area suggested that someone on horseback had opened the gate and led my horse out of the paddock and into the forest. It was getting late in the day, and when the trail we were following intersected a well-traveled road, we gave up as it was getting dark, and the hounds were having trouble picking up the scent. It was, of course, my own stupidity, leaving a valuable horse alone where it would be easy to steal him, but I never thought anyone would try to steal my hunter straight out of my paddock. It rather shakes one up when something like that happens, don't you know?

"I have been intending to come over to Dipton to talk about getting a replacement, but somehow I haven't had a chance to do so. I should get a new horse soon because our next hunt is coming up, and riding Dipton Thistle was much more exciting than being mounted on the horse I formerly used for hunting."

"You are welcome, Mr. Gossling, to visit Dipton Hall any time," Daphne said. "We did come over to learn what had happened to Dipton Thistle since Mr. Griffiths had spied the horse elsewhere, and we found it hard to believe that you had sold him. Some other information we had also did not fit that interpretation of his being at Wallingford, where Mr. Griffiths discovered the matter. I will let him take up the tale."

The stable master explained how he had seen Dipton Thistle while on business and had discovered that he had been sold by his original owner. "It surprised me because I know you were excited and pleased with your purchase, Mr. Gossling. But the new owner explained that he not only had a bill of sale for his purchase of the horse from the owner but also that he had been given the original bill of sale by Dipton Stables in case anyone disputed that the horse was a genuine Dipton Stables horse. This was now very strange, indeed, since when I saw the bill of sale, it looked like one of ours, except that the writing was not in my hand. It said just 'Richard Giles,' without any title, which is how Lord Camshire likes to sign documents, but he doesn't have such a flamboyant signature, which would make it easier to copy. Even stranger, the bill of sale claimed the name of the horse was Dipton Rover, which I know is a name we have never used.

"I've brought the document with me, for I gave the man who now owns your horse a substitute to say that the horse is indeed Dipton Thistle, though the man signing the bill of sale that had transferred ownership had not been the owner. The present owner of your horse was happy with that, for it did validate his ownership of the horse, even though it had been stolen. Our solicitor told us that when someone buys a horse in good faith from someone who he has good reason to believe owns the horse, such as a valid-looking bill of sale, the horse belongs to the buyer. It doesn't matter that it was actually stolen. Any restitution or penalty for the theft lies with the original thief, who may have produced fraudulent documents. The new owner does not have to give the horse back."

"Yes," said Mr. Gossling, "I already learned from my lawyer that it might be impossible to get my horse back, even if we could find him. Only if we could show that the final buyer knew that the horse was stolen and not owned by the seller could I hope to retrieve my horse if the thief had already sold the stallion. If I still wanted the horse, I would have to negotiate a price for him. But I am curious about how this false bill of sale compares to my genuine one. I was just looking at it yesterday to refresh my memory on the price I paid before visiting Dipton Stables again.

"Trent," he called to his butler, who must have been waiting just outside the door in case he was needed, "bring the gray folder which is on my desk."

When the folder arrived, Mr. Gossling took from it the bill of sale that showed that Dipton Thistle had been transferred from Dipton Stables to himself. It was clear that the paper used for the two documents was the same as were the printed contents. Only the blanks for the name of the horse, a brief description of it, and the price had been filled in with different content and in different handwriting, though the description was identically worded. It was also clear that the signatures were not the same.

"It is quite clear to me, since the documents are on identical pieces of printed paper, that we must be to blame in some way for what has happened to your horse,

Mr. Gossling," said Daphne. "We did nothing wrong that I can see, but somehow I feel that we bear some responsibility for your loss. We should definitely make it up to you in some way. I suggest that you visit Dipton Hall and choose a new hunter, which we will sell to you for half the price we would normally charge.

"You will want to try the horse, of course, or several of them, before making up your mind. I suggest that you and Mrs. Gossling visit Dipton Hall when the Ameschester Hunt next has a meeting. You can see our horses and try one out in a real hunt before making up your mind.

"Do you ride to hounds, Mrs. Gossling?" Daphne asked.

"I am afraid not, my lady," replied their hostess. "I occasionally follow along with some other women and some of the less active men, but I don't do it frequently, and certainly, it involves nothing adventuresome for me. My old riding mare is good enough for me, though I don't think I have ever seen her jump a hedge."

"You will be more than welcome to borrow one of our horses if you don't want to bring your own. My niece-in-law, Mrs. Bolton, often follows the hunt's progress while keeping to the roads and tracks, but she never rides cross-country. I am sure that she will be happy to introduce you to others who follow the hunt more safely."

"Oh, Mr. Gossling, please say that we can accept this gracious invitation," their hostess responded. He nodded his agreement.

Without waiting for further discussion, Daphne declared, "That's settled! I will look forward to your visit. I'll drop you a note when we get home about the dates.

"Now, gentlemen, we must bid goodbye to our hosts if we want to get home this evening. Thank you so much for your hospitality, Mrs. Gossling."

Daphne, followed by the two men who accompanied her, swept out of the sitting room, leaving Mr. and Mrs. Gossling to absorb how substantially their plans had been changed because of the unexpected visit.

The visitors had spent much more time at Summit Manor than they had intended, which, together with their break at the inn, had meant that it would be impossible to get home before dark. Soon after their arrival at Summit Manor, dark rain clouds had moved in, and it promised to be a dark, wet night, so they wanted to get home as soon as possible. Trent was rushed to make sure that their horses were ready and that servants were present to help the visitors into their outer clothes. However, they were mounted and rode away very soon.

"Your offer was an unexpected development, Lady Camshire," Mr. Griffiths said as the horses settled into a steady miles-devouring gait. "Both the offer of a reduced price for Mr. Gossling's new hunter and the invitation to visit Dipton Manor."

"Yes, I suppose it was a spur-of-the-moment decision, but the more we talked about the situation, the more I realized how these thefts could do real harm to our business if they are not countered by strong responses. My concern is not just this one theft; it is the reports that there may be others that we have yet to find time to investigate. Even if we do not know about them, other people may hear that Dipton hunters are being singled out for stealing and may avoid buying our horses because of the theft problem.

"I am, indeed, starting to wonder if that raid on our horses was actually made by gypsies. It is not like them to go into such an elaborate scheme as selling the stolen horses with apparently valid certificates of ownership. Steal when the opportunity presents itself, that's what I have always heard about gypsies, and this is something quite different. I have also never heard of them using guns when people try to get them to move on, though I guess that we did more than that. Still, if they were gypsies, I would expect them to flee rather than to try to protect their loot.

"The more I think about it, the more I believe that it is possible that the gang stealing our horses just happened to stop for the night in that clearing where gypsies may have been camping already. The fact that the gypsies gathered up their camp and took off when we showed up does not indicate that they were part of the theft. After that gun was fired, I would expect any bystanders to leave as fast as they could, even if they had nothing to do with the theft. If it is a gang and not gypsies who wander about haphazardly, they may try again in the future.

"It won't do us any good to have it known that buying one of our horses puts the buyer at hazard of having the creature stolen even though there is proper documentation. Taking action to counter losses that occur because people have had horses stolen because they are particularly good ones will help us sell at prices that match all the work that goes into breeding and training superior hunters. What I offered the Gosslings will help that endeavor, for I am sure they will tell others about it.

"Besides that, I rather liked both Gosslings and would be happy to have them as friends even if no horses were involved."

The three companions rode on, chatting about hunting and what was happening around Dipton, Daphne's canal-boat interest, with which Major Stoner was involved, and the implications of Daphne's brother's death. The rain started as the daylight dimmed, and it was evident that there would be no moon to light their way. They were getting close to the Major's estate, and he broke into a discussion about ponies to suggest that the others spend the night at his house. The others welcomed his invitation. They knew they would be welcomed warmly, despite the lateness of the hour, and entertained royally. Soon the group of friends was riding up the Major's drive.

Lady Marianne, Daphne's half-sister-in-law and Major Stoner's wife, had spent years in Army camps trying to balance insufficient resources with her first husband's haphazard and irresponsible spending habits. When she married Major Stoner, she realized that they would both be happier if she always made sure that last-minute guests could be accommodated and that she now had the money and servants to do so easily. Being already for visitors meant that she could happily enjoy not having the lonely evening which she would suffer if the Major had gone on to stay at Dipton Hall as he sometimes did. That evening would now be enlivened by her husband, her sister-in-law, and Mr. Griffiths without Lady Marianne worrying about what to serve them or whether there was enough wine. Somehow, her time in army barracks and with Major Stoner had taught her to value people of inferior status, such as Mr. Griffiths, for how interesting they were rather than for their position in society. Not to mention that someone worthy of attention by a countess was certainly to be more than tolerated by the wife of a former Indian Army Major, even if she was also an earl's daughter. Lady Marianne sat back as the dinner conversation about stolen horses continued, content that her dinner was more than sufficiently elaborate for a countess, even if her sister-in-law was not particularly fussy about such things.

Listening to the conversation about the horse thefts made Lady Marianne realize that the others seemed to be missing the obvious. "Where do these bills of sale come from, and who fills them out?" she asked in a lull of the conversation.

"They are printed at a printing shop in Ameschester. They have quite a bit of engraving on them, particularly the Camshhire coat of arms, so it would not be easy to replicate them," said Mr. Griffiths.

"Did the print shop do the printing while you waited?"

"No. The people there couldn't do the job right away – they had to first make the plate for the engraving following our sketch and then run off the copies."

"Did you get the plate back when they were finished?"

"I don't think so. I think we left it with the printer for the next time we needed more copies of the document. We only printed twenty-five. Lord Camshire wasn't sure that they would make much of a difference to the reception of our horses and thought that it would suffice just to write out a bill of sale when one of our horses was sold. Why do you ask, Lady Stoner?"

"Listening to you, I wondered where the thieves got the form they used, which must have made it much easier to sell the stolen horse at a high price. That made me wonder where you got the forms in the first place. Knowing that might lead you to what has gone wrong."

"By Jove!" burst out Major Stoner. "I think you are on to something, old girl! Yes, that is very perceptive of you! Very perceptive!"

"Yes, I think you have taken us the next step, my lady," agreed Mr. Griffiths. "I don't know how I have missed the question of how the form for the false bill of sale was obtained. We will have to look into the printing shop being linked to the thieves."

"True," said Daphne, "but Marianne's insight suggests we also look closer to home."

"What do you have in mind, my lady?" Mr. Griffiths asked in a tone of voice that indicated that he had guessed what Daphne was about to say and was not happy about it.

"I was thinking about how the false bill of sale had the description of the horse's hunting skills right. That suggests that at least one of the culprits has close knowledge of our horses as well as having access to the printed papers."

"That thought is very alarming, my lady. But I hate to think that anyone in our stables is involved in the thefts."

"I hope not, Mr. Griffiths, but we must consider the possibility," Daphne replied. "Now, we have had a long day and an excellent dinner to complete it, thanks to your hospitality, Marianne," said Daphne, suppressing a yawn. "I think a good night's sleep will allow us to better assess how to deal with the situation in the morning.

The travelers headed for their bedrooms without even considering passing some time in the drawing room. Lady Marianne might have liked to prolong the time with the guests, but she could see that the Major was tired. He wouldn't admit it, but he was no longer the tireless young man who won his rank in India by hard work, not by purchasing his commission using funds his family provided, and had made his fortune the same way. However, though they did not dawdle before retiring, none of them fell asleep at once.

Mr. Griffiths reflected on the day, especially on what had emerged at dinner. He was getting old and had to think about what would happen if he were dismissed. The position at Dipton stables was better than any others he could aspire to. Daphne and Giles were good employers, very good ones, indeed. They were encouraging, sympathetic with difficulties when they arose, and willing to do their part to clear them up. They included him in possible plans to improve the enterprise. But he knew that owners could be capricious. After all, he only got his present position by the unanticipated event that Lady Giles needed a riding horse just when Captain Giles was thinking of getting into the horse-raising business. But he also wouldn't have got the position if he hadn't had that excellent mare ready for selling just when Lady Giles came looking. If he lost this position, he would have trouble finding another one at his age. He realized that he had not been careful enough when he had the income to make sure that he and his wife would be comfortable if he was out of a position and a home. He knew that the theft from Dipton's fields would have been reason enough for dismissal with many masters. While that had not happened, Lady Giles was still distressed by what had happened and was unhappy about the possibility of the theft being repeated. Lord Camshire worried that it could happen again when he was not home, feeling that the safety of his home was his responsibility. And now, the other thefts of Dipton-raised horses might be traced back to his stables. Could they solve the problem, and would the solution show that he was not at fault? Furthermore, if they couldn't find the source of the problem, would it convince Lord and Lady Camshire that they would be happier if they did not have a breeding stable when such a thing could happen again? There was nothing he could do about any of it by thinking about the problems over and over again that night. Still, that consideration did not prevent Mr. Griffiths from going over the situation again and again until he finally fell asleep.

Daphne's sleeplessness was more straightforward. She had asked for some paper from Lady Marianne to continue her series of letters to Giles, which she wrote every evening no matter what had happened during the day. Her dilemma was how to explain the conundrum she faced over the horse thefts without making him conclude that he had made a mistake leaving her to deal with the matter, even though they had not known that it was on the horizon. She had to choose her words delicately, for emphasizing the difficulties too strongly would make him conclude that running the estates was too complicated to expect her to do it by herself while minimizing the situation opened the possibility that he might think that she was not giving a serious situation enough attention. Adopting the right tone was difficult because she knew that Giles was more than half tempted to give up the Navy. She wanted that, but only if he could do it without regret or blame his family commitments for preventing him from doing his duty to the country and his ship's crew. Of course, it was not the first time she had faced this problem, nor would it be the last if he continued to believe in the importance of the contributions he could make. Still, it took time to make the careful writing of the letter look easy while recognizing that her problems were not frivolous. In the end, she just gave up trying to think of how she framed her sentences and wrote as she felt. That still took time, but she knew that Giles would give her a favorable interpretation if anything wasn't quite right.

Major Stoner was awake for quite a different reason. He was pleased with life. He had been lucky to marry Lady Marianne, a wedding of convenience that, for him, would raise his status and, for her, would take her out from dependence on her much younger sister-in-law. To their surprise, they found they were compatible, so compatible that they occupied the same bed even though intense passion was not something that they enjoyed together. However, the major remembered with delight how Daphne had accepted him as the suitable candidate for the presidency of the hunt, indicating, without saying it, that she regarded him as of as high status as any of the more established men who had tended to treat him as an inferior newcomer. He also took pleasure remembering how he had held his own in discussions of the affairs of Daphne's horse farm. He realized that he was now fully accepted as a member of the landed gentry, as indicated by the respect shown to him by the Gosslings. These thoughts kept the Major from his well-earned sleep.

Lady Marianne realized for the first time that she was proud of her husband and not embarrassed at having to settle for someone beneath her. She wanted to savor her contentment as she snuggled against him. When they drifted off to sleep, sharing the warmth of the bed as the fire diminished to ashes, she had no pressing concerns about the following day, unlike the others.

Chapter XVIII

Glaucus was cleared for action before the first hint of daylight appeared, as she always was when at sea. The anchored frigate pointed straight at the middle of the bay on the little island with a slight current holding her in place, for there was not a breath of wind. *Freedom* was similarly anchored off *Glaucus*'s larboard quarter. Their night had been tranquil, undisturbed by wind, rain, or other ships.

When it was light enough to see the shore of the little island clearly, Giles called for his barge and, with Midshipman Jenks, went ashore. They landed on a shingle beach that sloped up to a well-defined low bank. Giles and Midshipman Jenks, equipped only with telescopes and signal flags, set off to climb to the top of the hill that occupied the island. From the beach, they scrambled up the low bank that marked the highest place where storm waves had eroded the shore. There they found a barren field with some small clumps of gorse. They set off, heading straight towards the top of the hill, for there were no well-worn paths to guide them to an easier route. As they advanced, the hill became steeper and the gorse denser. Before long, they reached the first of the stunted Scotch pines that had seemed to define the island from a distance. As they continued to climb, the trees became denser while the gorse petered out so that they walked on a cushion of pine needles as they approached the summit.

The trees at the top of the island were stunted and twisted but provided adequate cover so that they would not stand out on the skyline if anyone was looking. Even so, they lay down on their bellies, but a careful survey of the scene in front of them suggested that the precaution might be unnecessary. There was no sign of life along the shore of Pendrag Island, and there was no ship in sight. The shoreline across from them was a low bluff that looked like it was part of a long ridge that protected the land immediately behind it from the worst of the winter storms. As a result of this barrier, they could see nothing of what lay farther inland, including the fields where the rebel forces were supposed to gather.

A fog bank to the northwest hid everything at sea more than a league away. There was a light breeze from that direction, just enough to ripple the ocean's surface but not enough that it was likely to break up the fogbank; the wind was more likely to move the fog toward Giles's lookout position.

Giles and Midshipman Jenks settled down to watch the area in front of them to see if there would be any change, but the morning wore on with no sign of life on either the shore or the sea. Giles was about to go back to *Glaucus*, leaving Midshipman Jenks to watch for any developments, when he noticed that the fog bank to the north was beginning to break up, with misty gaps appearing and then melting away. Emerging from the fog, first as a ghostly suggestion and then as a definite presence, was a frigate. She had set all sails to the royals, but the ship was moving very slowly. Somehow, the fog bank was not crossing some invisible line in the ocean but instead broke up there while the ship kept coming towards them.

The frigate looked British to Giles, a guess that was contradicted when an errant gust of wind spread her dangling flag for a minute or two. The French flag's broad red, white, and blue bands were unmistakable. Giles presumed that the ship must have something to do with the planned insurrection, but she was certainly much more powerful than a brig of war, stronger, indeed, than two brigs. The French plan, he had been told in London, called for two brigs; maybe the frigate had taken their place. If so, it was bad news. It was much easier to beat two brigs than one frigate.

Giles trained his telescope on the French ship. Near the wheel, there was a small cluster of four officers. Two of them, he guessed, were the officers of the watch of the frigate. They were dressed better than the ordinary crewmen scattered about the deck engaged in various tasks. The third officer was in a much more elaborate uniform. He was wearing a blue frock coat and britches rather than trousers. All he lacked was a sword to make it clear that he was the vessel's captain. The fourth man looked like he must be a high-ranking army officer. His uniform had an unmistakably French military flair.

Giles focused his telescope on the bow of the French frigate. As he expected, there was a sailor with a leadline taking soundings. That made it clear that the ship was deliberately approaching Pendrag Island, probably with the intention of anchoring.

"Captain," said Midshipman Jenks, his voice breaking in excitement, "there is another frigate emerging from the fog.

Giles changed where he was pointing his telescope. Yes, there could be no doubt about it. It was another frigate. She looked familiar. Surveying her through his telescope, Giles realized that she was the frigate he had seen in the Mersey a few days ago. Yes, certainly, the ship was Captain Blenkinsop's *Cicero*. What she was doing here was revealed when he focused on *Cicero*'s masthead. There the Union Jack flew beneath the three broad stripes of the French flag. Somehow, Captain Blenkinsop's frigate had been captured by the French — and Giles could see no evidence of a fierce fight on either ship, which one would expect if she had been taken by the enemy in a fight.

The breeze was dropping farther, and the lead frigate seemed to be losing steerage way though the current was still carrying her along the shore of Pendrag Island. A scurry of activity on the foredeck of the French frigate accompanied by a hoist of flags, presumably directed at *Cicero,* marked the moment when the sails flapping indicated to the captain of the French frigate that his ship was no longer under control. Down splashed the anchor, and Giles could see the anchor cable slide out through the hawse hole until it was cleated off so that the frigate stopped and swung to face the current. Training his compass on *Cicero*, Giles watched as she soon followed suit, anchoring a hundred and fifty feet to the northwest of the French ship.

Giles glanced back at *Glaucus*. She and *Freedom* were anchored with their reflections stretched out on still water that had not a single ripple. The ships were held in place by the current that must be pulling at them without revealing its existence to the casual observer. Lovely as the picture was, it troubled Giles. He was supposed to appear from behind the little island and descend on the French ships when they were involved in landing their army passengers and gear on Pendrag Island. Now was the time when *Glaucus* should be getting ready to fall on her prey. Instead, she was helpless. If she raised her anchor, she would drift helplessly away from where the French frigate was anchored, and she would have no effect on the outcome of the French landing. This failure would have been particularly serious if the French had brought more troops than the London planners had expected. There had been many French soldiers lounging on *Cicero*'s deck as well as on the French frigate's. Was Cicero's being used to transport French soldiers indicative that they had brought a larger force than expected by the British? Then, without *Glaucus*'s decisive intervention, the planned snuffing out of the Jacobite uprising would prove much more costly than expected. Indeed, the invasion might succeed because *Glaucus* was becalmed. If she could not interfere effectively, stopping the rebellion could become very costly. Surely there was something Giles could do. There was no point in his watching from the top of the little island when the information he gathered could not be used.

Giles told Midshipman Jenks to inform him by flag signals if the situation changed materially and left the lookout to return to *Glaucus*, being careful to avoid being seen if, at that moment, someone on the French frigates was looking at the summit of the little island. He quickly made his way back to the beach where his launch was beached and was rowed to *Glaucus*. He didn't board his frigate but ordered all the senior officers, including the master, to join him on *Freedom*. Once all the officers were assembled on *Freedom*'s quarter deck, Giles called Dixon to join them.

"There is a French frigate anchored off Pendrag Island," Giles announced. "She has a captured British frigate with her — our old antagonist *Cicero*. The French are about to land troops and, probably, military supplies to further a rebellion among the Scots to the detriment of our efforts against the French.

"Our mission, as some of you know, is to interfere in that operation and capture the French ship. While we were expecting only two brigs of war and not frigates, we still have to intervene in their activities. The problem we face is that with the lack of wind and the current setting away from Pendrag Island, we cannot reach the French ships to interfere with their scheme. At least, we cannot use *Glaucus* since she is becalmed. But we might row *Freedom* to attack her.

"Now, the question is whether we have the ability to do so. As you know, we have been using the slave drivers to try rowing her. That has been a rather mixed success. The question is, 'do you think that we could row her against the current to reach our target?' Luckily, she has not rigged a spring on her anchor line, so we can approach from the stern and take her by boarding without facing her broadside guns. Once most of her crew and the soldiers currently aboard her have gone to Pendrag Island, we should have no problem capturing her if we can reach her.

"Dixon, you know the most about rowing this ship. What is your opinion?"

"Well, sir, I doubt we could get any distance rowing with these men at the oars, especially not against the current. There are two problems, sir. First, our new rowers have yet to learn how to manage the oars as an effective team. We have already seen what a mess we get into when one of the oars catches a crab. Second, these men are not used to hard labor; they will tire easily and probably collapse if their mistakes do not stop us first. With the current, sir, we can't let up or row very slowly if we want to get anywhere."

"Could we use our regular crew members to row, especially those who have experience rowing our boats?" asked Giles

"That would be better, sir," replied Dixon, "but becoming effective at rowing a galley is a lengthy process. The teamwork needed to handle the long oars takes a while to learn, even when a new rower is introduced into an existing team. It would take a lot longer if everyone was inexperienced. While it might be possible for your men to learn to row the ship, it would not be possible to do so in the next few days."

"So, Dixon, are you telling me that we can't move *Freedom* under oars."

"Yes, I suppose so, sir, not in the way you were suggesting, but let me talk to the other former rowers; they might have some ideas."

Dixon took the group of former galley slaves to one side, where he must have explained the situation to them. Heated discussion ensued. 'What could they be arguing about?' Giles wondered. He didn't have long to wait to find out. The discussion broke up, and Dixon returned to the group of officers.

"We've discussed the situation among ourselves, sir," he began. "You have been more than fair to us, and most of us figure that we should help you because, otherwise, things might become a lot worse. We were talking about doing the rowing for you. Most are willing, but a small group refuses ever to have anything to do with rowing: too many bad memories of being whipped and beaten while chained to the oars. I can understand them, sir, and trying to force them would be a bad idea. One angry oarsman can completely interrupt the smooth rowing of this ship."

"So, you can't solve our problem for us?"

"No, sir, that is not what I meant. The rest of us are willing to take the oars, though we can't make the ship go as fast as it would if everyone were pulling. But we could still make more than enough progress to overcome the current quite easily."

"Would it help if some of the seamen rowed with you?"

"Not really, sir. The problem with inexperienced rowers would remain. We do have some experience rowing with reduced crews."

"All right, Dixon. Tell your men I am very grateful for your offer and will accept it. Of course, first, we must get ready before raising anchor to attack."

Giles issued a string of orders about moving all the Irishmen to *Glaucus* and bringing her crew and marines to *Freedom*. Though it was early in the day, he also ordered that everyone be fed. He then took his barge back to the little unnamed island.

Midshipman Jenks welcomed Giles to their lookout with the news that the French seemed ready to start landing the troops. All the boats were alongside the two frigates, and many soldiers with their gear had been mustered on deck, presumably in anticipation of boarding the boats. Furthermore, even as they watched, a piece of field artillery had been hauled from the French ship's hold and was being lowered into one of the boats. The French intentions seemed much more threatening than Giles had expected from his conversations in London about the Jacobite scheme. There had been no mention of French artillery on that occasion.

"I wonder how many guns they have with them," Giles wondered out loud. "Originally, I intended to let the French all get ashore, but if there are many more of those guns, I should interfere with their activities sooner.

"Mr. Jenks, keep watch here, and when that boat with the gun is near the beach, signal to *Freedom*. Then come down and have yourself rowed to *Freedom* rather than *Glaucus*.. I'll leave the jolly-boat at the beach for you."

It took a while before Midshipman Jenks was ready to go to *Freedom*. During that time, Giles's crew had been busy. They shifted all the passengers to *Glaucus* while *Glaucus*'s seamen and marines, except for an extended harbor watch to take care of the Irish visitors, crossed to *Freedom* with their weapons. The capstan was readied so that there would be no wasted time raising the anchor. Giles had considered buoying it to make for an easier departure but then reflected that he was unlikely to want to bring the xebec back to their present anchorage. The order was given to raise the hook before Midshipman Jenks reached the entry port and had a chance to report.

When the anchor was aweigh, the oars were unshipped, and the rowers prepared for their first stroke. The skill of the rowing crew was evident as, with a minimum of shouting from Dixon, the larboard oars pulled while the starboard ones backed water. Mr. Brooks, who had the helm, waited until the bow pointed beyond the headland, defining the south end of the east side of the little island. "Pull both," the Master ordered, using the commands that he had agreed upon with Dixon. It was new territory for both of them. The xebec gathered way rapidly, as fast as if she had sheeted home her sails in a stiff breeze. Dixon shouted out the stroke, and in keeping with his calls, the oars on both sides rose, moved forward, fell into the water simultaneously, were drawn back in harmony, and then rose again for another stroke. The rowing was a little ragged at first, but then it smoothed out, and the xebec surged ahead. Dixon called out the stroke, and the ship slid through the water faster than she would have in a fresh breeze. Reaching the eastern corner of the little island, Mr. Brooks put the helm over. The larboard oars were held clear of the water for the next few strokes, and *Freedom* changed direction much more easily and quickly than if she had been under sail.

Now the French frigate was straight ahead. It appeared that most of her boats were on Pendrag Island or close to it, still heavily laden. There were also many people, both soldiers and sailors, on the beach already, presumably taken there in earlier trips. They did not seem to have spread out yet, and it looked as if they might be waiting for all the troops to be ashore before moving inland. It was an ideal situation for the British. At the speed she was going, *Freedom* would reach the French frigate long before any of her boats could return, even if they turned around now. Better yet, it did not seem that anyone on the frigate, or in her boats, or on land had yet spotted the approaching ship. Giles couldn't be happier. The xebec was advancing rapidly on the French frigate, much of whose crew must be on shore.

Freedom kept charging ahead. She was only a few yards off the French ship's quarter when a cry indicated that someone on the French frigate had seen her. It came too late to matter. At a prearranged cry from Mr. Brooks, the starboard oars were shipped before they could be splintered by crashing into the French frigate. The larboard oars backed water to slow the xebec. *Freedom* slid smoothly along the French frigate's quarterdeck. Grappling lines were thrown and pulled tight, and *Glaucus*'s seamen and marines surged across to the enemy.

The French, caught completely by surprise, raised their hands in surrender. A young officer, possibly the only one still aboard, shouted, "Je me rends, monsieur le capitaine."

Giles wasted no time rounding up the few French sailors on board. Looking at *Cicero,* there were fewer French seamen on her than were on the French frigate. Of course, the French would have some crew members aboard their prize to prevent *Cicero*'s crew from retaking her. While it was common for officers to give their parole, the crew and the petty officers were usually bound by no such constraints because they were presumed not to be gentlemen who would keep their word. As a result, they could be ready to retake their ship if an opportunity occurred, and guards would be needed to prevent that outcome.

Giles left a quarter of his seamen on board the French frigate and set off for *Cicero,* with Dixon again calling the stroke for the volunteer rowers. Giles would not have been surprised if the French made a serious attempt to repel his men boarding their prize, but no effort was made. The very young officer who had been left in charge while *Cicero*'s boats were landing her share of the French soldiers realized that resistance would be futile. He surrendered as soon as grappling hooks were thrown from *Freedom.* Giles wasted no time having the marines round up the small French crew. Next, he released *Cicero*'s crew. They who had been confined to the fo'c'sle. Giles replaced them with the Frenchmen he had just captured. He found *Cicero*'s officers, except for her captain, in the wardroom, where they had been confined while the invasion of Pendrag Island was underway.

"I am Captain Richard Giles of *Glaucus*. Who is senior among you?" Giles asked when he found the officers.

"I am, sir," one of them replied. "George Lester, First Lieutenant of *Cicero*. The others here are the rest of her officers, with the exception, of course, of Captain Blenkinsop."

"Have you given your paroles to the French?"

"No, my lord. Our capture was so shameful that we did not think we should promise not to continue fighting the French if we had the chance."

"Glad to hear it. I see that Mr. Lester has recognized my name, but I only use my title on land. At sea, I am simply 'Captain Giles.' There will, of course, be a court marshall about how this ship was captured, but that is a matter for another day. You can all resume your positions. Where is Captain Blenkinsop?"

"Confined to his cabin, I expect, sir. He did give his parole," replied Lieutenant Lester.

"I suppose that I had better see him now. Assemble on the quarterdeck, please, and I will give you orders for what I expect from *Cicero* now that she is in the right hands. You can assume command of this ship, Mr. Lester, since Captain Blenkinsop cannot continue in that role because he gave the French his parole."

Giles took Mr. Macauley, whose marines were busy replacing in confinement the captured crew of *Cicero* with the newly defeated French crew, with him to the captain's cabin. He found Blenkinsop sitting in an armchair near the stern windows, looking quite content with his lot.

"Captain Blenkinsop," Giles began. "You will be glad to know that your ship has been retaken from the French."

"I guessed as much, Captain Giles. You certainly took your time coming to our aid. Now that you are here, I shall resume command. We have no further need of your assistance."

Giles was taken aback by this declaration. He had trouble believing that Blenkinsop did not realize how serious was his position.

"Captain Blenkinsop, that will not happen. You don't seem to realize what the situation is that you find yourself in. I understand that you gave your parole to the French Captain."

"Yes, of course I did. It is a mere formality, of course, of no consequence."

"I do not agree. In fact, I am horrified that a captain of His Majesty's Navy could make such a statement. You promised not to fight with the French until the terms of your parole were met, probably that you were exchanged for French prisoners. While it is true that your ship and you, yourself, are now in British hands, you are still bound by your oath given to the enemy. Until you are formally exchanged, you cannot participate in the activities of this ship which is again engaged in war with France.

"Furthermore, you must face a court marshall over your loss of your ship. Since there is no evidence that *Cicero* has been in battle with the French ship, that will not be a formality, I can assure you. I presume that the court will hang you, and in view of that, I place you under arrest and will take you to my frigate, *Glaucus*, to await trial when we return to port.

"Mr. Macauley, place Captain Blenkinsop under arrest. When we return to *Glaucus*, arrange for my cabin to be divided into two, and place Captain Blenkinsop in the smaller one with a marine guard posted at the door. Confine him to this cabin, again with a marine at the door, until *Glaucus* joins us and we can move him."

"Damn you, Giles!" shouted Blenkinsop, "you can't do this."

"Oh, yes, I can. And if you don't cooperate, I'll have you thrown in irons until we reach Portsmouth!" Giles replied. "Now I have to deal with stopping the French."

On deck, Giles took little time instructing Mr. Lester and the other officers about preparing for an anticipated French attempt to retake the frigate, for which they would need to clear for action and be ready to use the broadside guns to counter any concerted attempts to attack them.

Giles returned to the captured French frigate, noticing as they approached her stern that she was called *Dordogne*. On board, he found that Mr. Macreau had everything under control and had prepared the starboard guns to fire.

"They are loaded with round shot right now, sir," he reported to Giles, "in case the French appear to want to use their boats to recapture their ship."

"Very good," replied Giles. "Have grape shot ready in case they press home any attack. The real danger may come after it is fully dark. This is when I would assemble all the boats to try to retake this frigate, or maybe *Cicero,* if I were in charge of the French operation."

"Now, I will go aloft to take a look over that ridge to see what the French are up to."

Giles climbed the mainmast of *Dordogne.* There was a large number of French sailors on the beach, with most of them lounging about while waiting for their officers to decide what to do. The French soldiers were no longer milling about. Their officers must have decided that there was nothing they could do about the naval fiasco that had unfolded, and their troops were forming into columns. Clearly, they intended to march across the ridge onto the flat land that lay beyond. That must be where they were to meet up with the Scottish renegades.

Looking beyond the coastal ridge, Giles could see some groups of men scattered in places where the gorse had been cut back or failed to grow. These men must be the rebels who were supposed to meet here. This part of the plot must be going well as more and more small groups filtered onto the flatter land from the north. The men all wore skirts — what were they called? — kilts, that was it. The kilts came down to their knees and were made of heavy cloth with a geometric pattern. All the kilts had the same pattern and colors. The men wearing them looked like the caricatures of Scotsmen that sometimes appeared in the newspapers. Each carried a large, curved sword, and many had muskets slung over their backs. From how they walked in uncoordinated groups, it was obvious that they were not some trained military brigade. Still, if the groups all came together, they could already make a formidable force, and there was as yet no end to the groups appearing.

Giles would like to bring *Glaucus* to join the other three ships off Pendrake Island, but he could not ask his volunteer rowers to tow her with *Freedom*, and he could hardly expect *Glaucus*'s boats to tow her against the current. He looked towards the little island behind which his ship was hiding. Focussing his telescope on the peak, Giles spotted where he and Midshipman Jenks had kept watch that morning. Now he could see no signs of life there. The trees, so stunted and bent by winds, showed no sign of any wind now, but then Scotch pines would not respond to light airs. Turning his telescope on the water around the island, nowhere could he see the ruffles that might signal that the air was moving in preparation for the wind to blow. Like it or not, *Glaucus* would have to remain at anchor for the time being. In fact, with the day fast fading, she would have to wait until morning to join the rest of his small fleet. Surely at this time of year, the winds could not remain calm for more than one day. In fact, he was amazed at the day they had just experienced. In thinking of this voyage, he had been more worried that it would be impossible to get anywhere near the coast of Pendrag Island because of storm waves and had wondered why the plan hadn't called for landing on the island's eastern side rather than on its western coast.

Looking at the horizon all around, Giles could see what looked like the top of clouds to the south-southeast. That was the direction from which the prevailing winter wind along this coast came, he had been told, and it was only a westerly storm that would be disastrous to the planned French landings.

There was nothing he could do about how unperceptive he had been about the obvious difficulties of the mission. Like it or not, he had three ships exposed to the weather on the westerly side of Pendrake Island. He could, of course, have his vessels stand out to sea in anticipation of a storm, but he would have a hard time justifying such a decision, even to himself, if it stayed calm for the night.

Giles came down from the masthead, having decided on the orders to give. First, the jolly-boat should return to *Glaucus* with a message to stay where she was until morning and to take precautions against a storm in the night from the southeast. He ordered three ships anchored close to the coast to prepare for a strong wind that might require them to let go another anchor to reduce the danger that the ones they were presently using might start to drag. But in the expectation that the storm might not arrive before the French ventured from the shore, he ordered all the starboard guns to be loaded with round shot and have grapeshot, as well as round shot, available for subsequent broadsides aimed at any approaching boats.

With the orders all given, Giles could relax or, at least, pretend to. He went to the French captain's cabin and ordered that some food be prepared using the cabin supplies the French captain had brought along on the voyage and that a bottle of wine from the same source be opened.

The sun had set before the table was laid. Giles asked Mr. Macreau to join him as they waited for information about boats approaching. The time dragged on. Both had thoughts about what might happen during the night, but neither had any thoughts worth sharing. A bright moon was illuminating the water between their frigate and the shore so, at present, the French could not get close to them without being seen. Later in the night would be the real danger when the moon had set, and only faint star shine would allow them to see approaching boats, but there were enough sharp-eyed members of the crew that they should be safe from surprise. Except things would be a lot trickier if it clouded over.

The dreaded message came at four bells of the first watch. A ship's boy, whose voice was just changing, announced, "Mr. Jenks says that clouds are moving in from the southeast," with the last word coming out as a squeak.

"Very good, lad," replied Giles. "We'll come on deck."

On deck, Giles discovered that a brisk southeast breeze had sprung up, just the one to produce an uncomfortable night in *Glaucus*'s safe harbor. The wind had enough east in it that it only produced a mild chop where Giles's three ships were anchored, not enough to make the frigates' decks unstable, so conditions were still ideal for the broadside guns to hit whatever they aimed at. However, billowing clouds were moving in with the wind. Right now, the water between the ships and the shore was nicely illuminated by the moon, but very soon, the moonlight would be extinguished by the moving clouds.

"Mr. Richardson," Giles ordered the only midshipman he had kept with him on *Dordogne*, "prepare to fire our flares when ordered. Only one at a time, followed by others one at a time and not too quickly since we have only a limited supply. It may be a long night — if I were in command of the French forces, I would make several false attacks to get us to waste our flares and then attack in earnest when we can no longer see."

"Aye, aye, sir — but —"

'What is it?" Giles demanded irritably since midshipmen did not say 'but' to captains.

"On Mr. Marceau's orders, sir, I searched this ship's magazine to see how much powder and shot we had acquired. The French kept the flares in the magazine, and I found several dozen. Their flares look like ours, sir, and I think that they would work in the same way. If we use them, we would not have to limit how many we fire when we think we need them."

"Very enterprising of you, Mr. Richardson. We will wait for the time when we need flares and then try one of theirs, followed by one of ours. If their one works, you can continue to use them but remember that they may try to get us to fire all our flares before they make their determined attempt to board us. Space them out."

It was now pitch dark. Giles ordered the crewmen to take up their stations, ready for an attack by boat from the starboard side, and then extinguish all lamps or shutter them so that no light would be visible from the starboard side where the attack would come. When all was set, *Dordogne* went quiet. As the clouds thickened, what little light was still coming from the moon disappeared. Looking to the west, Giles could just make out the horizon and a bright strip between it and the clouds. If he could see that, *Dordogne*'s outline would be clear to anyone in a boat approaching his ships from the east. In whispers, he warned his crew that the attack might come soon.

Giles remembered that, in this area, motion in the water, even if not visible or audible, usually left trails of phosphorescence. He went along the line of guns, warning each gunner to watch the water where his gun was pointed and to fire if he saw any significant lights dancing in it. Then he could think of nothing else to do in preparation and settled down where he would have a good view of the water close to the ship on the starboard side.

Would it be a long wait or a short wait? Giles didn't know. But he was sure the attack would come sometime in the darkness. He could not imagine that the French commander would be happy to engage in a very problematic invasion of Scotland without a means of escape if things went wrong. That meant, by Giles reckoning, that they would bring soldiers in the boats they had used for landing to try to recapture their frigate and the other ships too.

Waiting for an enemy to respond is always nerve-wracking. Giles was not a patient man, so for him, it promised to be an unpleasant and anxious time.

Chapter XIX

The attack came at seven bells of the second watch. Giles discovered it because he had reminded himself that late in a watch, on a dark night, was the time sailors were most likely to be drowsy and inattentive. That was when he would have attacked if he were trying to capture anchored ships using a small number of boats. Giles, of course, was not the only man on the captured frigate keeping watch on the sea between *Dordogne* and the land; even so, Giles had gone around warning everyone to be particularly alert. It paid off as he was returning to his post.

"Sir," said one of the midship gunners. "I think I see a hint of movement out there."

Giles examined the indicated bit of water. At first, he could see nothing. Then he saw little sets of sparkles in the water. Could they be made by oars dipping into the sea while rowing a boat? 'Better to be safe than sorry,' he thought.

"Mr. Jenks," Giles said quietly. "Fire a flare."

The flare rose into the air, leaving a trail of sparks, and then burst, illuminating the area to the starboard of *Dordogne* with light. There they were, clear as day! The French were attacking with eight boats, possibly all they had available to mount the attack.

"Adjust your aim," Giles bellowed. "Fire when you bear."

All of *Dordogne*'s broadside guns roared out simultaneously. Three of the advancing boats were struck directly, and a fourth looked like it might be swamped. *Dordogne* reacted to the explosions by being rocked to larboard; then, she swung back again.

"Load with grapeshot," Giles ordered. "Fire as you bear."

The next volley was more ragged as some targets were rowing to shore as fast s they could, and the gun's aim had to be adjusted, while others were still wallowing where they had been hit and could be fired at as soon as the ship's recoil faded.

"Mr. Macreau, Mr. Macauley," Giles ordered, "take our boats to rescue as many as you can and capture any seaworthy boats out there."

The order was expected, and within moments the three boats that Giles had brought from *Glaucus* started to search the sea.

"Keep sending up flares to illuminate the area until our boats are finished," Giles told Midshipman Jenks.

Only three of the attacking boats were now rowing towards the shore, and, in one of them, the ragged way in which she was being rowed suggested that the guns had done significant damage even though she was mobile enough to be getting away.

The boats which Giles sent from *Dordogne* quickly reached the waters where the damage had occurred. Their first priority was to rescue any men swimming in the water or clinging to bits of destroyed boats. It was hard to see how many they rescued and distressing to see many bodies being looked at and then abandoned, presumably as clearly dead. Before long, the jerry boat returned with as many men as it could safely carry, and the others, larger craft, soon followed.

The survivors were all chilled to the bone; some had drunk more salt water than was good for them and were violently sick in the boats rescuing them or after being helped onto *Dordogne*. A few appeared to be drowned but had been brought to the frigate in the hope that they could be revived. Giles had always made sure that several sailors on Glaucus knew the techniques for reviving drowned men, and they set to work immediately. One by one, those who could be saved sputtered and vomited their way to life, but all too soon, the seamen trying to revive some of the victims had to give up and declare that they could not be brought back to life.

Meanwhile, Mr. Maclean, *Glaucus*'s surgeon, was hard at work in the orlop trying to patch up the many Frenchmen who had been injured by gunshot or by deadly splinters slicing out in all directions when the cannon balls struck something wooden. As often happened in war, several of the surgeon's patients died even as he was trying to help them. The corpses were laid out on the main deck, awaiting burial after the sailmaker arrived from *Glaucus* to sew them into canvas for burial at sea.

Nothing more of note happened that night. With the heavy overcast that now prevailed, it was well into the forenoon watch before Giles could see the beach clearly. There was no one on it. All the evidence indicating that it had been used as the landing place for French soldiers consisted of three boats pulled up on the beach above the high water line, one of which appeared to be seriously damaged by the night's gunfire. Clearly, the French soldiers would not be returning home anytime soon if the rebellion failed.

"*Glaucus* emerging to the east of the little island," a lookout called.

"Mr. Jenks, signal her to anchor to the southeast of us." Giles reacted.

With visibility increasing quickly, it was time that he went aloft to see what was happening on Pendrag Island. The beach and the side of the ridge towards *Dordogne* were clear of people. Farther away, he could see French soldiers milling around. They appeared to have set up camp after a fashion, but there were only a few tents. Some distance away, a group of French sailors must also have slept rough, if they had slept at all, for no tents or bedrolls were in evidence. Not surprisingly, since it was highly likely that they were supposed to return to their ships when the landing was complete. In a third location, some kilted Scots appeared to be in a proper camp with tents and what appeared to be an adequate set of provisions. But did the Scots have supplies to feed the Frenchmen for long, and were they supposed to provide blankets and tents to the French? Had the French arrived, presuming that they could not only live off the land but also find shelter that they did not bring with them? That seemed likely since they were supposed to be landing in a friendly place with people whom they were assisting.

Giles climbed down to the quarter deck and told Mr. Macreau to check what was in the hold of *Dordogne*. He also told Mr. Jenks to signal the same order to Mr.

Lester on *Cicero*. Etienne was the first to come up with the answer. *Dordogne* was carrying several stands of muskets and bayonets together with musket balls and gunpowder. Dordogne's hold also had some field rations, blankets, and tents. Mr. Lester took longer to reply, partly because he had rowed over to *Dordogne* from *Cicero* to gather the material for his report.

"Captain Giles," Mr.Lester reported, "I checked *Cicero*'s hold. When *Cicero* was taken, our hold contained everything you would expect of a frigate near the beginning of her cruise, and we had not been at sea very long. The main items that the French added are the materials for a large field kitchen, several bundles of tents for camping, a considerable amount of bedding to go with them, though there are no cots, some field rations, many cases of wine, and several crates of cutlasses. I imagine that that was in the hold of their ship that got into trouble somewhere near the northwest coast of Ireland. She was accompanying this ship when she ran into trouble, and we heard things being loaded onto *Cicero* soon after they captured us. I believe that *Dordogne* went hunting for another merchant ship but found us instead. *Cicero* did not have space to take her cargo without wasting more time unloading what we were carrying.

"I see. I don't suppose you know what the French intended to do with all this stuff."

"No, sir, not in any detail. None of our crew members or officers speak French, and hardly any of *Dordogne*'s crew speak English. One chap who was friendly and had a few words said that they were carrying soldiers to capture some place in Scotland, though he didn't know where."

"The French," said Giles, "clearly left much of their gear on the ships when they landed their troops yesterday. I suppose they must have sent most of the men ashore with the first boats going to the island intending to make further trips to bring the gear. They must also have taken their marines ashore in the first batch since we didn't find any when we took *Dordogne*. We also have not captured enough sailors to provide even a minimal crew to sail the two ships, so the missing crew members must be on shore with the soldiers.

"The lack of equipment will put the French in a very awkward position for any lengthy campaign. However, they could have brought as many as four hundred armed men to contribute to the Scottish rebels, but they are seriously short of supplies now, including the muskets and shot we have discovered still on board the ships. That can mean that they will be quite a drag on their hosts as well as being a help. We can't presume that they are badly supplied with weapons, but we hope that is the case. I am sure that the number of French troops is far larger than our planners expected. The Catholics will be eager to proceed with their rebellion in order to acquire supplies from the other Scots on the mainland so that they are in a better position to use their extra forces to stop whatever response our government makes to the rebellion. Well, we should be able to put a spoke in their wheel before they get that far. We have more marines and seamen than they expected, and our broadsides may be able to contribute.

"Now, to change the subject, I see that *Glaucus* is almost here. We'll need to coordinate our forces. Mr.

Jenks, signal *Glaucus* to anchor behind us and for all officers and the gunner's mate to report on board this frigate. Mr. Lester, I will also want you, your officers, and your gunner to be here when *Glaucus*'s other officers arrive. Do you need to return so that you can arrange for as many of your people as possible to participate in our land excursion while still making sure that Captain Blenkinsop and the French prisoners are safely kept out of things?"

"No, sir, I anticipated that we might be required to go ashore. But we have very few boats."

"I realize that," admitted Giles. "I'll explain how we will deal with that in a moment."

Giles turned to the marine officer from *Cicero*, "Mr.?"

"Finch, sir, Everley Finch."

"Mr. Finch," Giles continued. "Do you have the usual complement of marines on *Cicero?*"

"Yes, sir. We are at full strength."

"I don't suppose that you have rifles."

"No, sir. They are not standard issue for marines, sir."

"Pity, but not surprising. *Glaucus*'s rifles are a gift from my wife's uncle's factory. It is very convenient to have him in the family.

"All right, everyone. I should tell you more about what is happening. The French are trying to stir up trouble between the Catholics and Protestants in Scotland, largely to induce our government to divert resources away from fighting Napoleon. The Catholics have a man who they claim should be the King, and he has arrived on *Dordogne* to lead this uprising. He was supposed to come in a brig with only a small honor guard of French soldiers. Unfortunately, the French changed their plans and sent this Pretender in a frigate with a merchant ship loaded with troops. The merchant ship got damaged, but the French captured *Cicero* to fill in for her. I was told to expect only a small French honor guard to indicate Napoleon's approval of their plans. Instead, we are facing a substantial number of well-trained French soldiers.

"*Glaucus* was supposed to arrive and capture the brig after the Pretender had gone ashore, so he could not use it to escape when the revolt was nipped in the bud. The quick ending of the uprising was supposed to happen because a group of Protestants, who would outnumber the local Catholics, knew about their intentions and would come to defeat them. I am sure the Protestant contingent is on the way, but they will be no match for the well-trained French troops and their Catholic allies here.

"The Protestants should arrive shortly if their plans have not changed. We must intervene to even the odds and defeat the French and Catholics. To do that, I will land the marines from *Glaucus* and *Cicero*. In addition, we will use as many of our seamen as we can spare while still being able to fire the guns on our three frigates. I reckon that our guns can fire over that ridge and cause mayhem among the enemy. Mr. Macauley, your men should bring their rifles as well as their muskets. They can add to the chaos produced by our guns by picking off French soldiers before they can engage either the Protestants or our own forces."

"Now, how are we going to get that many people ashore? We will first land the marines from *Glaucus,* who are actually on *Dordogne* now. Then those from *Cicero*, followed by all the seamen we can spare. On the first load, we should seize the few boats still on the beach and use them as well as the ones we now have. If we have to retreat, it will be in reverse order.

"We'll need people at the mastheads of the frigates to direct the broadside guns, which will fire over that ridge. The gunners must be sure they are clearing the ridge to be effective. Even if they don't hit much of significance on any one broadside, they should sow consternation among the enemy that will soften them up for our marines and the Protestants.

"All right. Get ready to carry out these plans as soon as I say to go ashore. First, though, I want to check what is going on behind that ridge myself."

Giles again climbed to the masthead of *Dordogne*. The activities going on beyond the ridge were getting more orderly. The Scottish men were gathered into four groups in the northeast corner of the open space. They seemed to be getting instructions from French officers.

The French troops were in the middle of the northern part of the field, well away from the Scots. They were practicing musket drills, with the soldiers instructing the marines and seamen on how to fight on land. There was no evidence that any supplies to make a proper camp for them had yet been assembled from the residents of Pendrag Island. Had they even been given better rations by their hosts? But that was idle speculation, and Giles had to concentrate on what he could see. Finally, a small, separate group caught Giles's eye. It was between the Scottish and French groups who were practicing for battle and consisted of some high-ranking French officers who appeared to be talking to some Scots who were better dressed than the others. Included in this group was a middle-aged man dressed in a kilt of a quite different pattern from the one on the other Scots' kilts. This man's whole Scottish outfit looked like it had never been worn before. He wore highly polished riding boots that looked more used than the kilt. They did not go well with the knee socks that were part of the Scottish costume. Somehow his stance suggested that he was uncomfortable being in the present situation. This must be the Pretender who was central to the nascent Scottish rebellion. When Giles focused on the man explicitly, the Pretender did not seem at all comfortable being with the leaders who intended to commence the campaign to put him on the throne of Scotland. Giles felt that he certainly did not have that mysterious personal appeal that had shaken Scotland in the previous century.

Giles turned his telescope to the southeastern corner of the field where he expected the Protestant forces to arrive before the Pendrag Island Catholics got well organized. Sure enough, he could see a couple of men dressed in kilts of the same pattern as those worn by the Catholic Scots, surveying the scene from behind a screen of trees. He realized that, while he could see these men, their position was such that they were invisible to the rebel forces. It was time to get his own men in position and prepare for the bombardment he hoped would disrupt the Pretender's plans.

"Deck there," Giles bellowed. "Send the gunners to me."

Soon the petty officers in charge of the guns on Giles's three frigates made their way to the masthead. Mr. Abbott, *Glaucus*'s gunner who had transferred to *Dordogne* to handle the guns on the French frigate, and his mate, as well as *Cicero*'s gunner, crowded rather unhappily together with Giles at the masthead. None of them had been aloft for some time and were no longer comfortable in their unstable positions.

Giles took no notice of the gunners' unhappiness. "Your targets will be those groups of French and Scottish soldiers at the northeast side of that field. It is important that your shots not hit that ridge, at least not the part to the right, where our marines and some seamen will be landing. Can you do it?"

"Aye, sir, we can fire with a high enough elevation to clear the ridge. We can fire on the uproll. It may take some adjusting to get the charge right. How accurate we can be about where the shots fall is another matter. We may scare the enemy more than harm or kill them."

"That should help confuse them so our allied Scots can get at them. They will be coming from that southeast corner which is somewhat hidden from where the other Scots and the French seem to be practicing. Can you get the guns to shoot where I pointed out?"

"Aye, sir. We may scare and confuse them more than kill them, but it should help overcome whatever they have planned."

“Mr. Abbott, Will you manage the guns on *Glaucus* or on this frigate?”

“This one, sir. My mate, Barley, is very familiar with *Glaucus*, while my wider experience may be more useful in dealing with these French guns. Can you believe they use slow-match to fire them, not flintlocks?”

“All right. Let’s get the guns ready. I’ll give the order to start firing when the shore party is in place.”

Giles returned to the deck and assembled his officers around him. “We can’t see much from the deck here, so I’ll explain what we face over there. Let me sketch out the situation.”He pulled the notebook he always carried from his coattail pocket and started to sketch.

“Here is the shoreline. At the south end as you can see, it curves around like this to the east. Our four ships are here.” Giles sketched some rough shapes to indicate his little fleet.

“There is a ridge running along the shore like this,” he continued. “We can’t see over it from the deck, but I could see it from the masthead. The ridge falls away on the other side, so the land beyond is not much higher than the shore. The ridge curves around to the east and then ends. The land beyond the ridge is a rough meadow that ends in scrubby bushes and small trees like this.” Giles added some rough scribbling to indicate what he was talking about. “The meadow should be the battleground today.

Giles returned to the deck and assembled his officers around him. “We can’t see much from the deck here, so I’ll explain what we face over there. Let me sketch out the situation." He pulled the notebook he always carried from his coattail pocket and started to sketch.

"Here is the shoreline. At the south end as you can see, it curves around like this to the east. Our four ships are here." Giles sketched some rough shapes to indicate his little fleet.

"There is a ridge running along the shore like this," he continued. "We can't see over it from the deck, but I could see it from the masthead. The ridge falls away on the other side, so the land beyond is not much higher than the shore. The ridge curves around to the east and then ends. The land beyond the ridge is a rough meadow that ends in scrubby bushes and small trees like this." Giles added some rough scribbling to indicate what he was talking about. "The meadow should be the battleground today.

"There is an opening in the scrub here, at the northeast corner. I suppose it's a path going to the village. Some men were emerging from it when I was looking. They appeared to be Scottish for they were all wearing kilts. They are armed with large swords or other implements and a few guns, muskets as far as I could make out through my telescope. I imagine they are the Catholics who are unhappy with the present government. The men are milling around hereafter they arrive." Giles drew a circle and labeled it 'Catholics.'

"The French are assembled here, quite a distance from the Catholics." Giles drew another circle and labeled it 'French.'

"There is quite a bit of space between these two groups; they certainly haven't joined together into a single force yet.

"There is a small group of men, who I guess are officers, between the two forces, about here." Another circle appeared on the sketch with 'command' scribbled in it.

"Finally, there is a second group of Scots who are just emerging from here. I don't know how many of them there are because of the scrub, which is hiding where, I guess, they have come ashore." This time the circle was labeled 'Protestants' in the southwest corner of Giles's sketch.

"I don't think the other groups can see this one, the Protestants, yet because of the scrub. It must extend further into the meadow than I first indicated, more like this." Giles drew a single additional line to indicate where the view of the Protestants might be blocked from the others. "It shouldn't be very long before this new group is gathered together, and I expect the battle between them will start soon.

Pendrag Island Battle Ground

Captain Giles's Sketch

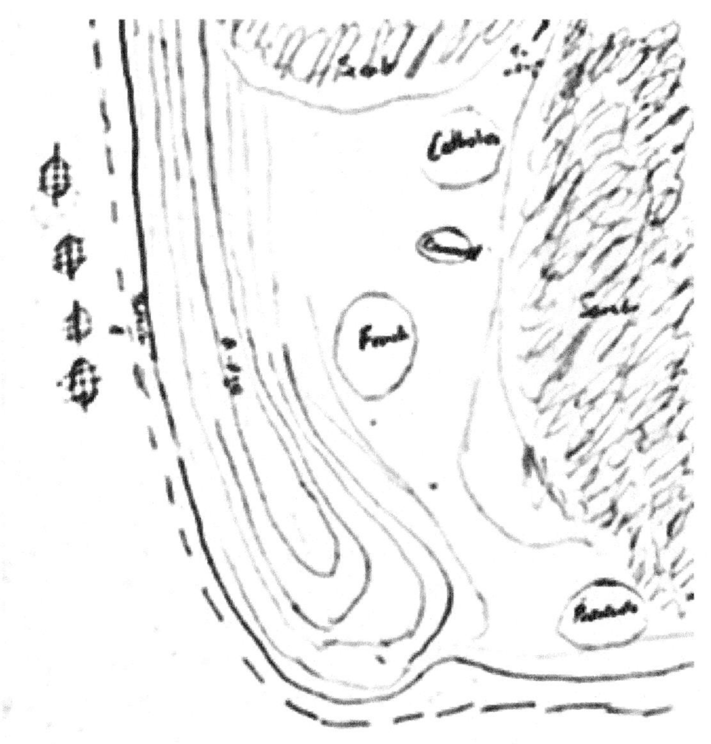

"What we are going to do," Giles continued, "is to try to disrupt the rebels so that we can defeat them with our small force. First, I want to land our marines and any sailors we can spare on the beach, pretty well abeam of *Freedom*. When our people are ready, I want the frigates to open fire on the rebel groups, and then the marines assisted by the sailors will attack the French by coming over the ridge over the ridge." With luck, they won't be ready for us and will be confused by the bombardment, so we can remove them from the battle. Then I hope that the Protestants will defeat the Catholics as originally planned. There are far more French troops than we expected, but we also have more people thanks to our getting *Cicero*'s marines unexpectantly. With surprise, I believe we will defeat them and end these Jacobite revolts once and for all."

It took a while to get the landing party ashore because of the lack of boats. The first group found that only one of the boats still on the beach could be used, the damage to the others from the cannon balls being too great for them to be seaworthy. Eventually, however, all sixty-nine marines from *Glaucus* and *Cicero*, together with their officers and weapons, were ashore. Only eighty-two seamen could be spared since so many men were required to sail the four ships in Giles's little fleet, and the eighty-two had only pistols and cutlasses.

Giles's force had assembled just in time. From his lookout place on the top of the ridge, hiding behind a couple of stunted trees, Giles observed how the Protestant forces had assembled out of sight of the Catholics. They appeared to be more numerous than the rebels, but the large and well-trained French soldiers would probably make short work of defeating them. Through his telescope, he could see that Lord Pendrag was among the leaders of the Protestant contingent, probably in command though he had no military background. Turning to survey the Catholic forces again, Giles saw that the group of officers had dispersed. Over at the group of Catholic Scots, who were standing at ease, ready for the action to begin, he saw a man who was appeared to be giving instructions to the group who looked a great deal like Lord Pendrag. Could that be Percy MacCarthach, who was trying to grab his twin brother's position?"

Shifting his gaze back to the Protestant group, he saw them lining up in a coherent formation. No doubt they would be attacking soon. It was time for Giles's surprise. He wriggled back from the top of the ridge and had Midshipman Jenks signal to the frigates to fire. Almost immediately, the bombardment from the three frigates commenced. All three fired simultaneously, despite the gun crews on *Dordogne* having to use slow match to fire their weapons.

Giles turned to see what damage the broadside created. The cannon balls had not yet arrived on their targets, but devastation struck the crowded soldiers seconds later. Giles didn't have time to count how many shots hit their targets as lines of fallen soldiers appeared in the mass of French soldiers. Indeed, he had hardly taken in how effective the broadside had been when a second one struck at a slightly different angle. Unlike the first onslaught, it missed the front edge of the crowded French enclave. Instead, its presence was first noted by taking off soldiers' heads with the efficiency of the guillotine. This gruesome happening was too much for the French soldiers' discipline. Having no idea what had happened, those who still could move broke ranks and fled toward the far edge of the clearing.

Giles had hardly succeeded in taking in the disaster that had affected the French when his attention was caught by the Catholic group. That is where the broadside from *Cicero* must have struck. The mayhem it produced was less precise than the results from the other two frigates, for the height of the cannon balls arriving was less precise, but their effect was just as devastating. Exactly where the shots had landed within the crowd was obscured by most of them skimming over the men on the edge of the massed Scots before delivering their lethal blows. As Giles had already observed where the earlier shots had landed on the French, here, again, the arrival of the balls produced several moments of stunned inactivity. Then to a man, the Scots broke and ran towards the sheltering scrub trees, their enthusiasm for the Catholic cause and restoring the throne to the Pretender completely extinguished.

When Giles understood the extent of the damage and confusion that the unexpected artillery fire had produced, he signaled for the frigates to hold their fire and was relieved to notice that his order was received and obeyed even as *Dordogne* was running out her guns for the next salvo. Glancing to his right, he saw that the Protestant force was heading to overwhelm the Catholics before they could disappear. They left the remaining French soldiers to be dealt with by Giles's men.

The marines advanced at a half run. The confused Frenchmen turned to face them, pressing together to form a column to march over the approaching marines in the standard infantry movement for Napoleon's troops. The French had even brought some drummers with them, and their doomsday rattle accompanied the thud of marching boots.

Mr. Macauley's marines, by contrast, spread out in two long rows. The front row unslung their rifles and knelt on one knee. The second row remained standing as they also got their rifles ready. Meanwhile, from the sides, the marines from *Cicero* extended the marines' line. Beyond them, the seamen from the frigates formed the wings of the line. The sailors were armed with cutlasses. Now, the French were marching into a cup. Their soldiers were so closely packed together that most could not use their muskets quickly, even if they wanted to. The marines were still too far away for the French muskets to be much of a threat, even if they stopped to fire them. Had they been English infantry, they would have formed an impenetrable defensive square, but possibly the French did not appreciate the hazard they were marching into when it was composed of a thin line that would be easy to snap.

On came the French into the trap that was closing on them. Giles wondered out loud, "Do the French not realize that Mr. Macauley's marines have rifles ready to fire?" Mr. Macauley waited to give the order. With muskets, one had to be very close to the enemy for the weapons to be effective

The threatening French column kept advancing, making no adjustments for the maneuvres of the marines and seamen. The marines stood firm, their rifles already loaded, showing no sign of the terror that had defeated so many of Napoleon's enemies when confronted with the juggernaut of a marching French column that could not be diverted from its prey.

Lieutenant Macauley cried in a loud, but calm, voice, "Ready."

The marines took their rifles from their shoulders. They were through with maneuvering. Now the French were in range; it was time to kill them.

"Aim," was Lieutenant Macauley's next order. His well-trained men unhurriedly positioned their rifles on their shoulders and took aim at the enemy, each man choosing a particular trooper to follow as calmly as if they were choosing which grouse to slaughter.

Moments later, the Marine lieutenant completed what he seemed to consider a routine drill by calmly shouting, only loud enough to be heard over the racket the French were making, "Fire!"

Both rows of marines fired simultaneously. The front rows of the advancing French column disintegrated, and its edges crumpled to the ground. However, the column closed ranks and kept coming. The marines unslung the loaded muskets that they had also been carrying. They cocked their flintlocks and waited for the French column to get close to them.

On a bugle call, the French column, still marching like clockwork soldiers, unslung their muskets.

That was the signal Lieutenant Macauley had been waiting for. "Fire," he bellowed. Then he didn't wait to see if his men should reload or even if they had hit the enemy. “Charge” was his next order.

With bayonets at the ready, the marines advanced at a run to skewer the remaining Frenchmen before they could recover, closing in on the sides of the column and the front. The seamen attacked the rear of the column, catching their opponents still taking their muskets from their shoulders, quite unprepared to parry the English cutlasses with their bayonets. A junior French lieutenant, who was the only French officer still standing, ordered his men to throw down their arms, even as he bellowed for mercy. In rather an anti-climax action, the British marines switched from trying to kill the French soldiers to disarming those enemies who were unharmed and treating the many who were wounded.

Giles, with Midshipman Jenks, had followed the marines at a safe distance. There was no point in his joining their ranks; Lieutenant Macauley knew his business, and Giles would just have been in the way. When the marines’ line started to curve around the marching column, Giles skirted behind them to continue towards where the French officers had been standing with the man who he presumed was the Pretender. Just before the marines opened fire, Giles was able to see that the Pretender was still in the same place, but now there was only one French officer with him. Giles couldn’t tell how senior the officer was, not being familiar with French uniforms, but the man was middle-aged and exuded authoritative confidence that suggested he was of senior rank.

Giles and Midshipman Jenks were still some distance from the Pretender and his companion when the roar of the first marine volley sounded. Instinctively they looked to see what was happening. They could see the effect of the rifles, and when it was followed by the marines' muskets firing, it was obvious that that part of the battle was won. Turning back to look at the French officer, Giles saw that the man's first reaction to the defeat of his forces was to pull out his pistol.

Giles wasn't worried about being confronted with a firearm. He was still too far away for the pistol to be a serious threat. Maybe the French officer thought to offer it to Giles as an indication of surrender. Giles was still some distance from the officer whose presenting his firearm might indicate that he wanted to surrender, or maybe he intended to use it to keep Giles at bay while trying to join his Scottish allies, not realizing that the destruction of his company of soldiers had put paid to any successful rebellion.

Neither of these possibilities turned out to be the Frenchman's intention. Instead, he turned his pistol on the Pretender, who had been standing motionless next to him, stunned by what had just happened to the invading force. The distance between the two men was such that there was no chance that a shot to the head would fail to kill the victim immediately. Before Giles could react to this change in the situation, the French officer shot the Pretender in the head.

Even in the middle of battle, deliberately shooting an unarmed man was unacceptable.

"That's murder!" Giles yelled.

The Frenchman spun on his heel to see who uttered the objection. Spotting a British naval officer, he threw away his pistol, drew his sword, and attacked. Giles was taken by surprise. He did not have his cutlass with him though it was his preferred weapon for boarding operations. Instead, Giles was wearing his sword, a rather ornamental accouterment given to him by a group of appreciative merchants for rescuing merchant ships while he was patrolling the North Sea looking for pirates and privateers. Now, he drew the weapon just in time to counter the Frenchman's attack, knocking his rival's sword aside as it was about to skewer him. Giles realized that he was in trouble in the short period before his enemy could attack again. The Frenchman handled his sword easily, like someone who had spent many hours practicing with it, while it was a long time since Giles had handled any weapon other than a cutlass. He was bound to lose in any duel with swords, especially as he felt his sword's blade was already coming loose from its hilt.

All Giles could do was go on the attack and hope that the suddenness and fury of his attack would startle the Frenchman enough so that he could win. Realizing this, he swung his sword wildly like a madman, forcing the Frenchman to parry his sweeps and giving him no chance to safely break through Giles's violent attack. Giles could only keep up his terrorizing attack for a few minutes. His sword was becoming heavier in his hands, and somehow the blade felt looser. In a minute, he would be too slow to prevent the Frenchman from going on the attack, and then he would have no hope of preventing his more skilled opponent from breaking through Giles's wild attack to end it.

Giles sprang back to give himself a moment to shift from attack to defense. It was long odds that his opponent would give him an opening to beat him, but it was his only hope. Then something tore at the Frenchman's left shoulder, and blood immediately appeared. Whatever had happened distracted the Frenchman for a moment.

Giles did not wait. Leading with the point of his sword, he charged the Frenchman. He used his left hand to push his opponent's sword aside, not even realizing that his action had cut his hand. He put all his weight into his charge. His sword struck the French officer in the middle of his chest and deflected upwards. A moment later, it found the man's throat and penetrated it. Giles's forward movement halted when the weight of the collapsing Frenchman tore the hilt of his sword from his hand. Spurting blood covered Giles's face and clothes. He stood shaking. He was very tired suddenly and disoriented. Slowly he recovered, but he still felt shaky.

Giles looked at Midshipman Jenks. "Did you shoot the French officer?"

"Yes, sir, but I only hit him in the shoulder."

"That was enough. Thank you for saving my life."

"I wasn't sure, sir, if you would want me to interfere when I had a chance."

"Of course, I would. Don't be fooled by all that chivalric nonsense of letting individual contests continue uninterrupted on a battlefield. The object is to kill your opponent. It was especially so here because, if that Frenchman survived, whether he killed me or not, he would swing for murder. Deliberately killing unarmed men, even on a battlefield, is not justified or permitted. So thank you again, Mr. Jenks. You have done very well today."

Giles realized that he had lost all track of how the other battles were going while he was fighting for his life. A glance behind him showed that the marines had captured all the French soldiers who were still alive. Those not so involved were forming up again. Lieutenant Macauley came running to him.

"Captain Giles, are you all right? You're covered in blood. Shall I call over the surgeon to patch you up, sir?"

"No need, Mr. Macauley. It's all my opponent's blood. I only need a damp rag to scrub the worst of it off. I see that the doctor has arrived to look after the wounded. He is busy right now. All I have sustained is a cut on my left hand."

"Yes, sir, I was about to form up the unoccupied marines to go over to see what help is needed with those Scottish men."

"Good. Mr. Jenks and I shall come with you."

The fight between the two groups of the Clan MacCarthach had ended. They were standing together watching some sort of spectacle. Since the tartans of their kilts were all the same, it was not obvious who had won or why they were not still fighting. Could the Catholics have lost heart when they saw that the Pretender had been shot, but then what were they all watching? The answer became clear when Giles and Midshipman Jenks pushed their way to the front of the crowd. The Scots let them pass when they saw the English captain was so horribly covered with blood that their immediate reaction was to shy away from this avenging monster like some creature from fables told to scare children.

The spectacle the men were watching was a sword duel between two kilted warriors. Their kilts were made with the same tartan and looked very much alike. Giles realized that one must be Lord MacCarthach and the other his brother Percy, the Catholic renegade, but it was hard to tell who was who even though he had seen Lord MacCarthach recently.

The two men were fighting with what must have been Scottish claymores which were huge, two-handed swords with rather elaborate cross pieces protecting the grip. Giles had never seen such a sword before though he had heard of them and knew that they were some form of cutlass that played some ceremonial role in Scotland. Here the two men were taking giant swings at each other and parrying the attacks with other swipes of the swords. There was no attempt to use them as pointed weapons, though their points looked deadly. “Clang, clang, clang, clang,” went the weapons as the contestants swung and parried with no attempt to stab their opponents. Sooner or later, one or the other fighter would break through their opponent’s defense and slice him in two.

That is not quite what happened. Instead, one of the contestants jumped back at the last moment without meeting his opponent’s sword. Immediately, while his opponent was off balance from not meeting resistance, he stepped forward and gave a great backhanded slash. That didn’t literally slice his enemy in two, but the wound he inflicted was unquestionably fatal. Pausing only to be sure his opponent was finished, the victor turned to the crowd, waving the claymore above his head as the crowd roared.

"Thank heavens you arrived on time, Lord Camshire," he called to Giles, confirming that the winner was not Percy MacCarthach.

Lord MacCarthach, the victor, surveyed the crowd waving his claymore above his head and turning around slowly as if the weapon had no weight. He then stopped and leaned on it.

"Men of Clan MacCarthach from Pendrag Island. My brother misled you about the Pretender. He had no claim to the throne, for he was not a legitimate son of Prince Charles. The only legitimate Stuart claimant to the throne is an old man who is a Catholic priest. Any King of England is also now the King of Scotland. The restrictions on you Catholics, which Percy MacCarthach claimed are very harmful, actually produce little hindrance to our ability to thrive. We hurt ourselves by having our clan split. Protestants, Catholics, that doesn't matter. We are all of Clan MacCarthach. United. We gain and are stronger together than when we are divided by religion. Let bygones be bygones. What we all need now is uisge baugh*."

That met with a roar from all sides of the circle. It was obvious that all the Scots felt that way. Whisky was the only proper way to finish off such a day.

"Then let us all go to Pendrag town to celebrate that we are again an undivided clan," Lord MacCarthach concluded his speech. He came over to Giles as the crowd broke up and headed towards the northern exit from the battlefield.

“Lord Camshire, thank you again for saving our endeavor. If it had not been for your presence and the contribution of your guns and your men, today would have been a disaster for me and for all of Scotland as England responded to Percy’s uprising. But I think it would be best if your men now left rather than joining in the celebration. Memories of Collodden* are still too fresh for my clansmen to welcome your men.”

Lieutenant Macauley had been waiting at the back of the crowd for Giles’s orders. “I saw your sword fight, Captain Giles. Well done!” he said. “Now, what do you want us to do?”

“It’s time to return to the ship, Mr. Macauley. Make sure that all the wounded are cared for and transported to the ship, ours to *Glaucus*, *Cicero*’s to her. That goes for the seamen as well, of course. Bring all of our dead back to the ships so that they can be given a proper burial. Yes, and we had better take all the living French soldiers, including the wounded ones, to the ships too. We can leave the French bodies for burial by the Scots. Mr. Jenks and I will go back to our landing place to help with loading the boats.

It took many trips to get everyone back on board. The French surgeon and his loblolly boys* were routed out of the makeshift prison on *Dordogne* to help with the casualties among the French troops. A moment of relaxation occurred when several barrels of whiskey arrived from Pendrag village, compliments of the Chief of Clan MacCarthach. Under careful supervision, tots of the precious liquid were measured out for everyone. Giles was not surprised when it turned out that most of the crew members preferred rum, which they would get normally, to the Scottish tipple, but that did not stop them from draining every drop of the precious liquid. Giles knew that he much preferred brandy to whisky when enjoying distilled drinks, though he had found in the past that there was no point arguing the relative merits of other drinks with devotees of Scotch whisky.

Night had fallen before everyone was on board again with all their gear. Giles found that he was too exhausted to compose more than a brief note to Daphne before collapsing into his cot. The note did not mention his fight with the French officer or Midshipman Jenks's role in its outcome, how his arm hurt, or how he came to be drenched in someone else's blood. She would be worried and concerned: worried enough to discourage him from pursuing a naval career.

Chapter XX

The big day had come: Hugh would get to ride his pony all by himself for the first time. When the ponies arrived at Dipton Hall, Hugh had wanted to jump on the larger one at once, but Mr. Griffiths had prohibited that. The pony had not been trained properly, and Hugh had not been taught how to ride. The instruction for both of them commenced immediately. It turned out that the pony had already been trained almost up to Mr. Griffiths' exacting standard, while Hugh took quickly to the lessons. Now he would have his first ride without someone holding the bridle or telling him what he had to do.

Mr. Griffiths was a stickler for riders being taught everything about handling their horses. Though most aristocrats' children might expect anything menial to be done by servants, the stable master believed that you should understand all the equipment if you expected to ride a horse. Hugh, young as he was, had been trained in harnessing the pony, even starting by catching him so that he could be harnessed. Daphne watched as the lad went to the pony, soothed the animal enough that he could lead him to where the gear had been set out and harnessed the pony accurately.

Daphne recalled how she had learned to ride, not assisted by her father or his stable master but instructed by one of the stable boys who thought her rebellious nature was amusing. She had only received a mild warning from her father about not being so trusting; the stable boy had been sacked because he let her ride. Daphne had felt sorry about what followed for the servant, but there was nothing that she could do after his crime had been discovered.

Hugh, of course, would not learn to ride bareback as Daphne had learned to do on her own. Could she show the boy how to do it sometime when no one would know about her behavior? She was certainly tempted. But she would not be surprised if Giles would be equally in favor of teaching the lad things that most gentlemen were not supposed to learn.

Hugh was ready to mount unaided, but he was a little hesitant about how to push up so that he could swing his leg over the saddle and settle down. Mr. Griffiths had chosen the pony well, for it stood patiently until Hugh finally was able to swing his leg over the horse's back, hook his foot into the stirrup, and settle into the saddle.

"Well done, Hugh!" Daphne and Mr. Griffiths called at once. Hugh's next task was to get the pony walking, which he did without trouble. Then he made the animal walk sedately around the paddock, making him change direction as he pleased, not as the pony wanted.

Hugh patted his steed on the neck when he stopped it in front of Daphne and Mr. Griffiths. "Well done, Titan! Good pony!" he declared. Then Hugh looked at the adults. "Can I practice with Titan some more?"

"Yes, you can," Daphne told him. She then turned to see what Mary was doing.

While Hugh demonstrated his new skills, Mary had been petting her little Shetland pony. She was still too young to ride her pony yet, or so Daphne decreed, but the little girl should be introduced to her. At least, that was the idea. However, when Daphne's attention was directed at Hugh's activities, Mary had a different idea. When Daphne next looked, Mary was sitting on the pony's back, holding onto its mane with both hands, her legs spread wide apart, heels dug in to prevent her from sliding off. The pony, called Petunia, seemed to be quite content with her burden. She was standing placidly as she had been trained to do when her reins were loose.

"***What*** do you think you are doing, Mary?" Daphne demanded.

"I'm sitting on Petunia," the child answered perfectly accurately while not really answering the question that Daphne was asking.

"I see that. How did you get there?"

"I pulled myself up by her hair." Daphne supposed that Mary meant the pony's mane, which was long and thick.

"Did I say you could?"

"No, but you didn't say I couldn't, Aunt Daphne," was the reply.

Daphne was flummoxed. This conversation was not going at all as she wanted, and she was about to lose her temper at Mary's saucy replies.

"And how do you think you are going to get down?"

Without saying anything, Mary slid off the pony's back holding onto Petunia's mane until her feet were only a couple of inches above the ground when she let go.

Luckily for Daphne's temper and Mary's bottom, Mr. Griffiths came over to them at that moment. "I see that Mary is getting on very well with Petunia," he said, ignoring the ill humor that Daphne seemed to be in. "We must get her riding now that Master Hugh's practice can be left to the stable boys for a while."

"Surely she is too small to ride a pony, isn't she?"

"I don't think so, my lady. As you have seen, she can get on and off the creature, though not in a conventional way. I'm told that children as young as three can sit safely on a Shetland pony while it is in motion. With your permission, my lady, I will have Geoffrey, the senior stable boy, harness Petunia and adjust the tack so that Miss Mary can try it. She is, I think, a little young to be able to harness Petunia herself, at least until they are more comfortable with each other, so I'll make an exception on what should be taught first."

"Well, let's try it. Mary, would you like to ride Petunia?"

"Oh, yes, please, Auntie Daphne. Please, please, please!"

"All right." Mary didn't wait for someone to lift her onto the pony. Instead, she pulled herself back onto the pony's back. Mr. Griffiths told one of the grooms to walk the pony around the enclosure. "While we are waiting, Lady Camshire," he declared, "there is one subject I would like to raise."

"Yes?

" It is about tracking down how our horses have been stolen. As you may have heard, the Honorable Mr. Patterson-Baker wants to buy one of our hunters. He has an estate to the northwest of Ameschester, roughly seven miles from the town. He is a member of the Ameschester Hunt. You may have met him."

"Yes. A rather burly and presumptuous man, always complaining about how the Hunt is run, but still coming to it and never offering to help in running it. I avoid him if I can; he believes that women should always ride sidesaddle and never jump."

"That's the man. The Major cannot stand him, and I can't say I blame him. Patterson-Baker rides a brute of a horse, hard mouth and unresponsive. Not well trained as a hunter. Just a riding horse that someone half-trained to jump and sold the beast to Patterson-Baker. There have been complaints about the horse from members of the Hunt, and Mr. Summers has had some rather ineffective discussions with him about it. Major Stoner has been more forceful in talking to him, and as a result, Patterson-Baker claims he is in the market for one of our horses. As you know, my lady, we have several which will be ready for sale very soon."

"That is very good to hear."

"Well, it is, yes and no."

"Oh?"

"Yes, Patterson-Baker claims that we charge too much. He hopes to get a Dipton-Stables horse secondhand from someone who has lost interest in hunting or got injured too badly to hunt."

"I don't see why this is relevant? Why should we be interested if a boor bad-mouths us about what we ask for our horses?"

"Ah, this is where it becomes interesting. I must say that I learned of this from the Major, who may have more details. Apparently, Mr. Patterson-Baker's estate is as close to Haverton as it is to Ameschester, and while he is a member of our Hunt, he does most of his business in Haverton. That may be because, the Major knows, Paterson-Baker has a mistress — or, rather, a concubine — in the town, if you will pardon me mentioning such an inappropriate subject to a lady."

"Of course not, Mr. Griffiths, when it is part of a story. Much as we pretend not to, most gentlewomen are fully aware of what many men get up to when not at home. When we wives get together by ourselves, there are many complaints about unfaithful husbands whose adultery is well known. None of us are truly shocked at its being mentioned casually. Of course, we all pretend otherwise in polite society, just as we also pretend that we have no idea how babies are made."

"I suppose that is true, though I was not aware that a husband's infidelity was a subject of gossip among ladies. I must declare that I do know that Captain Giles does not indulge in such activities — ever. Anyway, the point is that this 'gentleman,' after taking his pleasure, repairs to the nearest alehouse, which is not a very elevated establishment. While in his cups with his cronies there, he reveals all, both about his mistress and about his complaints about his treatment in the Ameschester Hunt. Recently, Mr. Patterson-Baker has been boasting that soon he will get one of our Dipton horses, which will show the Major and others — including you, my lady — what a superior huntsman he is when not held back by the deficiencies of his mount, and how he doesn't have to put up with the ridiculous prices — as he calls them —that we charge.

"Now, as you may recall, I bought Petunia from Mr. Chester Bryant. His estate is quite close to Mr. Patterson-Baker's, near Haverton. You probably don't know him since he does not hunt, though his daughter is a great admirer of yours."

"Oh, yes. I think that I met the Bryants at an Assembly in Ameschester not very long ago. Giles and I went there while he was home earlier this year. They have a daughter who has just come out, as I recall. Yes, she was very keen on some things she had read about me, much to my surprise. For most young girls, Giles is the one they most admire."

"Anyway, my lady, on returning from Mr. Bryant's estate after arranging for Petunia and her gear to be brought here, I stopped at an alehouse in Haverton, the one that Mr. Patterson-Baker patronizes, though I didn't know it at the time. He came in with another gentleman and took a table near mine. I could hear quite clearly what the two were discussing, despite the noise in the alehouse —or maybe because of it, for there were several quite rowdy men at a table not far away from me. That meant everyone else in the taproom had to speak louder to be heard by their companions. Mr. Patterson-Baker thinks I am a servant, so even if he had recognized me, he would think I was quite incapable of overhearing him or having anyone important believe me if I told them what he said.

"Certainly, what they said was of great interest to me, though I pretended to be reading a racing paper that the landlord keeps for his patrons. They were discussing hunting horses, Dipton Stables horses in particular. Mr. Patterson-Baker was complaining about how expensive good hunting horses are, particularly the amount that Dipton Stables demanded for their horses. His companion — a man named 'Prescott' — pointed out that we produce the best hunting horses. I was tempted to join in at that point to confirm the statement, but I restrained myself.

" Patterson-Baker — I dislike having to call such a man 'Mister,' my lady."

"Very understandable, Mr. Griffiths," Daphne replied. "He is certainly no gentleman from what I have seen of him. Do continue, please."

"Patterson-Baker stated that he had heard that it was possible to get Dipton-Stables horses at a much lower price on resale from men who had acquired them — that's the term he used, 'acquired' rather than 'bought' — and that Prescott was the man to talk to about it. Prescott asserted that he could arrange such a sale at a considerable saving to Patterson-Baker. When pressed for the price, Prescott said that, usually, it would be about forty percent of what would be charged by Dipton Stables. However, at Haverton, they had to be more careful because of its proximity to Ameschester, so the price would be a bit more. He noted that Patterson-Baker wished to ride in the Ameschester Hunt, which would ensure that questions about the provenance of the horse would arise since many people in that hunt were fully aware of Dipton Stables and its reputation. It would be likely that someone would recognize the horse itself as one we had raised. Mr. Patterson-Baker was bound to be asked how he obtained the horse, and his story and records should make it plausible that the horse had come to him through honorable means, even though it could not be shown to have been acquired legitimately."

"So this Prescott creature admitted that it was a stolen horse?"

"Not in so many words, my lady, but it was clear that both men understood what he was talking about."

"Prescott then launched into a description of how, for a price, he would get around the problem. First, he could provide a bill of sale from Dipton Stables to the first supposed owner; it would be on the distinctive, engraved form that we use, only, in this case, it is not made out to the man who actually purchased the horse, but to someone else, who was known to have gone to America sometime after the sale was supposed to have occurred, which was earlier that it had come into Prescott's possession. The horse's name would not be the one under which he was sold by Dipton Stables in the genuine transaction.

"The provenance of the horse would then be further muddied by having the first owner sell it to a second one, according to a well-executed sale. This one would not indicate where that man resided, nor would the record of the next sale to another fictitious owner. This would be followed by yet another bill of sale to Prescott. None of the other men after the first could be traced. Still, it would appear that Patterson-Baker, and Prescott before him, were the victims of being sold the horse under false pretenses that Patterson-Baker could not be expected to recognize. Prescott, the last seller in the record, intended to move away from the area soon. As a result, he could not be questioned about how he came to acquire the horse. As a result, Patterson-Baker's rights to the horse would be vindicated since he had purchased it from a seller in the area whom he knew.

"My lady, that confirms what little we know about how they can sell our horses to gullible — or not-so-gullible — buyers without the transaction being canceled when it turns out that the earlier papers were bogus and the horse had been stolen from us,"

"It seems that this man, Prescott, must know everything about the ring of thieves. What should we do about it, Mr. Griffiths?"

"Let's get to that in a minute, my lady. There is still more to the story," responded Mr. Griffiths. "Prescott next announced that he could arrange for all that was required, though he would expect an additional reward. Because of the risks, Prescott would have to be paid in sterling, not bank notes or other bills. Patterson-Baker agreed but said he would have to get the cash for the transaction from his bank in Ameschester. He would do that today, he said, and then Prescott could bring the horse to his estate tomorrow."

"Well, Mr. Griffiths, we will just have to find a way to stop this criminal by tomorrow or, better yet, today."

"That's all very well, my lady, but do we have the authority? We can't just arrest someone because we know that they are crooked, can we?"

"I suppose not. We need a magistrate, I imagine."

"I believe that we do. I also know that the magistrate who was helpful with that previous horse theft is away at Bath."

"Drat!" Daphne exclaimed in a very unladylike way. "Heaven knows where Lord David is; certainly not at Dipton. I wonder how we can find the other magistrates in time to be of use."

"Could we just bluff our way through it, my lady?"

"Yes, but then whatever we accomplish might just unravel later. Let me think."

"We don't have much time before the chances of catching them in the act may evaporate, my lady."

"Yes. Just let me think," Daphne said again. "Yes … yes, I know what we can do. Giles arranged for Major Stoner to be made a magistrate before leaving for his ship. He set all the necessary steps in motion before he left. I wonder if the Major has had his appointment confirmed yet."

"Let's hope so. But, my lady, we both know that Captain Giles doesn't use his influence often, and so, when he wants something, it always goes through. Just the presumption that the Major is a magistrate should see us through if we can get him to join us, whether he has had confirmation of his appointment or not."

"Right. Assemble some of your men, Mr. Griffiths, and we will pay this Prescott fellow a visit. We can go by the Major's estate to get him to join us."

Daphne returned to Dipton Hall, gave orders for everything that needed to be done while she was away, and quickly changed into riding clothes. Even so, she felt annoyed that she had to change her clothes for the adventure while most men living on an estate could wear the same clothes for all their activities during the day. She also had to tell Hugh and Mary that they would have to wait for the next day for their next riding lesson, though she wished, not for the first time, that she could do two quite different things simultaneously. In this case, it was to catch a horse thief and watch the children learning to ride.

Major Stoner had received the confirmation of his being appointed a magistrate. He was eager to join the expedition to deal with the horse thieves to use his new authority. As they waited for the Major's horse to be harnessed, Daphne and Mr. Griffiths told him everything they knew about Prescott and Patterson-Baker .

"Never trusted that man, Patterson-Baker, never! Always thought he must be up to no good. Certain of it! Certain!" the Major exclaimed.

"Well, now that I am a magistrate, we can put a spoke in his wheel. We certainly can! Received my papers in the mail yesterday. Have to swear before a judge at the next Assizes, but that is a technicality. I can take on the full duties now. All of them! All!

"Just let me get my horse harnessed and tell a few of the stable boys to get ready to ride with us, and we can go and deal with this rotter — what did you call him? — ah, Prescott!"

As they waited for the horses to be readied, Lady Marianne provided spirit cups of mulled wine to the group from Dipton. That helped produce the feeling that they were off on a pleasant adventure rather than on a grim mission to uphold the law. That happy feeling was reinforced by its being a sunny day with no wind or other hint that rain might be on the way.

The Major assumed the leadership of the group as if it were obvious that he should be in command. His taking charge came as a surprise to Daphne, who was more used to him being a rather backward and nervous participant in various activities. In particular, she thought he had been too ready to give way to Mr. Summers on matters concerning the Ameschester Hunt or to treat casual suggestions by Giles or herself as orders. This development came as a relief to Daphne since she knew that she had no experience in dealing with thieves and little in the way of plans as to what they should do when they got to Prescott's estate. Without question, she was very happy to have the Major be in charge of this expedition.

When Mr. Griffiths announced that they were getting close to Prescott's estate, the Major called a halt so that everyone would know what their role was to be as they took over the buildings and captured any men who were there. In crisp terms, he detailed the jobs assigned to each of the three groups he formed. The first would head directly to the stables to prevent anyone from using the horses kept there to escape. Another group would go to the back of the mansion to apprehend anyone who tried to escape from a back door. Only when these two groups were in place would the principal members of the expedition go to rouse out Prescott.

Before taking over the manor, however, the Major's forces would secure any horses that might be in the paddock where Mr. Griffiths had spotted the horse called 'Dipton Charger.' Hopefully, that horse would still be there. If it were not, that would put an end to the dubious seizure that was planned. Mr. Griffiths, with two of his stable boys, went off to see about capturing the stolen horse. Everyone waiting was nervous, for this was one of the centerpieces of their plans. Before long, however, Mr. Griffiths returned. He brought Dipton Charger and four other good riding horses with him as well as his stable boys

"Very good, Mr. Griffiths. We will leave these horses with your two grooms," the Major stated. "You men," he addressed the two stable boys, "take the horses to that empty field we passed a few minutes ago and keep them there. If anyone should ask what you are doing, tell them that you are complying with the orders of the magistrate who can be found at Mr. Prescott's estate."

Daphne was amazed. She had never heard the Major talk without his annoying habit of repeating or rephrasing everything he said as if no one would believe him if he didn't hammer home what he was saying. Now, as a man with legitimate authority, he could make his decisions and needed no one else to confirm the value of what he said. She just had to hope that the Major's new authority would not go to his head. After all, what Giles had arranged, he could cancel just as well, but there would be hell to pay with Lady Marianne if Giles had the Major's appointment rescinded

"Mr. Griffiths," said the Major. "It's time for you to take your men around to the back of the mansion. I will give you a few minutes to get into position, and then Lady Camshire and I will go and meet this Prescott fellow in his lair. Incidentally, if there are any side doors, station some people at them to intercept any attempt to flee.

Daphne and the Major waited for Mr. Griffiths and his men to get into position. Apparently, their movement about the property had roused no suspicions. Then the two leaders rode up to the main entrance. Without waiting to see if any servants would emerge to help them and hold their horses, they dismounted and proceeded up the short flight of stairs to the portico. Surprisingly, no one appeared before they reached the front door.

Major Stoner strode to the front door and knocked loudly. A man wearing the livery of a butler opened the door after a few minutes. His clothing looked well-used, and he had a sour, unwelcoming expression, not what you would expect from the butler of a prosperous estate.

"What do you want?" the man asked in a surly tone.

"I am Magistrate Major Welcomb Stoner here to see Mr. Prescott on an urgent matter," the Major replied.

"Are you? I'll tell him you want to see him. Wait here while I see if he wants to see you."

The butler turned away while at the same time swinging the door to close it. He didn't notice that the Major moved his boot so the door could not close. Major Stoner put his index finger to his mouth in the universal signal for quiet and whispered to Daphne, "I think we should not wait for an invitation."

The Major and Daphne tiptoed down the passage and saw the servant turn into a doorway. They speeded up in time to hear the servant say, "Mr. Prescott, sir, there is a magistrate and some woman here to see you."

"Tell them I am not available, Ferson. Close the door on them and then get away from here. Tell the same thing to anyone you meet. I'm leaving now."

The Major and Daphne burst into the room just in time to see a man rise from a chair behind his desk. Before they could do anything, he had opened a French door onto a terrace and rushed through it. Though he had a head start on the Major and Daphne, he didn't get far.

"Where do you think you are going?" said Mr. Griffiths as he and one of his grooms seized the man who was trying to escape. "I am sure that Magistrate Stoner needs to talk with you."

Mr. Griffiths and his assistant frog-marched their captive back into the house and positioned him in front of the desk from which he had just fled. The Major sat in the seat that Prescott had just abandoned.

"Mr. Griffiths, is this the man you overheard in Haverton yesterday?" the Major asked.

"Yes, your honor. He was plotting to sell a horse stolen from Dipton Stables to Mr. Patterson-Baker."

"I protest," broke in Prescott. "I have a document that shows I obtained the horse honestly.

"Oh, do you?" said the Major. "Show it to me."

"It's in the desk drawer."

"Ah, yes. Here we are. A bill of sale from Dipton Stables for a horse called 'Dipton Dreamer.' Signed by Geoffrey Griffiths and 'Camshire.' Presumably, that is supposed to be the signature of the Earl of Camshire. It is written on a most impressive piece of paper showing the Camshire Coat of Arms and a sketch of some stables. Most impressive, Mr. Prescott! Most impressive! Tell me, Mr. Griffiths, is this your signature?"

"No, your honor. And the name of the horse we found here is 'Dipton Charger,' not 'Dipton Dreamer.' I have never heard of this Mr. Harold Dumstable, who is supposed to have bought the horse from us. This is a bogus bill of sale, just as the conversation I overheard suggested it would be."

"I see. Well, Mr. Prescott, this is clear evidence that you are in possession of a stolen horse. I already know that you are in the process of selling it to Mr. Patterson-Baker. Horse theft and selling stolen horses are both capital offenses, but I am sorry to say that we can only hang you once. I'll just have to arrest you and have you held in Ameschester Gaol while awaiting the next assizes in Ameschester. I have no doubt that you will swing for your offenses. Well deserved, I would imagine."

"Yes, indeed, Major," Daphne broke into this speech, "but what about that cretin? Does he just get away scot-free?"

"I don't see how we can prevent it."

"But surely he was conspiring to get a stolen horse cheap. And he knew what he was doing."

"Yes, but he didn't actually do it, did he, my lady? No money changed hands, and we have no compelling proof that he would go through with it."

"But … but," Daphne sputtered.

"No, my lady. Without evidence, we will have to let Patterson-Baker go. Even pretend at meetings of the Ameschester Hunt that he is perfectly respectable, even though we know better. We'll just have to hope that having a very public execution of this man, making sure that his neck doesn't break in the drop so that he has a long, painful death, puts a stop to these horse thieves."

"Well, that doesn't sound right to me. Surely we can get more out of our discoveries beyond hanging this wretch, whose lack of prosperity suggests he is just a tool of men that benefit more from horse stealing and will continue to do so."

"Well, I suppose that we could ask for some clemency if this man really helps us. Depends on how much use he is to us. I know that the judges who come to Ameschester love to ride to hounds. You may remember how much they enjoyed coming with us the last time they were here in hunting season."

"I do. What can we offer this man, Major, to get him to help us?"

"All I can do is recommend clemency to the judges. But Prescott will have to give us very substantial assistance to make an example of Patterson-Baker to discourage others who want to buy stolen horses. If we get only a little help, then it might only be enough to allow him to hire someone to speed his death after the trapdoor opens, and he is kicking pointlessly at the end of the rope as he strangles to death," Major Stoner proclaimed gleefully. "More assistance might allow me to arrange better treatment in gaol while awaiting trial, access to better food, perhaps, or things like that."

"Is that the best we can do?"

"Well, we would have to demonstrate to the judge that something very constructive could come from his help. Remember, these judges will want to impose the maximum penalty. They don't like horse thieves, especially ones who take hunting horses. For the criminal providing really major assistance to us, the judge might consider commuting a sentence to something lighter—maybe transportation to Australia or something of that order. For very, very effective aid, they might allow him to serve in the army or navy, where I am told survival is much better than being sent to Botany Bay or left to rot in some prison. Getting clemency of that sort would probably require the exercise of Lord Camshire's influence with the judges, and you know he is reluctant to squander it, Lady Camshire."

"Yes, that's true. This wretch's help would have to be worth a lot for my husband to be interested," Daphne asserted, even though she knew that Giles would be horrified at even the idea of his influence being for sale.

"What sorts of things would you consider worth enough to try to get clemency from the courts, Magistrate Stoner."

"Let me see. We'd have to get information to make a case that stands up in court, wouldn't we? And full details about all the people involved who I think are relevant. To start with, I would need to know from whom he got Dipton Charger — the horse he calls Dipton Dreamer — and was he the man for whom this fake bill of sale was prepared? If he isn't this person, who is, and where does he live? That is the sort of thing I would expect to work for to get clemency when backed up with all the details about the operation and who is involved. If he gives us all that information and helps us to round the culprits up, I would hope that the judges would look favorably on giving him a more lenient sentence. But it would have to be a major help to us. Remember that at Ameschester Assizes, the judges are a blood-thirsty lot.

"Prescott," said the Major, "tell me about this Harold Dunstable to whom the first sale was made according to this 'document.' Is that his real name?"

"If I'm to answer any questions, will you go to bat for me with the judges?"

"Only if your answers are true, complete, and helpful."

"All right, I'll have to trust you, I guess. 'Harold Dunstable' is one of the names I use. I took it because I owned Dunstable Hall, an estate in Wiltshire, for a time. I won it at cards a few years back. Things were going well for me then, but I have been losing steadily ever since. Dunstable Hall is heavily mortgaged, and I am likely to lose it soon since the tenants don't pay because I have not kept up my side of the leases. My creditors are foreclosing on it and other properties I bought when the winnings were coming in all the time. I also won this place at cards; it is all I own, free and clear now. It's too miserable a place to have warranted a mortgage."

"So you are the center of this horse-stealing ring?" asked the Major.

"Yes."

"Then you had better tell us all about it. Mr. Griffiths," added the Major, "can I persuade you to take notes on what Prescott says? I imagine that there is paper in the desk drawer, and there is an inkwell and quills on the desk."

The next couple of hours were spent by the Major and Daphne questioning their captive. The whole story emerged, including the name of the stable boy who had helped him to acquire the false documents of Dipton Stables. This man had already been dismissed by Mr. Griffiths for other failings, though he expected that they could still find him and make him pay the price for his treachery. Prescott also told them where he had stolen the other horses they found in the paddock.

After about an hour of questioning, Daphne and the Major decided to take a break. They needed to evaluate what they had learned and see what other information they needed.

"We'll pause for a while, Prescott, and then we will expect more answers from you when we have evaluated what we have."

"Have I given you enough to avoid the gallows?"

"Possibly," Daphne replied. "Major, do you think that we could recommend a very long prison sentence instead of hanging him?"

"I believe so," replied the Major in a reluctant voice, "though I am not yet sure how vigorously we should argue for some leniency. But we should be able to get the judges to reduce the sentence to life in prison or something equivalently less fatal if we actually nail Patterson-Baker. Of course, you know, Lady Camshire, that if one doesn't have a lot of money, chances of survival in prison are pretty bleak, and I don't imagine that Prescott has some hidden source of wealth that won't be seized as being forfeited on account of his crimes. You know, as well as I, that horse theft is one of the crimes that is treated most harshly. Only high treason has more brutal punishments. So if the sentence is reduced, we will need a lot more help to be confident that our intervention will prevent this man from swinging. Transportation or something milder will require more assistance, with him telling us everything we still need to know and helping us to arrest some of his associates."

"Well, I know that Lord Camshire only uses his influence in cases like this when there is substantial benefit to the community from what he obtains. I am pretty sure that the judges would listen to him if I can convince my husband that Prescott here is cooperating fully. Right now, we have no way of nailing Patterson-Baker, and people who knowingly receive stolen goods are at least as guilty as people who steal them. I think I could ask my husband to arrange leniency if Prescott helps us bring down Patterson-Baker and break up this horse-stealing ring."

"How would you do that?"

"Well. Let me think. Suppose we had Prescott deliver Dipton Charger tomorrow, but with us there as well. It might be enough if Prescott could get Patterson-Baker to incriminate himself while we hear him do so. Of course, Prescott would have to get Patterson-Baker to make it crystal clear that he knew he was dealing with stolen goods, maybe by repeating what you heard him say yesterday. Then we could swoop in and apprehend that cretin."

"Sounds like a splendid idea to me, my lady. Splendid! What do you say, Prescott? Will you do it?"

"All right. If you promise to try to get me clemency. I know you can't guarantee it, but I do know you are a gentleman whose word can be trusted."

"Mr. Griffiths," Major Stoner changed the topic. "Can you arrange for the people we have captured here to be brought to Ameschester gaol and for the stolen horses to be taken to my stables or your stables? There is probably a cart and some cart-horses here that we can use to transport the prisoners."

"Yes, Major. We can do it. We'll take the prisoners to the gaol and the livestock and cart to Dipton Hall. We can straighten out what to do about the horses later."

"Very good, Mr. Griffiths. I wish my lieutenants in India had been just as ready to make suggestions and take responsibility. Lady Camshire, we will take Prescott to my estate with the men I brought with me. We can work out how we will get him to incriminate Patterson-Bakertomorrow ."

Daphne, Mr. Griffiths, and Major Stoner rode away from Prescott's estate accompanied by their prisoner and the stolen horses they had found there. As they passed the road to the Major's estate, he left them, taking Prescott and the men he had brought with him on the raid. Daphne and Mr. Griffiths continued to Dipton with the horses, content to ride in silence. The winter afternoon had darkened completely before they reached Dipton Hall. They agreed to meet again before dawn when Mr. Griffiths would bring their horses to the Hall so that they could join the Major in completing the ruination of Patterson-Baker.

As agreed, Daphne and Mr. Griffiths set out before dawn the next morning. He had again brought some men with him, though not as many as had accompanied Daphne and him on the previous day since there were tasks around the stables that could not be put off any longer. He also brought Dipton Charger, who was a central part of the plot to demonstrate that Patterson-Baker would knowingly receive stolen goods. They met the Major as the sun was rising. He also was not alone. Now they were confident that they could overpower whatever staff Patterson-Baker might have.

They reached the turnoff to their target's estate before nine in the morning. The major organized some small bands of people to make sure that their dealing with Patterson-Baker was not disturbed by any outside workers. Then they let Prescott go by himself to the large, rather ornate front door, leaving Dipton Charger quite obviously tethered to a hitching post near the entrance. He was to ask to see Mr. Patterson-Baker and say he had brought the horse. When he met with their target, Prescott was to ensure that listeners outside the door could hear a clear admission that the provenance of the horse involved horse theft.

The plan was carried out without a hitch. The butler admitted Prescott to the mansion without checking with his master. Mr. Griffiths had stationed himself so that any sudden attempts to flee could be stopped, though it turned out to be unnecessary. His position did have the advantage that from the smoke escaping from the chimneys, he could guess where Prescott-Baker would meet with Prescott. One window in that room was open, and Mr. Griffiths stationed himself near it where he could hear everything that was said.

Daphne and the Major were equally lucky. They placed themselves to one side of the main door where they would not be seen by anyone opening the door unless that person exited and looked around. As instructed, Prescott bellowed that he was hard of hearing, so could the butler speak up? As a result, Daphne and the Major knew that the butler proclaimed that he had to inform his master of Prescott's arrival while the latter was to wait to see if his master would see Mr. Prescott. Later, they heard the butler tell the horse thief that his master would see him and invited Prescott to follow him to the office where Patterson-Baker received visitors who came on matters of business.

After hearing that development, Daphne and the Major waited a couple of minutes. Then they tiptoed through the door, where they found it easy to follow the butler and Prescott since he continued to chatter at the top of his voice. Soon the butler showed Prescott into a room and returned, not fully closing the door behind him. He had hardly turned to return to the main door when the Major grabbed him and rendered him unconscious.

"How did you do that, Major," Daphne whispered. "Is he dead?"

"Of course not! It is just a trick I learned in India. Very useful, often. Very. He'll recover in a short while."

The Major then crept up to the door so that he could hear clearly what was said inside. Daphne followed him, wondering what Major Stoner had been doing in India besides making a fortune. The ability to soundlessly render someone unconscious was not, she thought, a standard part of an army officer's training.

She turned her attention to what was going on beyond the doorway.

"So you brought the horse, did you, Prescott?" Daphne heard. She was little acquainted with Patterson-Baker's voice, but she deduced that he must be the speaker.

"Yes, sir. All I need is the money we discussed, and the horse will be yours," Prescott replied.

"And you brought the papers you mentioned."

"Of course, though, as I warned you, they are not quite genuine."

"I understand, but the end of the chain involves you, does it not."

"Yes, but the person before me on the ownership path is someone who has gone to Halifax in Canada, so he can't be questioned," Prescott asserted. "I would not be surprised if the people from Dipton Stables recognize the horse, though they know him as Dipton Charger, not as Dipton Dreamer, which is how the paper names the horse. But that is why you need an unusually impossible-to-follow record to be safe with owning a stolen horse."

"Yes, I see that. The people at Dipton don't respect me, though I won't mind if they suspect me of knowingly getting a stolen horse as long as others, especially the magistrates, are prepared to recognize that they couldn't prove that I knew he was stolen. In fact, I'll be glad if they know I have put one over them, and there is nothing they can do about it."

"Then it's all settled, isn't it?" asked Prescott. "All I need is the money we agreed on."

"Here you are. I got this bag of thirty-five guineas from my bank yesterday."

"Is that all?"

"It contains all that I am paying you. You didn't expect me to pay what you asked for a horse that you stole, did you? You are lucky to get this."

At that point, the Major came through the door into the portico. He gave a piercing whistle that could be heard outside where men were hidden, ready to take control of the estate.

"Mr. Patterson-Baker, as a magistrate of Amesshire, I arrest you for knowingly receiving a stolen horse from this thief. This is a capital crime like stealing a horse, so you will be held in Ameschester gaol until the next assizes.

"Lady Camshire, Mr. Griffiths, thank you for your assistance. I will be getting all the information I can about the horse thefts and the false documents. I would appreciate it if you would take Dipton Charger with you. I will be consulting with Mr. Snodgrass, our lawyer, about what to do about the properties of these two miscreants and will let you know what should be done with the other stolen horses. I will come by Dipton Hall when I have all this straightened out."

"Very good, Major," Daphne replied. "I must say that my husband made a very wise decision in recommending that you be appointed as a magistrate. Do bring Lady Marianne with you when you come. I am sure that she will be just as curious as we are about the outcome of all this."

Daphne and Mr. Griffiths rode to Dipton Hall in companionable silence, each glad that such a satisfactory conclusion had been reached to the problems of horse thefts from Dipton Stables.

After her two strenuous and often tense days, Daphne would have liked nothing better than to have settled into her workroom and lose herself in the figures that told her so much. However, that was not to be. Hugh must have been on the watch for her, and as soon as Steves opened the door, he dashed out.

"Aunt Daphne, can I go riding now? Nanny Weaver said I couldn't when you and Mr. Griffiths are away, but you're back now. Please, can I go riding? Please!"

Daphne was trying to think how to refuse without damaging the child's enthusiasm when his sister snuck around Steves and joined in.

"I want to ride 'Tunia. I like riding her. Nanny said I couldn't, but you are here, so I can."

Daphne thought that she couldn't refuse them. Picking up Mary, who seemed to be getting heavier by the day, and with Hugh coming alongside her, she went down to the stables where Mr. Griffiths was giving orders for the care of Dipton Charger.

Daphne had rather hoped that Mr. Griffiths would announce that his staff were too busy dealing with the results of the horse thefts to see to the riding pleasures of the two children, but there was no such luck. Mr. Griffiths and his wife were childless, and Mr. Griffiths was rapidly adopting Hugh and Mary as surrogate grandchildren.

"Certainly, you can go riding," he answered the children's request. "One of the men has adjusted Petunia's saddle so that you can ride her properly, Miss Mary, and you should ride every day that you can, Master Hugh."

Daphne felt that she had to watch for a while before telling Mr. Griffiths to bring the children to the Hall when they were finished. Going back to the house, she realized that she had not been seeing as much as she wanted of her own three children. She had observed in other noble families how easy it was to ignore young children except for a brief time before dinner when they were put on display. That wasn't good enough for Daphne. Nanny Weaver was an expert at taking care of her charges, but she wasn't the children's mother. Daphne was determined to make sure that they knew her from an early age as more than a remote figure in the drawing room. Besides that, she had found that she greatly enjoyed playing with them in the nursery and shouldn't let other matters prevent her from seeing her children often or for significant periods.

Then it was time to change for dinner. That is when Daphne discovered that Lady Clara had invited her father and her uncle for dinner. They were all curious about the strange activity around the stables and yards of Dipton Hall, the visits of the Major, and their disappearance for long periods the last two days. All three wanted to know everything that had been happening, and they were not content with the information they could pry out of Steves and other servants who knew hardly more than they did about Daphne's recent activities. They wanted to get it from the horse's mouth, so to speak. Daphne had no choice but to comply. The discussion and comments lasted long into the evening since, as had now become their habit, the two men were to remain at Dipton Hall for the night. Betsey, Daphne's lady's maid, had felt it her duty to inform Daphne that her father usually left the men's corridor to visit Lady Clara's room. However, if it didn't bother the lady of the house, the other servants knew better than to gossip about this pattern.

Daphne was exhausted by the long day, but her duties were not yet over. As always, her evening ritual when Giles was away consisted of composing a letter to him. But she did skimp on the details of the busy and stressful day.

"How was Giles's voyage to Scotland going?" she wondered in her letter. The main event of his expedition was supposed to have happened two days previously, but she had realized long ago that naval plans were all subject to wind and weather and rarely unfolded as intended. Well, Giles would be home soon surely and could take over much of the horse business. It would also be his turn to be grilled by their senior relatives. He certainly would have enjoyed taking part in her adventures this day more than she had. But she did not include those thoughts in her letter, just a summary of her achievements that day. She didn't want him to feel guilty about going to sea when his duty required it of him, even though domestic matters also needed him to be at home. If he were to leave the sea, that would be his choice, not the result of her pressuring him.

Chapter XXI

Daphne settled into her desk chair soon after dawn, though she had nothing urgent to deal with. Everything was caught up with after the hectic days when thc three friends arrested Prescott and Patterson-Baker. She had even found time to look into the accounts of Patterson-Baker's estate and had her solicitor in Ameschester look into the property. Why she was considering the property, she couldn't really tell. It was just that she was pregnant, she was pretty sure, and she felt that it would be desirable to have real property to leave all her children, not just the first-born male. Anyway, she was getting ahead of herself. She hadn't even had the pregnancy confirmed by Mr. Jackson. And the eventual disposal of all their property would be up to Giles in any case.

She turned to the one minor task that she had to perform that day, namely confirming her choice of an orchestra for the Ameschester Hunt Ball. In principle, she just provided the facilities for the Ball while all details were the task of the executive of the Ameschester Hunt, in reality, of Major Stoner alone. He was quite happy to have Daphne make all the arrangements since she (or, rather, in theory, the Earl of Camshire) paid all the bills. What had to be dealt with was a letter from the manager of the orchestra that she had hired for the event, confirming their arrangements. It was a group that Daphne had never employed before. She had heard it play at a not-very fashionable ball that she and Giles had attended right at the end of the previous London Season. She had been impressed by the orchestra's sound and their choice of new pieces that enlivened the traditional dances without being so far from traditional pieces that no one knew how to dance to their offerings. Newness was desirable, but only if everyone knew how to dance to the new rhythm and structure. Otherwise, everyone would be left hovering uncomfortably on the sidelines and the places on their dance cards wasted. Daphne thought gleefully that she would not be surprised if her choosing this orchestra for the Ameschester Hunt Ball would mean that they would be fully employed in the coming London Season. Yes, she would ensure that their dance card was full for the coming Season. How she wished that she could share that thought with Giles. He always enjoyed wit even though neither of them was witty.

The orchestra leader confirmed all the arrangements that Daphne had requested, including a broad outline of the types of dances that they would be playing. Daphne was delighted but did want to offer some suggestions. The main one that she was hesitant about was her request for some varieties of the Mozart dances she had seen in their piano transcriptions but knew had been written for dance orchestras. She phrased her request in polite and not binding terms but such that she was sure that, if the orchestra was comfortable playing them, they would perform a good selection. Daphne loved to dance, but she preferred to dance to music that pleased the brain as well as the feet.

She had just finished the letter to the orchestra when Steves came in with a large parcel of mail that had just been delivered. Only one event ever produced such a large packet. Giles must have reached an English Port.

Daphne opened the covering letter first. Yes, Giles had returned and was well. The mission had been a success. Such a success that he would have to stay in Portsmouth for a couple of days to deal with captured ships and people, but he should be back in Dipton in less than a week. That already was only five days away, Daphne calculated. 'What had happened?' she wondered. Usually, Giles came home almost as soon as his ship arrived in an English port. The rest of her morning would be taken up reading his letters in order. She rang the bell for Steves to bring her some tea and then settled back to read about Giles's adventures in *Glaucus.*

Daphne read and reread Giles's letters over and over again in the next few days. She didn't want to pester him with silly questions about what had happened that he had fully explained in his letters, and she wanted to make sure that she was aware of areas he had skipped over, possibly to save her from worry or because they involved matters that he was not facing. He was bothered by how much larger than he had expected was the force provided by the French. Was he suspecting some systematic failure somewhere in the government about collecting and evaluating material? Certainly, he had been surprised by the force opposing him, and it was only by good luck that he was able to nip the Jacobite rebellion in the bud. The other thing that stood out was how little he had to say about his fight with the Frenchman. His very reticence about the whole business led Daphne to suspect that Giles had been in much more peril than he let on. Giles was not an old man by any calculation but did he still have the strength and agility of a younger man that the risks he took were acceptable? She had never urged him to give up his naval position. Was it time to let him know that she was worried about him going as well as missing him when he was away, or would he resent any attempt on her part to affect his actions? Giles was not nearly as prone to think that he alone knew what was best as were the husbands of her friends and acquaintances, but he was not immune from the common presumption that men always knew best and needed no advice from their wives about major matters.

The time dragged on. It shouldn't; Daphne had a great number of things to keep her busy, things that she usually enjoyed doing. But she kept glancing at the clocks and peering down the drive even though she knew there was no chance that Giles would suddenly appear. After a couple of days, Daphne realized this was stupid. She just had to get on with whatever she was doing. Giles would arrive when he arrived. He would come as quickly as he could.

Daphne decided to watch Mary ride Petunia using the new saddle that had arrived the previous afternoon. The field where Mary was learning to control the pony by herself was out of sight of the drive and portico of Dipton Hall, so Daphne's first indication that Giles had arrived was seeing a man walking towards her from the mansion. The sun was behind him. All Daphne could see clearly was his outline, but she would know that walk anywhere. For a moment, she forgot all about Mary, who was, after all, having no difficulties controlling the horse, and dashed up the track to fling herself into his arms. Giles was ready for her: there was nothing new in the exuberant way she greeted him when he returned from a voyage. They hugged fiercely. He hadn't been away very long. 'Why did she make such a fuss of his return,' he wondered. It certainly did make homecoming very special.

Petunia took this moment to test how firmly her rider would control what she could do. The pony stopped and dropped her head to graze on some particularly attractive grass. Mary was mortified. She didn't know how to get Petunia going again, and Auntie Daphne had gone up the track to hug some man. However, before she could let out a wail of distress, Giles looked up.

"I think Mary needs you even more than I do," he told Daphne.

Daphne spun around and looked at Mary and the pony. The problem was immediately clear, and she called to Mary instructions on how to get the pony to behave. At once, Petunia raised her head and turned as her small burden directed.

"What a lot of progress she has made since I left," Giles exclaimed to Daphne. "What else have I missed?"

"A great deal," Daphne replied, "The most notable was that Major Stoner, Mr. Griffiths, and I have solved the mystery of the horse thieves praying on our stables, and the guilty men have been apprehended and await trial."

That summary was not enough to satisfy Giles's curiosity. In fact, for most of the day, Daphne had to recount what had happened while Giles was away, interspersed with discussions of what were matters of urgency in their various properties. She held back on questioning him about the details of his voyage. She knew that he would be asked many questions at dinner by her relatives.

That is exactly what happened at dinner. Daphne's father and uncle were there, and so were her sister–in–law, Lady Marianne, and Major Stoner. Catherine Bolton, Giles's niece, was also in attendance, though her husband was away. Lady Clara, Giles's mother, who lived with Daphne and Giles in Dipton Hall, was also in attendance. Daphne had added some special friends. The only family member who was not present was Lord David. But that was not all the people at dinner, for Giles's closest friends in the neighborhood were present, namely Captain Bush and Mr. Jackson. It was lucky that two of those, who would be present if they were available, had to be absent. The small dining room was filled to capacity, and it would have been much harder to have a table-wide conversation in the cavernous main dining room of Dipton Hall.

Dinner started in the normal way. General conversations of a very inconsequential nature occupied everyone's attention until the major meat removes had been served. Then came the demand that Giles recount his adventures in Scotland. Giles told the tale in detail up to the end of the Battle of Pendrag Island. He had learned from past presentations that if he tried to minimize some event either because it painted him as having been in danger or was of a nature usually considered unfit for female ears, his audience would demand more and, in fact, over-emphasize what he had been trying to minimize. Even so, he was often interrupted by questions of clarification. That he minimized his own part in the battle was evident to all, but no one wanted to have him make clear what dangers he had been in until Daphne had a chance to grill him in private.

Giles had intended to skim over the return to Portsmouth, which he did not regard as being of much interest. That was not what his audience felt. It started as soon as he tried to skip over the return from Pendrag Island to Portsmouth, which he didn't regard as being of much interest. How wrong that presumption had been.

The first question came from Captain Bush. What had happened to the strange ship he had christened as *Freedom*. Had he scuttled it?

No, Giles replied. One had to remember that he needed to remove the French sailors and soldiers from the scene of the battle. Destroying *Freedom* would mean that his remaining three ships would be badly overcrowded.

"What happened to the Irish people who had been torn from their homes," asked Lady Clara, to Giles's surprise. He had not thought she would be concerned with the fate of ignorant peasants, especially Catholic ones.

Giles replied that his little flotilla had passed down the east side of Ireland, stopping wherever there was a cove from which the Irish captives had been taken. It had been slow progress. While he had thought that all that was needed was to take the captives ashore, in every case, the villagers turned out to welcome the people whom they had never expected to see again and to thank their rescuers. Giles himself had gone on the first one to make sure that all was well, and he and his crew were overwhelmed by the response of the villagers. They were feted, and nothing would do but that they all had a drink together. The toasts were drunk with the Irish version of whiskey, which was just as potent as the Scottish one, though of a slightly different taste. He found he couldn't refuse a second tot. Nor could his crew. At the next cove, he had to bring a different set of rowers to make sure that they would still be capable of rowing after celebrating with the villagers. And so it went as they progressed down the coast until all the captured Irish people had been returned to their homes.

Other details emerged from other questions. No, Giles had bypassed Dublin. He was pretty sure that a stop there would only delay his completing his assignment. He had yet to learn what had happened to the merchant ship that his officers had sent into that port. Hopefully, it would be condemned for trading with the enemy. He had no idea of what the prize-money implications would be.

Would there be prize money for the recapture of *Cicero*? Again, it wasn't clear. If she had been taken formally into the French Navy, there would be prize money. Had she been captured and then recaptured in the same battle, there would not be. He was sure that there was some rule to deal with the situation, possibly several different rules. Mr. Snodgrass would be looking into it.

It was late in the evening when the party broke up. As was usual with family parties at Dipton Manor, the ladies had not withdrawn so that the men could drink their fortified and distilled drinks. Nor had the whole party moved to the drawing room where they could enjoy music or cards as well as talk. Indeed, it was so late that

Daphne invited everyone to stay the night, though the offer was only taken up by the Major and Lady Marianne and by Daphne's father and uncle.

Daphne and Giles still had plans to make and news to exchange, but that could wait for the next day or later. In Daphne's opinion, what could not wait any longer was her big announcement: she was pregnant. All the symptoms were present, except she had escaped morning sickness so far. Mr. Jackson had confirmed the situation for her. It was, of course, early days, yet; miscarriages were all too common. But both were excited and delighted with the news. Daphne stressed that she would not even be showing before the coming London Season was over. Giles could easily fulfill his duties in the House of Lords before thinking of his wife's health. Before retiring for the night, however, they resolved to not move to their London House until after the Ameschester Hunt Ball had taken place. Most of the London Season would still be ahead of them at that time, and Giles thought that nothing was pressing in the House of Lords that demanded his attention before then.

Author's Notes

Chapter I: Jacobite

The Jacobite movement was concerned with reversing the (Glorious) Revolution of 1688 in which King James II was overthrown and replaced with the joint monarchy of Queen Mary II, the closest Protestant in the line of succession, and King William III, her husband, the Dutch Prince of Orange, a protestant, a notable military commander, and the nephew of the deposed King.

James II fled to France, where he remained for the rest of his life, despite various plots to restore him or his successors. These plots were egged on by the French King. Those who supported the restoration of King James II and his heirs to the throne of England and Scotland were called Jacobites.

A rebellion occurred in 1715 to try to overthrow King George I, who acceded to the throne as the closest protestant in line to the thrown. He was from a minor German state and had no real ties to Great Britain. The 1715 uprising was suppressed, and the plotting returned to France, kept alive by expatriate British nobles and the French King with some support from Catholic aristocrats and others in England and disgruntled Scotsmen who were not happy with the new regime.

Thirty years later, in 1745, a serious rebellion occurred in Scotland to put Prince Charles (Bonny Prince Charlie), the grandson of James II, on the throne. The rebellion had initial success, but that ended at the Battle of Culloden, in which a predominantly English army was victorious. That victory was followed by a brutal campaign to stamp out the lingering embers of revolt. That effort left strong pockets of resentment for years.

Nevertheless, the Jacobite cause had become pretty well a dead issue by 1807, though resentments in Scotland resulting from the putting down of the insurrection of 1745-6 still lingered. This novel takes place only sixty years after the end of that rebellion, and the brutal events following the decisive battle of Culloden had not been forgotten.

The main obstacle to keeping the Jacobite cause alive was that Prince Charles had no legitimate sons to follow him. The next in line was a Roman Catholic cardinal who could not be pawned off as a Protestant and had no interest in the throne. Furthermore, he had no legitimate sons, and next in line would be the man who was already the king. However, there were rumors that there was a legitimate one among the illegitimate sons of Bonny Prince Charles (who was dead by this time). The French could have tried to stoke the fires of revolt in Scotland. However, the pretender and the events described here are entirely fictitious.

Chapter II: Smallpox

Smallpox was a terrible scourge during the period in which this novel takes place. Some estimates claim that smallpox counted for half the deaths in England in the eighteenth and early nineteenth centuries. Many victims not killed by the disease were rendered blind, and almost all were badly scared, in many cases hideously. The disease strongly affected the upper classes as well as the lower. We are less aware of its prevalence because portrait artists of the time usually did not include the pockmarks of their subjects, and the impression that so many ladies of the period had unblemished, clear complexions is misleading. Similarly, pictures of the men, though sometimes having lined visages, as being unscarred, are highly misleading. Jennings's discovery of a very effective vaccination using (live) cowpox eventually led to the eradication of the disease, but that was still years in the future.

Chapter VI: The payment of Clergymen

The payment of the clergy at the beginning of the nineteenth century is a highly complicated story. In a very simplified description of the system, the country was divided into a very large number of parishes, even cities and towns. Each parish had a church with a minister in charge, whose job was to arrange for Sunday and feast day services and carry out some religious ceremonies such as baptisms and weddings.

The minister was paid by a local tax, called a tithe, basically ten percent of the production of the parish. These tithes in rural parishes were divided into great tithes, being ten percent of the field crops of the parish, and the lesser tithes, which in an agricultural parish were ten percent of the value of livestock, milk, eggs, etc. In most cases, by the early nineteenth century, these had been converted to monetary payments rather than being in kind, as was generally the older practice. Tithe barns, some of which still exist, were where the clergyman stored the great tithes if they received them. Usually, the great tithes were worth three times the lesser ones, but this varied widely, depending on the parish's location.

The ministers in charge of the parishes were divided into two main types, rectors and vicars. Rectors got both types of tithes; vicars only got the lesser ones. Both types of clergymen were entitled to a house to live in and, often, attached land that could be used for crops and livestock. Just what was included and how large and in what condition were the house and associated property varied widely among parishes. In exchange for these rewards, the minister was required to perform (or have performed) various religious and civic functions. This package, the duties and especially the rewards, was called a living. A living was granted to a parson for life.

A clergyman could hold more than one living, and he (women were not eligible for appointment) did not have to perform the associated duties himself. Instead, he could appoint a curate, with the approval of the bishop in whose diocese the parish was located, to perform these duties. The curate was paid, by the incumbent of the living, a salary that depended on how much the parson wished to pay, often a very small pittance. In the period covered by the books in this series, there was a bill before the House of Lords to require a minimum wage for curates. It was strenuously debated, for many vested interests were allied with the proposition that curates did not need to be paid enough to live like a gentleman.

The right to appoint parsons to a living was held by individuals or, in some cases, by institutions such as university colleges. The right of appointment was considered property that could be sold or passed to the next generation through wills. It was often held by a major landowner in the district, but this was not always the case. The owner of the right did not necessarily have any association with the parish involved.

An individual could own the rights to several different livings. The right of appointment did not involve a corresponding a right of dismissal. Only the bishop could dismiss. An incumbent had the right to keep the living until he died, no matter how infirm he might become. The right to appoint for a particular living which was vacant could be sold for that one time without transferring subsequent appointments to that living. In consequence, someone who did not own a living, or only owned ones that were filled, could purchase a living for a relative or client.

In this book, the curate of Dipton is stuck in his low-paid job unless he can find a sponsor with a vacant living or a better-paid position as a curate elsewhere or by taking up another occupation. Giles does not have a vacant living for the curate and cannot fire his brother, which is why he needs other means to get his brother to resign.

Chapter XI: Horse Theft

Horse theft is probably as old as the use of domesticated horses. It was a very difficult crime to counter before the days of good and widely available records or ways of recognizing horses. In England, horse theft had been a capital offense for a long time before the events of this book took place.

Likely, the punishment was so severe because it was so difficult to establish that a particular horse had been stolen. Branding horses, though not unknown, was not a common practice. This was partly because horses could be dispersed easily since horses were regularly shuffled from one place to another because of the need to change horses on lengthy trips. It was also because horses, including trained horses broken to the rider, the carriage, or the plow, were always in demand. The "second-hand" market flourished, even though a horse represented a major purchase for many owners. A horse bought in good faith was the property of the buyer, even if it was stolen, unless the buyer had good reason to know that it was stolen.

Chapter XI: Gypsies

Gypsies were a feature of rural life in early nineteenth-century rural England. They had the reputation for being light-fingered (possibly deserved, but possibly not, in reality, more so than any other group of dubious honesty.) They were also known as knowledgeable horse traders. I have seen no evidence that they were more prone to horse theft than any other group.

Principal Characters

Betsey	Daphne Giles's lady's maid
Blenkinsop, Hector Fitzroy	Captain in the Royal Navy, captain of *Cicero*
Bolton, Mrs. Catherine	Giles's half-niece and married to Captain Bolton
Bolton, Captain	Married to Giles's niece Catherine
Beaver, Mr.	Designer of the changes to Camshire House
Breecher, Mr.	Coroner
Brooks, Mr.	Master of *Glaucus*
Bush, Captain Tobias	A Royal Navy Post Captain, formerly Giles's first lieutenant
Bush, Midshipman	Nephew to Captain Bush, midshipman on *Glaucus*
Carstairs	Giles's Cockswain, operator of the Dipton Arms Inn
Chapman, Mr.	Lawyer in Norwich
Lady Clara Giles,	Dowager Countess of Camshire. Mother of Sir

Richard Giles and Lord David Giles

Darling, Mrs. — Cook at Dipton Hall

Downing, Mr. — Chief Magistrate of Westminster

Duff, Master and Commander Jeffrey — Commander of *Falstaff*

Dunsmuir, Mr. — Midshipman on *Glaucus*

Edwards, Randolph — Giles's former agent, guilty of embezzling funds.

Emery, Sir Titus — A High Court Justice, who spends much of his time as an agent of the government

Evans, Garth — Carpenter on *Glaucus.*

Findlay, Michael — Portrait and landscape painter

Forsythe, James — Giles's agent in Norfolk

Foster, Rev. Angus — Curate at Dipton

Giles, Daphne — Countess of Camshire

Giles, Captain Sir Richard, Earl of Camshire — Captain in the Royal Navy and husband of Daphne

Henry Griffiths — Stablemaster at Dipton Hall

Hatcherley, Lord	First Lord of the Admiralty
Jackson, Mr.	Apothecary/physician
Jamieson	Steward at Dipton
Jenks, Roger	Junior midshipman on *Glaucus*
Lester, George	First lieutenant on *Cicero*
Little, Sir Humphrey	Previous owner of Sallycove estate in Shropshire
MacUther, Lord Robert	Scottish Baron and Chief of the Clan MacUther
MacUther, Percy	Twin brother of Lord Robert
Macauley, Lieutenant Hamish	Lieutenant of Marines on *Glaucus*
Macreau, Lieutenant Etienne	Second lieutenant on *Glaucus*
Marianne, Lady	Giles's half-sister and Major Stoner's wife
Marsdon, Mrs.	A bawdy house keeper and procurer
Matthams, Mr.	Proprietor/ innkeeper of the Woodbridge Inn, Shropshire
Matthams, Mrs.	His wife
Miller, Lieutenant	First lieutenant on *Glaucus*

Moorhouse, Daniel	Daphne's father, Owner of Dipton Manor
Moorhouse, George	Daphne's invalid uncle, owner of a gun factory in Birmingham
Moorhouse, Harold	Son of Daniel
Moorhouse, Nancy	Daniel's wife
Moorhouse, Hugh	Son of Harold and Nancy, eight years old
Moorhouse, Mary	Daughter of Harold and Nancy, five years old
Newsome, Mr.	Second Secretary to the Admiralty
Philman, David	Giles's servant on *Glaucus*
Reeding, Earl of	Giles's friend in the House of Lords
Richardson, Joseph	Midshipman on *Glaucus*
Shearer, Bill	Bosun on *Glaucus*
Snodgravel, Mr.	Lawyer in London, starting to become Giles's agent in place of Mr. Edwards
Snodgrass	Lawyer in Ameschester
Steves	Butler at Dipton Hall
Stoner, Major Ralph	Retired Indian Army Officer, married to Lady Marianne

Struthers, Lady Gillian	Giles's maternal aunt
Struthers, Lord Walter	Giles's uncle-in-law, a member of the government
Stewart, Lieutenant Daniel	Officer on *Glaucus*
Summers, Edward	President of the Ameschester Hunt
Ted	New coachman at Dipton Hall
Tisdale	Butler at Dipton Manor
Walters	Dispatch rider at Dipton Hall
Weaver, Nanny	Giles's and Daphne's nanny
Whitley, Ralph	Master's mate on *Glaucus*
Wilson, Mrs.	Housekeeper at Dipton Hall
Worthington, Mr.	Builder in Shropshire

Glossary

Admiral Byng's fate	Admiral Byng was executed for lack of aggression for, in Voltaire's words, "pour encourager les autres."
Amiens, Treaty of	Treaty between Britain and France ending the Napoleonic wars, signed in 1802.
Back a sail	Turning a sail so that the wind blows against the back side rather than the front side so that the ship stops.
Belay (v.)	Tie down. Regularly used by mariners to also mean stop. Belaying pins were stout, removable rods that were often used as makeshift weapons.
Board(ing)	(1) Refers to attacking another ship by coming side to side so that men from one ship can attack the other one in an attempt to capture it. (2) in 'on board' it means present on a ship.
Boarding-nets	Loose nets hung from the spars of a ship to prevent enemies climbing aboard from boats.
Brig	A two-masted, square-rigged ship.
Carronade	A short gun, frequently mounted on a slider rather than a wheeled gun carriage, only used for close-in work. They were not usually counted in the number of guns by which a ship was rated.
Close (verb)	Closing with another ship (or fleet) was to sail towards it by the quickest path.

Close to the wind — A ship is sailing close to the wind when it is going upwind as much as it can without stalling. Slang meaning is that the action is almost illegal.

Cloth (drawn) — Refers to the stage of a meal when the final dish had been consumed, the tablecloth had been removed, and the men in attendance gathered together to imbibe liquor stronger than wine, usually accompanied by nuts and fruit. When ladies were present, they withdrew to the drawing room just before the cloth was drawn. It was often a time of more pointed conversation than occurred during the meal.

Consol — A bond issued by the British Government with no stated redemption date, paying the holder a specified amount per annum. The term is short for Consolidated Fund.

Crosstrees — Two horizontal spars at the upper ends of a topmast to which are attached the shrouds of the topgallant mast

Cutting-out — Entering an enemy harbor in boats to capture a ship and sail her out to sea where the warship would be waiting.

Entail — A provision that the inheritance of real property would go to specified members of a family (or another specified group) usually to the closest male relatives. An entail typically prevented the present owner from leaving the property to someone else, and it was usually put on a property to prevent the immediate heir from dissipating the inheritance but would

	pass it intact (more or less) to the next generation.
Exemptions	Documents issued to merchant seaman and some other so that they would not be pressed into the navy. Even with them seamen were often forcibly taken from merchant ships to serve in the navy.
Fight both sides	Occurs when a warship engages two (or more) enemies using the guns on both sides of the ship. Doing so requires a very large crew.
Fighting top	A Platform on the mast where the main part met the top mast from which marines could fire their muskets on to the deck of an opposing ship.
Full and Bye	A sailing ship is sailing full and bye when it is as close to the wind as possible without danger of the sails flapping with small changes to the wind. The same as 'close-hauled,' but the latter indicates adjusting the course for every small change in the wind.
Gammoning	*Rope lashings on the bowsprit of a ship.*
Grapnel	A metal hook or set of hooks attached to a line that could be thrown and hook on to the edge of another ship or a wall or other object.
Gunroom	Place where the midshipmen berthed.
Helm alee	Turn a ship into the wind. (It sounds backwards, but originates from the time when ships had tillers which were pushed in the direction opposite to the desired turn.)

Holystone	On naval ships, the decks were scrubbed each morning using sandstone blocks. Since the crew had to perform the task on their knees, they were called holy stones and holystone became the verb to indicate the activity.
Jolly boat	A small lapstreaked boat often suspended from the stern of a ship
John Company	Nickname for the East India Company.
Leeway	The sideways drift of a ship down wind of the desired course.
King's hard bargain	Refers to crew members who are ineffective or insubordinate.
Knighthead	One of the two mitred timbers rising from the keel of a sailing ship at the bow to support the side planks and the bowsprit. Sometimes used as the plural noun for the pair of timbers.
Larboard	The left-hand side of the ship looking forward. Opposite of starboard. Now usually called "port."
Lead-line	A thin rope knotted at six-foot intervals with a piece of lead at the end. Used to measure the depth of water under a ship.
Line abreast	Vessels sailing together in parallel.
Loblolly boys	Assistants to the surgeon
Lubber's hole	A hole in the top (q.v.) of a mast so that access can b e gained from below, either to get to the top of to be able to reach the next set of shrouds to clime farther up the masts. Experienced topmen avoided its use when

	climbing the mast, preferring to climb up the ropes on the outside of the top.
Luffing up	turning into the wind to take stop a ship
The Nore	Anchorage in the Thames estuary off the mouth of the Medway River. A major anchorage for the Royal Navy in the Age of Sail.
Quarterdeck	The outside deck of a ship at the stern.
Raft	Ships or boats are rafted together when they are tied to each other.
Rake (a ship)	Fire a broadside into the bow or stern of an opponent who would not be able to return the fire.
Remove	Different dishes served at dinner. The more removes, the more elaborate and elegant the dinner was thought to be
Rout	A large, formal evening gathering. It had a slightly risqué connotation.
Shrouds	A rope ladder formed by short lengths of rope tied tightly between the stays of a mast.
Sheet	A line controlling how much a sail is pulled in.
Slave Coast	The part of the Subsaharan coast of Africa which was the main source of slaves to be transported to the Americas
Slowmatch	The slow-burning cord used as a fuse to delay explosions for some time.
Stay(s)	(1) A line used to prevent a mast from falling over or being broken in the wind
	(2) Corsets

Steer by the course	Usually sailing ships would adjust the direction they were sailing according to vagaries of the wind to avoid have in alter the set of all the sails frequently. "Steering by the course"indicated that the ship would keep heading in the same direction as indicated by the compass and the sails would have to be adjusted to suit that course as the sind varied.
Stern sheets	The after part of an open boat.
Step	Promotion from lieutenant to commander.
Spring (line)	A line attached to the anchor cable leading to the aft of the ship that can be used to turn it
Tack	(a) Change the direction in which a ship is sailing and the side of the ship from which the wind is blowing by turning towards the direction from which the wind is blowing.
	(b) (as in larboard of starboard tack) The side of the ship from which the wind is blowing when the ship is going to windward.
Taffrail	Railing at the stern of the quarter deck.
Ton	That part of London society most interested in adhering to the latest fashions.
Toulon	The main French naval base in the Mediterranean. It was under loose blockade both in 1805 and also earlier when it slipped out of the harbor and evaded the Britsih Fleet under Nelson to go to Egypt. Nelson's ability to contain it was no greater in 1805.
Tubs	Liquor was not usually smuggled in regular barrels but in smaller containers, made like a barrel, which could be carried by one man.

Tumblehome The part of the hull of a ship that slopes inward toward the deck.

Turn of the glass Time during the day on ships was measured via an hourglass – or rather a half-hour glass. It was counted from the start of each watch, and a bell was rung each time a half hour had passed when the glass had to be turned. The number indicated how many half-hours had passed since the start of the watch. Eight-bells was the signal that a watch had ended.

Uisge baugh Scotch whisky

Wadden Sea The part of the North Sea whose coast stretches from the Netherlands to Denmark.

Wardroom The area in a ship used by the commissioned officers of a ship when off-duty.

Watch (1) Time: A ships day was divided up into fur hour watches with one further divided into two. The watches were

First watch: 8 p.m.- 12 midnight

Middle watch: 12 midnight - 4 a.m.

Morning watch: 4 a.m. – 8 a.m.

Forenoon watch: 8 a.m. – 12 noon

Afternoon watch 12 noon – 4 p.m.

First dog watch 4 p.m. – 6 p.m.

Second Dog watch 6 p.m. – 8 p.m.

In each watch, time was marked off in half-hour segments so the one bell of the First watch would be 8:30 p.m., two bells would be 9:00 p.m., and so on.

(2) Division of the crew. The crew was divided (usually) into two watches, the starboard watch and the larboard watch, which alternated when they worked (in normal circumstances) and when they were at leisure or asleep.

(3) the time when officers were on duty. Referred to as "being on watch" or "watch."

(4) Police force on land.

Wear (referring to a ship) The opposite of tack where the maneuver of changing which side of a ship the wind is coming from is accomplished by turning away from the wind. Sometimes spelled ware.

Withers The place where a horse's shoulders meet is neck; the place where a horse collar rests.

Yellow admiral A Naval officer who has been promoted to the rank of Admiral without being given a command. Largely created to allow the promotion of a captain with less seniority.

Printed in Great Britain
by Amazon

38883783R00235